The Hidden Sister

HISTORY UNVEILED

OLIVIA OSBORNE

MARGON PRESS
LONDON, ENGLAND
WWW.MARGONPRESS.COM

Published in the United Kingdom
Margon Press Ltd
London, England

Cover design by Bobby Dawson
Interior design by Commercial Campaigns
Photographs of the Collegiate Church of Saint Martha, Tarascon, France
compliments of www.dreamstime.com
Photographs of the Church of Saint Martha on the Hill, Chilworth,
England compliments of Olivia Osborne

ISBN: 978-0-9563635-1-0

DEDICATED TO YOU

All of the characters within this story are true to life, and most are highly renowned. The mentions of documented historical events are accurate, as are the references to places, buildings, and fine art; most of which is still in existence today. The first two chapters set the scene by providing historical information that is not well known, and to establish a more personal sense of the individuals being brought to light, first-person narrative and dialogue will be utilised on occasion throughout.

The story itself is probably the most famous in the world, and one that has been interpreted in many ways before. However, the development of this version includes an element of poetic license, but that is not to say it is untrue; quite the contrary. When revisiting the most renowned story of all time an entirely unique perspective is required if new horizons are to be found, since that which remains elusive could develop into a mechanism for revolutionary change on an inconceivable scale.

My research has been unstinting and included the work of many reputable theologians and historians, and while the conclusions they suggest do not always coincide, they leave similar and often identical loose ends and curiously inexplicable outcomes. It is the 'loose ends' I determined to make sense of, and as my investigations progressed, and my sensibilities and intuition took hold, a story emerged from evidence that is both compelling and intangible, which to this day continues to astound me.

Where is the proof, some may ask. You will not fail to see it, is my response. In demystifying the past, I trust that an understanding of the present emerges with a clarity not witnessed before.

Olivia Osborne
April 2010
London, England

CHAPTER ONE
THE TRUTH IS LONG OVERDUE

*I*n satisfying the ambition of dominant political and religious leaders of the past, the characterisation of certain legendary figures from history was systematically distorted. The far-reaching and enduring effect of such deception has impacted generations to an inconceivable degree; as the resolve of a select few to deliberately prevent advances the human race was capable of achieving, altered the entire course of history for mankind.

The remarkable men and women whose life stories were fundamentally adapted to meet the needs of a specific agenda, acted with the most selfless, altruistic motivation. In supporting the man who ultimately rose to iconic status in symbolising the world's most influential religion, these individuals became unintentionally implicated in creating an impression that is far-removed from the truth. Each of them was driven by a determination to effect monumental change for the generations that would succeed them, yet the prospect they envisaged is something we have been denied, and the cost we abide is beyond measure.

The majority of challenges the world faces at present are the consequence of impediments put in place by single-minded, powerful religious and political leaders who lived some two-thousand years ago. The perpetuation of such obstruction continues today, as those yielding the authority of their predecessors intensify an already intolerable state of affairs. Until the truth of our history is uncovered and the barriers thereby removed, the progress of mankind will not come close to achieving its potential.

As each year of this century succeeds another, a conscious realisation of the depth of atrocity that has befallen mankind emerges in the most transparent of ways. As influential religious leaders unwittingly reveal their true selves when acceptance of responsibility becomes inevitable, *the truth will out* ceases to be a mantra of the defeated. As exposés of fraudulence and impropriety verify what most have always known to be true, those who believed their authority would never be questioned are finally being held to account. However, their incrimination exposes only a partial truth – it is the ominous nature of their influence over mankind as a whole that needs to be examined and laid bare.

The iconic symbol of Christianity has forever been perceived as someone he was not. Jesus had no desire to establish a new religion; his objective was to simplify what had become so complex as a result of religious indoctrination. His ambition was to encourage an enhanced perspective on life; a way of conducting life that could be incorporated into the doctrine of any religion, or adopted by those who felt no need for religious affiliation. However, those who falsified his intentions to establish an influential, wealthy empire had profound and covert ideas in mind. They could neither tolerate people feeling understood, nor the possibility they may one day understand: sentiments that guaranteed independent thought were for centuries perceived as blasphemous ideology, rather than a naturally evolving intellect.

A grave social injustice has been perpetrated by man against mankind. The misrepresentation of the most prominent story of all time has affected the perspective on life of billions of people across the world. My objective is to redress the balance of such injustice by providing new insight into the reality of our history, while establishing with certainty the truth – Jesus walked the earth for the benefit of humanity, not the institution of Christianity.

CHAPTER TWO

MARTHA

PART I – THE HIDDEN SISTER

*T*he decision to remove the story of Martha from history was made during the Christian church's formation in the early centuries after the crucifixion. Tens of thousands of people were in uproar opposing many aspects of the direction of the early Christian movement, and the disappearance of Martha contributed much to this commotion. Those who dared to object were condemned as blasphemous heretics, and in their thousands were hauled away and murdered. Their outrage at what happened to the memory of Martha, and the rest of Jesus's family, was something the early Christian leadership was not going to tolerate. The female role model of Martha, and the actual teachings of Jesus, did not remotely coincide with how the early Christians viewed the future of society or their ambitions as an institution.

To refer to Martha as the hidden sister is probably quite an understatement. Martha was the second child of Jesus's parents, Joseph and Mary, and was born some 14 months after Jesus. In the Bible, however, she is relegated to being the sister of Mary of Bethany and Lazarus, and depicted as having a minor role in the life of Jesus as one who served. The Bible briefly mentions that Jesus visited Martha's home and she cooked for him, thereby minimising the extent of their relationship. However, had the true account of Martha's life been communicated throughout the ages, her status in the world would have been comparable to that of Jesus.

The story of Martha was to have personified the role of the female for the future of mankind. As a sister to Jesus, his working partner, and closest confidante, they were the embodiment of how a man and a woman complement and need one another: how each individual brings inborn skill-sets to a relationship that the other does not possess. Their association was supposed to demonstrate that it was neither acceptable nor required for one individual to dominate another, and that the function of women within life should be as respected as that of men. Had the true story of Martha been told, men and women would have accepted an equivalent and instrumental role in the church, which would have carried over into other areas of life. We would not be in a position some two thousand years later where equality has literally had to be fought for, with compensation for history often being sought by women striving and succeeding to achieve the extreme of dominating men, which is as destructive as the subservient role they were historically forced into.

The lost true representation of this relationship, as well as that which existed between Joseph and Mary and Jesus and Mary Magdalene, has blurred the lines for us all, which is why we fail to see where those lines are drawn.

PART II – TEXTUAL REFERENCES TO MARTHA

The brief mentions Martha receives in the Bible are in the gospels of Luke (10:38-42) and John (11:1-44) (12:1-11). References to Martha in the gospel of John relate to the miracle of Lazarus being raised from the dead, but it is the mention of Martha in the gospel of Luke that creates much interest. Scholars who study and interpret the Bible appear confused when attempting to comprehend the relationship between Jesus and Martha, which is perfectly understandable: their curiosity is intuitive but they have no evidence to assess, thus they have yet to draw the correct conclusions. Nevertheless, proof of their concerted effort can be seen in their debate.

The focus of most interest for theologians is a heated exchange that occurred between Jesus and Martha at a time when Jesus was visiting the House of Martha in Bethany. It was surprisingly candid and inappropriate, particularly as it began by Martha reprimanding Jesus. The dispute occurred when Martha displayed resentment towards Mary of Bethany for not assisting in the kitchen with food preparation and other responsibilities. Martha was upset with Jesus for encouraging Mary to spend time relaxing with him, rather than helping her. As would any sister when frustrated with her elder brother, Martha did not hesitate in telling Jesus what she thought.

Jesus's response to Martha's rebuke is often interpreted by biblical scholars as an angry admonishment − in other words, they had an argument. It appears from such analysis that Martha did not revere Jesus in the usual way and, likewise, he did not falter in his reaction and proceeded to give Martha a piece of his mind. Despite this understanding, however, no clarification of worth has emerged regarding this exchange.

The level of familiarity demonstrated in this encounter could only exist in a close or intimate relationship, or between immediate family members such as siblings, but certainly not between a hostess and her important male visitor. The reality is that the dispute was no more than a typical brother-sister spat. Martha and Jesus were among friends and felt familiar enough with one another to say what they thought without fearing it was out of place to do so. Scholars, on the other hand, have succumbed to interpreting the story as Jesus using Martha's predicament to demonstrate the importance of listening to the word of God by prioritising spending time with him over participating in one's work. A highly unlikely scenario, particularly when bearing in mind that Jesus was always grateful and humbled when anyone showed interest in his philosophies on life, and would never be so conceited as to insist his 'word' was that of God and should therefore be ranked above everything else.

While the true relationship between Jesus and Martha explains the level of familiarity that made it acceptable for such a disagreement to occur, it does not explain why Jesus would be so unthinking as to publicly rebuke Martha and apparently humiliate her in such a manner. However, what will be revealed throughout this story is that Jesus had no alternative but to navigate his predicament in this way: he had to placate Mary of Bethany and remind Martha to leave well enough alone. There was an accord that could not be broken under any circumstances, and it was for this reason only that Jesus appeared to be taking Martha to task for a non-existent offence.

* * *

Many renowned biblical scholars and professors of interpretation of the New Testament, suggest that Martha and Mary of Bethany were so close to Jesus throughout his life that only his relationship with his mother can be compared. It is also often asserted that Jesus loved Martha, Mary of Bethany, and Lazarus, but in particular that he loved Martha 'as though she were family'. Such opinions beg the question as to why the church has essentially ignored the significance of Martha in Jesus's life; relegating her to someone who has barely been heard of by most people.

PART III – THE HISTORY OF MARTHA

Along with other family members and followers of Jesus, Martha escaped Jerusalem after the crucifixion and travelled via land and sea across Europe, eventually settling for the remainder of her days in the small town of Tarascon in the south of France. The relics of Martha were discovered in 1187, buried beneath the ruins of an ancient church. The sarcophagus appeared to have been hidden by the people of Tarascon some 400 years earlier to avoid damage during the 8th century Saracen invasion. While that foray saw the destruction of the church and all its contents, the discovery that occurred in 1187 proved not all had been lost. The hidden relics of Martha were identifiable due to an inscription on a marble plaque stating, *Beata Martha jecet hic – Here Rests the Blessed Martha.* However, the inscribed plaque was not all that was discovered; manuscripts, inscriptions, and primitive altars were also unearthed.

It was previously believed that these treasures had been lost during the 8th century invasion, so what was revealed alongside the remains of Martha in 1187 must have been startling to the townspeople of Tarascon. The discoveries no doubt evidenced Martha's relationship with Jesus and her involvement in his life and ministry; including corroborating the family's opposition to the early Christian movement.

The people of Tarascon were so moved by their findings that they established The Cult of St. Martha and built a new church in her honour, which stood directly above the original. The Church of St. Martha was consecrated in 1197 – some ten years after the relics were uncovered – but that building was unfortunately destroyed during the French Revolution. The conclusion of that assault saw the church reduced to the remains of an entranceway and small bell tower, which were later incorporated into a new structure that was built and extended throughout the centuries following the Revolution. The house of worship standing on that site today is a beautiful building known as The Collegiate Church of Saint Martha.

The evidence of the life of Martha discovered in her tomb in the late 12th century was vast and is probably still in existence. However, elements of any real consequence would no doubt have been seized at some point, and either destroyed or preserved within the vaulted Vatican archives. The ancient testimony contained the truth, but the truth was not allowed to be spoken then, any more than it is today.

If there is such a thing as the Holy Grail, this is it. What Martha knew and documented for posterity would shake the foundations of Vatican City to its core.

* * *

The Collegiate Church of Saint Martha, Tarascon, France

The following information about the interior of The Collegiate Church of St. Martha in Tarascon, France has been extracted and paraphrased in parts from various informational websites and promotional leaflets.

The Collegiate Church of St. Martha houses considerable art depicting the life of Martha, including seven paintings that were produced in the 18th century by French artist, Joseph Marie Vien. He was First Painter to King Louis XVI and Director of the French Academy in Rome, and it is this series of paintings that granted him membership to the Royal Academy – *The Resurrection of Lazarus, St. Martha Receiving Jesus Christ at Bethany, St. Martha leaving Palestine by Boat, The Arrival of St. Martha in Provence, St. Martha Preaching, St. Martha Dying,* and *The Funeral of St. Martha.*

When descending the steps leading to the crypt of St. Martha, there is a painting directly ahead by Charles Parrocel, which is aptly named, *St. Martha, Our Lady of the People.* Immediately beneath that painting is a cenotaph in honour of Martha – *The Gothic Tomb of St. Martha.* The memorial was commissioned by King Rene and completed in the 15th century by artist, Francesco Laurana. Intriguingly, the front of the cenotaph bears three reliefs memorialising St. Martha, St. Magdalene, and St. Lazarus. As the story unfolds, it will become apparent why this memorial in particular is so significant, and demonstrates that the truth of these individuals was well known and respected in this part of the world for many centuries after they lived. The aforementioned *reliefs* are more than a casual hint at the true legacy of Martha, and are in fact evidentiary fragments of an elaborate mystery, which will be fully revealed in upcoming chapters.

★ ★ ★

In addition to the historical and biblical information available on Martha, there is a well-known mythological tale of her taming a dragon that dominated the streets of Tarascon, terrifying its citizens. Unbelievably, to this day the tale continues to be told in a literal sense and the important metaphorical aspect remains unnoticed and unreported. In the few churches that exist in Martha's name, the story is recounted as an actual event, and the dragon-taming episode is exhibited in art and literal form. The story relates that Martha paraded a dragon throughout the town of Tarascon to prove it was no longer a threat, and in some instances the myth extends to describing the fabric she allegedly used to tie around the dragon's neck. Needless to say, Martha did not actually tame a dragon at all; rather, the dragon was a metaphor she used when preaching. It was symbolic of the threatening energy that existed among the townspeople, and the fear and insecurity that possessed them all and wreaked havoc with their lives.

Martha set out to 'tame the dragon' of Tarascon by changing the lives of its citizens and introducing them to the philosophy of life that she and Jesus had instilled in so many. She brought forth the suggestion that the atmosphere they created was equivalent to the presence of a monstrous dragon living among them, and used the imagery to demonstrate the negative effect of people mistrusting one another and fearfully suspecting that their neighbour was dishonest, or in some way plotting to gain the upper hand. Martha inspired people to trust their intuition and eradicate the irrational fears that controlled their lives. She encouraged them to embrace honesty, learn to trust one another implicitly, and work together as a community towards creating a unique and harmonious environment. The end-result was that Martha taught the people of Tarascon how to experience bliss and dispose of negativity. They each received the gift of inner peace by learning there was nothing for them to fear but fear itself. The mythological *dragon* was tamed.

The people of Tarascon felt it was a miracle that a woman could achieve so much with an entire community simply by speaking calmly and peaceably to them. As a result, Martha was revered: she changed their lives, and the transformation that occurred within the community was considered miraculous.

In addition to the high esteem in which Martha was held by the townspeople of Tarascon, she was worshipped for centuries by pilgrims and Kings alike. Many privileges were bestowed upon the town due to its connection with Martha, and over the centuries fifteen convents were established in and around Tarascon because of her association. Despite these well documented facts, the powers that be within the Christian religion have ensured Martha remains a virtual unknown on the world stage. They have downplayed her existence to such a remarkable extent, that those who maintain churches in her honour respond to enquiries by stating very little is known of her, other than she tamed a dragon.

* * *

The Church of Saint Martha on the Hill, Chilworth, Surrey, England

There are very few churches around the world that honour Martha, but the most beautiful is a church named *Saint Martha on the Hill*, which can be found in the village of Chilworth, south of Guildford in the county of Surrey, England. The church was built and consecrated in the late 12th century; around the time that the Cult of St. Martha was established in France, and simultaneous to the Church of St. Martha in Tarascon being built. It is located on top of a hill and is only accessible by foot, but is visible from many locations throughout the surrounding Surrey hills. At Christmastime the church is floodlit, creating a heartwarming view from many vantage points, which is somewhat appropriate — a mark of the celebration of the birth of Jesus in this beautiful part of England is projected like a beacon from a church honouring Martha.

Along with the handful of churches around the world established in Martha's memory, those who maintain this building admit to knowing little about her history, and quote the dragon-taming story in literal terms rather than as explained herein. Nevertheless, despite the lack of information that is apparent, this little church atop a hill must have been constructed by individuals who knew of Martha's true identity, but the fear of retribution by church authorities no doubt dictated that the secret be upheld. It is a wonder that it was permitted for a church such as this to be built at all, but as will be discovered in due course, a fear of the wrath of God instilled in the followers of Christianity is something that possessed those in authority. Permitting the determined few to memorialise Martha in what appeared to be a harmless way, no doubt put their conscience at rest.

Due to the confusion about the church's history and that of Martha herself, it appears to have become fashionable in recent years to propose that this beautiful building may actually have nothing to do with her at all. In suggesting that the name *Martha* could be derived from the word *martyr*, an attempt to create a more legitimate history for the church has brought about the unsubstantiated idea that it was originally named the *Church of Martyrs on the Hill*, due to the fact that centuries ago a number of Christians were martyred nearby.

However, the truth is, Martha was a highly significant individual from history and should be revered for who she was and all she accomplished. Those who worship in a church of her name ought to recognise that the guardian of their prayers is someone they should proclaim the entire world needs to learn about.

* * *

The straightforward interpretation of the dragon-taming myth remaining undetected for more than two thousand years is an astonishing fact, particularly in view of the lessons it contains, which are of vital importance to us all. Nevertheless, the manner in which this unlikely tale cleverly disguises the true story, and the fact that the myth even exists and has survived so many centuries, is proof of the determination of those who knew Martha. In creating such a unique storyline, and using the oral tradition of folklore as a means of guaranteeing it would be maintained, it is clear that those involved devised a unique and ingenious way of upholding Martha's memory. By capturing the imagination of people with a story of a woman taming a dragon, they avoided the wrath of the church by associating Martha with what appeared to be a harmless tale. Her followers no doubt decided they had no choice but to rely upon the metaphor being discovered one day, and such a revelation heralding the beginning of a search for the truth.

CHAPTER THREE

HIS LIFE BEFORE HISTORY WAS MADE

PART I – CHILDHOOD

*I*n the months following the birth of Jesus, his parents, Joseph and Mary, did as many young families of that time felt compelled to do, and took refuge in several different localities in an attempt to avoid much of the political uproar occurring at the time. The atmosphere was intimidating to say the least, and Joseph felt it advisable to ensure his wife and son were safely secluded in the homes of various extended family members.

When Joseph and Mary's second child was born some fourteen months after Jesus, the family had still not returned to their hometown, but the birth of Martha made it more difficult to be accommodated with relatives and they felt obligated to turn their attention towards putting down permanent roots. The contentious situation that prevailed in the area was becoming less so as each month passed, but Joseph felt certain that when the time was right for him to return his family permanently to Nazareth, he would instinctively know.

The newly born Martha became the primary focus of her brother's life – he would not leave her side for a moment. Jesus seemed to think that Martha was his baby and his responsibility, and this depth of devotion became mutual as the brother and sister grew. They often admitted that their lives would have been intolerable without the reciprocal support and companionship they were able to offer one another, which they knew could not be provided by anyone else.

Jesus was almost three years old before the family felt it was safe to settle in what became their permanent home in Nazareth. It was a secluded town that lay in a basin surrounded by hills of white limestone, and inhabited by some 15,000 people. Even though the location was remote, roads to Jerusalem and the seaports of Egypt were easily accessible. The atmosphere in the town was both contentious and serene, and people generally chose to be part of one or the other; either becoming heavily involved in local politics, or choosing to live a quiet life focused upon family and work. Joseph and Mary were unassuming people who sought a simple way of life. In preferring to keep very much to themselves, and desiring only to live their lives as best they could, they prioritised creating an atmosphere of contentment and love in their home.

The myth surrounding the relationship of Jesus's parents would suggest their marriage was somewhat unique, and in fact it was. It was exceptional in that their love for one another was true, and their emotional and physical relationship was something most of us yearn to achieve. It is regrettable that in satisfying the desire of the church to generate mystique surrounding the birth of Jesus, we have been denied the illustration of true love and intimacy that Joseph and Mary were destined to portray, and from which we could all have aspired. (A detailed account of the relationship between Joseph and Mary, and the conception and birth of Jesus, is presented in the PostScript section at the rear of this book.)

* * *

Once the family became fully integrated within the community of Nazareth, Joseph and Mary felt comfortable with their decision to settle down and raise their family in this setting. Joseph established himself as a gifted carpenter and managed to provide well for his family, and throughout the early years of their marriage they joyfully welcomed four more children – James, Joseph, Simon and Ruth. The boys were typically rambunctious and certainly kept Joseph and Mary on their toes, but the baby of the family, Ruth, was the apple of everyone's eye. All of the children wanted to be her protector – they could not get enough of their darling little sister.

The early years of Jesus's life were quite a challenge for Joseph and Mary, and while no one would deny that the raising of six children presents more than its fair share of interesting situations, the responsibility of being the parents of Jesus alone was enough to test the most patient. Having to navigate the risks he was driven to take was often overwhelming for these gentle, unassuming people. Jesus's considerable intellect, coupled with a lack of maturity, meant he often missed important social cues. His use of humour and irony was way beyond his years, and without intention on his part others often felt inadequate in his company, creating many social reactions for Joseph and Mary to resolve. Jesus could not understand why he caused offence, but it often related to what he did not do, rather than what he did. He was unable to comprehend the importance to others of what he supposed were trivial issues: matters he felt were of no significance were upsetting to his peers, whereas complex social concerns he attempted to debate with them, went in one ear and out of the other. Forming and maintaining friendships and interacting with his peers on a level playing field did not come naturally to Jesus: they viewed him as strange, while he perceived them to be equally so.

In Martha's Voice:

"We were a 'normal' family, if there is such a thing; life was no different for us than for everyone else. We had our fair share of disagreements and conflicting personalities, but there was always an abundance of love and compassion to overcome difficulties. Our home was a sort of well-organised chaos, but we each had responsibilities that contributed to everything running smoothly, and most of the time life was more organised than chaotic. Mama could always be found in our home, and I can barely remember there being a moment when she wasn't. I suppose when we were very young she must have shopped at market, but as we grew that became each of our responsibilities, so there was little reason for her to go anywhere. She was somewhat like the captain of a ship — she wouldn't think of abandoning her post. Papa's carpentry workshop was immediately behind our home, so he was always there when we needed him. It was a luxury none of us appreciated when we were growing up; like most children, I suppose we took things like that for granted.

"However, there was one thing I remember we all appreciated — how we celebrated the end of each day. We did actually celebrate it, and Mama and Papa used that word to explain what they meant. Each evening we would gather around for dinner, which was always cosy and welcoming because there were so many of us. Rather than Papa merely saying a blessing before we ate, he always said, 'Let's celebrate the success of another day and look forward to the next.' The success being that we had each learned something new, while the celebration was that we'd all arrived home safely to share what we'd learned. Papa would then say a blessing over our *food and we would all tuck into dinner, but throughout the meal and into the evening we talked constantly; each sharing details of something we'd done that day, as well as something about life or about ourselves that we'd discovered. Needless to say, most of our stories created lots of conversation and laughter, often lasting throughout the evening until it was time to retire. I think the main benefit of our time spent together as a family was on the occasions one of us had not had such a good day; we always felt comfortable bringing up our worries, and somehow a problem didn't seem to be such a predicament after we'd all had our say."*

* * *

Even though Jesus participated in the normal activities of childhood, his favourite pastime was talking at length with Martha. They would compare their observations in human behaviour, and reflect upon how adults seemed to complicate life. As children, they could not understand why their elders would do such a thing, since life seemed to be problematical enough as it was. In an attempt to make sense of it all, Jesus was enthusiastic about visiting synagogue and listening to what preachers had to say. However, Joseph and Mary were concerned when he showed interest in so many serious issues at such a tender age and tried to discourage it; they were afraid he would speak out publically in the manner they had witnessed in their home.

As a compromise, Joseph and Mary insisted that Martha accompany Jesus at all times to keep a watchful eye on her brother. Being quite mature for her age, it was felt Martha was capable of reining Jesus in should he overstep the mark when expressing opinions to outsiders. However, even though Jesus had promised his parents he would keep a low profile in synagogue, Martha's ability to successfully manage her brother was hampered by his determination to push the boundaries at every opportunity.

On one particular occasion, a preacher had noticed the eleven-year-old Jesus in the crowd and decided to have a little fun. In view of how interested he seemed in the ongoing activities, the preacher asked Jesus his name and presented him with a question. Not really expecting Jesus to be able to comprehend much of the goings on, the preacher enquired of Jesus in a playful, childish way, which was probably his biggest mistake. To Jesus, this approach felt like an insult to his intelligence, and that was how he took it. Like most young boys, Jesus had a sensitive ego and did not take kindly to it being trivialised: any level of restraint he may have possessed disappeared instantly.

Looking around synagogue and noticing that all eyes were upon him, Jesus slowly moved in the direction of the preacher. Aware of everyone's amusement as he climbed onto the podium, Jesus nevertheless maintained his dignity, turned to the crowd, and addressed them by gently stating, "My name is Jesus of Nazareth." He waited in silence for people to notice he was serious and wanted their attention, but rather than respond to the trivial question posed by the preacher, Jesus used the opportunity to speak his mind. In a profound but innocent, calm, and articulate way, he said:

"I observe with great interest your commitment to synagogue and the respect you show to those you engage. Clearly, you feel it appropriate to conduct yourselves with grace in the presence of scholars and elders while in a house of devotion to scripture, but why is it that same grace is not exhibited outside these walls? I ask because I'm curious, and I don't understand. Why is it I see so many of you nodding your heads and groaning in agreement as the words of scripture are considered, yet in everyday life I do not see such attitudes conducted with sincerity. As a child this concerns me. Is this what happens as we grow up? Is this what I have to look forward to — a life of confusion and fear?

"It appears that many of you cannot live up to the standards expected in scripture. Do you think that perhaps those who wrote scripture knew that? Do you think they set standards you could not attain in order to make you fearful, insecure, and self-loathing? Being so angry at your own weaknesses makes you dependent upon preachers: it leaves you with a need to attend synagogue to feel some semblance of good about yourselves. But I do not see that this works. I see you take out your confusion and anger on others you come into contact with — others you should love and provide for — your family, your neighbours and those who are less fortunate than you.

"Do you not think that if scripture presented us with ideals that were actually attainable, we would all conduct ourselves with confidence? We would not be confused and angry and find ourselves compensating for insecurities by being condescending towards one another. If what we were taught was something we could actually achieve, I believe we would be able to teach others by way of example.

"When I observe you attending synagogue, I see many serious faces with expressions of concern and confusion. I do not see peace and joy emanating from your hearts or emerging from your eyes; often there is fear, jealousy, insecurity, as well as a pretense of sorts; a need to be seen as someone you are not. Some of you greet one another respectfully when you arrive and

depart, exuding an impression of peace, but you return to your homes and do not show that same level of respect towards those you purport to love. Do you think this is because you feel 'less' when you arrive home? Knowing, deep down, that you cannot attain the ridiculous heights of piety scripture requires must be disheartening."

The crowd stood in silence: no one was smiling or laughing at Jesus now; rather, they were in shock. Even the preacher was motionless, unable to speak with any level of coherence. Martha had witnessed the entire episode but had remained hidden in the background. She was terrified at what the reaction of the crowd might be, and was certain they'd both be in trouble with their parents for this outburst. Martha urgently signalled to Jesus to get down from the podium, but he took no notice.

In Martha's Voice:

"I held my breath wondering what was going to happen next. Jesus looked intently into the eyes of the people he faced, as he had done throughout his short speech. I knew this was his way of learning — it wasn't a way of teaching, although I think some teaching took place. He had wanted to learn what their reaction to his questions and opinions would be. Jesus told me later that throughout his presentation he had observed an occasional and momentary relaxation of facial expressions among those gathered — a sort of relief appeared in most of their eyes for brief moments as he spoke.

"When Jesus had finished, I noticed everyone appeared to be in a trance-like state — it seemed as if they were waiting for more. However, the silence was broken when someone spoke out, exclaiming, 'How dare you!' At that point the entire crowd suddenly came to their senses, as if being rapidly brought out of hypnosis. Joining their fellow citizen, several others began calling for the blasphemous young boy to be evicted from holy temple.

"As the taunting became more determined, I waved furiously at Jesus, desperately urging him to get down from the podium, but he took no notice. He stood silently, carefully observing the behaviour of the gathering. As he later explained, he was fascinated by the reaction — his words had affected them all, but what disturbed him the most was seeing fear in their eyes more so than anger.

"Despite the chorus of dissenting voices, Jesus remained on the podium facing the crowd, and in a humble but somewhat authoritative manner he slowly raised his right hand with his palm facing the people. By now I was in a state of panic — I felt certain they were not going

to take this from an eleven-year-old boy. But irrespective of my continued pleas for him to come down, Jesus remained in his hand-raised position on the podium.

"When eventually the people stopped debating among themselves, they looked up at Jesus in a curious and confused way. After a few moments he simply addressed them by saying, 'My name is Jesus of Nazareth.' His tone and demeanour took them off guard. It was full of such understanding, love, and compassion that even I was brought to a sense of numbed silence. The panic I'd felt suddenly disappeared. I knew instinctively that this was all supposed to have happened. It was that moment when I began to comprehend what this was all about. This was the beginning. Where this journey was going to take us was somewhere no one had ever been before."

* * *

With the crowd looking on in astonishment, Jesus stepped down from the podium and moved among the people in the direction of Martha, and together they went on their way. It was cold and becoming dark; they knew their parents would be concerned, but they were in no hurry. Quietly absorbed in thought, they walked together in silence, while trying to grasp the enormity of what had just occurred. Martha spoke only briefly, suggesting they should tell their parents what had happened, and Jesus agreed to do so, but the remainder of the journey home was undertaken in an atmosphere of calm.

Both instinctively knew what had just occurred: the historic beginning of an historic life.

PART II – THE TEENAGE YEARS

A significant turning point occurred in Jesus's life at around the age of fourteen, when his cousin of the same age, Judas Iscariot, joined the family. Judas's mother had passed away, and it had been agreed by extended family that Joseph and Mary's home would be the most suitable for Judas to be raised. His father travelled extensively to earn a living, so it was thought that the stable environment Joseph and Mary provided was somewhere he could thrive.

From the moment Judas arrived, the entire family felt he had always been there, and it was not long before close friendships were established among the children. Over time, a particular bond developed between Jesus and Judas, which was a huge relief to Joseph and Mary – finally they could relax a little, knowing there was someone capable of helping Jesus view life from a more relaxed standpoint. Judas possessed a simplistic and innocent take on life, which brought levity to situations that may otherwise have become intense. Jesus developing a sense of detachment from matters he found upsetting was a coping mechanism that did not come naturally, but thanks to Judas it was something he learned to appreciate the merit of.

About two years after Judas's arrival, and when both boys were approaching the age of sixteen, Joseph and Mary decided they would benefit from some travelling. It was arranged for them to spend a few months at a time with various relatives and family friends, and earn their keep by gaining employment at the carpentry trade they'd been taught by their father. Mary was not entirely happy to be sending the boys away, but she felt that Jesus's reputation within their community was becoming too widespread for someone of his years, and for that reason she convinced herself the break would be of benefit to everyone.

Jesus and Judas were excited about the plans, and as soon as arrangements were in place they set off. They weren't travelling too far, but the experience gave them a sense of freedom, and they loved the idea of that. Both boys worked hard at their carpentry jobs during the day, helped with their host family's chores, and attended the local synagogue. However, what was missing was a little fun, and the best way they knew to achieve that was by teasing and challenging preachers.

The antics of Jesus and Judas in synagogue and around town were mostly for the thrill of seeing a reaction, but they made it more interesting by placing a wager. The challenge related to whether or not they would be thrown out of synagogue for being argumentative, and as both boys assessed the target and placed a bet, Jesus purposely triggered a debate. However, Judas failed to realise that Jesus was manipulating the level of antagonism to ensure he won the bet each time, and it was several months before he sheepishly admitted the truth. As a frustrated Judas counted the cost of being a little too slow to catch on, the boys making the acquaintance of a more worldly-wise cousin presented him with an opportunity to retrieve his losses. In meeting a relative who later became known as John the Baptist, Jesus and Judas not only thoroughly enjoyed the company of their slightly older cousin, but benefited from his more sophisticated approach to certain matters. When Judas warned that John not be taken in by the antics of Jesus, John came up with the idea that they join forces and encourage other teenagers to participate and place small stakes of their own. Needless to say, this team-effort worked well and they cleaned up every time, with Judas winning back his losses several-fold.

As the years progressed, John became more involved in Jesus's life, and it was during this time that the idea of a ministry began to be formulated. As the normal rebellion of someone in their latter teens took hold, Jesus determined that he had to do 'something' to put the world to rights, and many years of debating political and social issues with John, Martha, and Judas formed the basis of what eventually became the ministry that consumed every day of his life. John was an integral part of this process and became involved in nurturing Jesus's temperament, which was a great support to Martha and Judas. His home was not too far from Nazareth, and after the boys had become so well-acquainted during their teenage years, they visited one another frequently. The debates about plans for the future were often intense, and John offered much needed guidance and insight. In fact, John the Baptist eventually became so involved in the ministry that Jesus credited his perception and encouragement as being akin to having a personal guardian, who ensured he never put a foot wrong when making important decisions.

Joseph and Mary neither learned of the betting game antics, nor did they realise for some time what these rebels with a cause were planning. Jesus was no different than other teenagers, and was excellent at pulling the wool over his parents' eyes.

In Martha's Voice:

"Even though Jesus and I saw ourselves as ordinary teenagers, in many ways we knew we weren't. Throughout our teenage years we continuously discussed with one another, and with Judas and John, our ideas about the future and what we thought we were supposed to achieve. At times we both felt that what we discussed seemed ridiculous and far-fetched, and every so often we came to our senses and questioned our reasoning and the harsh reality of our fantastical plans. Then somehow we'd suddenly come to terms with it all; we'd get on with life, while remaining connected to this other part of us that was emerging from within. It often seemed as though another person existed inside each of us. We were the teenagers everyone could see, as well as someone they could not.

"I can't imagine how we'd have coped with the way our minds worked if we'd not had each other to talk to. The truth is — we probably wouldn't have coped."

PART III – A YOUNG MAN EMERGES

Jesus and Judas visited their family in Nazareth frequently during the four-year period they worked away from home, and returned permanently as they approached the age of twenty. Joseph needed help from his sons in supporting the family, so everyone was reunited for the foreseeable future, which brought a sense of comfort and stability to the home. Jesus had matured considerably over the years and was taking his responsibilities at home seriously, but deep down another persona was evolving. Working alongside Judas in their father's carpentry workshop, he often found himself thinking seriously about the future, especially as he became more consciously aware of what his role in life was to be.

Jesus would discuss his thoughts with Martha and Judas, and with John when he visited, but not with anyone else. He didn't want to worry his parents with talk of what he believed the future held; they were such gentle people and Jesus thought they'd be upset if they discovered the sort of plans he and Martha had. They both knew their lives would be in danger once the ministry began, but were determined to succeed at whatever cost.

It had been agreed between Jesus and Martha that if anything untoward happened to Jesus before his goals reached fruition, John was going to take over and carry through the plans. While his personality and demeanour was quite different to that of Jesus, he had a similar energy and commanding presence: it was felt he could comfortably step in if required, and he was more than willing to do so.

John purposely distanced himself and took a back seat when it came to the detailed ministry preparation and the recruiting of followers. It was decided that maintaining discretion regarding his association would avoid the possibility of his arrest should that fate befall Jesus. However, John knew and understood every aspect of what was to be achieved, and was more than capable of effectively carrying on where Jesus left off should the need arise.

★ ★ ★

In Martha's Voice:

"As things turned out, our efforts to keep Mama and Papa in the dark about our plans were unnecessary. We were astonished to discover that they'd known all along what we were up to, but had chosen not to interfere, while keeping a distant, watchful eye on proceedings. In fact, we didn't think they were paying attention to our conversations at all — little did we know. It wasn't until about six years before the ministry began that Mama confessed she'd known what our future held since long before we were born. I remember being so shocked when discovering that.

"On one particular day, Mama had been quietly sitting in a room adjacent to ours, and was listening in to our conversation. Jesus and I had been going over ideas for the future and questioning the wisdom of everything we felt so driven to pursue. While reflecting upon the strategy we had in mind, we were anxiously considering how on earth we could believe it was feasible to achieve something that often seemed so completely absurd. Sensing doubt, anxiety, and fear in our voices, Mama suddenly appeared in front of us in a manner we'd not witnessed before. She momentarily looked at us both, and then bluntly stated, 'You have nothing to fear, but fear.'

"We looked up in amazement — Mama rarely, if ever, made such comments — she kept her thoughts to herself. I remember glancing towards Jesus, hoping he would respond, but he didn't utter a word — I don't think he knew what to say. In deciding I had better break the silence, I gently asked: 'How can you be so sure?'

"Looking towards Jesus, Mama seemed to wait a few seconds for his reaction, but he continued to maintain eye contact and didn't say a word. Jesus told me later that he didn't speak because he felt this let Mama know that we really needed to hear whatever it was she had to say.

"As we both looked up with uncertainty in our eyes, Mama walked over and took Jesus's left hand and my right, and said, 'Before you were born, Papa dreamt of your futures. The dreams are coming true, and that is all you need to know. I listen quietly to your plans, but would only speak out if they were not in accordance with what Papa and I already know. I am intervening now because you've allowed fear to enter your thought processes. As you are both aware, one of the main things you are to teach is that fear is an impediment to succeeding in life, and that is something you need to keep in mind yourselves. Fear not — you are on the right path, and the only thing you need to be fearful of, is fear itself. Do not forget to do as you teach, Jesus.'

"Of course, we had umpteen questions, but we didn't say a word in response. When Mama walked out of the room, we both looked at one another in astonishment — there'd been so much we wanted to ask, but neither of us knew where to start. Jesus became very quiet; as if he was absorbing what had just taken place. I could tell he was a little taken aback, so touching his right arm I quietly asked, 'Aren't you going to say something?'

"Jesus seemed to sigh to himself in an almost reluctant way, and appeared deep in thought for a few moments, but eventually he looked directly at me and said, 'Martha, I think we've just learned one of our most important lessons, and we must not forget what Mama has said about permitting fear to enter the equation. We have also received confirmation that we are doing what we are supposed to be doing, but I don't think we should ask anything more of Mama, or tell her the specifics of our plans. I sense she only wants to know what she needs to know. I think anything more may be too distressing for her. We need to respect that, and trust that when it is important for us to be provided with more information, Mama will do so.'

"I completely agreed with everything Jesus said, and as I acknowledged that he was right, he stood, and slowly walked outside. Those few moments had left us reeling: something had changed and we both needed time to take it all in. We always knew a ministry was our destiny, but I think we'd also thought it was something we could choose. Suddenly, it felt as though we didn't have a choice any more — it was as if our future was mapped out whether we liked it or not. There could be no more questions or doubts. There was no going back."

* * *

By the age of twenty-two Jesus had completely overcome his youthful impatience; he'd matured beyond his years, and now understood that people needed to know he appreciated what they were coping with. He had learned that expressing his beliefs in a compassionate, persuasive, and straightforward manner, as well as bringing lightheartedness to situations when needed, was the only approach that would succeed. He hoped that by reaching out to people in this way they would begin to accept him; ultimately trusting and understanding that what he was attempting to teach would dramatically alter the course of their lives. Jesus was convinced that if he could teach humanity to be humane, there would never be another war, and every person on earth would be taken care of and provided for.

* * *

One of the decisions made during the many hours and days spent planning for the future, was that Jesus and Judas would leave home once again when they reached the age of 24. By then, their younger brothers would be old enough to take over their responsibilities, which meant that travelling further afield for an extended period of time would not affect the family. Jesus needed to experience the world from many different perspectives if he was going to have the impact he desired, so it was appreciated that this trip could last up to five years and would take the young men to lands they knew very little about. While the logistics involved in such a journey were consuming, they were not the priority that occupied Jesus's mind. This experience needed to encompass many things, and after much deliberation regarding the most vital aspects of such a trip, the main priority became obvious – it was simply to learn. Jesus needed to know precisely what it was people needed to understand to facilitate succeeding in life.

Leaving the town of Nazareth, with its comparatively small population and narrow, insular visionaries, Jesus and Judas journeyed to larger cities where they would have opportunities to meet people from more diverse backgrounds. Their travels began by land to the north of Nazareth, and then west by sea towards Greece, Italy and France. Upon reaching the northern coast of France, they sailed to southern England, and eventually travelled on to Wales and Ireland. Their return journey brought them through France, Spain, and a small area of Portugal, and Morocco, and by sea through the Italian and Greek islands, returning to the mainland of Egypt before travelling north through Israel and on to the town of Nazareth.

Throughout the five years that Jesus and Judas were away, Martha assisted her mother in running the household and spent much of her time observing the climate of change occurring around her. In her spare time she drew up plans for how the ministry could most effectively be conducted, which created a good foundation for when the actual plans were put in motion.

In Martha's Voice:

"I missed Jesus and Judas so much during those years; it's a period of my life I really wouldn't want to relive. I kept myself busy helping Mama and continued with my own research in preparation for their return, but despite my life being very full and occupied, I began to feel anxious from time to time and doubts crept into my mind. To seek a little reassurance, I made some casual enquiries of Mama. I wanted to know why she and Papa had not told us what they knew about how our lives would evolve.

"It was obvious Mama was reluctant to discuss very much in the way of specific details, but what she divulged was helpful: 'At first, we didn't want to believe it' she explained, 'Papa had dreams that were quite vivid and detailed – they couldn't be ignored. But we'd not been given the impression we were to tell you. The proof was provided when we saw you both emerge into the young adults we had been told you would become. It was astonishing for us to watch your progression and listen in to your conversations and plans. We left you alone because you didn't need our input; you were doing everything we'd already dreamt you would. There was nothing for us to say or contribute, and to this day that remains the same.'

"I suppose this is what I needed to hear to feel reassured. I needed to learn once again that we were on the right path, and that Jesus's plans weren't just those of a rebellious young man, but those of someone who had a destiny to fulfill."

* * *

The eventual return of Jesus and Judas was well prepared for, and the long term plans to combine what Martha had learned with the information gathered during their years of travelling, created a well-rounded foundation for the ministry's beginnings. Throughout the five-year excursion Jesus had engaged people from all walks of life and encouraged them to speak from the depths of their heart; letting him know what it was they needed to understand. As had been expected, people from every culture and socio-economic background presented Jesus with the same questions — no doubt the same questions we would ask of him today. What is the purpose of life? What are we supposed to be achieving? Does God really exist? If so, who or what is God, and where can he be found? People also wanted to understand what life was really for; who are we, and why are we here? What happens, if anything, when death occurs? Why is there such discord and why is there not enough of everything for everyone? Why do so many seem to suffer, while some benefit from the suffering of others? What is life really about, and how can we do better at whatever it is we are supposed to be doing?

* * *

Jesus and Judas were both turned twenty-nine by the time they returned to Nazareth for an emotional reunion with their family. To some extent they were all aware that the homecoming ushered in a new era, although nothing specific was discussed at first. Everyone seemed to instinctively know what was ahead, but no one was ready to speak of it – it would have made it too real. For the first week or two of being back together, they each satisfied a shared desire to reconnect and become used to the family dynamics returning to what they had always been, but the joy of being reunited was tainted by a terrible sadness that encompassed the entire family. The timing of Jesus and Judas's return coincided with their father's deteriorating health, and without hesitation all matters of business were put aside as the priority became supporting and caring for their beloved father, as he reached the conclusion of his life.

Joseph was relieved to see his sons return safely to Nazareth, and in witnessing how much Jesus had matured after all he'd experienced and learned, he felt liberated and at peace. As if sensing that his main life purpose was complete, Joseph permitted himself to relinquish the struggle to survive, recognising there was no longer a need. Jesus had evolved into the most splendid personification of a human being: his role as a father was complete.

Only a few days after the brothers had returned to the family home, Joseph passed away peacefully in his sleep, causing the entire family to suffer enormous grief: this gentle, unassuming man had been a consummate illustration of modesty and strength of character to all. On the day before he died, Joseph became lucid enough to notice that Jesus was by his side. Not forgetting the many dreams he'd experienced throughout his life regarding what the future held for his son, Joseph enquired of Jesus's plans – it was as if he could not go until he knew his responsibility was complete. Jesus gently reassured him:

"Papa, our time spent travelling was highly successful and Judas was a great support; he came up with many observations and ideas that complemented my own. I learned the skill of reaching people by using the most straightforward vocabulary, which cannot be misinterpreted: my use of language and argument has to be based in absolute commonsense, and needs to be instantly recognised as such. I discovered how powerful words can be, and I learned how to reach a person's soul: I need to accept them for who they are, and not judge them in any way. I now know what I have to do, and it's really much less complex than you might think. People need to know who they are and the purpose of their existence. Sometimes it's difficult for people to see those things, and even more difficult to understand. It wasn't so bad for me. I've always known I had a very specific purpose in life, but it took me quite some time to realise that most people do not appreciate that about themselves. I used to become impatient, but now I understand. I know it's not going to be easy, Papa, and I think I know how it's going to end. But I don't have a choice. What else could I possibly do with my life? I only hope it's not all in vain and that people benefit in the way I intend. It's an uncertain process, but Martha and I have been working on this for our entire lives. I only hope we get it right.

"Papa — thank you for being such a perfect example of humility and for not judging me when things were so difficult and I didn't understand. You never told me what to do; you showed me. That is what I hope I can achieve. I need to show people what to do, not tell them. God bless you Papa."

Joseph's last words to his much-loved son were: "You know more than I what you have to do. I will be with you, as I always have."

* * *

In Martha's Voice:

"It took us all quite some time to come to terms with the void we felt at the loss of Papa; he had always been there for us in every sense possible. For so long we could not fathom that he was gone. He was still in our hearts, but the lack of his physical presence was so difficult to bear. Momentarily becoming distracted in thought, and suddenly being brought back to reality, served as a painful reminder. Eventually, the realisation that his voice was no longer present accompanied the understanding that it actually was. We all learned that if we listened, we could hear. He never really left; he couldn't, and we wouldn't let him.

"After a period of mourning, Jesus, Judas and I began to discuss in detail everything we had learned during the previous five years. We drew up plans and discussed with Mama that it was time for us to leave Nazareth to make preparations for the ministry. We wanted to distance ourselves from the family completely at this stage; we didn't want Mama or our younger siblings to be involved. There was no telling how things were going to turn out, or whether we would even be permitted to continue for very long. All we knew was that we had to try. What the outcome would be, and whether or not we would all survive, was something we were unable to predict."

CHAPTER FOUR

THE PLANNING PHASE

PART I – A MAN NAMED SETH

*P*rior to the official beginning of the ministry, Jesus authorised a man named Seth to seek out secure locations for he and Martha to conduct their undertaking in relative safety. Seth had encountered Jesus towards the end of his five-year excursion with Judas, and had been impressed by what he witnessed. There were many people like Jesus who travelled from town to town and engaged people, but there was no one with the astonishing presence and captivating vitality of Jesus. Seth had noticed he was unique, and discreetly followed him for some time to learn of his philosophy firsthand. Approximately six months before Jesus and Judas were due to return to Nazareth, Seth approached them to discuss the possibility of becoming involved in the ministry. He explained that he represented an emerging influential movement of people with similarly held convictions, who could offer considerable support. Seth further suggested that by joining forces with the individuals he represented, the philosophy of the ministry would be promoted and incorporated into the group's ideology, thereby ensuring that Jesus's message would be spread far and wide effectively and quickly. By way of further encouragement, Seth offered the use of his group's well-established network, secure housing, financial support, and protection from the authorities while the ministry was being conducted.

Jesus considered the offer Seth presented, which in many ways was an attractive one. He knew that without the support of someone like Seth and the movement he claimed to have behind him, the ministry would be in serious jeopardy. During his final year of travelling, Jesus had succeeded in creating quite a following, but he had also succeeded in acquiring enemies from within the religious establishment: while they feared his unorthodox views, their main concern related to how many of their congregation embraced them. This made Jesus aware that he needed to institute contingency plans to protect himself, Martha, Judas, and followers who may work alongside him. However, the need for plans and support had become even more urgent since his trusted and beloved cousin, John the Baptist, had recently been murdered by King Herod.

The sudden and unexpected death of John meant there was no longer a Plan B — there was no one else who could possibly take over Jesus's role if there was a sudden arrest prior to the completion of the ministry. As well as feeling bereft at the news of John's death, Jesus felt that this further highlighted the danger he and his immediate family members were in: overstepping the mark at the wrong moment could provoke an arrest without warning. The fate of John the Baptist made Jesus feel more vulnerable – he knew he could afford to take very few risks. However, failing to reach his potential was an inconceivable outcome: Jesus was determined his end would not be upon him before the ministry had succeeded.

* * *

Unbeknown to Jesus, the group Seth represented comprised of individuals from all walks of life who were set upon establishing a new world order. Their leaders were from a wealthy, influential community of people, determined to expand their collective voice using whatever means it took to establish emotional control over the masses. Although remaining underground, they had become quite well organised, with effective communication techniques and clear mandates in place. However, what they lacked was an individual with appealing magnetism and strength of character: someone who was not afraid to speak his mind, and was capable of evolving into an iconic symbol of what they referred to as the 'Movement'.

While this aspect of the Movement was not disclosed to Jesus, it was similarly not understood to be as such by Seth. He was convinced he'd discovered someone quite unique in Jesus; an individual with the necessary charisma and presence, who he believed would complement the ideologies of the group he'd been indoctrinated into. Seth did his utmost to persuade Jesus they were of like mind, and to achieve that end he used Jesus's own expressions, which he'd been inconspicuously listening to for many months. Seth was desperate to convince Jesus to accept his offer and was certain his superiors would be highly impressed with such a find, for which he hoped to personally reap the reward of promotion within the Movement's ranks.

Jesus thought long and hard about the arrangement and discussed the pros and cons in detail with Judas. Ultimately, it was concluded they actually had little choice. Jesus had to survive and see the ministry through, but without some form of support and protection his fate could quite easily mirror that of John the Baptist. Once the ministry became official, and if a serious following emerged, there was every possibility his life would be in jeopardy. When Jesus meditated on this decision, he intuitively felt he should accept Seth's offer. If it ever transpired that the Movement had ulterior motives, Jesus felt sure they would pay for such indiscretion – he was convinced that God was on his side.

* * *

Jesus and Seth hammered out the basics of an agreement, and Seth promised to relay the details back to his superiors before a firm commitment was reached. In addition to what Seth had offered, Jesus asked that protection be provided for his family in the event of an arrest, and that a separate location be established for Martha to live and operate. He also asked that an alias be established for Martha to assume in the event of an unexpected change in circumstance. He wanted to avoid at all costs the potential of an arrest befalling her.

It was always appreciated that the ministry could cause disruption, and possibly an arrest and prosecution, but Jesus and Martha needed to feel assured that matters would not move beyond their control. With the Movement's support, Jesus felt the message of the ministry would spread far and wide expeditiously, but before making a final decision there were many issues to contemplate. The possibility that the Movement may not fulfill its commitments, and thereby create a situation where the ministry may have to be abandoned, was something that needed to be looked at seriously.

It was going to take some weeks for Seth to travel to his superiors, convince them he had discovered someone unique, work out an agreement to accommodate Jesus's requests, and arrange for leaders of the Movement to meet with Jesus in person. This allowed sufficient time for Jesus to give the pact further consideration, but with the added benefit of being able to inform Martha of developments so she could provide input. Conveniently, even though the brothers were not scheduled to return to Nazareth for another six months, they were located only seven days journey time away. It was therefore decided that Judas would travel to Nazareth to discuss Seth's offer with Martha, since she would be able to take into account the prevailing atmosphere in Galilee and anything else that may be pertinent.

For Jesus, the most attractive aspect of this agreement was the fact that the Movement seemed to have a massive following that was well-structured and in place. If they could be utilised to work alongside him and his own followers, this would indeed ensure that news of the ministry could be spread very effectively. However, far more than this needed to be considered, and including the thoughts of Martha in these deliberations was considered paramount.

* * *

Seth and Judas set off towards their respective destinations, and for the first two days of the journey they travelled together. This was convenient for both in that they had an opportunity to learn a little more about one another. Judas wanted to make certain of Seth's trustworthiness and strength of character, while Seth used the time to discover more about Jesus, his life, and his plans for the future. Judas found Seth to be quite an affable man; some ten years older than himself, and a person of sound mind and good conscience. Seth talked of his outrage at the various authorities in existence at the time, and what he believed the Movement hoped to achieve. Reading between the lines of conversation, Judas learned something important: Seth was clearly a very small cog in a big wheel. He had originally given the impression that the Movement was something he had been a founder of, but as Judas assessed — he was no more than a follower trying to make a name for himself. Seth had made a number of promises to Jesus, which Judas now appreciated would have to be negotiated with his superiors. Judas also discovered that Seth had little to no power of command, which meant he would be subject to much control by people neither he nor Jesus had personal knowledge of — an important aspect to bear in mind when making their final decision.

Seth was charmed by Judas and decided he could not have met a more honest and forthright individual. This eased his mind considerably — if this was Jesus's closest companion, it was a very positive indicator of Jesus's character. Seth was fascinated by the stories Judas told regarding how Jesus and Martha had always known what their destiny would be, and what part Judas had played in their life since he was fourteen. He began to gain an understanding of why Jesus had so many distinctive characteristics that set him apart from anyone else, and the more he learned from Judas, the more he appreciated how significant his find had been. Seth was determined to persuade his superiors that this was the man they had been looking for.

* * *

Martha was thrilled to see Judas after being apart for so many years, and was keen to hear of everything that had transpired throughout the long journey, but was particularly interested to learn what arrangements Jesus and Seth had provisionally agreed. While concurring with Judas's apprehension regarding a lack of firsthand knowledge of the people Seth represented, Martha felt somewhat assured by his description of the Movement's beliefs, which appeared to correspond with their own. Judas portrayed Seth's engaging personality, openness, evident passion, and apparent good character, which suggested he'd more than likely be involved with people of similar moral principle.

Martha confided in Judas her growing concerns regarding an arrest befalling Jesus once he began conducting the ministry; the prevailing atmosphere within the religious authority meant they were certain to initially view his ideas as controversial. Consequently, she agreed that Seth's offer be seriously considered, recommending an accord be reached if at all possible, but also suggested it be made clear from the outset that the Movement failing to produce what they'd promised would justify the agreement being abandoned, and Jesus and Martha proceeding as originally planned.

* * *

During subsequent months, founding members of the Movement travelled with Seth to observe Jesus for themselves. Initially, they did as Seth had done when coming across Jesus, and gathered anonymously within the crowd and listened to him speak; affording them the chance to determine the most influential approach for when the time came to be formally introduced. Needless to say, the Movement's leaders were decidedly impressed with Seth's find, and once they were comfortable and fully prepared, they entered into discussions with Jesus regarding how they could work together.

Jesus's appraisal of Seth's associates was that they seemed open minded, interested in his observations and techniques, and thought similarly regarding changes he felt needed to be encouraged. Jesus explained his philosophy and expressed his ambitions for the ministry, while assessing their disciplines and beliefs throughout the conversation. The leaders of the Movement convinced Jesus they were of like-mind, and willingly agreed that he be given full authority over how the ministry was conducted; offering to support his endeavours in whatever way necessary. It was also agreed that Jesus's ideals and personal characteristics be used to symbolise the Movement, which Jesus did not consider was problematic at the time. Before long, both parties reached agreement on all the finer points, and Seth was assigned the task of overseeing security arrangements and acquiring accommodation as per Jesus's request.

* * *

Several months after Jesus and Judas returned to Nazareth, and once the mourning period for their father had progressed, precise plans for the future began to take shape. Seth was rewarded handsomely for persuading Jesus to allow his ministry to be incorporated into the Movement's philosophy, and his superiors agreed he would be an invaluable resource when co-coordinating matters. Seth was granted the coveted position of chief liaison between his superiors, Jesus, and Martha, and was assigned a large house within a secure compound known as Barbelo, located to the north-west of Jerusalem. To facilitate his part in the operation, Seth was provided with several staff and guards, with more at his disposal if required. Needless to say, Seth was elated at such a promotion and entirely confident in his ability to carry out his responsibilities.

Seth's first task was to locate secure housing for all parties, which he achieved with little difficulty and in a timely manner. It was decided that Jesus and Judas would be based in Capernaum, located to the north of Jerusalem and Nazareth, on the north-west shores of the Sea of Galilee. Seth arranged for Martha to be based initially in Bethany, two miles east of Jerusalem, in the home of wealthy siblings Mary of Bethany and her brother Lazarus. In addition to the Bethany house, Mary and Lazarus owned a second home located on the western shores of the Sea of Galilee; a few miles south of Jesus's base in Capernaum. This second home became Martha's base throughout the actual three-year ministry, with the Bethany house being used during this time for planning meetings and social gatherings between Jesus, Martha, and their followers.

The two homes Martha shared with Mary and Lazarus provided her with a safe haven from the authorities, and the private locations were perfect for Martha to discreetly carry out her duties. She acquired a separate identity for the benefit of those who lived in the two communities; portraying herself as a family member of Mary and Lazarus, which created a situation where Martha could assume that identity in the event of a sudden change of circumstance. While Jesus and Judas were prepared to accept the potential fatal consequences of the ministry, they did their utmost to ensure Martha's safety. One of her responsibilities was to record and maintain a diary of the entire work of the ministry, since it was imperative to provide manuscript evidence to pass on to future generations. For this reason, it was vital that Martha's life be preserved at all costs.

Jesus, Martha, and Judas prepared for the beginning of the ministry by assigning themselves roles and responsibilities. It was agreed that Martha would liaise with Seth, be responsible for logistics, and coordinate how best to present their case to the people. Prior to the official start of the ministry, Jesus and Judas spent their time travelling and preaching in communities and synagogues. Jesus needed to establish a climate of trust before moving into the actual ministry phase, while simultaneously recruiting a following to support him throughout this period. Judas was responsible for observing the reaction of the crowd from a distance, and paying attention to anything unseemly occurring that may become a threat. Throughout this period, all three regularly met at the Bethany house to share what they'd learned, review developments, and introduce new followers to the ministry.

* * *

The Movement Seth represented is what eventually became known as the movement of Christianity. They were a well-organised group, comprising of individuals from many walks of life and religious affiliations. These people were disenchanted with just about every authority, religious and political, and were determined to develop an establishment that incorporated politics and religion in equal measure. Religion and politics have always been linked, but the early Christian movement's founding policies were to ensure that politics remained dependent upon religion, and religion maintained control over politics. This is one of the reasons so many political disputes in the world are religion-based, and why religious intolerance manifests into political disputes. In this century as much as any other, religious interference in political processes is rampant.

Jesus and Martha had no idea this philosophy was behind the Movement. They had been offered protection and encouraged to believe their respective ideologies were compatible. They had been convinced that participating with the Movement would ensure the rapid spread of the ministry's message; eventually reaching people throughout the entire world. However, they were unaware that the Movement was recruiting from the disenchanted of every nation, much in the way radical organisations do today. They inspired the angry and resentful to join its ranks, using indoctrination procedures that were highly persuasive to those with no sense of direction or purpose in their life.

Jesus's perception of the Movement's objectives when compared with their true intentions was entirely conflicting. He assumed they had been encouraged by his theories and were intent upon spreading his message to effect change in the way Jesus imagined. His impression was that these wealthy, influential people wanted to support achieving the enlightenment of minds, while helping individuals resolve personal conflict, but he had been completely misguided. Jesus was oblivious to the fact that the Movement had incredible plans for the future, which did not come close to coinciding with his own.

Without any knowledge of the history or foundation of the Movement, Jesus and Martha had placed themselves in a highly vulnerable position. The impeccably presented leaders had been encouraging, and convinced Jesus their intentions coincided. They promised not to interfere with the ministry itself, and persuaded they were in total agreement with its principles. The enthusiastic Seth had ingratiated himself with Jesus's family, all of whom believed him to be genuine in his desire to support the ministry. Understandably, these impressions created a false sense of security, for which Jesus, Martha, and Judas would later forfeit far more than could have been imagined.

Unbeknown to Jesus and Martha, the dilemma they were yet to comprehend was further compounded. Their only liaison with the Movement throughout the ministry period was their new acquaintance, Seth. While recognising that Seth was not the senior official he had initially portrayed, Jesus was unaware that Seth had been recruited into the Movement as a consequence of their indoctrination techniques. Therefore, Seth too had no real knowledge of the founding principles of those he'd represented to Jesus; he believed wholeheartedly in what he thought was their ambition. However, Seth also believed passionately in Jesus and his ministry. He respected his commitment to succeed at any cost, and was determined to support him in whatever way he could. The man named Seth was destined to face some very difficult choices of conscience.

PART II – THE INTRODUCTION OF JESUS
AND MARY MAGDALENE

The living and working arrangements Seth organised for Martha, accommodated her with the siblings Mary of Bethany and Lazarus. It was a consequence of this association that Jesus made the acquaintance of Mary Magdalene.

Mary of Bethany and Lazarus were wealthy young people, but rather lazy and lacking in direction. Seth discovered these young, impressionable siblings during his search for a secure location to house Martha. He persuaded them to provide accommodation by explaining that Martha was responsible for organising all aspects of the ministry of Jesus, and that ultimately they would achieve personal laudable status for their contribution to the cause. This was an exciting prospect for both Mary and Lazarus when compared to their normal everyday activities, so they agreed to house Martha and go along with Seth's plans.

About six months after Martha had taken up residence with Mary and Lazarus, and immediately prior to the official start of the ministry, Lazarus became gravely ill. For several days he lay in an unconscious state, suffering the effects of a high fever. Mary of Bethany was beside herself with grief, and no amount of reassurance from Martha could convince her of Lazarus's condition. She had concluded her brother was dead, and only because Martha insisted he was not did the 'body' remain in their home. They were anticipating a visit from Jesus, and Martha maintained that a final assessment of Lazarus's condition be made at that time.

Much to Martha's relief, Jesus arrived at the Bethany house to conduct meetings with his disciples on the fourth day of the illness. Explaining the condition of Lazarus and that Mary was inconsolable, Martha asked Jesus to examine him and confirm her appraisal. When Jesus and Martha walked into the room where Lazarus lay, they found him sitting up in bed complaining of thirst. An exhausted Mary of Bethany had fallen asleep on the floor next to her brother's bed, and at that point she suddenly awoke. As she looked up, the first thing she witnessed was Jesus sitting at her brother's bedside wiping his brow and conversing with him. Mary jumped to her feet screaming for joy that Lazarus was now alive and claiming he must have been brought back from the dead by Jesus. In a state of hysteria,

Mary raced outside telling everyone that her family had been blessed by the miracle she had witnessed.

Jesus and Martha tried to ignore the commotion, knowing there was nothing they could say to convince Mary of anything other – she had been so sure her brother was dead. However, when excitable crowds began gathering at the house, Jesus felt obliged to step outside and address them. He attempted to dismiss the miracle aspect of Lazarus's recuperation by explaining he had simply overcome a serious fever. Mary, enthralled at being the centre of attention, insisted Jesus was being modest and convinced her neighbours otherwise. The people of the little town of Bethany loved the idea that a miracle had occurred in their domain and preferred to believe Mary's version of events. From that moment on, the miracle of Lazarus being raised from the dead became 'gospel'.

* * *

The experience of Lazarus's recovery was Mary of Bethany's first personal connection with Jesus, and this caused her to adore him in more ways than one – as Jesus of Nazareth, but also as a man. Mary of Bethany now had a direct association with Jesus; she was the central witness to the miracle of Lazarus, and thus felt she had rights to a closer involvement with him.

Not long after the illness of Lazarus had passed, it was decided that Martha and the two siblings should move permanently to their second property on the shores of the Sea of Galilee. It was closer to Jesus's base, which for some time had been at Capernaum, and because the ministry was about to begin, Martha needed to be more centralised to her brother's location. It took little persuasion for Mary and Lazarus to agree to relocate to their coastal home since they would now do anything to be near Jesus – their miracle association had brought them much-desired attention, which they revelled in.

Because Mary of Bethany was determined to attract the attention of Jesus, she chose to reinvent herself as one of his disciples. Now feeling reborn as a devout follower of Jesus of Nazareth, Mary decided to give herself a new name. It was common practice in such times for people to take the town of their birth and incorporate it into their name. The town where Martha,

Mary, and Lazarus relocated to on the western shores of the Sea of Galilee was where Mary of Bethany felt her 'rebirth' occurred: the town was called Magdala – Mary of Bethany became Mary Magdalene.

* * *

Mary Magdalene had been a handful in the early days – always desiring to be the centre of attention and more than a little afraid of hard work. Her initial motive for becoming a devout follower of Jesus was not particularly convincing, but at least it created a positive outlet for her vital energy and an opportunity for her to contribute to the ministry in her own way. Judas thought she was charming and amusing. He could see she'd not yet matured into thinking beyond self, and correctly observed this was due to receiving no such guidance during her life. Judas took Mary under his wing, realising he needed to make sure she did not antagonise the other followers. Mary Magdalene had a tendency to insist she was the most dedicated disciple, benefiting from the closest relationship with Jesus, which disastrously impacted the egos of the ambitious followers, all of whom competed for attention.

The transformation of Mary Magdalene was a gradual process that occurred over several years. However, her gregarious personality, creative, active mind and determined nature, contributed much more to the life of Jesus than has previously been understood. The persistent insinuations of romance are untrue, but her effort and involvement in Jesus's life was impressive, which will be revealed in more detail as the story unfolds.

Mary Magdalene and Judas were, in essence, loathed by the other followers; the common ground for such discontent being their closeness to Jesus and their relationship with each other. Jealousy prompted the followers to direct their hatred towards the two, but particularly towards Judas, which made his life quite unbearable at times. While the followers knew there was no point in complaining directly to Jesus about Judas's close involvement in matters, they did not hesitate in making his life miserable when Jesus was not present. However, they felt no such restraint over their right to complain and exert more influence about the presence of their other main rival for Jesus's attention – Mary Magdalene.

The rumours surrounding the relationship between Jesus and Mary Magdalene were distracting to many, but it was well known among the followers that Jesus was not participating in a romance. However, Mary Magdalene did her best to create the impression that a close relationship existed, which the followers used as an excuse to condemn her while persuading Jesus to distance himself from such talk.

Mary Magdalene worked diligently to persuade Jesus to fulfill her desires, eventually submitting to the destiny of a love that would never be. However, neither Mary Magdalene nor the followers succeeded in their efforts to usurp one another's position, and the status quo was maintained. The followers were informed in no uncertain terms that Mary Magdalene was an integral part of the ministry, since Martha was being accommodated in her home. Her cooperation was of vital importance, and the followers were instructed to tolerate her presence among them.

CHAPTER FIVE

PART I – THE MINISTRY BEGINS

*T*he Bible is comprised of numerous stories depicting the life, ministry, and death of Jesus, and is believed by many to portray such information faithfully. However, the *real* ministry was never included in any aspect of the Bible: along with many other features of the life of Jesus, it has remained completely unknown to the world. Designed to teach precisely what we need to understand to facilitate conducting life effectively, the real ministry was divided into three specific areas: *Who we are, and why we are here; who or what is God, and how to communicate and interact directly with God.* These are issues that today remain the subject of considerable mystery and debate, due entirely to the suppression of the real ministry.

When Jesus and Martha planned out their endeavour, it was estimated that each stage would take approximately one year to teach, with each subsequent stage beginning once they had established the climate was right to do so. The three-year ministry was conducted close to the home bases of Capernaum and Magdala, on the north-west shores of the Sea of Galilee. It was not required for Jesus to travel great distances because the learning was a process, conducted as an ongoing experience over a specific period of time. The disciples were taught by Jesus precisely what to teach on his behalf, and they were each allocated an area to cover, which was in close proximity to Jesus's operation at the central base of the ministry.

The offer of support accepted from the Movement facilitated the dispensing of the teachings far and wide. Jesus taught the Movement's recruits how to present each stage of the ministry, and they were individually assigned a location further afield in neighbouring areas. Everything was coordinated in such a way that Jesus, his own disciples, and the Movement's recruits were teaching the same aspects of the ministry concurrently, which facilitated the message being spread simultaneously among many thousands of people.

Initially, it appeared as though Martha's dedicated work of coordinating the programme was paying dividends; more and more people were becoming interested in what was being taught, evidenced by the increasing crowds Jesus and the disciples attracted. However, only a few months into the first year, Jesus and Martha learned of something disturbing taking place in the areas being administered to by Seth's men. The Movement's recruits were not only presenting a message that did not entirely coincide with Jesus's instructions, but embellishments were being added that created enormous excitement and curiosity.

The Movement's recruits had so impressed their audience that people began travelling in the hundreds to the central base of the ministry to see Jesus for themselves. Initially, Jesus and Martha did not understand what was happening, but assumed that perhaps the sudden influx of travellers attending Jesus's own presentations was due to them not being content with the preaching of the recruits. However, when the number of people arriving into the area began to cause disruption, Jesus asked why they were so curious about him personally. It was then that it transpired that Seth's men were including remarkable tales of miraculous occurrences within their teaching agenda; persuading people they had witnessed such events, and strongly emphasising that this evidenced the divine son of God walked among them. Needless to say, Jesus was horrified to learn this news, but there was little he could do – people had been easily convinced by the tactics of the Movement's highly trained recruits, and Jesus's denial was merely assigned to gracious humility.

To complicate matters further, these rumours spread rapidly to the people Jesus and his own disciples were administering. Continuously having to deny such assertions distracted from the ministry teachings, and it became increasingly difficult to encourage participants to maintain focus. Predictably, Jesus and Martha met urgently with Seth to discuss these developments, but it registered fairly quickly that matters were way beyond their control. Seth was adamant that the stories enhanced the message of the ministry and reminded Jesus that one of his closest followers, Mary Magdalene, in witnessing the miracle of the resurrection of her brother, established his status in the town of Bethany. Seth was genuine in his approach and really believed that what his superiors instructed was a positive addition to the ministry. However, what Jesus saw was a terrible dilemma: he personally was becoming the focus, alongside the associated magic trick element of the miracle stories. People were in awe of Jesus, rather than what they could learn from his teachings and incorporate into their lives: the message of the ministry was being relegated to secondary status in everyone's mind.

Jesus and Martha disagreed strongly with Seth; they felt that claims of miracles and son of God theories could stir up considerable ill-feeling within the religious authority. They also thought this developing situation would actually discourage those who were genuinely interested in learning a new way of conducting life. However, Seth completely disagreed and suggested they were overreacting. He made himself clear in stating that he firmly believed the miracle stories would bring more people to the ministry, not turn them away. While Jesus agreed that such antics may attract more people, he argued it would be for the wrong reasons: they would be seeking to satisfy their curiosity rather than learn what he had to teach.

Despite ardent protests by Jesus and Martha, Seth continued to insist that it was necessary to create mystique surrounding Jesus, since there was a need to establish memorable associations that would support his eventual evolution into an iconic symbol of the Movement. Jesus, on the other hand, did not want to be remembered for fantastical stories of miraculous occurrences, which totally diminished the straightforward message of his ministry.

The recruits had been very successful and were highly trained by their superiors – no matter how much Jesus tried to alter impressions, people continued to believe what they wanted to believe. Seth's men had achieved their goal, and Jesus's public denials only served to establish him as one of immense modesty — he could not win. It began to register with Jesus and Martha that the Movement may have motives they had been completely unaware of.

* * *

Most of the well-known miracle stories can either be simply explained or dismissed as pure fabrication. However, many were actual events that did occur but were enhanced by the early Christians to create a twist that included a magical element, and by so doing the message Jesus tried to deliver literally disappeared. By way of example, I will translate into reality one well-known biblical story known as *the feeding of the five thousand.*

The Bible states that Jesus blessed and miraculously multiplied a few loaves of bread and several fish, producing sufficient fare to feed 5,000 people. However, what Jesus actually did was much more impressive, but Christianity chose to portray an event that would be viewed as an astonishing miracle, which only the divine son of God could perform. Here is the true story.

Jesus presented himself to a large group of people who, like him, were hungry, tired, and weak from travelling. In front of them he laid out the small amount of food he possessed, and in an attempt to motivate the gathered crowd he said, "Those who present themselves as the hungriest are very welcome to my food." Standing quietly to one side, Jesus awaited a response, but despite their hunger nobody moved forward: no one could possibly be so shameless as to stand up among a gathering of hungry, tired, and weak people and claim to be the hungriest.

Silence fell over the crowd as they meekly glanced towards one another while deep in thought. Jesus knew that many of the travellers would almost certainly be carrying supplies. He also knew it was most likely they were keeping their supplies to themselves and were unwilling to share with those around them who had nothing – to do so would mean they too would have nothing, or so it seemed. The human conscience had clearly not been engaged, since those with supplies were thinking only of themselves and were determined to emerge from the group as stronger, while knowing that those without food would become weaker and therefore need to depend upon the others for leadership.

Eventually, a man from the crowd slowly came to his feet, and as Jesus gestured towards him, he asked, "Are you the hungriest in this crowd?"

The man responded that he was not, stating he had sufficient supplies for his needs, but then asked, "I would like to request that I too be permitted to offer my food to the hungriest."

Jesus thanked the man for his humanity and generosity, and signalling that he step forward, he accepted the food and placed it alongside his own.

As the crowd continued to remain silent, another man eventually stepped forward and Jesus enquired of him, "Are you the hungriest in this crowd?"

The man responded in the same manner as the previous, and offered his personal supply of food to be added to the table for the hungriest. After a further short period of silence, approximately twenty men slowly came to their feet one by one, and as Jesus asked them the same question, they each provided the same answer. Gradually, the conscience of many more became engaged by the generosity they had witnessed, and in their dozens people came to their feet and walked forward to the table for the hungriest, depositing all they possessed to be shared equally among those in need.

Eventually, when those with plenty had felt humbled by the example Jesus had shown and learned from him a lesson of humanity, enough food was accumulated to share among all those gathered; sustaining everyone for the remainder of their journey.

The miracle was not that Jesus used a magic trick or a miraculous blessing to multiply a few loaves and fish and provide sustenance for 5,000 people. The miracle was Jesus, with his love and humanity, changed the minds of hundreds of tired, hungry, and weak people by setting an example for them to follow. Those who emulated his gesture were so moved by the gratitude and love shown by those in need, they could have lived off that feeling for several days. No longer was it a matter of the strong attempting to control the weak; rather, they all worked together and supported one another throughout the rest of the journey.

Had this simple story been told in this way, and instilled into the consciousness of mankind from an early age, imagine how different our experience of life would be today. The magic trick version established awe and contributed towards intimidating people into following the doctrine of those who represented Jesus. The true version would have been inspiring, and enabled people to see clearly what they could do to achieve such civility with grace, while learning for themselves the lesson of humanity that Jesus demonstrated throughout his life — *in giving you shall receive, since the gift is in the giving*. Perhaps by now we would be living in a world where the strong were not trying to control the weak, and nobody went hungry because we all shared what we had. We would each feel loved and respected, which would sustain us throughout our journey in life. Our individual strengths would complement one another's, while our weaknesses would not be viewed as such. This is just one small example of the massive injustice dealt to humanity at the hands of history's Christian leadership. The message for mankind was completely missed because the true story was never told.

* * *

As a result of what transpired during the early months of the ministry, Jesus and Martha debated whether they should abandon their plans to work with the Movement. They were now highly suspicious of their agenda and unhappy with recent events, not to mention being concerned with how little control they possessed over the direction of their programme. However, Seth had been provided with all the details of the three-year ministry and how it was to be conducted. If they walked away, it was certain the Movement would continue on their own terms, and do so in the name of Jesus.

Ultimately, they decided it was too late to back out. They would have been left to go it alone, and the protection provided by the Movement would have been removed. In addition, Jesus and Martha had become increasingly aware that the Movement had much influence with those in legal authority, and felt that Seth's superiors would almost certainly arrange for Jesus's arrest to ensure he did not interrupt their agenda. A serious following had already emerged and it was clear the Movement was not about to let that go. In fact, Jesus and Martha felt it likely they would not only orchestrate Jesus's arrest, but use it to gain further momentum for their cause by declaring Jesus a martyr, and subsequently use his memory to represent their doctrine.

All Jesus and Martha felt able to do was pray, while maintaining the belief that there must be a purpose for what was transpiring. They decided to remain committed to the ministry as per the original plans; continue to deny the miracle stories and son of God theories, and hope that in the end this is what people would instinctively believe. What they did not appreciate at the time, however, was that over two thousand years would pass before the *real ministry* was revealed.

CHAPTER SIX

THE REAL MINISTRY

Introduction

*T*he *real ministry* was never intended by Jesus and Martha to become a religion; rather, it was a philosophy of life that was cleverly designed to be incorporated into the principles of any religion, or embraced by those who desired no religious affiliation. The purpose was to create a school of thought that would enhance the experience of life; providing greater understanding of an individual's life purpose, while producing the personal freedom associated with a superior level of instinctive, informed intelligence. Encouraging those in religious authority to embrace such a philosophy was a vital component of the real ministry; without their support Jesus knew he would not succeed. He attempted to convince influential elders to unite with him, and encourage their faithful congregations that the ministry was nothing to fear.

To achieve unity and the cooperation of religious elders, Jesus needed to persuade them of the benefits of not exerting emotional control and influence over those they administered to: Jesus believed that such attitudes being maintained would eventually lead to resentment and rebellion. He believed that as the intellect of mankind evolved over time, the constraints of religion would be considered an insult to intelligence. While Jesus did not agree with the way religions administered to their faithful, he did believe they had a vital role to play in the evolution of humanity. However, he was serious in his conviction that religions should *only* provide spiritual and emotional support to those who sought such provision throughout their lives, and not be tempted to enter into the world's political arenas. Convincing religious leaders that they should distance themselves from the business of politics and focus only on the spirituality of mankind, proved to be one of the most difficult challenges Jesus faced: a challenge he failed to overcome.

In working diligently to convince religious elders that the temptation of political power and influence should be avoided entirely, Jesus tried to persuade that irreparable harm to the evolution of mankind would be the consequence of such ambition. He knew that if religious leaders were tempted in this direction, it would be impossible for them to know where to draw the line: the opportunity to achieve a more highly regarded status, coupled with enhanced power and influence, would be too great for them to resist. The boundaries of their spiritual responsibility to mankind would eventually become an invisible line they would confidently cross, thereby diluting the purpose of their existence in exchange for the rewards of political prowess.

Even though Jesus understood that religious leaders may feel a responsibility to involve themselves in political situations, particularly where they felt an ethical or human rights issue was being violated, Jesus specifically encouraged that they should not. He felt it was not within the confines of their responsibility to align themselves with or against any world or local political force, or any issue that was not purely spiritual in nature. Jesus was certain that the temptation would be considerable for the agenda of a religious institution to be disguised as a political, ethical, or human rights campaign, and believed that religions establishing influence within world governing bodies was a path that would lead to many complications, and ultimately contribute to the downfall of mankind.

Jesus firmly believed that if religious leaders focused upon incorporating his philosophy into their own doctrine, and eventually allowed such principles to transform their own methodology, mankind would evolve at an incredible rate: becoming sophisticated and confident enough to form oppositions to tyrannical governments in an intelligent, non-combative way, and seek to overturn human rights atrocities wherever they existed. Jesus was convinced that if people changed the way they viewed life, and their individual role and responsibility in the world, conflicts negotiated through battle would be delivered to history, with no single race or creed ever seeking to overrule another. Jesus felt the role of religion should be to encourage and strengthen a belief in self and in God, while discouraging a victim mentality. However, his perception was that most leaders of religion encouraged dependence; enforcing rules and customs to be abided, while sanctimoniously seeking dominance over each other. He was confident that if the message of his ministry became an inherent part of humanity, it would in time create a society that confidently believed in itself and intensely cared about others — matters of importance would become the focus; asking what we could contribute, rather than what we need or deserve to receive, would by now be second nature to us all.

Institutions of religion have missed their calling by diluting their provision of spiritual counsel that is pure in nature, and ignoring the persuasions of Jesus by interfering on the world's political stage. A situation now exists whereby religions are viewed with suspicion by the very people who need their counsel the most; their spiritual advice is often thought to be tainted by the political agenda of religion.

* * *

The focal point of the real ministry demonstrated what individuals were capable of, not what Jesus was capable of. His ambition was to instill a belief in self, not a belief in him. Jesus did not seek out followers who would be impressed by him personally; meekly agreeing with his philosophies and blindly accepting his word. He encouraged people to question and challenge so he could be certain they understood. He wanted not only to *hear* that people had correctly interpreted his teachings, but also to *see* that they had. Words are spoken and can be heard, but actions are seen and speak volumes. Jesus would not rest until he could see that people understood. He believed he was here as our servant, and that his life purpose was to teach what we needed to know, thereby removing the constraints imposed by a fear of the unknown.

Jesus was fully aware that the consequence of not succeeding in his endeavour would be a world lacking in direction, with very little understanding of the meaning of life. However, the long term plans of the early Christians were astounding, and Jesus and Martha were oblivious to the fact that their goals were not remotely in line. They were dealing with a highly organised political force that was determined to create a new world order. Jesus and Martha had no idea what they were up against.

PART I – WHO WE ARE, AND WHY WE ARE HERE

Throughout the first stage of the *real* ministry, Jesus provided information relating to *who we are and why we are here*. He believed this knowledge was the foundation people needed to support them in succeeding at life, and felt that confusion and anxiety would prevail if such understanding was withheld. Those who participated in the lessons were taught in such a way that they were able to examine the facts, and privately take the time to consider them.

In essence, Jesus taught that each of us is an entirely unique individual, inhabiting a physical body that accommodates what is generally referred to as *soul*. By and large, the soul is perceived to be an integral part of who we are, but despite its association with religion it has little to do with such beliefs. The human soul has been in existence for an infinite period of time, whereas organised religion is a man-made enterprise that commandeered the soul of humanity for its own purposes.

Soul is fleetingly visible in the form of a tiny fleck of light as it enters the body upon the birth of a child and departs at the moment of death. It does not consist of physical components; rather, it is an energy composed of light that possesses the faculties of awareness, thought, emotion, and memory. The soul is a reflection of our true self and can be likened to a microchip that encompasses information detailing every aspect of an individual. No single thought or occurrence is ever erased from soul, and once its journey on earth is complete and the physical body is no longer required, the soul returns to an inspirational light energy that exists within the universe. It is this light energy that those in religious authorities chose to name God, and by cleverly making a connection between themselves and something that is an inborn part of us all, religions created a situation whereby people were drawn to them in the belief they were making a connection with God.

As we each return to becoming the soul we were before birth, our lifetime experiences become a part of its memory. It is hoped that the learning occasions presented throughout the duration of life, which also include opportunities to contribute to the lives of others, society, and the world in general, result in a fuller awareness and greater maturity being developed and attained.

* * *

When people question *life* and ask, *what's it all about* – this is it – this is what it's all about. There is no reason to embark upon an undertaking to find something that does not exist. The ability to recognise precisely *who you are and why you are here* brings intense peace of mind to most people. With the acceptance of this basic principle, the constant strive for the irrelevant ceases to exist, along with many of the psychological ailments associated with such aspirations. By acknowledging that the difficulties we all face in life are experiences designed for our long-term benefit, irrespective of how challenging they are, the widespread victim mentality that causes chronic depression, resentment, and anger would no longer be part of the human mindset for anything other than a fleeting period of time. As a result, challenges would be overcome more quickly, and those of a longer duration would be dealt with more effectively. Examining the changes within self as the years progress proves this point, but if resentment, jealousy and despair remain a feature of the mindset, it is a given that the lessons contained within the challenges faced have not been learned.

With the knowledge that the purpose of our existence is continuous growth, carefree periods in life would be appreciated as the reward for a challenge overcome and the necessary respite in preparation for the next 'learning experience'. The life of most people falls into such a pattern, but the lack of knowledge about the journey of life itself means that the pleasant periods are often only fully appreciated in retrospect, and the difficult times are not respected for what they are; resulting in many not living in the moment, and never actually experiencing happiness.

The experiences of soul are not only those that have arisen in the life we are currently living, but also other *phases* of life that we participated in before birth and to which we will eventually return. Understandably, many people are skeptical regarding what occurs after death, but I think most would at least agree that for what we have to endure here on earth, there has to be more to *life* than we consciously experience: there has to be a purpose, or what would it all be for?

The fact is, soul is essentially who we are and is really all we have. It is a wise man who remains in touch with who he truly is, and beginning the process of acknowledging *who we are and why we are here* is the only way to achieve that.

* * *

A presentation by Jesus from the Real Ministry - Stage I

"Do not give up on yourself is one of the most important initiatives I would like to instill. If you give up, nothing will ever be achieved — there has to be hope in your heart no matter how difficult circumstances become. The only way for hope to remain when challenges are overwhelming is to believe in yourself; to know who you are, and why you are here. To know with absolute certainty that whatever is occurring at any one moment in your life is precisely what is supposed to be occurring. Life is facilitating the necessary opportunities for your soul to learn and evolve. If you can learn to understand this and accept it, your life will become less complex.

"It is my hope to teach you how to examine and understand the difficult life experiences we all endure from time to time. Furthermore, it is my wish that you will eventually learn to accept them for what they are, rather than become resentful that they have happened. All challenges and difficult circumstances are opportunities to learn; it is as simple as that. Within every challenge there is a purpose. That purpose provides you with an opportunity to learn something about yourself and the world, thereby establishing growth, maturity, and wisdom. It presents the possibility for you to effect change within yourself and the world around you. Do not ever let a challenging life experience pass without examining and understanding the lesson it held. If you ignore the lesson and remain resentful of the experience, the same lesson will need to be presented in a further challenge until learning has taken place. Otherwise known as history repeating itself — something I think we would all prefer to avoid. The key to discovering what can sometimes appear to be elusive lessons is to remember that denial is not an option, and the truth can sometimes be unflattering.

"Reconciling painful life experiences by learning to understand them for what they are, is far more preferable to remaining resentful, confused, and disorientated. Everything you desire to understand can be learned, and it is my hope that you will permit me to demonstrate what I have discovered, and allow me to support you in finding your true self and appreciating the meaning of life. This, I honestly believe, will create within each of you a peaceful sense of 'knowing' who you are and why you are here."

PART II – WHO OR WHAT IS GOD?

Once Jesus was secure in the knowledge that those he was teaching precisely understood the lessons of Stage I, he progressed towards the second stage of the ministry and provided a straightforward explanation relating to who or what God is.

Essentially, the God that is referred to as a 'he' by most religions, more closely resembles an 'it'. God does not possess human characteristics, but is comprised of a mass of light energy that has absolutely nothing to do with religion. Our individual souls can be likened to seedlings grown from this field of energy, which is why it is often said that God is *within us* or we are *at one* with God. Both are correct, since the soul at our core is an offshoot of the energy that is known as God – we are all a part of God whether we like it or not: it is where we came from, and it is where we will return at death.

God is a topic that at some point in every individual's life will become significant to a degree. From the deeply religious to the outspoken atheist, God is an issue because there is no escape: *it* is who we are to the core of our being. However, what has confused the matter and created such discord is the way in which the authorities of religious institutions have chosen to identify the energy that connects us all, while using it to harness the emotions of their followers with indoctrination techniques that have conspired to cause astonishing levels of confusion and anxiety.

Historic leaders of religion were highly intelligent, intuitive people, as are the religious leaders of today. They precisely understood the meaning of God, but also knew that the fearful, uneducated masses had no way of comprehending the energy they could sense within. People were afraid of what they could feel; they knew they possessed an intuitive intelligence of sorts, but they could not discern what it meant. However, rather than teach the simple truth, powerful and persuasive individuals from history formed religions to encourage dependence, establish control, and create profitable and opulent empires. They used the energy of God to harness people on an emotional level, impacting their sensitive inner voice with quite terrifying rhetoric that ultimately became absorbed into their thinking.

The energy of God is an intrinsic part of who we are, but religion is an external entity that was created by man and, as such, became an extended part of our being. Because religion is external and can be seen clearly, our less educated, fearful ancestors agreed to adopt religious philosophies rather than embrace the invisible, inborn part of themselves, which the majority simply did not understand. This lack of understanding was entirely due to the fact that it was never explained; it was of no benefit to those in religious authority to do so.

Most of us at some point in life have embraced religion for one reason or another. However, in epidemic proportions we have become disillusioned and walked away, but that does not mean we have abandoned our spiritual nature. Mankind has merely developed a higher intellect as the centuries progressed. We have begun to question and doubt the integrity of the external entity known as religion, as a consequence of their chosen practices past and present. We have instead embraced our own spirituality and undertaken a journey of personal discovery. As a result, we now have a curious generation that seeks the truth, which is why the truth is being presented.

* * *

When we return 'home' at the time of death, we rejoin the energy field mankind has named God and are welcomed back into its fold. Possibly for the first time since before we were born, we will feel the most amazing energy imaginable and will know with certainty that we are 'home'. It is unfortunate that only those who have experienced a near-death or similar episode are consciously aware of this feeling, but their perception of life from that moment is forever changed. They have seen the light and felt its energy. They know exactly what it is like to go home, and know there is nothing to fear from death. Their way of dealing with life after such an experience is usually dramatically altered, and they begin to look upon life's challenges in exactly the manner described in stage one of the real ministry, while appreciating for the first time what matters in life, and what does not.

Had the real ministry of Jesus been an active part of the human conscious mindset for the past two thousand years, we would all by now have experienced peace of mind; it is what he taught and what we should have been educated to understand. There would have been an element of faith required to believe in this massive light energy, but that would have been proven by reaping the benefits of dealing with life's challenges from the perspective already outlined, with further proof being discovered when experiencing the results of communicating with the energy of God as demonstrated in the upcoming stage three of the real ministry.

* * *

A presentation by Jesus from the Real Ministry - Stage II

"While I believe that experiences can be less burdensome if one possesses a faith that there is something or someone to rely upon for support and guidance, I also believe it is important that people understand faith in God for what it is. Believing in God is not the same as being faithful to a religious authority, but unfortunately possessing 'faith' has, in general, become synonymous with being religious. I believe that the light energy commonly referred to as 'God' is an intrinsic part of our being and connects us all to one another; therefore, having a belief or faith in God is, to me, the same as having a belief or faith in yourself and one another.

"Those who do not possess a faith towards a religious authority should not be looked down upon by those who do. There are many people succeeding in life without any religious affiliation; similarly, there are many who do maintain such associations yet their conduct is not a reflection of what they proclaim. Establishing a belief or faith in self is what will connect you to the energy of God. As long as you are living your life in good conscience, desire to give to those in need, have the ability to listen to your intuitive voice, feel content with your experiences, and are learning from the challenges your life presents, that is all that matters.

"To proclaim an affinity to a particular religion is acceptable as long as two things are adhered to as part of that commitment. One being that we each respect one another's right to choose which religion meets our needs and fits within our cultural environment, and the other is that individuals should retain the right to think for themselves freely and with an open mind. If institutions of religion insist upon dictating people's beliefs and choices in life, rather than merely providing a spiritual home for individuals to retreat when in need, a desire to rebel will ultimately prevail. Accompanying that rebellion will be a departure from those who constrain, thereby disabling religious institutions from fulfilling their true role within mankind: to provide spiritual guidance and nourishment to those who seek it, and nothing more.

"As evolution occurs a greater intellect will be acquired, which will be accompanied by the freedom to question and distaste for being controlled. Rebellion brings with it a sense that there are no boundaries, but without boundaries of conscience in place mankind will eventually lose its sense of direction. A free-for-all will reign; nothing will matter and everyone will be looking

out for themselves. *The resulting confusion will provide justification for those who seek to control rather than educate, and the truth of why the rebellion occurred in the first place will be masked by the call for more restrictions to counter the unsavoury aspects of a revolt. This response in and of itself will produce further uprising, with the conclusion of a decline into quite an unpleasant existence.*

"At some point in the history of the world, the controlling has to end and the teaching has to begin. Let it be now. Surely it is preferable to teach people the truth of who they are and why they are here, and show them how to deal with the challenges they face throughout life. Those in religious authority need to think with their hearts. The long term effects upon mankind of the circumstances they are creating by perpetuating the falsehoods they have established, demonstrates a blatant disrespect to the evolving intellect of mankind."

PART III – HOW TO COMMUNICATE AND INTERACT WITH GOD

The guidance provided by Jesus in relation to communicating with God was straightforward in nature, but in the same way that other crucial knowledge was corrupted, it underwent the required changes to satisfy the ambitions of religion. The teachings of the real ministry would have affected individual lives to such an extent that religion as we know it today would not have come into existence, and the level of control and influence that still survives would never have been established in the first place. The teaching of stage three of the real ministry has at its core the creation of a society of highly intuitive, independent-thinking individuals, possessing purely altruistic motivations. There is no doubt that for some the words *naïve idealism* come to mind at such a suggestion, but the reality is that had the ambitions of Jesus been fulfilled, we would by now be benefiting from a society incomparable to that with which we are so familiar.

Jesus's teachings did not require us to be controlled and adhere to the regulations and traditions of a religion. All he actually provided was what we needed: an explanation for who we are and why we are here; information relating to who or what God is, and how to communicate and interact with the energy known as God while living here on earth.

By the beginning of the third year of Jesus's ministry, those who'd participated in the previous two stages had achieved a new perspective, but the third stage was an opportunity to discover the proof of what had been learned so far. It had been quite effortless to clarify who we are and the reason for our existence: such information only had to be reflected upon to be understood. It had also not been difficult to describe God as a significant intuitive intelligence that we are each a small but integral part of. It explained our opinionated fascination with the subject of God, irrespective of whether or not we are religious. However, the third and most essential facet of the ministry was to teach that by communing directly with the energy of soul, a relationship with God could be developed, which in turn would see substantial changes to the way in which we conduct life. Jesus believed that if he succeeded in this approach, the centuries that came to pass would see humanity enlightened to such an extent that the world would achieve 'peace' within a reasonable period of time, and certainly by the time of our existence.

When Jesus outlined his objectives at the outset of stage three, people responded as they would today and suggested it was entirely implausible. However, those who decided there was nothing to lose by listening and learning, ended up agreeing wholeheartedly with Jesus's beliefs once they'd experienced the effects of his ideas for themselves. They understood why he had such aspirations, and could see the long-term potential of such an approach being adopted and becoming part of everyday life. However, those in religious authority realised that should this aspect of the ministry become mainstream, it would seriously reduce their ability to be regarded as the font of all knowledge, and directly affect their goals from the point of view of creating dependence and maintaining emotional control of the indoctrinated. To counter this risk, the authorities chose to do as they had with all facets of the ministry, and utilised the convenient characteristics of what Jesus prescribed but removed what was deemed unpalatable. Jesus's ambitions were condemned as being too unorthodox, so the impression was given that an adapted approach was not only more sensible, but easier for people to embrace. However, this process removed the need for individuals to make decisions about moral or ethical issues since they were surrendering their basic sensibilities – their capacity to respond in favour of their own thoughts became extinct. They were persuaded that their commitment to the Movement was likened to surrendering themselves to God, but in truth they had surrendered to the ethos of being told what to think, do, and say, while abandoning their soul and intuitive voice in the process.

* * *

Jesus's *controversial* recommendation was for each of us to take a few moments alone each day and form a connection with our soul, while using the time to share our deepest thoughts, concerns, and hopes for the future. Because the soul is an offshoot of the energy that has been named God, focusing the mind within creates a direct connection with God. Jesus believed that the more frequently we practiced such brief moments of thought, the more peace of mind would be achieved. This observance alone causes a substantial shift in perspective, which is apparent once the practice becomes a habit or routine in the way of other activities. When Jesus convinced people to experiment with this idea, they achieved complete success. The third stage of the ministry complemented perfectly the lessons of the previous two, and brought with it the fulfilling enlightenment so desired.

Once the benefits of these suggestions had been experienced, Jesus expanded his initiative and introduced the prospect of receiving guidance and reassurance directly from God. He also proposed the idea that positive thinking and visualising the helpful outcome of a difficulty, could bring about a conclusion that provided for the soul's needs. However, this is not the same as visualising what you 'want' to transpire, but is more akin to what you 'need' to occur to assist with whatever learning is ongoing. The saying, *be careful what you wish for*, is very true – what you wish for, and what you truly need, are not always one and the same.

Having observed the enhanced intuitive capabilities that occur when a closer relationship with self and God has been developed, the leap of faith required to ask a question and expect to receive an answer is entirely feasible. This phase of the teaching requires that the concerns or questions be focused upon during the time spent alone with soul, and at a relevant point the guidance required will appear as a sudden thought, idea, dream or inspiration, or a turn of events will transpire that had not been anticipated but ultimately resolves the situation. However, these *moments* are not earth shattering, miraculous events, but are subtle thoughts and alterations to previously held convictions that over time contribute to resolving a particular issue, while helping the individual gain benefit from the learning encompassed in the challenging episode they overcame. They occur naturally in most people from time to time, and are akin to experiencing a moment of clarity when we find ourselves asking, *why didn't I think of that before.* However, we all experience many distractions in life, and it is often difficult for the sensitive, intuitive inner voice to be heard above the daily commotion that prevails. Those familiar inspirational moments would flow more fluently if the practice outlined became an everyday occurrence, since the intuitive voice works independently of the conscious mind, and both need to be provided with an opportunity to relate.

Discovering how our two minds work and interact would prove highly beneficial in every area of life, and practicing the third stage of the real ministry on a daily basis would achieve that. A clear mind prevents panic from setting in; permitting guidance and information from the sensitive inner voice to flow effortlessly, even during the most trying of times.

* * *

It is the practice of praying rather than meditation that is very much encouraged by the Christian religion, and even though the difference between the two may appear to be slight, it is yet another example of how selective and subtle changes were made to Jesus's ministry to facilitate the requirements of religion. Praying does not focus upon becoming more self aware and gaining a greater understanding of life, but is primarily geared towards seeking forgiveness, praying for the well-being of another, or asking for help regarding some aspect of life, but stops short of encouraging anything more in depth. In addition, traditional praying mostly consists of repeating memorised prayers that are taught from a young age and include the dogma of religion, rather than an intimate or personal conversation with God. While it is true that many do 'talk' to God during prayer, most do not expect to receive a response, and do not take the conversation to a level that is beneficial to soul and the emotional wellbeing of the mind.

The difference between private meditation and prayerful contemplation may on the face of it appear negligible, but in truth it is vast. The changes made to what Jesus prescribed appear to be minor, but not only did the adapted system ensure that people became dependent upon the church, but it also ensured they did not establish a belief in self by discovering the unique benefits of what Jesus endeavoured to teach. This directive alone is responsible for more individual harm than any of us can truly contemplate, but the outcome for mankind as a whole is visible for all to see.

Two thousand years is an awfully long period to sanction any group to experiment with the welfare of the world without being held to account, particularly having been proven so wrong. Even though Jesus's methodology sounds too good to be true and too simplistic and straightforward for words, it deserves to be taken seriously. Our less than enlightened ancestors were easily manipulated, and their fears and insecurities were compounded by the frightening rhetoric of the influential leaders of the past. Today, we are paying the price for their choices and the transgressions of those in power, yet to consider retribution is a futile proposal. It is the road less travelled that we should take, and by privately participating in the real ministry, its uncomplicated nature will bring our individual journeys to a peaceful and fruitful conclusion, and the world as we know it will finally begin to change as a result of the example we set.

* * *

The final presentation by Jesus from the Real Ministry - Stage III

"Well, here we are. I see different expressions than I saw when we first met three years ago. You are not anxious or fearful as you were then, but these are not the expressions I had hoped to see on our final day together. In general, you appear angry and frustrated, and this is not what I aspired for you to attain: I did not set out to turn anxiety and fear into anger and frustration, rather I had hoped by now to see peace radiate from your eyes.

"I know we've seen success because I know you've been transformed. You have listened and understood, and acted by integrating new philosophies into your life and sharing your newly-

acquired awareness with those you love. Why then do I see negative emotions among you all? Now your heads are bowed — have I made you feel guilty? You certainly look as though you're experiencing the emotion of guilt — coupled with anger and frustration; this is not a good thing.

"Don't look so worried — I understand why it is that you've not arrived at our final gathering in celebration for what we have achieved; rather, there is a sense of disappointment prevailing. I know what I've done. I have created the anger and frustration you feel, which is not how I want my ministry with you to end. You are not at peace, despite this long journey we have been on together. Would you like me to explain why you feel the way you do?

"The frustration and anger you feel is not directed towards me or one another, and it is not because of what I have attempted to teach. You are feeling this way because you feel helpless. You have now been enlightened to the truth about life; you know who you are and why you are here. You know who God is and how to communicate directly with him. But what else do you know? You also know that this invaluable information is not understood by most people. You can no longer conduct your life in the way you did previously, but your frustration is at watching those who have not benefited from this ministry continue in their self-destructive ways. Your anger is at observing those within the religious authority benefiting from the grief of those around you, and your disappointment is at feeling helpless to do anything about it.

"I can see relief in your eyes for the first time today. Hopefully you now understand why you feel the way you do, but please be assured — go ahead and enjoy your life and graciously accept the benefits you have derived as a result of your participation in this ministry. Do not feel frustration towards your neighbours who have not shared in this process; it is not their fault. Their choice not to do so was based upon fear — the fear of retribution at the hands of those they believe are empowered by God. What they do not understand is that the words retribution and God have no connection; they do not belong in the same sentence since the energy that is God does not know of such a thing.

"Show compassion, support them, and help them, but do not preach to them; do not become angry or tell them where they are going wrong. Rather, live your life by example; that is the best and only way to teach. Remaining intolerant and frustrated with their ways will achieve nothing. They will not then be able to see how you have benefited; rather, they will see a frustrated and angry person, and that is not something they will aspire to.

"It is not your responsibility to teach; your purpose here on earth is to learn. However, when we learn something new it instinctively becomes our desire to teach, but please do so only by setting an example of the way in which you conduct your life. If others choose to learn from you, that becomes their choice, and they will benefit accordingly. Make a stand and choose to live your life in absolute good conscience, and as a result you will not fail but to teach, and you will not fail in succeeding at life.

"Go in peace for you have earned it."

CHAPTER SEVEN

THE ONLY ENDING IN SIGHT

The entire three-year period of the ministry was fraught with the most tumultuous of times. The impact from external interference produced a series of events that no one had been prepared for. It had always been anticipated that the ministry would be subject to challenging circumstances, but it was the source of those challenges that was unforeseen. Jesus had participated with the Movement to alleviate potentially harmful scenarios, but had not anticipated they would be the origin of such. The very people committed to supporting Jesus and Martha transformed the entire endeavor into an intolerable series of endurance trials.

It became apparent within the first three months of stage one of the ministry that leaders of the Movement had a significant agenda of their own. The discovery that their recruits were spreading rumours of Jesus performing miraculous acts brought chaos to the functionality of this meticulously coordinated programme. Jesus was left to deal with the fall-out of thousands of people travelling miles to see him in person, and as a result needed to develop a plan to avoid total breakdown of the ministry. This was no small feat, particularly since the Movement's recruits were preaching a series of captivating, imaginary tales, which made the message of the real ministry seem like a non-event by comparison.

By using humour to dismiss the rumours as meaningless, rather than vehemently denying them, Jesus was able to keep everyone's focus on his message. Even though he did not see the funny side of this situation at all, he recalled from his childhood how effective humour could be in desensitising situations, and used it to successfully minimise the impact of the Movement's efforts.

The travellers were more than content to listen to Jesus, believing they were in the company of the miracle-performing son of God. But thanks to his well executed plan, Jesus managed to engage people, and over time the 'magic tricks' became secondary in their minds. However, simultaneous to Jesus doing his utmost to cope with this situation, enormous pressure was mounting from the authorities: the continuous influx of travellers into the area had caused much anxiety, and the confusion as a result of the Movement's imaginative 'accompaniments' to the ministry, created even more discord.

* * *

The real ministry necessitated thought, effort, and commitment, whereas the Movement's alternative version simply required individuals to abandon a responsibility to self, and surrender to a persuasive doctrine out of fear of doing otherwise. The fearful masses being indoctrinated by the Movement were succumbing to their philosophy, while those administered to by Jesus and his disciples were very content with their experience: week by week they were establishing a new awareness and inner peace, which was exciting as well as humbling. However, the groups administered to by the Movement were developing a sense of camaraderie; mixed with a feeling of superiority due to being convinced they had become part of something unique, resulting in quite a passionate and toxic outlook. Both groups argued intensely about the message of the ministry, and as a consequence the religious authority was outraged at such discord. They blamed Jesus entirely for the disruption, and such controversy was more than they could stand. In their outrage they called for the arrest of the person they supposed was the cause of such distress.

The Movement, of course, was delighted with all aspects of this outcome. The angst created among citizens and the authorities was precisely what had been hoped for. Maximum impact had been achieved at great speed. They had succeeded in infuriating the establishment, as well as those not participating in the ministry. A serious divide developed among the area's populace, intimidating and threatening the position of those in religious authority. The Movement had much to celebrate.

Jesus, on the other hand, had no desire to bewilder people or antagonise the authorities. He sought only to teach those who wanted to learn, and achieve his aim in a civilised, orderly manner. For his entire adult life, Jesus did his utmost to alleviate concerns by showing respect for religious beliefs. He was convinced that not only was his philosophy compatible with religion, but it could be utilised by the religious and non-religious alike.

While Jesus was in basic disagreement with the conduct of those who dominated within religion, he recognised that their main problem was a lack of awareness of a more meaningful way to administer to their faithful. He hoped that once he'd established a following, religious leaders would eventually appreciate that he was not trying to usurp their position, but only wished to demonstrate how they could more effectively serve people. However, that was not the aim of the Movement. They were intent upon dividing public opinion, and ultimately overthrowing those who held positions within the religious authority. The efforts of the Movement established fear and hatred among the passionately religious, and because Jesus was promoted as their symbol, he personally became the focus of revenge.

* * *

Unfortunately, the fiasco that was the first stage of the ministry was nothing compared to 'enhancements' that transpired in stages two and three. Jesus and his disciples continued to teach the real ministry, but the Movement's recruits, who far outnumbered them, established an entirely different version. Confidently speaking in Jesus's name, the Movement took his words and spun them into rhetoric far removed from the truth. Broadly speaking, the masses were convinced of the miracle stories despite Jesus refuting such declarations. They wanted to believe they had been in the presence of the son of God, and were encouraged to attribute Jesus's denial to modesty, which only served to enhance their opinion of him further.

Even though thousands of travellers had been taught by Jesus personally, the Movement decided to embellish those teachings once they returned to their hometowns throughout the second and third stages. They suggested that while the challenges people faced in life were designed to teach, such difficulties occurred because the majority of human beings were undeserving, worthless sinners, whose lives should be conducted in deference to the Movement's aims.

It was also impressed that an individual's 'inner voice' was not to be listened to, since suggestions such as this came from the darkness within; encouraging the celebration of success and the right to contentment. It was instilled that the *voice* of the Movement was all anyone needed to obey, since doing so assured eternal life within the kingdom of God; something most people were not prepared to risk.

If these victims of indoctrination had travelled to listen to Jesus during the second and third stages of the ministry, they would have heard an entirely different message. However, the naive masses were convinced Jesus was the miracle-performing son of God, and for the thousands who had met Jesus in person, becoming a follower of the Movement was no longer an option to consider: they willingly adhered to their ideals, in fear of the wrath of God if they did not.

* * *

The personal suffering these developments brought to Jesus and Martha was indescribable. Jesus would often withdraw to Martha's house in Magdala for some respite from the chaos. He was physically and emotionally drained; everything he had worked his entire life to achieve had disintegrated throughout the three-year ministry. During the many hours spent trying to comprehend why they had failed and the Movement had succeeded, Jesus and Martha exhausted every avenue in search of where they went so drastically wrong. They appreciated the many instances where decisions had created difficult situations to deal with, but they also knew that those decisions had not been taken lightly. Both had utilised the same depth of intuitive guidance they had used throughout their entire lives, yet when it came to the ministry, nothing they set out to achieve produced the hoped-for result.

As frustrating as this reality was, both Jesus and Martha eventually began to wonder if perhaps they had always been destined to fail: they supposed there was the possibility that people needed to experience negativity before they could appreciate bliss. If the Movement succeeded in their long term goal of world domination, this was precisely what was going to happen. They also wondered if this might explain their desire to create a record of the ministry: by so doing there would be something for future generations to consider once the direction of the Movement had run its course, and people were ready for something new and inspiring. They reasoned that perhaps mankind needed to try everything else first, before realising that the *real ministry* was the only way.

Jesus and Martha were certain that the lessons of the ministry were not difficult, and knew that the alternative of mankind enduring the negative consequences of a complex life would not be pleasant. Nevertheless, all they could do was pray, and hope that the human race would eventually evolve and become unafraid of embracing bliss and disposing of negativity. More than two thousand years have now passed since such sentiments were expressed — are we there yet?

* * *

As the Ministry drew to a close, the atmosphere was so contentious that Jesus resorted to holding the final sessions of the real ministry in various enclosed locations to avoid attracting attention. He was fully aware that once the Movement had obtained all of the support and power required, the protection placed around him would be removed. The Jews had been incited to such an extent that Jesus knew they would take matters into their own hands should the authorities fail to arrest him.

As a consequence of these developments, Jesus made some very important decisions. In an attempt to gain some control over his own fate and the reputation of the real ministry, he availed himself of an opportunity to be heard by the Jews and those in religious authority. Before his end was upon him, he was determined to set himself apart from the Movement as far as possible, and in Jesus's mind there was only one way to achieve that.

Confiding his plans only in Martha, Jesus proceeded to take command over what he believed was the only ending in sight.

CHAPTER EIGHT

EVENTS PRIOR TO THE LAST SUPPER

The truth regarding proceedings that occurred prior to the last supper could not be in more contrast with the Bible's assertion. Jesus was not concerned that one of his disciples would betray him to the authorities; he was neither in hiding and planning an escape, nor placing expectations upon those who'd supported him: he was not a coward. Jesus did not feel let down when his followers were unable to admit association; he would never have permitted anyone to put their life in jeopardy. Aware that his ending was imminent, Jesus took matters into his own hands. The rebel with a cause was to be immortalised into a martyr with iconic status, but plans already in motion to achieve that end suddenly became subject to negotiation. As the ministry drew to its conclusion, Jesus presented Seth with an ultimatum: he was determined to secure the right to orchestrate his own arrest, at a time of his own choosing.

The ministry had created much discontent among religious authorities, with Jesus's following escalating an already contentious atmosphere to unacceptable degrees. Knowing the inevitability of his fate, Jesus wanted to control the manner of his demise by organising his own arrest and trial with the certain outcome of crucifixion, as long as he was assured immunity for his family and disciples. He intended to use the spectacle to face those who feared him; letting them know he did not blame them for his downfall: it had been his choice to participate with the Movement – he blamed no one but himself. By securing an occasion to speak of his *real ministry*; what it stood for, and what he had hoped to achieve, Jesus was determined to convince people it bore no relation to menacing rumours that were so widespread. He viewed his trial as an opportunity to inform the authorities he'd neither sought to usurp their position, nor strived to establish a new religion: he was only attempting to teach a more beneficial way of conducting life.

Unwavering in his resolve to have the last word, Jesus insisted his death would be on terms dictated by no one but himself.

* * *

Even though Seth was not privy to the specific details of the Movement's plans, he certainly knew they included Jesus being murdered to establish martyrdom. Consequently, when Jesus presented his final demand, Seth had a choice to make: inform his superiors that Jesus may disappear due to anticipating their strategy, or permit his growing sympathy towards Jesus and Martha to support a decision to help them.

Jesus knew he had little to no influence when making such demands, and even though an attempt to escape the area was not viable due to the predicaments it could create for his disciples and family, it was also unlikely to succeed. Jesus was conscious of his lack of leverage, and knew he was totally dependent upon Seth choosing to stand in his corner. However, Jesus needn't have worried – it turned out that his request had played straight into Seth's hands. For some time, Seth had been trying to develop arrangements that enabled him to have complete control over the death of Jesus to assist with more complex plans he had in mind. Therefore, the decision to support Jesus had been an easy one for Seth – it gave him what he wanted – complete control over the ending of Jesus's life.

* * *

Recognising that an advantage of some sort was required for Jesus's request to be responded to positively, Seth suggested that Jesus and Martha go into hiding, proposing that he use their disappearance to influence negotiations on their behalf. While Jesus could see the sense in this suggestion, he agreed to cooperate only if he could use two of his own trusted men as go-betweens to communicate messages, while refusing to disclose where he and Martha intended to hide. He did not trust Seth's word to that extent, but meeting him half way seemed like the most sensible decision.

Seth was content with the idea of using trusted followers to communicate negotiations, and once all conditions were agreed, Jesus and Martha went into hiding. Judas and Mary Magdalene were instructed to remain at the Magdala house for their own safety, but were told nothing of plans that were afoot; believing only that Jesus and Martha had temporarily absconded for their own protection. As Seth and Jesus proceeded with negotiations they carefully worded their communication through the messengers, ensuring they had no idea of plans being developed. If word had leaked out in advance, much commotion would have occurred among the followers, and not only would such an eventuality have forced the hand of the Movement to proceed immediately with their own plans, it would also have put many of Jesus's most dedicated disciples in danger of arrest: an unacceptable outcome as far as Jesus was concerned.

* * *

Seth was anxious when reporting this turn of events to his superiors; he knew that if they so chose, an all-out effort to locate Jesus and Martha would produce results in a fairly short period of time. Therefore, it was vital he convince the leaders of the Movement that they were still in control, while portraying a scenario that was more compelling than their own proposal. Their yet to be implemented plan was to continue further deliberate incitement of the Jews, to the point of rousing them to take matters into their own hands. The call to arms was to be achieved by members of the Movement infiltrating the populace and calling for Jesus to be hunted down and stoned to death in a public display of outrage. This would have established the Jews as directly accountable for the death of the 'Messiah,' enabling the early Christians to legitimately depict and memorialise the horrific nature of Jesus's murder at their hands.

Seth did eventually secure an agreement in line with Jesus's request, despite the initial reaction being one of fury at the news that their soon to be iconic martyr had gone into hiding. However, once Seth persuaded them to listen to the details of the proposal he had in mind, his superiors became impressed by the argument that an arrest, trial, and agreed outcome of death by crucifixion was far preferable to Jesus's death occurring randomly at the hands of an angry Jewish mob. Seth convinced his superiors that historical records of the process would be highly beneficial; ensuring the circumstances surrounding the death could not be contradicted. There would be legal evidence showing that the Jews had called for Jesus's arrest and trial, which everyone agreed was a reliable way of proving their direct association.

Once these developments had settled into the minds of Seth's superiors, the planned scenario sparked many ideas regarding how they could develop the story further. The suggestion that the symbol of the cross be used to establish a direct association and represent all that Christianity stood for, was one of many innovative thoughts immediately embraced. However, Seth cared little about the enthusiasm his suggestions had produced, and instead focused exclusively on the way forward. He committed to further negotiate these arrangements with the authorities and the Roman Governor, Pontius Pilate, as well as communicating the outcome directly to Jesus and Martha.

* * *

While these final preparations were being put in place, Judas and Mary Magdalene were unaware an arrest was being formulated. They assumed that time was being allowed to elapse before a safe escape from the immediate area became possible. They had no idea Jesus was making other plans in a final attempt to rectify the damage the Movement had done to the ministry. For Judas, this was the first time he'd not been consulted regarding Jesus and Martha's strategy, but their reasoning for this was unyielding. They knew Judas would be devastated and argue to persuade Jesus not to permit his life to end in this way. In addition, they believed he would never have allowed Jesus to be arrested alone: he would have been the only follower to deliberately admit association, and insist upon accepting the same fate. While Jesus could not let this end befall his most faithful companion, he also felt that Judas was the only person he could trust to take care of Martha and ensure she was escorted to safety. Martha had in her possession the meticulously kept diaries, which recorded all aspects of the ministry; outlining what they had hoped to achieve, and what the early Christians actually achieved. Martha's life was in danger because of the knowledge she possessed, and Judas was the only person Jesus could trust to protect her.

* * *

Once Seth had begun implementing the agreed proposals, he met with Jesus and Martha at the Bethany house to discuss logistics and respond to any concerns they may have. The main issue Jesus needed clarifying was the safety of his family and disciples – something the Movement had promised to guarantee. While Jesus was reasonably satisfied with most of the arrangements, it was the plans for Martha and Judas that concerned him the most. They'd been intimately involved in all aspects of the ministry, and Jesus felt it unwise to trust that the Movement would permit them to survive. Therefore, while Jesus agreed that Seth could arrange their safe housing and passage away from the area, he felt he had no alternative but to secretly make other arrangements, which he confided only in Martha and his mother. Mary was the only person the Movement would be unlikely to interrogate, and by Jesus informing her of the arrest plans and Judas and Martha's whereabouts, he felt assured that if events took an unforeseen course, at least his mother would know where Judas and Martha could be found.

The other important matter needing attention was to secure Seth's agreement that the known outcome of the arrest be kept from Judas. Jesus and Martha explained their concerns regarding Judas's likely disruptive reaction, which Seth understood completely. Because he didn't want to contend with such matters, Seth willingly agreed to keep Judas apprised only of what he needed to know. It was agreed that Judas be told the arrest had an arranged outcome, with its purpose facilitating Jesus an opportunity to be tried; explain his vision and what he'd hoped to achieve, and for it to be declared he was not guilty of any crime. Judas was to be informed this process would ensure they no longer had to live in fear of arrest, and that eventually they would be able to move on with their lives.

The only remaining issue that needed resolving at this juncture was Jesus's outright refusal to declare he was the son of God. The Movement's determined approach in this regard was to support their obsession in establishing the cult as the only religion and the only way to God, and while Seth knew what Jesus's response would be to his proposal, his superiors insisted he work to accomplish such a pronouncement. It was vital for the Movement to set Jesus apart from other preachers and prophets, and a declaration of divinity being publically witnessed would add much weight to the argument they intended to present.

Seth went through the motions of explaining the importance of such a statement, suggesting Jesus speak of his divine status during the sentencing phase. Predictably, Jesus resolutely refused: for him to submit to such a claim would fly in the face of everything he intended to achieve throughout his trial and sentencing. Jesus also knew that such an announcement would be disastrous, causing even further division — an intolerable outcome for him to consider. In any event, Jesus and Martha had already agreed that if their lives were threatened due to a lack of cooperation on this matter, Jesus was not to succumb. They were each willing to give up their life rather than contribute to the influence the Movement was attempting to secure.

Seth did not struggle with this predicament for too long. He'd anticipated Jesus's response and had already decided to lie to his superiors; informing them he'd secured a commitment by threatening the lives of Jesus's family. He knew this would appease them for the time being, and intended to later report that Jesus had changed his mind and refused to cooperate. Seth knew it mattered little in any event — the Movement would invent history should actual events impede their aspirations in any way.

The only real point of contention that arose when making these arrangements was in relation to the future of Mary Magdalene. Seth was adamant on two points — firstly, he was concerned she could not be trusted with prior knowledge of events; believing she would be tempted to boast of a secret, which would encourage the followers to become inquisitive about what was afoot. In addition, Seth reminded Jesus that the Movement had only agreed to provide safe-haven for his family, but his followers were expected to remain and act as witnesses. Mary Magdalene was a well-known follower, and it was therefore imperative she be present throughout the proceedings and be informed of the arrest plans alongside the other disciples. However, Jesus had always assumed that Mary Magdalene would escape the area with Martha and Judas: he not only felt a responsibility to ensure she was taken care of, but was also aware she would be alone since Lazarus was preoccupied in starting a ministry of his own. In addition, Jesus could not understand why Seth was not grateful to have the often disruptive Mary Magdalene taken off his hands.

To reassure Jesus and Martha, Seth confessed that he too felt a responsibility to protect Mary Magdalene, particularly in view of how much she was loathed by the other followers. He promised that once the initial post-crucifixion phase was over, he would ensure she was escorted safely back to Magdala. However, he felt strongly that Martha and Judas would look far less conspicuous alone when escaping the area. Seth warned that Mary Magdalene's temperament, and emotional attachment to Jesus, meant she was unlikely to calmly accept the outcome in the way Judas eventually would, thereby possibly increasing the risk of them all being discovered.

Eventually, Jesus and Martha gave in to Seth on this point, despite not being entirely comfortable with the decision. They believed Seth was genuine in his assurance that he would personally arrange for Mary Magdalene to be escorted to her home, and when taking everything into consideration, they both agreed that this was probably the best outcome. Mary Magdalene had become part of their family to a large extent, but after due consideration they decided not to go behind Seth's back on this decision. They knew of the close bond that existed between Mary Magdalene and her brother, Lazarus, and felt that in the longer term she would probably be far happier and content to be in familiar surroundings and supporting her brother in his ministry. It was therefore agreed to keep Mary Magdalene in the dark regarding all aspects of the plans until she was informed alongside the other followers.

Moving the conversation towards explaining the timetable of events for the day of arrest, Seth confirmed that the last supper with the disciples would take place at the Bethany house in approximately three weeks. Roman soldiers would make the arrest on the morning after the final gathering, by which time Martha and Judas would be safely away from Bethany and the disciples would have left the premises and not be in danger of arrest. Seth's plan was to house Judas and Martha at a secret location in the southern outskirts of Jerusalem; keeping them there until it was safe for them to depart the area. However, unable to trust that Seth would do as he'd promised, Jesus secretly arranged an alternative location in the northern outskirts of Jerusalem, where it was planned that Judas and Martha would remain for approximately three days after the crucifixion and then proceed to the coast where their brothers, Joseph and Simon, were waiting. If everything went according to plan, the family intended to travel by boat to France and begin a new life. The additional contingency established to accommodate something unexpected occurring, was for the group to remain at the coastal location for up to one year, as long as it remained safe to do so. This would not only allow time to make specific plans for the future and earn a living in preparation for the journey, but it also gave other family members, who may find themselves in danger, the necessary time to make the journey and join the group before their departure for France.

* * *

When the day of the last supper arrived, an exhausted Seth was close to breaking point. Acting as mediator throughout all these years had taken its toll: the frequently distressed Jesus and Martha making their anguish felt, coupled with meeting the demands and expectations of his superiors, resulted in Seth looking forward to this whole ordeal reaching its conclusion. Over time, he'd discovered the unpleasant truth that the Movement's mission did not vaguely reflect what they had initially represented to him. He also believed that he had, in effect, conned Jesus and Martha into believing something that was entirely untrue. Seth felt remorse at the outcome they faced, but he knew there was no going back. By the time he realised what he'd become involved in, it was too late to walk away; he would simply have been replaced by some unscrupulous individual who'd have possessed no empathy towards Jesus and Martha's predicament.

By staying, he could at least ease his conscience somewhat; attempting to support Jesus to the end, while maintaining his position within the Movement. Even though there was much he disagreed with, Seth felt that by staying he could achieve more to effect change in the long term. Knowing he had been used and manipulated, Seth admitted his loyalties had been misplaced. However, it was already clear that the Movement would decide the facts history would record, and there was little, if anything, that could be done. By remaining involved, Seth felt he could at least speak out if events escalated beyond what had already become an obscene assault on Jesus's memory.

* * *

In Martha's Voice:

"I had been aware throughout the ministry that Seth seemed very curious about the fact that I wrote a tremendous amount. Part of my responsibility was to record every aspect of the ministry in detail, and this was done in diary format. I didn't hide anything from Seth; there seemed little reason to — we were not keeping secrets. However, I observed him on several occasions reading through my manuscripts and often witnessed a rather defeated expression when he'd finished. He'd go quiet, and I often wondered what he thought. His demeanour indicated he felt guilty, which made me wonder whose side he was actually on. Seth was unaware that each night I wrote a duplicate copy of the diary entries, which I kept hidden. I thought that in the event he 'arranged' for my manuscripts to be stolen, at least I would have another copy. Interestingly, Seth let me be, and made no attempt to dispose of the evidence.

"Obviously, the main purpose of the diaries was to describe in detail the process of the ministry. They outlined all of Jesus's speeches and how the three stages had been conducted and equally spread out over a three-year period. Unfortunately, as things turned out, they also revealed how distorted the ministry became.

"The diaries included more than the business of the day; they also presented details about us personally and the sort of lives we led. I included Jesus and Judas's antics and amusing jokes, knowing many would consider that to be the most interesting part. I wanted it to be real — I wanted anyone who read the diaries in the future to not only see what the ministry was composed of, but also what our life had been like and who we truly were. I knew the Movement would *never provide such intimate details, but I wanted to ensure that people eventually learned the full story behind the experience they were living. I am certain that one day a copy of these diaries will be revealed, when the time is right and the world is ready."*

CHAPTER NINE

THE BEGINNING OF THE END

PART I – THE DISCIPLES GATHER

With everything in place for the conclusion of Jesus's life to proceed, the disciples began to gather for what became known as The Last Supper. The location was the House of Martha in Bethany, situated two miles to the east of Jerusalem on the slopes of Mount Olivet.

Jesus was understandably a little anxious on this particular evening, but for more than the obvious reason. As the disciples began to arrive, he and Martha greeted them warmly while trying not to betray their primary concern – Judas was missing. He'd been apprised of arrangements to the extent it had been agreed, and understood his role was to be seen at the Bethany house before discreetly departing with Martha prior to Jesus beginning his presentation. However, Judas had not been seen all day, which was cause for more than a little concern. Experience had taught that the Movement would not stand by their word if it did not suit, and Jesus was becoming increasingly anxious they had anticipated he would make alternative arrangements for Judas and Martha's safety, and had taken matters into their own hands to avoid losing control over their fate.

Seth's presence at the last supper was to be brief and inconspicuous, serving only to verify that everything was ready for matters to proceed. However, with each passing hour Jesus and Martha became more concerned about Judas's welfare, hence Seth's arrival was now awaited with great anticipation. Seth, on the other hand, was oblivious to such concerns, and when he entered the Bethany house at the appointed hour, he did as had been agreed and discreetly glanced towards Jesus to acknowledge he could proceed. His intention was to depart almost immediately and he was somewhat taken aback when Jesus sternly signalled he should approach. Seth had not wanted to be seen in private conversation with Jesus, since any hint of collaboration on his part would forfeit the legitimacy of other plans that were in place. However, clearly recognising that Jesus was upset, Seth rather uneasily followed him to the rear of the house where he hesitantly enquired if something was wrong.

Making no effort to restrain himself, Jesus impatiently demanded, "Where is Judas - what have you done with him?"

Seth was confused and startled by such a suggestion and brusquely responded, saying, "Why would I harm Judas – is he not here? I told him to arrive prior to everyone else. I wouldn't do anything to jeopardise these arrangements – you of all people should know that."

Hoping to learn there was an explanation for Judas's disappearance, Martha joined in the conversation, but Jesus was unable to relieve her concern: "Seth claims he knows nothing of Judas's whereabouts, which leaves me to assume that someone has taken matters into their own hands – Judas would never let us down and disappear at this most vital time."

Already distressed because of what was about to unfold, Martha became even more anxious; she was beside herself and barely able to remain calm. She feared the worst – it now seemed likely that Judas was going to endure the same fate as Jesus.

Seth, however, was furious to learn that Judas was missing and that something as disruptive as this could have occurred. While Jesus and Martha contemplated what they should do, Seth moved among the gathered disciples enquiring if anyone had seen Judas on their travels. Of course, no one had, and no one much cared either.

Feeling angry and defensive, Seth returned to Jesus and Martha adamantly stating he was certain the Movement was not behind the disappearance of Judas: "They would not do this; they have too much at stake. They know what your reaction would be if anything happened to Judas, and besides – it was part of the agreement. In addition, I've taken the precaution of not telling anyone where I intended to hide Judas and Martha. They couldn't possibly know. Even my guard who is waiting at the hide-out has no idea who he'll be watching."

Jesus abruptly interrupted, saying, "Since when do those you report to ever abide by agreements, Seth? Please do not use that as an argument. They may not have told you what plans they had in store for Martha and Judas, but I'm sure you have a fairly good idea."

Leaning in towards Jesus, Seth responded in determined tones: "I would not allow anything to happen to them. You must believe that much about me after all we've been through. I know you're unhappy with the way some things turned out, but you know I did my best to support you ..."

Jesus interrupted again, saying, "Unhappy with the way *some* things turned out — a little bit of an understatement wouldn't you say, Seth? I'm giving up my life to prove in a very public way that I am not associated with your Movement. However, I also know they don't care what I do or say and will ultimately create the history they want to create. My only hope is that those who hear me remember the truth, and that one day, when your techniques have run their course and failed, people will be willing to listen to the truth."

Seth was livid, but did not want to enter a drawn-out argument with Jesus at this point, so hastily announced he would go in search of Judas; committing to return as quickly as possible with one of his men who would then escort Martha to the safe-house.

Confused and worried, Jesus and Martha retired to a secluded room where they could not be overheard. The dilemma they faced was not whether they could trust the Movement to keep Martha safe; they knew they could not. The decision to be made was which of the two remaining options available to Martha posed the least risk — accompanying Seth's guard to the supposedly secure safe-house and attempting an escape from there, or making her own way throughout the night to the secret hideout in the north. Both choices were fraught with danger: either becoming an easy target for the Movement's hit men, or travelling alone in darkened woods riddled with vagrants and criminals. While Seth's intentions may have been good, Jesus and Martha knew he was as disposable as they were; it wasn't reliable to assume he would even survive these proceedings, let alone be available to protect Martha.

While it was believed Seth's reaction to Judas's disappearance was genuine, a degree of panic was detected in his response. There had been many instances when it later transpired that Seth had been unaware of deceitful activities being undertaken, and the Movement's track record at ruthlessly obtaining the end-result they desired had been well established for some time. Therefore, trusting them with the life of Martha and her chronicle of the ministry was not an option either was willing to consider. As dangerous a pursuit as it was, Jesus and Martha decided there was no alternative but for Martha to gather her belongings and leave immediately; making her own way to the secret location they had identified in the northern outskirts of Jerusalem. Time was running out for them all, but the one remaining chance to save Martha had to be taken.

* * *

Jesus returned to the gathered disciples while Martha made preparations to leave. Neither could believe what was developing – as with the ministry itself, nothing had gone according to plan. In doing their utmost to ignore the reality of the situation, they each focused only on what had to be achieved.

With her belongings packed, Martha went in search of Jesus. Bewildered and overcome, she was deaf to the boisterous, pontificating debate actively engaging the followers. They were completely unaware of what lay ahead, but Martha's heart was breaking. With thoughts only for her beloved brother, whose life was about to come to a brutal end, Martha stood in a corner at the rear of the room upholding her composure while cautiously trying to attract Jesus's attention.

Excusing himself from conversation, Jesus made his way towards Martha and tenderly enquired if she was ready. As he led her away from the gathering, tears of sorrow and exhaustion began to flow and for a few precious moments the devoted brother and sister quietly held one another for the final time. As Martha slowly turned away from Jesus he placed a hand on her shoulder, gently whispering, "God walks with you." But she could not look back – it was finally over – an historic life had come to an historic end.

Jesus's words echoed in Martha's mind as she collected her belongings and walked into the darkness alone. Never before had she felt so isolated, uncertain, and defeated. The ministry had been disastrous, her beloved brother was about to be crucified, Judas had disappeared, her own life was in danger, and she'd said final farewells to her mother and family, knowing they would never see one another again. Martha felt vacant and without purpose for the first time in her life. All that remained was the small hope that the manuscript she carried would one day somehow find a way to make a difference.

* * *

Jesus did not want attention drawn to the fact that Martha had departed, so immediately became engaged in conversation, keeping everyone's attention on him. A short time later Seth returned to the Bethany house in an obviously distressed state, and in seeking out Jesus while cursing with rage, he bitterly announced: "I could find no trace of Judas at all – I'm distraught. I don't even know where to begin looking, but let me at least get Martha to safety – where is she? My guard is here and will escort her to the safe-house, and I shall return to Jerusalem to continue searching for Judas."

Jesus calmly responded, "There'll be no need, Seth. Martha has already begun the journey alone – you know how independent she is. She wanted to see if she could locate Judas on the route. She's hoping to find that he's made his own way to the safe-house."

Seth looked at Jesus in astonishment, saying, "Are you insane? You've allowed Martha to travel alone in the middle of the night? You know full well how much danger that places her in – what were you thinking?"

Jesus responded as nonchalantly as he could, saying, "Seth, you're over-reacting – Martha is more than capable of staying out of danger. The most important thing is for Judas to be found. I have no choice but to proceed as agreed, and all I trust is that you will do your best to ensure that Judas and Martha are provided for and safe from harm."

Seth was furious – not only had he lost track of Judas, but now he'd lost track of Martha – an outcome that seriously affected other more complex plans he'd had in motion since the day he was given control over Jesus's ending. Quickly instructing his guard to follow the route to the safe-house and catch up with Martha, he turned in frustration to Jesus, admonishing him for allowing such a thing to occur: "I have no idea why you would do this when I'd promised to take care of Martha. Despite our differences, you know how I feel. I did my best Jesus. I don't want to argue with you now – not at this moment. We may never speak again and I don't want things between us to end in this way. You have my utmost respect – I want you to know that. I will find Martha and Judas and I'll make sure they're safe – that is all I can promise. I can promise nothing more."

With his head bowed and no longer able to look at Jesus directly, Seth felt nothing but despair. He could speak no more – the reality of the moment was too much, even for Seth. In silence, he turned walked away.

* * *

Before facing his disciples with news of what was about to unfold, Jesus wandered away from the house for a few moments of private contemplation. The circumstances that had emerged during the evening could not have been worse. As with the rest of the ministry, these events were unforeseen and nothing had gone according to plan. As he tried to maintain his composure, Jesus reminded himself that there must be a reason for this outcome, although he had no idea what that could be. No matter how much he tried, he could see no purpose for the scenario of losing control over the fate of Martha and Judas – it was the one concern that had been his absolute priority since the arrest plans were instituted, yet not even this most basic of requirements had been met.

Even though he was besieged with worry over what could have happened to Judas and what may happen to Martha, Jesus forced himself to overcome his emotions and returned to the gathering where he proceeded to address the disciples.

PART II – THE LAST SUPPER

Positioning himself at a large, rectangular table central to the room, Jesus was immediately surrounded by the gathered disciples. Diverting conversation from familiar debate, he proceeded to inform the followers that he'd cooperated with the Movement and the authorities, and approved his own arrest and trial. He further explained that the outcome of his trial was also pre-agreed, in that he had surrendered himself to endure the punishment of crucifixion. Over gasps of horror and bewilderment, Jesus continued to explain that his arrest was imminent in any event, due to the disruption the ministry had caused. It was perceived by so many that he was personally responsible for the intolerable disturbance and provocative disputes erupting among the people. His whereabouts were constantly being sought by those who wanted to take matters into their own hands, and he believed that this reaction was something the Movement actively encouraged. In support of their desire to continue to incite division, Jesus felt he was being used as a political pawn to further enhance the prospects of the Movement. In encouraging his followers to understand that his time remaining was limited, Jesus suggested that anything other than surrendering to his fate in a sensible manner would not only place the lives of his followers and family in peril, but also facilitated the Movement gaining complete control over his ending.

He expanded further and in much detail, admitting that he had agreed to a civilised arrest to gain leverage. It would provide an opportunity to explain himself to the authorities, and the ability to speak out to the many who would attend such proceedings in view of his notorious reputation. Jesus put everyone's mind at rest by pledging that neither his family nor followers were in danger, but did warn that it may be required for many of those present to disown him to the authorities at some point in the coming days. He absolutely forbid anyone to give up their life for him, and stressed that under no circumstances were such heroics to be encouraged. Jesus's only request was that the disciples did their best to ensure the ministry was remembered for what it was.

Of course, everyone was shaken and appalled at such a revelation and vigorously refused to stand by and allow Jesus to be arrested. As they scoffed at the idea that they would ever disown him in any way, Jesus attempted to reassure them his decision was final, while being respectful of their concern and doubts. In an attempt to move the conversation along, Jesus proceeded to talk at length regarding how he would like his ministry to be remembered. He began by explaining that forgiveness and understanding are two of the most important components of his message; without them, humanity would never learn to be humane and compassionate towards one another. He stressed the importance of reminding people of the *real ministry*, despite the adversity they may confront for so doing. Along with the chronicle that Martha possessed, Jesus believed that the only hope of the truth surviving was if his followers had the strength of character to withstand the intimidation of the Movement.

Jesus then explained how the story of his life and teachings should be portrayed as a means to an end, but further emphasised that the *means* are not as important as the *end* of an individual's life. When the disciples asked him to expand upon what he meant by that, Jesus clarified that the *means* are his teachings, which should be viewed only as an available resource to support a person in achieving individual goals and living life to the full. His teachings, he felt, should be utilised to whatever degree was necessary for people to achieve success when proceeding towards their own ending. Jesus was concerned that his actual teachings would be distorted by the Movement, and that he personally, and the Movement as an institution, would be portrayed as the *way* to peace and fulfillment. The message of the *real* ministry was only supposed to be a contribution towards achieving a greater understanding of life, and discovering and enjoying the success that would be experienced as a result of this knowledge.

Jesus continued to engage the disciples by responding to questions, while expressing his lack of fear regarding his life coming to an end. He explained that when our ending is upon us, we will be presented with an opportunity to review our life and determine our level of success by how much we'd learned and evolved as souls. This is what he wanted us to understand – he did not want us to become preoccupied with his life or his ending – it is our own life, our progress and growth, and our own ending that we should be focused upon. Jesus did not believe the Movement's account of his life would truly reflect his personal struggles, shortcomings, and mistakes, but would create an impression of someone he was not. For Jesus, it was intolerable to imagine being represented as a condescending, infallible, self-proclaimed divine being. He was also horrified at the prospect of people being instructed that their first priority in life should be to listen to God's word by following a Movement that had portrayed such unimaginable falsehoods. He pleaded with his followers to do their utmost to prevent this from happening, and to do as they had throughout the ministry, and speak only of what he tried to achieve.

The room fell silent after Jesus had finished speaking. His message for them to carry forward was simple and straightforward – perhaps too straightforward. Most felt that if this was their last gathering, Jesus would surely have delivered a speech with more drama and gut-wrenching prophecy. Many of the disciples had doubts, and felt certain something was missing or not right. Immediately, they began debating among themselves; generating rumour in abundance by questioning whether Jesus was planning to disappear while pretending he'd been arrested, and asking how he could voluntarily accept his arrest when previously he'd been so compelled to live and spread his message. Did he no longer have a use for them and prefer to go it alone? Was he telling the truth, or was this some sort of complicated test they were expected to endure to assess their commitment to him?

The intense debate created many disagreements, and heated discussions continued well into the night. Eventually, most of the followers left the Bethany house and returned to Jerusalem, with only a few choosing to remain until sunrise to witness an arrest that many did not believe was going to occur.

Mary Magdalene was present during the address Jesus made to his disciples, and her reaction initially was of great distress. She was disturbed to learn that Martha and Judas were not at the Bethany house during such a significant moment in the ministry, and wondered if they even knew what was happening; she was astounded that Judas had kept this from her.

When Mary Magdalene asked Jesus why Martha and Judas were not present, he chose not to tell her of Judas's disappearance, or the fact Judas had no knowledge of upcoming events, saying only that he'd arranged for them to remain at a safe-house provided by Seth.

In spite of the fact that Mary Magdalene was deeply saddened and traumatised by the news, she felt privileged to be part of something so momentous. Deciding to be resolute in demonstrating her loyalty to

Jesus, she immediately entered the fray of debate, retaliating against anyone who suggested that Jesus was in some way being manipulative or not telling the truth.

* * *

If Jesus were here today, he would try to re-establish the very simple message he provided to his followers on the evening of the last supper, and would probably speak along these lines:

"Too often I am personally portrayed as the 'way' — the way to live your life, and achieve your goals. But I'm frustrated that the personal development of individuals is being restricted by this approach. As human beings coping with life on this earth, it is simply not possible for you to attain my way, since you are not me, any more than I am you. What I want you to understand is that the purpose of my ministry was to provide you with a resource to support you throughout life, in what is often a challenging and inhospitable environment. I wanted to enable you to achieve in your life at the level you would be expected and capable of achieving according to the maturity of your soul. There is such simplicity in that.

"I hope you hear me before it's too late. I do not expect people to set themselves up to fail by constantly asking, "What would Jesus do?" It was not my intention that you would be considered weak or a failure if you could not attain my 'way', lost your temper, made choices without conscience, or were unable to see what you were supposed to see. You are not sinners who need to repent; you are human beings who need support and understanding. This earth is here so you can experience and learn, but you are all so lost. You have either collectively given up on me because you have no idea what I represent, or have taken matters of religion so seriously that you are out of touch with reality. I am not a commodity or a thing. I am not a facility for those who enjoy being seen to be doing, while making others feel in some way 'less' if they are not. My true message was simply a means or a resource for you to utilise in achieving what you are capable of. It is not me who is important; it is not how you revere me that is of value; rather, it is your ending that is the key. The evolution of your soul is your purpose for existing.

"Everything I tried to teach was achieved with you in mind, so it could be used as a means to attain what you are capable of individually. It was supposed to enhance your experience of life. It was not meant to be something you could boastfully say you'd achieved, reached, or found by pronouncing your commitment to an institution. That does not mean you have achieved anything.

It is frustrating for me: I did not intend for people to feel so in awe of me as a person. I know I'm different, and I know who I am, but I also know who you are, and I know what you're capable of. If you make mistakes and fall short of either your own or other's expectations, that's fine — as long as you remember to learn from those mistakes. I too fell short of my own and other's expectations, but that aspect of me has never been revealed. I feel as though I failed you. I trusted people and was deceived, but I never imagined how far they would go. I am embarrassed to see the extravagant opulence and emotional control that has been established in my name.

"*Even today, when I attempt to reach you by using what is perceived by those in religious authority as non-conventional methods, they stand by what they have manipulated as my 'word', and use it against those who dare to speak the truth. Did they conveniently forget just how unconventional I was? Remember, I was crucified for being perceived as a blasphemous heretic. Is it not ironic that those purporting to represent me, react to those attempting to reveal the truth with assertions of blasphemy and heresy?*

"*If you claim to have 'found me', been 'saved' by me, or been 'born again', do not feel superior; a desire for such claims only proves you have yet to find yourself, and that is what counts. There will be many obstacles put in place before your ending in this life, and discovering my true message will be a significant beginning that will guide you throughout.*"

* * *

Arriving back in Jerusalem, Seth was absolutely determined to locate Judas. Frantic with worry and with little time to spare, he secured the help of several guards and organised a thorough search of the area. It was of paramount importance that Judas be found quickly and escorted to the safe-house — further plans were about to be unleashed, which would be seriously compromised if Judas could not be found. He was a vital part of those plans, but he had to be securely hidden for them to succeed.

With several men searching in many directions, Seth became more anxious as time progressed, but as he was about to walk beyond a clearly drunk man slumped in a heap in an alleyway, he pulled him over to one side in desperation and was astounded to discover Judas. As Seth shook him violently in an attempt to wake him, he threw water in his face while raging: "What the hell are you doing drinking yourself into oblivion when so much is going on? Do you have any idea how many problems you've caused? How could you let everyone down at such a vital time?"

As Judas attempted to focus and gather his thoughts, Seth ranted on and on about the trouble he'd caused, but as Judas looked up at Seth, he rather incoherently asked, "What do you want with me? Can't you just leave me alone – can you not see I'm of no use to you in this state?"

Seth was furious; dragging Judas to his feet he continued to give him a piece of his mind: "What I want is for you to abide by your responsibilities as we all agreed. Do you realise that Martha has journeyed alone to the safe-house because you were not in Bethany to escort her? Anything could have happened. I've sent my guard after her, but I don't yet know if she arrived safely."

As Judas became more aware, he impatiently shook off Seth's grip – he'd had enough. Sarcastically he retorted, "Oh, did I miss my important calling – a job anyone could do – stupid I am not. I know full well I'm being kept in the dark about something. There have been too many secret meetings that I've been excluded from. I know something is going on. I still don't know what it is, but I don't care either. It was the proof you see, Seth — proof that the followers had been right for all these years. Jesus doesn't really respect or value me; he just keeps me around because he feels responsible for his not-so-clever brother. I'm never given any tasks of substance, and being excluded from all of these recent proceedings and required only to be Martha's 'minder' was the end – enough is enough - 'Let's give that *job* to Judas so he feels important.' Well, guess what? I've had enough of being ridiculed by the followers; enough of having to rise above it all, and enough of convincing myself that what they say is untrue. I'm not going to burden anyone further with my presence because I'm clearly incapable of doing anything of value. I suggest you go to the safe-house and check on Martha yourself. Leave me to my own devices, Seth —I'm not worth worrying about. I'll be on my way if you don't mind."

Judas pushed past Seth and began staggering down the street, grumbling and cursing to himself. Seth had never before seen Judas in this state, and had no idea that he'd felt this way. He knew he couldn't leave Judas to go off on his own; things were going to unfold that Judas had no idea about. He had to persuade him to go to the safe-house.

Following Judas as he walked away, Seth talked compassionately, saying, "Judas, I have no idea where you got such ideas. There are lots of things that may be happening that none of us know about, and many events have transpired that I did not intend, but there is one thing I do know for absolute certain – you've never been so wrong about anything in your life. Jesus and Martha are distraught because they think my superiors have arranged for your end or the authorities have arrested you because of your association with them. They love you as their own. As such, I doubt if they thought to remind you of that too often – they probably assumed you already knew. Do you seriously believe that Jesus didn't need you throughout these years, Judas? You're so wrong. There was never a conversation that we had without him ending it by saying he'd ask your opinion first. You were his double check — you were his only check. You were with him for a reason, and whatever others may have thought or said – it wasn't true. There is also a very good reason you were asked to accompany Martha tonight rather than remain at the Bethany house with the others. It was to protect your life, but in addition, you are the only person Jesus could trust to protect Martha. You have to believe me, Judas, and you have to follow my instructions for your own safety. I know my people have let you all down, but I personally will not let you down – you have to do as I say."

Judas listened carefully to Seth's persuasions, but with tears streaming down his face, he replied, "You're saying what you think I want to hear, Seth. Mary Magdalene said the same, but being excluded from all of these recent meetings proves how little value is placed on my contribution."

Seth could see how Judas had arrived at such a conclusion, but tried once more to reassure him: "Judas, I attended all of the meetings you were excluded from, and yes, you are correct — you were purposely excluded — I'm not going to lie. But it was not for the reasons you assume – you have to believe me. If you accompany me to the safe-house we will hopefully find Martha there with my guard. She will explain everything, and then you'll understand. Believe me, Judas – you've never been more wrong about anything in your life. If you don't do as I say, you're not only putting your own life in jeopardy, but Martha's also. Please, will you accompany me?"

Judas thought momentarily, but suddenly became belligerent again. Pushing Seth aside and struggling to control his tears, he ranted, "I got a little drunk, but I didn't mean to end up unconscious in the street. I'm sorry

—I didn't mean to put Martha in danger. Things got out of hand, and I just kept drinking. I couldn't cope with being a burden to them any longer. I know I'm nothing, but for a while they made me feel as if I was someone, and I wanted to continue believing it until others convinced me otherwise."

Collapsing to the floor in tears, Judas begged Seth to leave him alone: "Go to the safe-house yourself and check on Martha — just leave me alone, please."

Seth now had no choice but to take action, so immediately ran towards the central square, summoning three of his men and instructing that Judas be physically escorted to the safe-house. Judas fought as his hands were tied behind his back and the soldiers marched him out of the city, but Seth could no longer concern himself with this situation. He hoped that Martha would be at the safe-house when Judas arrived, but knowing he was off the streets and safe was all that mattered. Seth had commitments to meet, which were integral and vital to his plans.

* * *

Positioning himself on the outskirts of Jerusalem for the remainder of the night, Seth focused on the task at hand. As each group of three or four disciples returned from the last supper at Bethany, he greeted them with an impression of distress and urgency, enquiring if they had come across Judas on their travels. As each responded that they had not, Seth informed them Judas had betrayed Jesus and provided the authorities with information to secure an arrest and prosecution. He further explained that Jesus was aware of these facts, yet did not want to betray his brother in the way Judas had betrayed him; hence he had chosen instead to convey a different scenario to them all in an attempt to protect Judas from their revenge.

This was music to the ears of the disciples — now they had a legitimate excuse for Judas to be disgraced. This development also made more sense to the followers than anything Jesus had announced, and actually explained so much of what they'd all questioned. They completely believed Seth's claim that Jesus knew he was about to be arrested because of Judas's indiscretion, but had fabricated a story of surrender to avoid a retaliatory attack on his brother. Having now generated considerable anger among the disciples, Seth motivated them further by asking if they'd assist in locating

Judas; forcing him to face his comeuppance for such atrocious insurrection. Needless to say, motivation was the last thing the followers needed – they loathed Judas with a vengeance; now they had the perfect defence to seek retribution for the years of pent up anger and jealousy they'd endured. The person they each believed had prevented them from acquiring a closer personal relationship with Jesus, was now officially a wanted man.

Seth's plan to deceive the disciples had succeeded with ease. He knew how little it would take to generate this response towards Judas, but Seth had actually achieved much more than that. By ensuring the disciples were all preoccupied on what was essentially a wild goose chase for an indefinite period of time, this facilitated Seth's ability to carry out the remainder of his plans without being questioned or disturbed by the followers of Jesus. They would never give up the search for Judas, and would likely become more ferocious in their desire as time wore on, thereby leaving Seth free to do as he wished.

* * *

Mary Magdalene was accompanying one such group of disciples when they came across Seth. She bore witness to his fabricated story, but knew instinctively it could not possibly be true – Judas had been Jesus's closest friend for most of his life; to her, this was simply inconceivable. Knowing that something was definitely not right with this situation, Mary Magdalene remained quiet within the small group of followers, and paid close attention to all that Seth revealed. She chose to keep to herself the fact that Jesus had disclosed to her in private that Judas and Martha had been safely housed by Seth, since that in itself told her something serious was amiss.

As Seth ushered the followers on their way, he took Mary Magdalene aside. While signalling for one of his guards to attend, he said, "I want you to remain at the house I have designated for Jesus's mother, Mary, and brother, James – my soldier will take you there. Under no circumstances whatsoever are you to share with them what you've learned tonight about Judas. You are to provide for them, organise their accommodation, ensure they remain hidden, and see to it that no one communicates with them until I declare they are safe to leave Jerusalem after the crucifixion.

Remember, they are not to be concerned about these things — do you understand?"

Somewhat taken aback at having this sudden dilemma imposed upon her, Mary Magdalene innocently questioned Seth when responding, and asked, "I understand they shouldn't learn of such terrible news at this difficult time, but what you've said about Judas makes no sense. How could it possibly be true?"

Seth took a tight grip on Mary Magdalene's arm and made himself clear: "I need you to ingratiate yourself with James and his mother. This is for their good and the good of Judas and Martha. If I need any further information in the event of anything untoward occurring, I expect you to obtain it. Do you understand? It is for their good. I refuse to answer questions at this point, but it is imperative I have your support."

Mary Magdalene was terrified; what Seth was asking of her did not bear thinking about. She was, in effect, being instructed to spy on Jesus's mother and brother; divulging their secrets to the Movement if Seth deemed it was necessary. In not believing for one moment that Judas could have betrayed Jesus, Mary Magdalene knew Seth must be lying and his intentions could therefore not possibly be good — this was an intolerable situation for her to accept. Taking a deep breath to calm herself, Mary Magdalene responded by saying, "I need more information Seth — what you are asking of me is to betray their trust should they share information with me. You don't understand — I cannot do that to the family of Jesus — not without you explaining precisely why it is so important, and why you are saying things about Judas that cannot possibly be true."

Seth knew that Mary and James must be privy to any secret contingency plans Jesus and Martha had made, but he did not want them aware of the rumours of Judas, since he feared their reaction would impact his plans. However, he did need someone in their midst who could be used should events take an unexpected turn. Tightening his grip on Mary Magdalene's arm while pushing his face up-close to hers, Seth threatened her again, saying, "Just do as I say — this is more complex than you understand. Leave this to me, and all will be revealed in due course. If you care anything for the family of Jesus, you will do exactly as I instruct."

Mary Magdalene was shaken and terrified by such a stern reaction to her questions, and decided it was best not to react to Seth's threatening tones. With tears streaming down her face, she passively agreed to do as he'd insisted. Remaining silent, she slowly removed her arm from his grip, and quietly accompanied the soldier to the house of Mary and James. True to her word, she did not reveal anything of these goings-on: she could not bear to cause upset with questions and doubts regarding the integrity of Judas. Nevertheless, Mary Magdalene was determined to get to the bottom of this situation; instinctively, she knew something was very wrong.

PART III – THE ARREST OF JESUS

The quiet streets of Bethany and the hillside beyond, afforded Jesus the privacy he sought during his final hours of freedom. All but a few of the disciples had departed Bethany in the early hours of the morning, and those who'd stayed behind intended to leave at sunrise. Even though Jesus was concerned that the remaining followers may become embroiled in his arrest, he was mostly preoccupied with the welfare of Judas and Martha. As he wandered among the scenes of tranquility on the outskirts of Bethany, he felt utterly frustrated at the predicament they faced, and at the fact he was helpless to do anything constructive about it. He could only pray for their safety, appreciating that their future was now out of his hands.

Returning to the Bethany house as the sun began to rise; Jesus sought out the remaining disciples and encouraged them to leave. In dismissing his concerns, the followers proudly alluded to being fearless and fully prepared for whatever fate they may suffer. Of those who remained, most were not entirely sure an arrest was actually going to occur and had, in part, only stayed in Bethany to discover the truth. However, the confident bravado of both the fearless and doubters alike, waned with the distant sound of approaching Roman soldiers. Within a few moments of everyone acknowledging an arrest could be imminent, a soldier appeared in the doorway demanding that Jesus of Nazareth make himself known. Stepping forward, Jesus said, "I am he." As two soldiers were summoned to arrest Jesus and remove him from the premises, the remaining disciples looked on in horror as the soldier in charge turned towards them asking, "Who in this room is a follower of Jesus of Nazareth?"

Before anyone could respond, Jesus announced, "I personally know none of these men. This house is a vacant property used as a refuge for travellers – we met for the first time when I arrived yesterday evening and we shared food and wine."

The disciples hung their heads, avoiding eye contact with Jesus – they were afraid – no one had the courage to speak out. With the room in complete silence, the Roman soldier glared suspiciously at the disciples while signalling for Jesus to be removed. Following his men out of the house, he ensured those remaining felt his defiant, threatening stare, as he purposely made note of their faces in the event of any future transgression on their part.

Jesus had attempted to demonstrate compassion and understanding towards his disciples by speaking out, ensuring they did not have to endure denying him. This was his way of saying, it's alright – he implicitly knew what they were capable of and did not expect such sacrifice. He hoped that this final expression of thoughtfulness would ensure they remembered his presentation from the previous evening. Jesus did not want people to feel pressured to emulate him as such; only to learn from his example, and incorporate those lessons into their own life as far as they were capable of doing.

* * *

The arrest of Jesus was the beginning of an arduous series of interrogations, taunts, threats, and provocations, but he managed to remain focused and rise above it all. His only concern was for the fate of Judas and Martha, but he had no way of discovering their fortune and could only pray for their well-being.

* * *

While Jesus was being transferred to Jerusalem for inquisition, an ever-increasing posse of followers searched the city and surrounding area for Judas, who by now was well-established as Jesus's betrayer. Seth convincingly conducted the mission with great urgency, but in truth he was reasonably relaxed: locating Judas and securing him in the safe-house had put his plans back on track, but he still had the problem of Martha to resolve. Seth had learned from one of his guards that there was no evidence she had arrived at the safe-house, so he immediately concluded that Jesus and Martha had made alternative arrangements and assumed they had not trusted he would provide for Martha's safety. Seth saw little merit in relying on Judas to divulge information since it was clear from his behaviour that he was unaware of their intentions. There now remained only one possibility — to persuade Mary Magdalene to encourage Mary and James to disclose the contingency plan, which he was certain they would know in detail. Seth knew they would never reveal this information to him, and even a casual enquiry would result in James suspecting Seth's motives and reacting aggressively. However, utilising Mary Magdalene so soon in the proceedings had not been anticipated, but Seth had no choice — she was his only hope of finding Martha.

While the followers continued the hunt for Judas in an open and public way, Seth's search for Martha had to be discreet. He sought out Mary Magdalene at the earliest opportunity and instructed her accordingly, but knew it could be some time before she was willing or able to acquire such information. It was necessary to keep the investigation regarding Martha's whereabouts a secret, since if the leaders within the Movement discovered she was unaccounted for, Seth's life would be in immediate danger. The fabricated search for Judas was part of the strategy, but as far as Seth's superiors were concerned, both Judas and Martha had by now been disposed of.

* * *

In Martha's Voice:

"It is difficult to put into words what I was feeling at that moment: leaving the Bethany house for the last time; knowing that Jesus was facing an unthinkable death, and having learned that Judas was missing was unbearable. I was oblivious to the potential danger posed by vagrants and criminals living in the woods; it was as if it didn't matter, or I didn't care. I felt bewildered

and numb with shock. The entire purpose of my life seemed to no longer matter; there appeared to be little point to anything. I doubted if there was any good I could do on my own. All I had were a few worthless diaries recording a ministry lasting three years that had turned into an absolute fiasco; resulting in me having to relinquish my freedom, abandon my family, and lose the two people who meant the most to me in the world. I felt as though there was no longer anything to live for.

"I began to wonder just whose side God was on; nothing seemed to have gone our way. My life seemed to have absolutely no purpose. An elaborate plan to escape the continent and ensure the diaries were safe, felt like a pathetic, limp ending to what had originally been life-long plans and hopes to effect so much change.

"As I put one foot in front of the other on what I knew was going to be a long, arduous journey throughout the night, I could only think of Jesus and Judas, but finding myself imagining either of them in the past tense was terrifying.

"It was the early hours of the morning before I found the hideout Jesus had chosen, and I was relieved when the journey was over. He'd stored bedding and enough food and water to last for several days, so it was good to find those comforts waiting. The cave-like dwelling was hidden by large trees and afforded me a view over the hillside looking down towards Jerusalem. As the sun rose, I knew that the arrest was imminent and my dear brother would begin to participate in the only ending he could foresee. I could barely stand to imagine the thoughts that must be passing through his mind at this time.

CHAPTER TEN

THE CRUCIFIXION

*P*rior to arriving at the office of Pontius Pilate for sentencing, Jesus was paraded from one place of jurisdiction to another as part of the process of trial. At each interval he responded to interrogators by explaining the true message of his ministry, while doing his utmost to distance himself from rumours perpetrated by the Movement. Even though most of those in authority initially appeared disinterested in what Jesus had to say, he sensed their increasingly subdued retorts and was hopeful his plea for understanding had been effective. His detractors on the streets had many opportunities to jeer at the apprehended heathen, who they believed was the blasphemous bigot entirely responsible for the disruption caused by the Movement. Despite such blatant opposition displayed by ranting throngs, Jesus was diligent in offering carefully chosen words and blessings of peace to anyone close enough to share in such exchanges.

Even though Pontius Pilate is held responsible for sentencing Jesus to death, he actually had no particular feelings about him one way or the other. He'd heard of Jesus as a result of the local disruption caused by the ministry, but viewed him not as a threat but an annoying young rebel about to receive his comeuppance. Sometimes depicted as the perpetrator of evil, Pontius Pilate was in reality a rather self-important figurehead who sought a quiet life and tried not to involve himself in too much turmoil if at all possible. He was bored and highly irritated at being required to spend time dealing with Jesus, and was only participating because of a substantial financial incentive offered by the Movement. He'd agreed to swiftly move proceedings along; thereafter passing control to Seth for the sentence to be carried out. Pontius Pilate knew the accord included an acknowledgement that his decision was to appease the Jewish citizens, but he was unconcerned about this technicality and viewed the entire procedure as a trivial, annoying matter he'd been handsomely paid to resolve.

However, Pontius Pilate had not anticipated the effect of personally meeting with Jesus in the privacy of his office. He discovered that being in the company of the most charismatic human being to have lived was highly unsettling, and it was not long before he began regretting his decision to cooperate with Seth.

As part of the required questioning of Jesus, Pontius Pilate asked that he defend himself against the accusations of blasphemy and heresy, but in a determined and respectful way Jesus refused to do so. He was then asked to confirm or deny the accusation that he had declared his status as the divine son of God, but once again he calmly declined to comment, choosing instead to use the opportunity to speak of his real ministry. These exchanges served only to enhance Pontius Pilate's increasing sense of panic at what he was participating in. Being faced with such a unique individual, willingly giving up his life for the chance to be heard, he did not feel obligated to administer what had been agreed, preferring instead to find a solution that would save Jesus from death.

Jesus could see that Pontius Pilate was anxious, so paid close attention to the emerging atmosphere and remained more focused and controlled than ever. Aware that the Movement had yet to overcome one final hurdle from their agenda – a person of authority stating he had witnessed Jesus assert his divinity – Jesus suspected that Seth may have persuaded Pontius Pilate to make such a statement. If it became apparent that he was moving in this direction, Jesus intended to do his utmost to talk him out of such a decision, and would even attempt an escape rather than be forced to stand alongside an authority figure while such a pronouncement was made. As it turned out, Jesus's concerns were unfounded since no such arrangements had been made, but the problem he did encounter was not one he'd anticipated.

Pontius Pilate did not fear Seth's superiors or the Movement as a whole, and as a wealthy, dominant leader he had no reservation in abandoning his agreement with Seth. Without notice, Pontius Pilate declared that proceedings be brought to an immediate halt and abruptly announced to Jesus that he could not progress the trial towards sentencing; informing him there was no evidence to support a guilty verdict.

While recognising it was his own approach that had disturbed the conscience of this powerful man, it also dawned on Jesus that Pontius Pilate was entirely unaware that he was as much a part of these arrangements as

Seth. Jesus could not understand why he was not privy to all of the information, particularly as his full cooperation was vital for the success of the plan – he wondered what possible diversions Seth and his superiors had in mind when deciding to keep something so significant from Pontius Pilate. However, with little time to deliberate such matters, Jesus had no choice but to turn his attention to resolving the immediate problem. Realising he had to provide reassurance, Jesus explained his reason for choosing this ending:

"You don't seem to understand – not only have I participated in these plans, but they were instigated by me. I have chosen to die in this way because I believe it will provide the only opportunity I can foresee to put the record straight in a very public way. By living, I am placing those I love, and those who have supported me, in danger: it is no longer feasible for me to continue. This ending is to ensure I am remembered, while providing an opportunity for me to convince people of the legacy I would like to leave behind. I wasn't attempting to establish myself or a religion throughout these years; my desire was to support and guide individuals. But my time here is now over, and my life is soon to be taken in any event – this trial is my way of retaining some control over that fate.

"If you bring these proceedings to a halt, the Movement will continue with their original proposal, which was to incite hatred to such a degree that I would be murdered at the hands of my own people. They were intent upon formulating outrageous assertions of my divinity, and condemning the Jewish people as perpetrators in the murder of the son of God. I cannot permit that to happen. It is my hope that after the event of my death, what I have explained to the authorities throughout my trial, and to individuals I have engaged along the way, will be debated with the help of those who followed the real ministry. Without this process, I would never be able to reach someone like you and have the opportunity to speak my mind. Please believe me when I say you are doing no wrong. I will not be forced into participating any further with Seth and his group, but by organising my own ending I now have the chance to speak freely while having my statements at trial registered for all time. I need this opportunity to ensure as far as possible that my ministry is understood for what it was, but due to the actions of the Movement, there is technically sufficient compelling evidence of blasphemy and heresy for you to convict without question. Please be assured – now is the time of my ending."

While Jesus had been quite persuasive, Pontius Pilate remained extremely reluctant. So reluctant, in fact, that irrespective of what Jesus had pleaded, he insisted on speaking to those gathered to assert Jesus's innocence; offering them an opportunity to reconsider their anxiety towards him. Jesus now had no choice but to stand back and permit Pontius Pilate to do as he wished, aware that this genuine and heartfelt approach could change everything.

Despite his best efforts, however, Pontius Pilate was unable to get anyone to see reason. With the encouragement of Seth's men planted among them, the people persisted in baying for blood; demanding the conviction they all perceived was a foregone conclusion based upon the evidence they had before them. Pontius Pilate could see that the gathered crowd were outraged at his suggestions, and recognised that Jesus was probably correct – if he went against their demands and released him, it would only be a matter of time before he was hunted down and murdered. In the end, Pontius Pilate conceded that by allowing Jesus to do things his way, he was at least able to retain some degree of dignity.

Before giving the final decree, Pontius Pilate hesitantly turned towards Jesus and enquired, "Are you certain this is the way you want it to be? I can send my soldiers to disperse this feeble crowd immediately and have you removed to a location that at least provides temporary safety. I don't care what arrangements we each have with Seth. It does not have to end here - that is what I want you to know."

Even though Jesus appreciated Pontius Pilate's efforts, he respectfully replied, "It does have to end here. You may be able to secure me for a period, but I have my loved ones and followers to consider – they will see retribution."

With a reluctant glance towards the crowd, Pontius Pilate approved their demands and sentenced Jesus to death by crucifixion. Summoning his soldiers, he instructed that Jesus be removed and prepared for execution before hastily leaving the room. He was consumed by remorse at being involved in such an episode, and could no longer bear to be in Jesus's company.

* * *

While Jesus advanced through the various stages of trial, Seth maintained a low profile to ensure nobody associated him with the arrest. He continued to incite the followers into believing it was Judas who had caused such an unspeakable development, and that Jesus's arrest was not the arranged event he had revealed. As part of the pre-trial negotiations with his superiors, Seth had insisted upon being responsible for supervising Jesus's sentence, but because the followers believed this situation arose as a result of Judas's actions and had no idea the Movement was involved, Seth needed to be circumspect regarding his role. It was therefore explained away as one of supervision, which Seth claimed the Movement had insisted upon to guarantee matters were correctly conducted, and to ensure that Jesus did not endure anything more than would be expected.

At this stage of the proceedings it was essential that Seth be vigilant in anticipating fringe activities that could undermine the plans. Knowing there were many followers who might decide to join forces and take matters into their own hands, Seth kept a close eye on those he believed were most likely to create a spectacle. However, his main priority at this point was making certain that Judas remained secure, while delicately engineering a search for Martha, despite having no idea where to begin.

With time on his hands during the trial phase, Seth travelled to the safe-house in the anticipation of finding Judas cooperative. He hoped to discover that he was aware of contingency plans, which he was now certain Jesus and Martha had made, but as he was not too surprised to discover, Judas had little to offer.

The moment Seth entered the room, Judas jumped to his feet, aggressively demanding news of Martha: "What have you done with her, Seth – where is Martha – you will get nothing from me until you disclose her whereabouts."

Seth was displeased to be on the receiving end of a verbal attack, not to mention finding Judas as quarrelsome as ever. He'd gone out of his way to ensure the safety of both Judas and Martha – it was their respective actions that had brought about this state of affairs, and Seth was in no mood to be argued with. Impatiently, he retorted, "I have not harmed Martha and would never do such a thing. She left the Bethany house alone because you were not there to escort her – let's not forget that Judas. One of my main concerns was to ensure the safety of you both, but neither of you abided by the agreement – that is why we face this predicament. I need your help if we are going to find Martha – I do not need arguments and demands. Jesus told me that Martha had made her own way to this house, which she clearly has not. Did they have another plan, Judas? Did they not trust that I'd provide for you both — did they intend for the two of you to hide somewhere else?"

Judas became a little more subdued after Seth's outburst — he knew it was his fault that Martha was missing. With a reluctant sigh, he responded by saying, "They told me nothing of other plans — only that I was to escort Martha to this house. I'm sorry — I've let everyone down. What could have happened to her? Can you not dispatch more men to search? Why can't you release me so I can help — what harm would that do? I will take precautions if you're concerned I may become embroiled in the trial alongside Jesus. Please, Seth, allow me to make up for my misdeeds by helping to find Martha. I could speak with James or Mother — surely they must know where she intended to hide. Seth — instruct your guard to release me — you know I can be of help."

Seth wandered awkwardly towards the exit, knowing it was entirely impossible to give in to such a request: "No, Judas, I can't let you go in search of Martha — it's too dangerous," he explained, "leave the search to me — I have plenty of trustworthy people at my disposal. It's not worth the risk to allow you to participate."

It didn't take long before Judas sensed there was more going on than he was privy to, and that once again he was being excluded from something important, but there was nothing that could be done to alleviate his concerns. The betrayal rumour was already widespread, and the disciples were feverishly searching for Judas. Not only would he be in serious danger if found, but of equal concern was his discovery ruining important, complex plans that Seth already had in motion.

"What are you keeping from me Seth," enquired Judas, "why can I not go in search of Martha? You have tried to convince me that I'm valued, yet now you appear to think I'm incapable of conducting a basic search. You would rather entrust such matters to the disciples and your men — isn't that what you're saying, Seth?"

Momentarily lost for words, Seth sighed to himself, saying, "It is not a matter of what you're capable of — I wish it was as simple as that. You have to trust me. Please leave the search for Martha to me. I will find out if she perhaps went to another location that we are both unaware of, but believe me — in a matter of days this will all become clear. My guard will remain and I shall return to update you on developments, but I implore you — please do not attempt an escape. I need your word on that – trust me."

Judas was so bewildered by all the secrecy and uncertainty. He knew that Jesus and Martha had trusted Seth for years, yet not once had that trust been justified. Judas was stricken with guilt that he may have misunderstood Jesus's intentions prior to the last supper when he'd been excluded from important meetings, but Seth not confiding in him only added to his insecurity. Observing the guard, Judas looked towards Seth, saying, "Do I really have a choice, Seth? You have me under armed guard, yet will not explain why. It's not a matter of me agreeing to stay – you have no intention of allowing me to leave, do you?"

Seth chose not to respond – he knew there was nothing he could say that would appease Judas. Walking away with his head bowed, he instructed his guard to secure his charge until further notice.

* * *

From the offices of Pontius Pilate, Jesus was escorted onto the streets where his torture awaited. Hundreds of people mocked and jeered as soldiers maneuvered him throughout the crowd, but Jesus tried to focus on what was now required. As the angry, ranting mob jostled for position, he witnessed up-close the fear and anger their faces portrayed. In a brief moment of clarity, he emotionally departed from the surrounding chaos, and quietly questioned his faith in God and the trust he had placed in his own intuition: "How could everything have gone so wrong? For my entire life I endeavoured to teach the meaning of inner peace and how it can be achieved, but now I am to die being loathed as someone who caused such fear and mistrust. How did my life come to this?"

In attempting to regain his composure, Jesus acknowledged to himself that he should accept his predicament and use whatever time that remained to make an impression. He proceeded to engage those closest to him; apologising for how he'd made them feel, while doing his utmost to convince them of his true intentions.

As he was jostled by soldiers trying to weave their way through the throng, Jesus observed Seth watching from a distance; seemingly staring directly at him, showing no sign of emotion. He also noticed several of the disciples among the crowd, but they kept quiet and stood back, observing in horror as events unfolded. When recognising his brother, James, his mother, and Mary Magdalene, Jesus struggled to reach them, pleading they not remain, but despite their utter devastation they insisted upon being with Jesus during his final hours.

Seth lingered in the background for as long as he could, while somewhat optimistically hoping Martha would make a last-minute appearance with the rest of her family. But as Jesus was being positioned for the flogging phase of his sentence, Seth had to move forward and assume his responsibilities. Deciding he had no choice but to attempt persuading Jesus to divulge the whereabouts of Martha, Seth approached him moments before his punishment began and demanded he reveal where she was hiding: "I have found Judas and he is safe, but you must tell me now – where is Martha? She should not be alone – you know that – tell me where she is and I will ensure she is reunited with Judas. If you do not, you will pay for this in more ways than you can imagine."

Jesus looked at Seth in utter disbelief and angrily retorted, "Threatening me at this juncture in my life is a little useless, Seth, don't you think? Leave Martha alone, she can take care of herself and has her own destiny to fulfill. You owe us at least that much."

Frustrated at knowing he would get nowhere by pushing Jesus further, Seth reluctantly accepted defeat and signalled for proceedings to begin. The beating of Jesus has been portrayed in many media re-enactments, and the brutality displayed is what occurred. However, throughout the entire ordeal Jesus preserved his dignity by trying to remain poised, while meeting the eyes of his detractors standing nearby. He struggled to be heard by as many people as he could, and did his best to speak of the true intentions of his ministry and offer reassurance to those willing to listen, saying, "I understand and I don't blame you. I was trying to teach, not change or control you. I wanted you to discover everything you need to know about life, and learn to believe in yourself above all else. Please know that I do not bear a grudge – it is I who failed you – I do not blame you for this reaction – I understand. I know it is time for my life to end – I am at peace with that."

* * *

As part of the agreement with Pontius Pilate, it was Seth who was to decide at what point the flogging would end and the march to the crucifixion site would begin. Onlookers observed that the lashing was considerably more extensive and violent than others they'd witnessed, and the recipient more resilient than any before. Consequently, the longer the process endured, the less resolute many of the witnesses became. They observed Jesus's strength and determination, and word spread of the utterances he'd struggled to project. As the cruelty prevailed, the crowd grew tired of jeering, and their relief was very apparent when Seth signalled for the second phase of the sentence to proceed. By now, the atmosphere had changed and the silence was conspicuous. No one openly shared what they were thinking, but many began looking into each other's eyes, searching for similar feelings of discontent.

Jesus was forced to march alongside soldiers to the crucifixion site, but often collapsed before being dragged back to his feet and forced to continue. He began the journey carrying his own cross until it was clear he could no longer do so, at which point a Roman soldier removed the burden and marched in front of him, creating a focal point as he tried to maintain his footing and remain alert. By now, Jesus was barely conscious, and the strength in his voice had almost gone, but so too had the voice of the people. The march to the crucifixion site turned into one of silence, interrupted only by the sound of Jesus's utterances being heard above the shuffling crowd walking alongside him.

Pontius Pilate was not in attendance for the first phase of the sentence, but was required to witness the crucifixion, which he did with great reluctance while closely observing Seth. His doubts about Jesus's guilt had been verified when he learned of his suffering and of the gestures he'd made towards the vociferous crowd. As a result, Pontius Pilate wanted the matter over with as quickly as possible – it was more than he could stand. While he had given Seth full control over proceedings, he had no intention of permitting this spectacle to continue for a moment longer than necessary.

Jesus's condition had deteriorated towards unconsciousness before being placed on the cross, which prompted Pontius Pilate to suggest that a crucifixion was futile. Ignoring his observations, Seth continued to instruct the soldiers to proceed; infuriating Pontius Pilate to such an extent that he stormed off in disgust, angrily shouting that he washed his hands of the entire proceeding. Seth sensed the very obvious weakening of his resolve, but remained focused on directing the soldiers as they securely strapped Jesus's wrists, feet, and upper body to large pieces of timber, and hoisted him to an elevated position facing the sun. Jesus momentarily opened his eyes, glancing briefly towards the crowd and using what little energy he had left to gesture towards James, his mother, and Mary Magdalene who were gathered in prayer at his feet. Jesus seemed to lose consciousness again within moments of this final exchange, as his head and body hung lifelessly forward for all to bear witness.

Those who had followed Jesus to the crucifixion site rather self-consciously observed the concluding part of his sentence from a distance. As the process unfolded, a river of doubt swept over them all as the words Jesus had struggled to utter replayed in their minds. Many quietly shared what they'd overheard throughout his ordeal, which served only to compound their apprehension. Even the Roman soldiers accompanying Seth had been moved, and were not at all at ease with their part in the dealings. Sensing he was not alone in such discomfort, one of the soldiers turned to Seth and enquired, "What did he do that was so harmful to them?"

Taking a few thoughtful moments before responding, Seth meekly informed, "He simply told them what they were not ready to hear."

* * *

There had been no sign of life within Jesus from the moment he was placed on the cross, and even though it was customary for criminals to be left for many hours or days until death, it was intended that Jesus be removed for burial as soon as possible. Due to his high profile, there was concern that his followers may try to recover the body and create a shrine of some sort, which was bound to cause even further unrest.

Pontius Pilate did not remain at the site for the period of crucifixion – his conscience made it impossible to do so – but approximately two hours later he returned to find the crowd still standing in silence observing Jesus's body. In his anxiety, he demanded that enough was enough, instructing that his soldiers disperse the crowd and that Seth oversee the burial. The soldiers did not wait for Seth's orders, but jumped to their feet and began to remove Jesus from the cross. While no one was in a position to object to Pontius Pilate's command even if they'd wanted to, it was clear they were all relieved that the episode had been brought to an abrupt end. In silence, people wandered away from the site and returned to their homes, while the family of Jesus prepared to bury their loved one.

Jesus's mother, his brother, James, and Mary Magdalene, prayed over the body for a few moments before wrapping it in a shroud in preparation for burial. Jesus was then laid to rest in a small cave-like area, which was secured and hidden by several large rocks and shrubs. Seth instructed two of his men to take turns guarding the tomb to avoid the possibility of Jesus's followers returning to claim the body, and arranged for soldiers to escort Mary Magdalene, James, and Mary to safety. However, as they were gathering themselves and preparing to depart, Seth called Mary Magdalene to one side.

"We need to talk as soon as possible," Seth urged, "did you discover whether or not there was a contingency plan in place? Martha is still missing and may be in danger – I need to know where she went. Mary and James will know – it is imperative that Martha is found – do you understand?"

Mary Magdalene remained stony-faced. She was overcome with grief; such a demand being made of her at a time like this was not well-received. Certain that Seth could not possibly have the best interests of Martha at heart, she responded by saying, "If you expect me to help you and betray Jesus's family, you will need to provide more insight for your requests. If Jesus had trusted you he would not have found it necessary to make alternative plans for Martha. And let us not forget the matter of Judas – his apparent betrayal does not sit well with me – until you are more forthcoming, it is unlikely I will be of any assistance."

Abruptly walking away and confident that Seth would not dare threaten her while in the company of Mary and James, Mary Magdalene felt empowered by standing up for herself in this way. She was not at all troubled by the news that Martha was missing; rather, she felt Martha was probably very safe and only missing as far as Seth was concerned.

CHAPTER ELEVEN

JESUS'S DIRECTIVE TO JAMES

*J*ames, the eldest of the three boisterous, younger brothers of Jesus and Martha, had been provided with strict guidelines by Jesus prior to the crucifixion, and instructed that under no circumstances was he to stray from these directives. Jesus knew that once the crucifixion was over, the agenda of the early Christian Movement would come rushing to the fore: people would not know what had hit them. Knowing James's temperament, Jesus put an obstacle in his path to prevent him from reacting and attempting to halt the Movement's progress. He insisted that James prioritise providing for their frail mother, and do nothing that would put either of their lives at risk. Jesus further maintained that James be responsible for returning their mother safely to Nazareth, where their sister, Ruth, was awaiting her return. As a result of this directive, James's hands were tied. He would now be unable to react to unforeseen developments after the crucifixion in the aggressive, confrontational style that was his, since doing so would almost certainly leave his mother at peril.

Jesus did not know precisely what would occur after his death, but he did know that the Movement's strategy would be extensive and geared towards capitalising on the situation. He was certain they would immediately engage in further disruptive and divisive behaviour, but Jesus believed that the most advantageous moment for James to make a stand would be once the Movement had developed a stronghold, as strange as that may seem. Jesus did not want their progress disrupted, and believed people needed to experience their tactics; enabling the truth of their motivations to be witnessed for what they were. Permitting the Movement to succeed was the only way that could be achieved.

Jesus was hopeful that once the consequences of the early Christian indoctrination strategies were fully understood, people would be in a position to make a well-informed choice: either join the opposition that

James would establish, or permit the early Christian Movement's intimidation to overrule. Even though this was a risky strategy, Jesus felt it was vital for individuals to see and experience their agenda and consider the opposition to it. This was their chance to practice his philosophy of trusting their own intuition, rather than bow in fear when faced with a threatening campaign. It was on this basis alone that Jesus felt people should decide whether to stand against or succumb.

While James accepted and understood his responsibility to his mother, he knew it was going to be difficult to abide by such restrictions. His natural tendency was to forcefully react to blatant injustices, while often neglecting to consider a plan until after the event. However, James eventually agreed that allowing matters to develop, while carefully structuring an effective opposition, presented him with the most likely path to success. He concurred that threatening the Movement's ambitions without a well thought-out plan, would likely result in his entire family being massacred.

Even though it was not appreciated at the time, it would later transpire that the direction of the future of mankind was entirely dependent upon the choices these individuals made. It was a turning point in our history, and a time for fear to be abandoned in favour of the courage to believe in self. Jesus had taught those who followed the real ministry that decisions made with fear overriding rational thinking and self-belief, would always produce a negative outcome. The same can be said of our choices today.

* * *

When placing these restrictions upon his brother, Jesus did not realise the extent to which such limitations would assist Seth in executing his plans. Being aware of James's temperament, Seth was always vigilant in his company, but as each day passed he knew it was only a matter of time before the story of Judas's disappearance and the betrayal accusation reached him. Seth knew he would be sought out by James in the first instance, and also knew he needed to be very convincing to prevent a substantial reaction. He had bought himself some time by having agreed with Jesus that James remain with his mother until the area returned to calm after the crucifixion, but Seth knew that state of affairs could only be maintained for a few days. He was walking a fine line, and Seth was very much aware that one aggressive move by James could result in his extensive plans falling into disarray.

Unbeknown to Seth, however, James had been rendered harmless. The time and space Seth needed had unwittingly been afforded by directives put in place by Jesus.

CHAPTER TWELVE

THE DESTINY OF JUDAS, MARY MAGDALENE, AND MARTHA

PART I – THE FATE OF JUDAS

everal days had passed since the arrest of Jesus, and the restrictions imposed upon Judas were becoming unbearable. Seth had not returned as promised to acquaint him with developments, which served only to increase his anxiety over Martha's fate. With little to occupy his mind, Judas became absorbed in making sense of recent events, while trying to determine what Jesus had been keeping from him, supposedly for his own good.

Seth had suggested to Judas that his life could be at risk, but he did not understand why the threat was more of a concern now than it had been for years. Nothing made sense to Judas, particularly as he felt Seth was being honest in his desire to locate Martha, yet evasive when Judas offered to help. Knowing that his family association would allow him of all people to secure information from James and Mary, Judas considered Seth's reaction as proof of something improper occurring. For that reason, he could no longer abide his confinement or continue to rely upon Seth for information. Intending to do his utmost to escape, Judas turned his attention to the guard's routine and his growing complacency towards what he believed was a non-threatening charge.

While deliberately spending most of his time curled up in a corner pretending to be asleep, Judas waited until the guard bored of standing over him and momentarily wandered away from the area. As soon as an opportunity arose, Judas piled a bundle of rags in place of his form, and escaped into the night.

With only the reflection of moonlight to guide him, Judas headed directly into the centre of Jerusalem. He disguised himself in a shawl, giving the impression of a pauper wandering the streets late at night, while carefully monitoring the occasional passer-by in the event that Seth or one of his guards was in the vicinity. With no particular plan in mind, Judas was relying upon coming across a group of followers in the hope they may know something of the whereabouts of his family. Recognising that the arranged trial would by now be over, Judas decided that wherever Martha had been hiding was likely to be where Jesus had gone. He was hopeful that some of the followers would be privy to that information, or at least be aware of the location of James and his mother.

It was the early hours of the morning when Judas approached the town centre, but the streets were unusually quiet for the time of day. Dawn was breaking on the morning after the crucifixion of his beloved brother, but Judas was unaware that the somber atmosphere was due to the broad disquiet caused by the event of Jesus's death. Observing a woman standing in a doorway, Judas casually mentioned the absence of the usual early-morning activity, and enquired further if she knew whether the trial of Jesus of Nazareth had been concluded. Hesitantly, the woman responded that it had, and proceeded to recount events leading up to the crucifixion, and the remorse she'd felt when witnessing Jesus's resolve and learning of the vows he'd spoken.

Judas stared in disbelief at the woman; his heart sinking further at every word – he could not believe what he was hearing. As the woman continued her account, she included the rumour that Jesus had been betrayed to the authorities by one of his followers, but it did not occur to Judas for a moment that anyone could suppose it was him. Judas was in such shock that he could not summon the words to question the woman further, and staggered the remaining distance into town; barely able to breathe as he sought out a secluded corner to sit for a while and gather his thoughts.

Distraught and bewildered, Judas eventually decided he could not take the woman at her word, and tried to convince himself she must have confused Jesus's crucifixion with that of a criminal. Now more desperate than ever for news, he set out to find others who may know of the trial or the whereabouts of his family, but more than anything else, he wanted to find Seth. He was no longer concerned about being discovered, but if what he'd heard turned out to be true, Judas decided it would be his responsibility to ensure Seth paid dearly for participating in the commission of such an atrocity.

Knowing that by now Seth's guard may have realised he was missing, Judas abandoned his careful approach as time was of the essence. In a forthright manner, he went in search of the truth, while oblivious to the fact that he was a wanted man. Judas had no idea of the peril he was placing himself in, or that the source of the threat was the followers of Jesus; the very people he intended to seek out.

As the sun began to rise over the hilltops of Jerusalem, Judas continued to pursue the followers, while praying that what he'd been told was no more than a rumour or falsehood, similar to that which flourished throughout the years of the ministry. Until he'd spoken with one of the more trusted disciples, he could not give up hope.

It was not too long before Judas overheard raised voices in the distance as he walked towards one of the familiar gathering places of his peers. As he approached the group, he was thankful when recognising them as disciples of Jesus and called out to identify himself; abandoning his usual more reserved demeanour in the process. In an emotional state, Judas rushed forward, pleading to be told the truth of what had happened to his brother, but the followers were astonished to see him appear out of nowhere in this manner.

Having been engaged in an exhaustive and determined search for Judas, the angry, despairing group were unable to comprehend how he had the audacity to reveal himself in this way. As they stared in disbelief at *the betrayer* tearfully begging for news of Jesus, their reaction was outrage. Turning on Judas, they taunted and accused him of treachery, which astonished and confused him entirely. Responding to their accusations with utter dismay and denial, Judas continued his plea for information, but the followers were rapidly losing patience. After several days and nights being spent in search of Judas, they were beyond exhausted and had no time for what appeared to be cowardly antics. They were exasperated when contrasting Judas's behaviour with the bravery they had witnessed in Jesus, and as a result the capacity to consider his proclamations simply did not exist.

Seth had instructed that if Judas were discovered he should be secured and brought in for questioning, but despite the followers being fully aware of this command, it took little to persuade them to conveniently dismiss it. Judas's pleas of innocence enraged the group, and his denial and tearful begging for compassion was more than they could stand. For years they had been frustrated by the mere existence of Judas; he was the closest confidante of Jesus, and each of them viewed him as an impediment to their own ascension within the ranks. Their resentment was, in part, because he qualified naturally for his close association, which they believed was without merit when bearing in mind he was an adopted brother. However, the root-cause of their feelings ran much deeper than irritation. Despite their lack of respect for Judas from an intellectual standpoint, they were highly irritated by his ability to so easily complement Jesus and contribute to the ministry; all while being seemingly oblivious to their overt attempts to make him feel less.

Many years of pent-up rage came to the fore as the followers each abandoned their usual more civil approach, sensing they were entirely justified in so doing. In satisfying their resentment by inflicting serious physical harm upon Judas, they were content that the person responsible for the death of Jesus, and for consuming them with such jealousy for so long, was finally on the receiving end of what he deserved.

Brutally beaten by the followers, Judas was left to die on the street; writhing in agony as a result of his wounds. As the group hurriedly departed the scene, they agreed among themselves not to admit responsibility for the deed, but to inform Seth they had discovered someone who appeared to be Judas in such a condition. The followers wanted to receive credit for discovering his whereabouts, but did not want to be held to account for their actions. As they set off to locate Seth, they were satisfied that justice had been served and felt self-righteously confident that they had done the right thing.

* * *

Judas did not die on the street that morning, but was found a short time later by a sympathetic woman named Elizabeth. He was in an appalling condition; barely conscious and unable to speak, but Elizabeth knew only that he was a young man in need of help. She asked a passerby to assist in carrying him to her nearby home, and did her best to make him comfortable. Judas drifted in and out of consciousness for several hours and was in severe shock and pain, and by the time he came around sufficiently to recall what had happened, he simultaneously remembered Martha's predicament. In realising he had made no inroads into discovering her fate, panic set in as he attempted to sit upright and tried to put weight on his feet. However, such was the extent of his injuries that the excruciating pain he faced caused him to once again lapse momentarily out of consciousness. When Elizabeth overheard his cries, she rushed to his side and reprimanded him for attempting to move; warning it would be several weeks before he could expect his legs to be sufficiently healed.

Judas was beside himself and tearfully exclaimed that he had responsibilities and important matters to attend to, but it was no use – he could not stand, let alone walk. Judas was going nowhere – he was inconsolable.

* * *

The followers responsible for attacking Judas came across Seth later that same morning and casually informed him they had discovered Judas; depicting him as appearing unconscious and assumed to be dead. Seth's stunned reaction took them by surprise, as he urgently ordered three of his men to accompany him to the location the followers had described. No one could understand why Seth appeared so concerned, and had expected his reaction to be one of jubilation in learning that Judas had received his comeuppance.

As Seth raced with his guards to the street of the suspected sighting, he was horrified to consider that Judas may have escaped and stumbled into a situation he could not fathom, but no trace of Judas could be found. While Seth instructed his men to search every house in the vicinity until Judas was discovered, he quickly headed towards the safe-house in the hope of finding him there, and thereby learning it had been a matter of mistaken identity.

In following instructions, Seth's men proceeded to burst into one home after another; questioning people and threatening the death sentence if anyone was found to be hiding the brother of Jesus. In claiming Judas was a fugitive desperately being sought by the authorities, they spread terror throughout the community as everyone denied participating in such an activity.

Elizabeth overheard the commotion and knew she was in real danger of being discovered. While fairly confident at being able to explain-away her predicament by admitting she did not know who Judas was, she was nevertheless concerned for his fate at the hands of the authorities. Finding it difficult to believe this gentle man could be guilty of anything, Elizabeth quickly resorted to the only distraction she could muster at such short notice.

As Seth's men arrived at the entrance to her home and pushed their way in, she screamed and chased after them, demanding they get out, while creating a huge fuss. Already frustrated with what they thought was a pointless investigation, the men could not be bothered dealing with Elizabeth's hysterics, and abandoned the house-search after only a casual glance around and without discovering Judas lying in an adjacent room.

For the first time, Elizabeth now realised who she was taking care of – the brother of the man she had just witnessed crucified. In reassuring Judas that the intruders had been dealt with, Elizabeth chose not to mention that she knew who he was, or that he was being sought out. Not wishing to cause him any further upset, Elizabeth decided her questions could wait until Judas had made somewhat of a recovery.

* * *

Having left his men searching the local vicinity for Judas, Seth arrived at the safe-house only to discover his distraught guard admitting he had slept throughout the night without realising that Judas had escaped. Seth was beside himself, particularly when the guard confirmed when he had last seen Judas, which time-wise coincided with the reported sighting in Jerusalem. Even though Seth knew it was most likely that the followers were responsible for the attack on Judas, he did not blame them; rather, he blamed himself. Seth had not wished Judas to come to harm, and could only hope he was in hiding and recovering from his injuries. As he returned to the town centre, Seth discovered his soldiers had not come upon Judas during their investigations, so instructed they continue the house to house search and not give up until he was found.

PART II – MARY MAGDALENE TAKES CONTROL

Somehow managing to rise above her own desperate feelings of grief, Mary Magdalene did her best to console Mary and James as the heartbroken group hesitantly departed the burial site. Returning to the house that had been reserved by Seth for their safety, she committed to providing the necessary emotional support, while putting aside her own needs for the time being. It was clear to Mary Magdalene that James and Mary had not yet heard the rumour of Judas's betrayal, since she was certain they'd have discussed such a matter openly. They also made no mention of the fact that Martha was missing, which suggested to Mary Magdalene that she was probably safe and in hiding. While she had no intention of ever betraying their confidence, Mary Magdalene decided it was best to keep what she knew to herself until there were solid facts to report, and saw no merit in burdening their grief further with scant information from a source as unreliable as Seth.

On the morning after Jesus's death Mary Magdalene chose to ignore Seth's directive to remain at the house, and returned to the cave where the burial had taken place. Having not yet tended to her own emotional needs, she felt compelled to be physically close to Jesus in an effort to make sense of her thoughts and bring about some much needed peace of mind. However, as she approached the site of the burial, Mary Magdalene was intercepted by two of Seth's guards and instructed to leave. As she attempted to explain who she was and that she sought only to spend time alone in prayer, the soldiers impatiently ushered her away, refusing to allow her to proceed. In tears, Mary Magdalene departed, but being prevented from benefiting from a few moments of prayerful contemplation was infuriating: her mood of forlorn grief altered rapidly to one of indignation. What she viewed as an absurd outburst by the soldiers only added to her suspicion that something unseemly was occurring. This unfortunate episode strengthened Mary Magdalene's resolve to put her own feelings aside, and do whatever was required to discover the truth.

* * *

Three long days had passed since the crucifixion, and Mary Magdalene was becoming increasingly frustrated. Remaining at the house with Mary and James meant she was oblivious to developments that may be occurring, but Seth had not returned to discuss his concerns regarding Martha, which led her to believe that perhaps she'd been found. Still feeling unable to burden Mary or James with rumours about their loved ones, Mary Magdalene decided she could no longer sit in wait for news. Disobeying Seth's orders once again, she left the house for a second time and headed towards the centre of town.

When Mary Magdalene came across a group of followers they rudely dismissed her, while remarking that it was no longer required for them to tolerate her presence. Ignoring their childish taunts, Mary Magdalene persisted in inquiring if anyone had news of Judas or knowledge of where Martha had been housed. The followers laughed raucously at such a request, mocking the fact that Mary Magdalene had been left out in the cold by the family of Jesus, and taking delight in suggesting that it was now obvious how little they thought of her.

As the followers continued to ridicule her pleas, they disclosed that a possible sighting of the lifeless body of Judas had been discovered in the back streets of Jerusalem. Horrified at such a revelation, Mary Magdalene demanded to know who had witnessed such a thing, but in scoffing at her anguish the followers refused to admit the source of the news; saying only that they awaited the return of Seth for confirmation of the finding.

Frantic that her much-loved friend could have been murdered, she begged the followers to describe where Judas had been seen, but having bored of her pleas the followers were about to depart when it was noticed that Seth was approaching. Much to everyone's surprise, Seth marched straight past them all and turned on Mary Magdalene; seizing her arm and pulling her to one side. As everyone stood back in shock at Seth's reaction, they could not help but overhear his demands: "What are you doing here? I told you to remain at the house. Where is Martha – did Mary or James tell you where she is hiding?"

The followers did not know what to make of this outburst, and as Mary Magdalene fell to the floor while begging Seth to release his grip, the onlookers were perplexed as they watched her struggle to respond through tears of frustration: "You know I have no idea where Martha is," she retorted, "and I've not told James or Mary of your accusations against Judas so they have no reason to share information with me. I have not said anything because I do not wish to upset them further and without any proof. You've not explained why you would say such things about Judas – what is the purpose of the stories of betrayal? Is that why Martha is in hiding – she must have had a reason for not cooperating with you. I beg you to tell me the truth."

Seth was outraged – in his fury he tossed her aside and cared not what anyone thought. The followers were standing by, aghast at his physical treatment of Mary Magdalene, and confused at overhearing the accusations and demands made between the two. Instructing one of his guards to escort Mary Magdalene back to the house, Seth absolutely refused to respond to any of her concerns; turning his attention instead to organising a larger search party for Judas, while assigning two of his more trusted guards to assist in locating Martha.

Beside herself in anger and frustration, Mary Magdalene begrudgingly accompanied Seth's guard back to the house. Rather than her venture into town providing answers, it had created more heartache and concern. No longer able to compose herself for the sake of Mary and James, she gave in to her emotions and fell into their embrace as the sentiments of the previous days came to bear.

* * *

Mary and James were sincerely upset at witnessing such distress, and did their best to provide comfort while insisting that Mary Magdalene explain what had occurred. As she reluctantly revealed the assertions of betrayal assigned to Judas; what she had learned about his possible fate; the fact that he did not arrive at the Bethany house for the last supper, and that Seth was searching for Martha, Mary and James were horrified. When further disclosing that Seth expected her to extract information regarding a contingency that may have been in place, they were outraged to think that such a burden had been placed upon someone so young and so committed to Jesus's cause.

James was now experiencing his first real test in maintaining the directive Jesus had put in place, but it was more than he could stand to hear such things being said about Judas. In addition, the possibility that he may have met his end, together with the likelihood that Martha was alone and could be in danger, was intolerable for James. Seth's despicable behaviour infuriated him – it became almost impossible for him to remain composed.

Deeply alarmed by all that Mary Magdalene had shared, James and Mary decided to confide in her. They told of the danger Martha and Judas could be in due to their intimate knowledge of the ministry and the diaries that Martha possessed, and further explained that Martha and Judas were supposed to have left the Bethany house together prior to Jesus making his announcement. They apprised Mary Magdalene of the longer term plans, but they were now concerned that it appeared they had fallen into disarray at the outset. James also mentioned that Judas did not know what was going to transpire, so would also not know where to find Martha in the event they became separated.

Recalling that Seth had questioned people during the early part of the evening at the Bethany house regarding Judas's whereabouts, Mary Magdalene suggested that something must have happened to him prior to the final gathering. She was able to confirm that Martha had been present initially, but disappeared before Jesus gave his presentation, which was of great concern to James and Mary. In concluding that Martha must have been left alone to attempt an escape with the diaries, they became extremely anxious about her well-being when contemplating what could have happened as she journeyed alone throughout the night to the hideout.

As they each came to grips with the situation at hand, James confessed that he'd promised Jesus he would not react to events that occurred in a way that would disrupt the Movement's progress. He explained Jesus's thinking on the matter, and how he understood his motives behind such a decision. Therefore, despite his natural tendency to immediately go in search of Seth and demand explanations, James felt he should at least try to abide by his commitment until matters evolved to such an extent that it became impossible or unwise to do so.

While Mary Magdalene understood the position James was in, she was fearless in admitting that she was not restrained by such promises, and committed to take the lead in getting to the bottom of what Seth was up to, using whatever means were at her disposal. With the support of Mary and James, Mary Magdalene was convinced she would succeed and secure the result they were each determined to achieve. Having known all along that things were not as they appeared, Mary Magdalene was relieved to be able to move forward and begin to discover what was going on.

* * *

Deciding not to concern themselves with the strategy of the Movement, they all agreed that their focus should be to discover what had happened to Martha and Judas. The most obvious place to begin was the hideout in the northern outskirts of Jerusalem, and James set off without delay accompanied by the directions Jesus had left with his mother. If he could find evidence of someone having been at the hideout, they would at least know that Martha had made it through the most risky phase of her journey.

It was considered unlikely that James's disappearance for a day or two would be noticed, and Mary Magdalene agreed not to create a stir while he was away. In the event of being summoned by Seth, she would keep the peace by giving the impression that she'd decided to be cooperative and say whatever was required. Feeling more confident now that James and Mary were on side, Mary Magdalene did not rule out reintroducing her womanly charms to assist in placing Seth into a false sense of security. She felt strongly that matters were not as straightforward as they appeared and did not believe that Seth's desperate search for Martha and Judas was simply to fulfill a command from the Movement to dispose of them. She knew that if this was the case, Seth could have made such arrangements swiftly and without incident. Mary Magdalene believed much more was at stake than anyone understood, and it became her mission to find out precisely what that was. The answers were with Seth, and that is where she intended to begin her investigations.

* * *

James travelled throughout the night in search of Martha, but could not promise to return for at least another day or two. This was an anxious time for Mary and Mary Magdalene, but they had no choice other than to wait patiently for news. If James reported there was no sign of Martha or Judas having arrived at the hideout, they would have to begin more extensive enquiries, which would no doubt create risk for them all.

Neither of the ladies slept particularly well that night, and the following day they could only continue to await James's return. However, as the day wore on Mary Magdalene became impatient and felt she should be making inroads of some sort. Concerned that matters may be getting ahead of her, and that it was important to re-establish relations with Seth, she obtained Mary's approval and left the house to see what, if anything, could be discovered.

PART III – THE MYSTERY DEEPENS

Believing that the men responsible for guarding Jesus's tomb would likely know where Seth could be found, Mary Magdalene decided to begin her search with them. Approaching the site in a determined and forceful manner, she noticed two guards in the distance; both of whom appeared to be as irritated by her presence as they had previously. As they hastily moved towards her while gesturing she retreat, a defiant Mary Magdalene continued to approach; assertively demanding to be told the whereabouts of Seth. Their excessive anxiety once again struck her as unusual, but as they physically turned her away she created quite a commotion; screaming and insisting they release her from their grip and respond to her question. At that moment, the angry outburst attracted the attention of someone else.

Seth suddenly appeared at the top of the hill and called for Mary Magdalene to be released, while signalling her to approach. Promptly regaining her composure, she boldly accepted the invitation, although somewhat anxious about how she was going to be received in view of their most recent encounter.

Dismissing his men to remain at a distance, Seth greeted Mary Magdalene warmly; gently taking her by the arm, and guiding her further in the direction of Jesus's tomb. Somewhat nervous and taken aback by such a respectful approach, Mary Magdalene began to feel troubled as they continued to walk in an increasingly remote location. Preferring not to go on, she came to a halt and casually removed herself from Seth's hold, while disguising her anxiety with a somewhat aggressive tone, asking, "Why are we walking this far, Seth – I came here to find you, not to visit the tomb of Jesus. I have something to say and questions that need to be answered. There is no need for us to continue on this path."

Seth did not respond initially, but signalled she should continue to move forward as he admitted rather awkwardly: "I thought you should be allowed to see what we've discovered."

At first, Mary Magdalene did not understand to what he was referring; unable to recognise anything in particular as she glanced around the rather untidy scene. But when Seth encouraged her to move a little further up the hillside, she realised they were approaching the tomb of Jesus.

As he gestured towards a pile of rocks and shrubbery laid out before a small cave entrance, Seth asked a bemused Mary Magdalene to approach the opening. Without knowing quite what to expect, she nervously knelt down before the entrance and peered inside. Perplexed and a little startled, she immediately looked back towards Seth, asking, "Why are you showing me this empty tomb — where is the tomb of Jesus?"

"This is the tomb of Jesus," Seth confessed, "we arrived here this morning to replace the rocks and shrubbery with a more permanent fixture, only to discover when we removed the rocks that the body of Jesus was gone."

Mary Magdalene almost collapsed in shock while crying, "Who would do such a thing? Why would anyone steal a body from its resting place?"

Seth responded, "It's impossible that the body of Jesus was removed. Two of my men have been on guard since the day of burial, and in my presence they removed the rocks this morning in preparation for securing the entrance more forcefully."

Mary Magdalene was bewildered by such news and could not comprehend what was happening. In calming tones, Seth continued: "The only explanation possible is that Jesus has risen from the dead and ascended into heaven to be with his father. He was the divine son of God, despite his protestations in that regard. There is no question in my mind that God has miraculously returned his son to his rightful place by his side. I believe that

Jesus will one day rise again; returning to teach his detractors and judge the conscience of his followers, and this miracle is the proof we needed – Jesus *was* the son of God."

Mary Magdalene was speechless and physically frozen in shock. There had been many scenarios she'd imagined regarding this meeting with Seth, but nothing even remotely close to a situation like this had entered her mind. While attempting to regain her composure, she looked directly at Seth and asked, "Why are you telling me this? You have never confided in me before, and if anything I am held in contempt. Why now, Seth – what is the reason for sharing this news with me, of all people?"

"It is coincidence that you arrived here today," Seth mused, "it was meant to be, I'm sure. It had been my intention that you should be the person to inform everyone of what has come to light, and your unexpected arrival here this afternoon has confirmed my decision. The followers treat you with such contempt, but I feel Jesus would want you to be the person to witness and spread the word of his divinity. You have now seen for yourself first-hand that his physical body has been resurrected from the dead. Forever more, you will be regarded as God's chosen one."

Mary Magdalene was stunned, and stared at Seth in disbelief as she struggled to come to terms with the position she found herself in. No matter how she tried, she could think of no reason why Jesus's body may have been stolen and began to wonder if what Seth had declared could possibly be true. Slowly gathering her thoughts, she countered Seth's suggestion, saying, "But I did not see Jesus's body resurrected from the dead – all I see is an empty tomb. No one will believe me. They'll accuse me of seeking attention as they always do. They'll say that his body was stolen, and that I'm imagining things in my hysteria. I cannot possibly lay claim to something like this without proof to support such a theory."

Seth attempted to reassure Mary Magdalene by admitting: "At first they may ridicule you, but I'll bear witness to your statement by saying I discovered you kneeling at the empty tomb, claiming an angel had appeared and informed you of Jesus's resurrection from the dead."

Mary Magdalene looked at Seth in dismay, saying, "But that would not be the truth Seth. How can you possibly expect me to say such a thing?"

Seth sighed to himself as he took hold of Mary Magdalene's hand before explaining: "If you want Jesus to become part of the consciousness of mankind, his divinity has to be established — there is no other way. You personally witnessed a miracle when your brother, Lazarus, was raised from the dead. Do you not think Jesus is therefore deserving of the utmost adoration and respect? Without his resurrection becoming well-known, history will remember Jesus as nothing other than an eccentric rebel who died for what he believed in. We need his divinity established, and we need proof of it. I know he has ascended into heaven, Mary Magdalene. I was here when the rocks were removed. But no one will believe me — I won't be able to convincingly portray the emotion, and my enemies will accuse me of fabricating a story to create intrigue. But they will believe you. It is well known that you love Jesus, and as a woman you are the only person who would not be accused of removing his body from its resting place. In addition, your responsibility will include persuading the followers, all of whom will be very untrusting of your claim, but that is what we want — it will add credibility to your story and discredit the theories of our enemies that you and the followers concocted this scenario. My job is to promote Jesus, but I cannot do so without your help. He will have suffered for no reason, unless you assist in establishing his true worth in the collective mind of humanity."

Mary Magdalene knelt at the entrance to the tomb while Seth continued his persuasive argument. He attempted to convince her of what she needed to believe, so she would feel capable of persuading everyone else of the 'truth'. Seth insisted that without her support, the life and ministry of Jesus would be declared a complete waste and forgotten entirely. He promised Mary Magdalene that she would be remembered in history as the one God chose to deliver this key message, and that her desire to be respected and taken seriously would no longer be in question, since her eminence would rise alongside the name of the man she loved.

Seth's forceful argument was overwhelming to Mary Magdalene; so much so that she momentarily forgot why it was she had been seeking him out in the first place. When she suddenly began to recall events of the past few days, she abruptly turned to Seth, saying, "I'm sorry, but I need time to absorb all of this information — you cannot expect me to make a decision on something of such magnitude without giving it further thought. Jesus's body is missing — therefore, either what you are telling me is accurate, or you've removed his body to create this scenario — a despicable act, if true, and one for which you will surely pay. However, I remain unconvinced and you will need to explain much more to change my mind. I recall that Jesus always denied the miracles and felt certain such talk destroyed the message of his ministry, but like many others I assigned his denial to humility, since I personally witnessed a miracle in the resurrection of my brother. Even though I agree that only I would be believed for the reasons you have explained, I would point out that the Movement has had no difficulty in persuading people to believe stories just as fantastical as this. Why can you not devise a plan similar to those previous?"

Seth began to grasp that Mary Magdalene needed more encouragement, so moved his expertise at persuasion to the next level: "I am pleading for your support because there is no other way – if this news is to be believed and travel far and wide, it has to be achieved in a spectacular and memorable style. My men preaching such a thing is not going to be anywhere near as effective as a well-known follower claiming to have witnessed evidence of a resurrection. Remember, Jesus's followers are not particularly renowned for telling stories of miracles, which is why there will be more legitimacy than if the story stems from one of my men, hence the reason using our tried and tested methods will not be effective for something of this magnitude. But let us not forget, Mary Magdalene, by cooperating with the resurrection miracle, you will not only have a very prominent place in history beside Jesus, but you would be directly contributing to his message being cast in stone for eternity. The Movement is committed to building and expanding upon his memory throughout time, until there is not a corner of the earth that has not heard it, but to achieve that end we need to establish this theory.

"However, I understand this persuasive talk is insufficient, since you are aware that Jesus was neither happy with the way the ministry went, nor agreeable to admitting to miraculous acts or his divinity. But what you have to understand is that we believe Jesus had no comprehension of what was required of him. In order to instill the message that he was unique in comparison to so many other preachers, much more needed to be proved. It is our intention that his name will be known by every person ever born on earth. His name and his word shall become synonymous with the word God – they will become one. The simple, humble style of his ministry was never going to achieve such grand status. It needed to be enhanced dramatically, and the proof of this fact is in how far and wide his message spread when conducted by my recruits compared with his own followers: almost instantly he became well-known. If we'd have left matters in Jesus's hands, barely anyone would have heard of him.

"I pleaded with Jesus to declare that he was the divine son of God, but he would not hear of it. What I'm asking of you, Mary Magdalene, is only to speak the truth. You witnessed the miracle of your brother, Lazarus, and you also witnessed Jesus humbly denying his part in that phenomenon. While his humility is admirable and certainly a trait we wish to promote, we will achieve nothing unless we can produce evidence that he is a unique and divine being. To endorse him only as a humble servant of God, is never going to establish him in the way he deserves."

Mary Magdalene listened intently to all that Seth explained, but needed time to think it through. Seth was certain he'd done well – he had at least achieved his offer being seriously considered, and felt his argument had been convincingly presented. However, unbeknown to Seth, Mary Magdalene not only had to weigh up his request, but also needed to learn what James had discovered during his attempt to locate the hideout. The outcome of the search for Martha would contribute a great deal to this decision, so until Mary Magdalene knew the result of James's mission, she could not arrive at a conclusion on this matter.

Explaining to Seth that she understood the reasons for his appeal, and confirming that she'd always believed Jesus had miraculously brought her brother back to life, Mary Magdalene promised to consider his plea: "I've heard all you have to say and understand your argument. However, I need to contemplate your request for my participation and consider whether there is another way for a greater awareness of Jesus to be achieved without this scenario being portrayed. I will return and meet you here tomorrow, at which time I will be prepared to give you my answer."

Seth was not entirely happy with this response as he'd expected Mary Magdalene to be won over far more easily, particularly with the promise of respect and recognition. He had not counted on her suddenly acquiring a sense of morality at such an inconvenient time. However, he had no alternative but to let her go and await her return. An affirmative decision on her part would dramatically help his cause, but a rejection of his proposal would create some serious obstacles to be overcome.

PART IV – THE SEARCH FOR MARTHA

Martha spent much of her time at the hideout sitting on a hillside overlooking Jerusalem, silently praying for guidance and struggling with the mystery of Judas's disappearance. She could neither accept that something must have happened to him, nor contemplate departing for the coast alone. When considering the pros and cons of returning to Jerusalem, she felt that for the time being it was sensible not to; preferring to place her hope in Judas seeking out their mother and James, and being provided with directions to find her.

While pondering the future and attempting to distract herself from what was happening to Jesus, Martha occasionally ventured a little further afield from the hideout, seeking reassurance that the area was secure and uninhabited. It was during one such excursion that she suddenly became aware of movement in the trees beyond the hillside. To have rushed back towards the hideout would almost certainly have exposed her whereabouts, so she quickly huddled down in the undergrowth; listening carefully to the sound of advancing footsteps and desperately hoping it was Judas approaching. As she heard the traveller move beyond her, Martha cautiously raised herself upwards and struggled to identify the passer-by, but with an obscured and distant view she only managed to assess that it was definitely not Judas.

Hoping the man would keep moving, she held her breath and remained as still as she could, but after a few moments it became apparent that the traveller had stopped. Terrified that her belongings and hideout had been discovered, Martha's heart beat rapidly as she prayed for the man to go on his way. As the footsteps once again became evident she felt momentary relief, but before long the man seemed to come to a complete halt, remaining silent for what seemed like an eternity. Just as Martha was beginning to consider that her only option might be to confront the traveller, he suddenly bellowed, "Is anyone here?" At first, she did not dare believe her instincts that the voice sounded familiar, until the man once again called out: "Martha it's me – it's James – are you here?"

Startled but relieved, Martha frantically scrambled from the undergrowth; calling out her brother's name and rushing towards him. Neither had ever been more relieved to see the other, and embraced as if their lives had somehow just been saved.

As Martha led the way towards the hideout she expressed her desperation for whatever news James could provide, and impatiently asked that he tell her everything he knew. However, as James proceeded to confirm the death of Jesus and describe the events that took place, Martha was shocked at the emotional impact this news had upon her. She had spent so many years planning for such an eventuality, but only now did it register that she had not actually prepared herself for it. The emotional force of listening to James describe what occurred was tortuous, and it was not long before Martha's mind became oblivious to whatever James was saying. Jesus had been her whole life, but the sudden realisation that he was no longer present made her entire being feel vacant.

After a while, James realised he was not being heard, particularly as he had begun to discuss Judas, yet Martha was not reacting. He took her hand in his when recognising how overwhelmed she'd become at the reality of Jesus's death, and gently suggested they could discuss Judas when she felt ready.

Glancing towards her brother, Martha tried to regain her composure somewhat, but feared she was about to be given the news she dreaded. Pleadingly she asked, "Don't say what I think you're going to say – please tell me that Judas is safe."

Reluctantly, James attempted to begin an explanation by tentatively, saying, "I'm uncertain about the fate of Judas at this point, but..."

At once, Martha could sense that James was being evasive and interrupted his speech in a quiet but deliberate manner, saying, "You may not know precisely what happened to Judas, but I can tell you know something, James. I am afraid of what you're going to disclose, but I have to know – please, do not be hesitant."

James took a deep breath, bracing himself for the reaction he knew was certain: "Judas is still missing. There is a rumour he was discovered on the streets in a bad way. It appeared to witnesses that he'd been viciously attacked, but he's still not been found. We're hoping that if it was him, someone is caring for him, but our real hope is that he was misidentified and has escaped the area. We really don't know, Martha, but we can't give up on him yet – anything could have happened."

While this was not good news, it was not as bad as Martha had feared. She waited, expecting James to explain what he had done to try and locate Judas, but when she looked into his eyes she saw defeat and fear; she knew he was still keeping something from her. Cautiously, Martha enquired, "I may be feeling fragile, James, but I need to know everything. What is it that you're not telling me?"

James sighed deeply, momentarily glancing away before revealing the details he knew would be devastating: "Seth informed the disciples that Judas betrayed Jesus to the authorities and that he was to blame for the arrest and crucifixion. He instructed his own men and the followers to search the city and bring Judas to him. If it turns out that it was Judas's body discovered on the street, this will explain why he was attacked. We believe that a possible development could be that some of the followers found him, and took out their rage and frustration on Jesus's presumed betrayer. Even though Seth had instructed that Judas be delivered to him, it is thought that those responsible may have chosen to ignore that part of Seth's orders; instead, grasping the opportunity to channel their anger and make Judas pay for what they believed was a dreadful wrongdoing."

As James continued to ramble on about all sorts of possibilities, Martha sat in silence without moving a muscle. Staring at James with bated breath, she waited patiently for him to finish; feeling certain that the story would conclude with an announcement that all was resolved in the end.

James, however, was only grateful for Martha's apparently calm reaction, and nervously continued hypothesising until noticing the blank expression on her face. When it finally began to dawn upon Martha that James was not going to inform her of a positive outcome, she slowly rose to her feet while remaining sternly focused upon James, and asking, "It was all resolved in the end, James, wasn't it? Am I correct? You explained to everyone that Judas did not betray Jesus at all – didn't you?"

Looking down in defeat, James nervously shook his head indicating he had not, and sighed deeply in resignation as he awaited the reaction he knew his response would bring.

As Martha shrieked in a manner James had not witnessed before, she hysterically demanded of him, "What do you mean, no? Why was this not dealt with? You know it's untrue!"

James tried to encourage Martha to remain calm before attempting to explain why it was not simply a matter of telling everyone the truth. He insisted she sit alongside him while he provide more detail, and in quiet, methodical tones he began to disclose the full extent of what he knew: "First of all, it is important you appreciate that Jesus warned me that unforeseen events such as this were almost certainly going to occur. They happened throughout the entire ministry, and they were bound to happen after the crucifixion. I was instructed by Jesus, in no uncertain terms, not to cause disruption by opposing such antics, but to allow situations to develop as the Movement intended so they could be seen for what they are. Jesus believed that people needed to learn precisely what motivated this powerful group so they would eventually be brave enough to join me and make a stand, and the only way that could be achieved was for them to be permitted to play out their proposals without opposition at this stage. In addition, Jesus left me in sole charge of mother, which I believe he did purposely to tie my hands, but you know what would have occurred if I'd made life difficult for Seth — there'd have been a massacre and we would have had no chance at all to secure the outcome we desire.

"Jesus was right, and you and I both know that Judas would never expect us to put ourselves in harm's way on his behalf. By disrupting whatever plans that are in motion, which may include something happening to Judas, would have endangered us all, including our beloved mother. We are moving towards resolving this terrible situation, Martha, but we are doing so carefully and with the help of Mary Magdalene. She is very involved in helping get to the bottom of what is occurring, and Seth has no idea she is engaged in supporting us."

Martha did her best to contain her mounting rage at learning how Seth had once again betrayed them all, despite his promise of protection. Her mind was busily determining what she could do and whether it was wise to return to Jerusalem to assist in the search for Judas, but as James continued to speak of their compromised position, it became increasingly apparent that she should not: "I did discreetly talk to some of the followers," James continued, "as did Mary Magdalene, but they were more than willing to accept Seth's story and had no interest in our protestations. You know they were jealous of Judas's close association with Jesus, so in many ways the tale woven by Seth was one they were pleased to learn. What also compounded the situation was that I was in hiding with mother prior to the crucifixion, and did not hear of Seth's perpetrated rumours for several days and until Mary Magdalene confessed what she'd been told. Not only was it too late to persuade the followers of something they didn't want to believe, but the hearsay of the attack on Judas had already circulated. By the time I learned what Seth had done, it was all over."

As Martha maintained a dignified silence, she continued to listen to her brother's sound counsel: "We still have hope, Martha — as I have said, someone could have helped Judas or it's possible he was misidentified. No actual body has been recovered, and from what we can gather, the victim presumed to be Judas seems to have disappeared. Mary Magdalene is determined to discover the truth, and I know she will not give up until she does. A thorough search of households in the vicinity was conducted, but no news of Judas surfaced, which suggests that he may have escaped and gone into hiding for the time being. He knew about the long-term plans to travel to the coast and escape by boat to France, even though he was unaware that the journey from Jerusalem was to be undertaken only by the two of you. I'm hopeful that because Judas has been unable to make contact with one of us, he may have made his way to the coast on his own in an attempt to find you. He knew you had no intention of remaining in Jerusalem for any longer than you had to, so he will not spend too much time here searching. I'm sure that if he's alive and well, he'll realise that his only option is to head towards the coast. Martha, we can't give up hope, and we don't want you to give up either — hope is all we have left."

Martha listened in astonishment to all that James disclosed, but was beside herself in grief. She knew that even if Judas had survived and escaped, it would be very difficult for him to locate her at the coast since he had no specific knowledge of where she was going. The hope that James described smacked of desperation to Martha, who felt certain that something must have happened to Judas before the last supper as he would surely have found a way to locate another family member by now. Crumbling into her brother's arms for reassurance, she tearfully whispered, "Judas was the epitome of dedication and commitment — how could God possibly allow something like this to happen to him?" Sobbing quietly, Martha gratefully accepted the comforting embrace of her brother as he encouraged her to release the utter sadness and desolation she felt. Having Jesus's death confirmed, immediately followed by such a discouraging and hopeless scenario, was heartbreaking.

The following morning James tried to persuade Martha to focus on the future and continue with her plan to journey to the coast. Jesus's instructions were clear in his mind: Martha and the diaries had to be secure, and the Movement had to be permitted to proceed for their tactics to be witnessed. James knew he had to keep Martha focused on the only hopeful element of this situation; the fact that Judas's body had not been recovered, which meant he could still be alive. She needed to believe in something for her own sake.

Martha listened to her brother's well-meant encouragement, but the task she had once believed in now seemed futile. The Movement had so easily manipulated every aspect of the ministry, and she felt her diaries would be of little to no consequence in preventing their ambitious plans. These people were powerful and persuasive, and Martha felt no one was ever likely to succeed in standing against them and say what needed to be said.

As the morning progressed, Martha accepted that she had no choice but to continue with the plans that were in place, but as she began to gather her belongings and prepare to depart, she found it heart wrenching to be faced with saying goodbye to her brother, knowing that he would one day likely meet a fate similar to that of Jesus. As she clutched onto the package that held an account of the ministry, Martha embraced James and promised she would not let him or Jesus down. She committed to fulfill her responsibility to protect and secure the diaries until her dying day.

Setting off towards the coast, Martha could not begin to fathom her grief. She tried to remain focused only on the future, while submitting the past to the back of her mind. To do anything other was unbearable.

PART V – JAMES AND MARY MAGDALENE RETURN

Although more than a little troubled following such a revealing meeting with Seth, Mary Magdalene had no intention of disclosing to Mary and James that Jesus's body had disappeared from the tomb: she could not bring herself to say something that could further enhance their distress. Choosing to take no one into her confidence, she determined that the responsibility for collaborating with Seth had to be hers alone.

Feeling relieved at arriving safely back at the house, Mary Magdalene was pleased to discover that James had returned and brought with him the only good news they had received in a long time. It was a welcome distraction from the experience of an afternoon spent engaged in negotiations with Seth, and with the entire evening being taken up listening to the account of James's journey and the discovery of Martha, Mary Magdalene had little time to consider the important decision she needed to make. She felt so deceitful to be enjoying the company of people who held her in such esteem, while knowing she could be about to mislead them in a manner she knew they would view as appalling. For most of the evening Mary Magdalene contributed little to the conversation, and once it felt acceptable to do so, she suggested they all retire. Her conscience was bothering her immensely, but she had to focus on the important decisions to be made, and needed to do so in seclusion.

Throughout the night, Mary Magdalene thought long and hard about what to do. This decision was not based upon rewards of personal recognition, as Seth had offered — the experience of the crucifixion had changed so much about her. She did not care about the promise of being revered, but did her best to make a decision based upon whether or not participating would actually assist in upholding the memory of Jesus. It seemed to Seth that proving Jesus's divinity was of paramount importance, although she did recall that Jesus and Martha would only deny such claims. As with many of the disciples, however, Mary Magdalene believed to a large extent that Jesus's rejection of his divinity was due to modesty and feeling embarrassed by the attention he received. Nevertheless, she knew that such facts could not form the basis of her decision; rather, it had to be whether participating with Seth would ensure that Jesus was remembered for all time.

As Mary Magdalene pondered her options, what she did not grasp was that her love for Jesus, and the possibility of an infinite association with him, was subconsciously contributing much more to her decision-making than she appreciated. This was an opportunity for her to feel connected and associated with Jesus forevermore: they would be 'together' for all time. However, even though she appreciated that Jesus and Martha had not trusted the Movement at all, she rationalised that in spite of this they had still participated with them; therefore, perhaps she too was expected to do the same. Instead of looking at both sides of the argument, Mary Magdalene was unwittingly looking for reasons to say yes to Seth: satisfying a desire to feel a deeper connection with Jesus was interfering with the reasoning behind her decision. She did not consider the reality of the no-win situation Jesus and Martha had faced, or that her decision did not include such consequences.

As the night wore on, Mary Magdalene eventually decided that participating with the resurrection story was the only way forward. She also concluded that if this plan was going to work, she would have to convince everyone; taking absolutely no-one into her confidence. In determining that this was a secret she would take to her grave, Mary Magdalene was convinced her choice would contribute towards ensuring Jesus's death, and all he had achieved throughout his life, would not be in vain.

PART VI – MARY MAGDALENE'S DECISION

Before committing to her decision and meeting with Seth at the appointed hour, Mary Magdalene went in search of the followers and enquired if there was any further news of Judas. Most had nothing to report, but others confirmed that the search had proved fruitless and it was generally accepted that Judas was dead. However, Mary Magdalene remained unconvinced – she could not give up hope that Judas had either escaped the area or survived the attack, and felt it was not necessarily a bad thing for the followers to presume he was dead: if anything was going to provide Judas with a chance at freedom, it was the relentless search being abandoned in the belief that it was futile.

Returning to the house later that morning, Mary Magdalene apprised James and Mary of the consensus regarding the fate of Judas, but encouraged them to have faith in her instincts that he could have survived. Until there was actual evidence of his demise she intended to pursue every possibility, and for that they were very grateful. However, it was with a heavy heart that Mary Magdalene bid them both farewell as she set off to meet Seth. She knew that her choice to participate with the Movement would not have met with their approval, and felt deep regret at such deception in spite of feeling certain she was doing the right thing.

* * *

Approaching the hillside, Mary Magdalene observed Seth standing alone in the distance with an intense, anxious demeanour that she fully intended to take advantage of. Arming herself with a calm air of superiority and emotionless, blank expression, she drew towards Seth in silence; confidently walking beyond him and directly to the entrance of the now abandoned tomb of Jesus. As she gently knelt down and prayed quietly to herself, Seth hesitated in his approach as he waited for her to speak. Fully aware that the decision she was about to make was momentous, Mary Magdalene prayed for Jesus's understanding that her intentions were only for the sake of his memory, despite the fact that she knew he would not have permitted her to take such action.

As Mary Magdalene became aware of Seth's presence, she turned and looked directly into his eyes with unconcealed dispassion, saying, "I'll do as you ask, Seth, but I do not want personal recognition or devotion for being the 'chosen one'. To me, that would be sinful and a gross injustice when bearing in mind what we both know to be true. I did not witness any of what you suggest has occurred, and cannot explain the disappearance of Jesus's body, but I will contribute to this scenario only because of your persuasion that doing so would assist in ensuring Jesus is remembered for all time. However, being adored and revered for this disclosure is not something I deserve or aspire to. I will participate only on the condition that you render me to the history books as a messenger of sorts, and maintain that the only reason I shared this witness with the world was to preserve the memory of the life of Jesus from becoming obscure."

Seth accepted Mary Magdalene's decision with relief and gratitude, and courteously reached out and helped her to her feet. He acknowledged her desire not to be honoured for bearing witness to this event, and suggested she spend some time in contemplative prayer before recounting for others the experience of discovering the empty tomb. In dramatic, meaningful tones, Seth explained: "When you are fully prepared, describe for them a miraculous visitation by an angel. Say you were informed that Jesus was the Messiah and that his body has been returned to its rightful place alongside God. Pronounce, in a determined manner, that the angel prophesised Jesus will come again to judge humanity based upon the lessons his life purpose it was to teach."

Mary Magdalene stared straight ahead in silence as Seth continued to instruct her. She needed to creatively visualise this process in her mind and establish an emotion within: one that would evolve into a convincing portrayal when the time came to perform. Seth promised he would support her claims passionately; convincing the disciples, as well as his own men, that word of this miraculous event should be spread among the people.

Mary Magdalene did not respond to Seth's instructions; she no longer felt comfortable in his presence in this most holy of places. Satisfied she had made her conditions clear, she walked away in silence and prepared herself for the performance of a lifetime: convincing the world that Jesus had risen from the dead and ascended into heaven to be seated at the right hand of God, while promising to one day return in judgment of us all.

* * *

Many years of over-dramatising events to attract attention had placed Mary Magdalene in good stead for this performance. Entering the town of Jerusalem, she expertly portrayed a traumatised woman; laying claim to discovering Jesus's empty tomb, and describing an angelic visitation that confirmed the miraculous event of Jesus's body being returned to reside alongside God. However, as she skillfully revealed the story of Jesus's resurrection, the townspeople felt certain she had lost her mind.

They listened to her screams and cries, but most believed her behavior was a consequence of losing Jesus, Martha, and Judas and feeling abandoned by those she had been so close to. Despite not being taken seriously, Mary Magdalene persisted; engaging her detractors and repeating the story to anyone who would listen. Before long, rumour had spread throughout the city that Mary Magdalene had lost her sanity and was making incredible claims. However, Seth had anticipated this reaction and timed his arrival into the centre of town to coincide with talk being of nothing but Mary Magdalene's apparent madness. As the followers approached him with their concerns, Seth boldly called for the attention of all those nearby; announcing that what Mary Magdalene had stated was true and suggesting they be respectful of her claims.

People were astonished at such a pronouncement, and rumour spread quickly of Seth's confirmation of the story the 'mad woman' had been portraying. While the mood of the people was at its peak of curiosity and surprise, Seth suggested that several of Jesus's followers and city officials attend the empty tomb to see it for themselves, which they willingly agreed to do.

Upon their return, the officials were pale with shock and unable to offer reassurances or explanations. As the townspeople gathered to learn of what had been discovered, the witnesses could only inform that the tomb had been guarded day and night and secured with many large rocks, but they could not imagine how the body had been removed. Of course, there were accusations of foul play, but these were countered by Seth's men and their fear-the-wrath-of-God rhetoric, condemning anyone who doubted Mary Magdalene's claims. The obvious distress displayed by the followers of Jesus indicated that nothing untoward had occurred at their hands, so the authorities were unable to offer an explanation for such an event, thereby paving the way for people to listen more seriously to what Mary Magdalene had to say.

Throughout the remainder of the day, Mary Magdalene engaged all those who enquired with intimate details of her story, and before darkness fell her declarations had spread throughout the city. With no evidence brought forth to oppose her claim, it was rapidly becoming generally accepted; particularly by those who'd previously been captivated by the miracle stories, as well as those who'd witnessed the crucifixion and felt remorse at their denouncement of Jesus.

* * *

James and Mary had been anxiously awaiting Mary Magdalene's return from what they believed was her initial meeting with Seth, and as darkness fell they became increasingly concerned for her safety. However, their relief at overhearing her approach was immediately extinguished when witnessing her exhausted state and the fact that she was accompanied by Seth.

For obvious reasons, Seth was more than a little anxious at appearing in front of James with Mary Magdalene at his side, particularly as she was about to expose her story in the way she had informed everyone else. James, who was immediately suspicious of the visit by Seth, was stunned into silence when Mary Magdalene disclosed the outcome of her time spent at the tomb of Jesus.

As Seth stood by and confirmed that he too had witnessed the empty tomb, James's eyes bored into him as he attempted to determine whether or not he was telling the truth. Seth's greatest concern was of James's reaction, so he avoided making direct eye contact as much as possible and talked only of Jesus's divinity now being proven beyond doubt. This was a dangerous time for Seth; he knew full well that the temperament of James was such that if Mary Magdalene did not convince him of her story, his reaction could throw into disarray all of his plans. However, Seth need not have worried. Unbeknown to him, Jesus had taken care of the problem of James – he was under strict instructions not to react to any of the Movement's antics, no matter what they were.

Even though James was highly suspicious of Seth's involvement in this outcome, and instinctively knew something quite unseemly was taking place, he could do nothing to prove it. He listened to all that Mary Magdalene had to say and she appeared to be entirely genuine, but James remained unsure. However, once again he had to swallow his pride; accept the situation, and maintain his focus on comforting his mother.

James behaved impeccably, much to the amazement of Seth, and neither he nor Mary openly questioned the integrity of Mary Magdalene, but both had one important concern. This aspect of the life of Jesus had never been revealed to Joseph in the many intuitive dreams he'd experienced regarding his family's destiny. As far as James and Mary were concerned, matters were beginning to move in a direction no one had foreseen.

CHAPTER THIRTEEN

THE 'MIRACLE'

PART I – LIFE AFTER THE CRUCIFIXION

*L*ife changed somewhat for the disciples after the crucifixion, and the account of Mary Magdalene's episode at the tomb certainly gave them much to consider. Now under the guidance of the Movement, they preached about their experiences and competed to tell the most fascinating and awe-inspiring tale. It did not take long for most of the followers to abandon what Jesus had encouraged them to achieve: falling in line with what was required by the Movement's leaders came almost as second nature. The safety in numbers mentality provided them with a sense of security and far greater influence than they would otherwise have had. Their rationale for so readily discarding the principles Jesus instilled was a belief in the resurrection; in addition to being subject to the same persuasion used to encourage Mary Magdalene's propagation of the myth in the first place. The followers wanted to be aligned with the iconic figure that the Movement was hailing as divine beyond doubt, so it took little effort to convince they should promote the sensationalist claims of the Movement.

Seth oversaw the entire process of establishing the beginnings of what became arguably the most successful institution in the world, while closely monitoring activities for evidence of an uprising. The followers were reminded that their preaching should impress the significance of the resurrection as proof of Jesus's divinity, alongside the promise that Jesus would one day return to judge all souls. These two vital facets of Mary Magdalene's account were an integral part of the Movement's long term plans to enlist support and sustain control, along with setting the tone of absolute and unquestionable certainty when establishing a reputation. For those indoctrinated into the following, or in later years born into it, the acceptance of this miracle was a non-negotiable condition that had to be adhered to and an issue no one dared counter.

* * *

The historical account of Jesus's death states that he died as a result of crucifixion and his body was enclosed in a cave-like tomb, which was then sealed and secured by rocks. After three days, Mary Magdalene discovered the tomb was empty and experienced a miraculous angelic visitation, during which she was informed that Jesus had been resurrected from the dead and was now residing at God's side. It is then claimed that some six weeks later Jesus appeared in front of his disciples, who declared witnessing him physically rise through clouds towards heaven, which was thereafter referred to as Jesus's ascension into heaven to be seated at the right hand of God.

For the past two thousand years many have tried to explain these events without Christianity's magic trick element, only to be condemned as blasphemous heretics for so doing. The various conclusions drawn do not establish an understanding of how or why these things happened, or what occurred during the six-week period between the phenomena known as the resurrection and ascension.

However, it has been argued for centuries that Jesus did not die on the cross: argued, due to many cultures claiming that subsequent to the time of the crucifixion a unique preacher named Jesus travelled in their land. It is reported that he talked of his ministry and encouraged people to consider his philosophy of life. For obvious reasons, however, Christianity will not entertain the idea of such a theory, irrespective of the historic evidence many cultures claim they possess to support it. To do so would annul their two established miracles of resurrection and ascension, and this in turn would declare the origins of their religion invalid. Without 'proof' of Jesus's divinity, their basis for claiming to be the voice of God, and the only true religion and spiritual representation on earth, would have no foundation.

* * *

The truth is, Jesus did not die on the cross as Christianity profess – Seth did not allow matters to go that far. He knew of Jesus's physical strength and mental capacity, and carefully tried to gauge how much he could withstand. Pontius Pilate was unaware of Seth's true intentions and, along with other witnesses, left the crucifixion site under the impression that Jesus was dead, but he was not. His injuries were vast, but nails were not driven into his hands and feet to hasten death as this was not routine as commonly believed – crucifixion was meant to be a long, drawn-out, painful experience lasting many hours or sometimes days, including the victim being exposed to the elements. Further punishments such as driven nails occurred only if the authorities felt matters were taking too long, or if it was deemed the criminal was deserving of further torture. Because Jesus was not subjected to the customary body-puncture to determine death prior to being removed from the cross, his internal organs were intact. Seth did not instruct it be conducted, and as Pontius Pilate and the Roman soldiers were appalled by what they'd participated in, and the witnesses were unnerved by what they'd observed, no one called for further retribution. In fact, most observers regretted their association and felt nothing but remorse. Everyone involved wanted matters concluded swiftly, and no one complained when Pontius Pilate abruptly announced the episode be brought to a close.

Jesus appeared to be deceased to everyone present, and no one witnessing the execution imagined there was the remotest possibility he could have survived. Seth had allowed the flogging phase to continue for much longer than usual, but this was done purposely in an attempt to render Jesus unconscious sooner rather than later. He knew that meant he would appear deceased in the early stages of crucifixion, and knowing that the authorities wanted to disperse the crowds and see the body of this controversial figure buried as soon as possible, Seth felt this was his best chance at succeeding with his plan.

At the time of the crucifixion, Seth was fully aware of the plans to institute the miracle of resurrection, yet keeping Jesus alive actually placed this vital component of the foundation of Christianity in jeopardy, which begs the question – why would Seth try to keep Jesus alive?

* * *

The series of events that transpired after the crucifixion were carried out under the watchful eye of Seth. Jesus was removed from the cross by the Roman soldiers and his body was carefully wrapped for burial. He was immediately taken to a secluded tomb where his family members were permitted to spend some time in prayer. After a short period, an escort of Seth's guards took Mary, James, and Mary Magdalene back to their house, and the Roman soldiers left the area while dispersing the crowd and ensuring onlookers departed the site. Seth's two remaining guards then prepared to place a number of rocks in front of the entrance to the tomb, with the intention of taking turns to watch over the burial place throughout the day and night for the immediate future.

However, once everyone had departed, Seth instructed that the body of Jesus be removed from the tomb prior to the rocks being put in place. While somewhat surprised at this development, the guards followed the command, which included transferring Jesus to Seth's compound in the realm of Barbelo. They were led to believe it was required that the body of Christianity's future icon be kept safe within the grounds of the compound, rather than a simple cave on a hillside in Jerusalem. The guards were unaware that Jesus was alive, and even Seth had no idea of his condition at this point. The guards were dispatched back to the tomb once Jesus had been safely transported, and were instructed to monitor the vicinity until further notice. Their mission was not to protect the body of Jesus, but to ensure nobody discovered it was gone. When the resurrection story was later revealed, the guards were rewarded for their silence, and assured that the miracle story was for the good of mankind and the future success of the early Christian movement.

* * *

To have permanently *silenced* the guards who participated in removing Jesus from the tomb would have been the usual directive of Seth. However, his conscience could no longer participate in such things. Consequently, when the resurrection story emerged, rumours regarding whether Jesus had actually died became widespread. It is likely the guards found it impossible to resist gossiping about what they knew, and along with the fact that many did not actually believe the resurrection and ascension claims in the first place, the rumours and theories that circulated at the time have no doubt contributed to the suspicion still in existence today.

* * *

When the body of Jesus was delivered to the Barbelo compound, the guards were instructed to place it in a private room in the lower part of the building. Seth then summoned a medical professional to evaluate the body, informing him the man was his brother, Jeremiah, and conveying an account of discovering him wrongly accused among a group of criminals and sentenced to a flogging – a common daily occurrence that would not be questioned. After a basic examination, it was declared there was a faint sign of breathing, so remedies were prepared to hydrate and stabilise the body and a potion applied to prevent infection from the horrendous lacerations to the skin. Seth was informed that 'Jeremiah' was close to death, and his survival could not be guaranteed for quite some time, and would be dependent upon the patient's ability to fight infections that would inevitably take hold. The physician was unable to make any promises, but Seth was not disappointed – this outcome was the most he could have hoped for.

Several days passed before Jesus began to show signs of regaining consciousness, but Seth was not there to witness this event. He was in Jerusalem conducting the search for Judas and Martha; ensuring the followers of Jesus kept his memory alive, and persuading Mary Magdalene to participate in the resurrection story. For the most part, things were working very much in Seth's favour. He still had the problem of Judas and Martha to resolve, but with his men searching in several directions, he was hopeful this too would eventually arrive at a positive conclusion.

Within one week of the crucifixion, Seth's highly organised plans had been successfully executed, but were not remotely close to anything Jesus and Martha could have anticipated. They were aware that the Movement would have many strategies in place to establish their authority after the crucifixion, but Jesus and Martha had no inkling it would include such a *miraculous* circus of events, or that their beloved brother, Judas, would be depicted as a betrayer.

PART II – JUDAS FINDS HOPE

Almost a week after Judas had been so severely dealt with at the hands of the followers, his condition had barely improved. In hiding at the home of Elizabeth, he was still unable to stand and spent many of his waking hours sobbing in despair. Even though Elizabeth knew he was the accused betrayer and much sought-out brother of Jesus, she was not afraid. She remained convinced he could not possibly have deserved such an assault or be guilty of the accusations he faced.

Each afternoon Elizabeth briefly left Judas alone and ventured into the town centre to purchase supplies, and it was during one such outing that she overheard talk of Mary Magdalene's claim of resurrection. When learning that local officials supported the declaration due to an inability to explain it away, Elizabeth became curious and could not resist visiting the site of the abandoned tomb. Most of those she accompanied were either in awe of the possibility or highly skeptical and seeking proof, but many seemed to welcome the news. It transpired that they felt less guilt for persecuting Jesus, and the prospect of a resurrection suppressed much of the regret they experienced at his death. Some of those Elizabeth encountered considered that perhaps death had been Jesus's true destiny, and in death he would find peace at the side of God. There were others, however, who felt quite differently – they now lived in fear of the wrath of God for vehemently opposing Jesus, should these rumours be proven to be true.

Elizabeth had previously shown little interest in such politically driven events, and had only the most basic knowledge of the disruption caused by the activities of Jesus and his followers. However, she was somewhat surprised at how emotional and moved she felt by the energy present at the tomb, and when observing those who'd been more closely associated with proceedings fall to their knees in prayer, she could not help but reflect what might have been had Jesus lived. She could see that he'd made quite an impression on those more familiar with his cause, but to have generated such depth of compassion among others, who'd previously been so ardently against him, she felt was quite an astonishing achievement.

As Elizabeth began the journey home she considered the idea of telling Judas of what she'd learned, and decided to casually inform him of events without disclosing that she knew who he was. Her only desire was to bring him some comfort at knowing the way Jesus had affected so many people, which she thought would benefit his recovery.

* * *

Judas listened in astonishment to Elizabeth's disclosures, and when learning that Mary Magdalene was still in Jerusalem, he became desperate to make contact. Without much thought about the possible consequences, Judas spontaneously shared with Elizabeth his true identity, and pleaded she act as go-between and seek out Mary Magdalene on his behalf.

However, when Elizabeth had decided to disclose to Judas all that she'd learned, she had no idea that Judas and Mary Magdalene had been so close. Consequently, she had not considered that revealing such information would bring with it an even greater burden of responsibility. Realising that to do as Judas was asking could potentially put them both in danger, she felt there was now little choice but to explain to Judas more than she'd intended.

Suggesting that he calmly listen to her plea, Elizabeth explained, "Judas, it would be too risky for me to tell anyone you're here, particularly not one of Jesus's most devout followers."

"Why ever not," enquired Judas, "you don't understand — we are very close. I worked alongside Mary Magdalene for several years – she is probably searching for me and is no doubt very concerned. I'm certain she'd want to know where I am."

Elizabeth sighed deeply before revealing: "On the first day you were in my home, a group of soldiers from the Movement did a house-to-house search in an attempt to discover your whereabouts. They threatened everyone should they be discovered hiding the brother of Jesus, and informed us you'd betrayed him to the authorities, resulting in his arrest and crucifixion."

Judas stared at Elizabeth, completely stunned. He was now more confused than ever. Only a day or so prior to being attacked by a handful of followers, Seth had been kind and understanding; had placed him in a safe location in his inebriated state, and promised this was for his own security until the trial was over, but now Elizabeth was telling him the Movement had violently sought him out. Shaking his head in dismay he replied, "I know the followers who attacked me assumed that was true, but I hadn't understood that the Movement was actually searching for me in this way, or for that reason. I thought those who assaulted me were merely mistaken – I thought they were making assumptions because I was not present at the time of the arrest. They'd always loathed me, and I felt they had drawn incorrect conclusions as a consequence of the trauma they'd experienced at Jesus's death and were purely venting their rage. Elizabeth, are you certain about this? Seth — a senior representative of the Movement — took me to a safe-house just days before the attack. It was because I was inebriated that I didn't fulfill my responsibilities on the evening prior to Jesus's arrest, and Seth knew that. He assured me that everything would work itself out as long as I remained in the safe-house until he returned. I became impatient and made an escape, which is how I came across the followers and endured an assault at their hands. Therefore, I find what you're suggesting very difficult to understand. If only we could find Mary Magdalene, I'm sure she'd be able to explain this more fully."

Elizabeth found herself in a precarious predicament that she had not foreseen. However, for the first time since they'd met she could see life in Judas's eyes. His persuasive pleading resulted in Elizabeth feeling duty-bound to try and locate Mary Magdalene, despite the personal risk of being discovered hiding a fugitive.

* * *

While prioritising not placing herself and Judas in danger, Elizabeth decided it would be advisable initially to simply seek out Mary Magdalene and casually engage her in conversation. If she discovered that her attitude towards the rumour of Judas's betrayal was to deny it was true, she would then consider taking matters a stage further. However, before confiding in Mary Magdalene, Elizabeth had to be absolutely convinced she could be trusted — both Judas's life and her own were at stake.

Judas, on the other hand, did not believe for a moment that Mary Magdalene would have lost faith in him, and knew without doubt that Elizabeth's approach would succeed. At long last, Judas had found hope.

PART III – FINDING MARY MAGDALENE

Mary Magdalene was very much in demand by the curiosity-seekers, who were keen to discover first-hand the more intimate details of her angelic visitation. Most afternoons she could be found preaching in the centre of town as per Seth's instructions, while debating those who argued against her claims. Finding Mary Magdalene was not, therefore, going to prove difficult for Elizabeth, but deciding how and when to make an approach was altogether more troubling.

Merging into the crowd presented Elizabeth with an opportunity to assess Mary Magdalene's demeanour before surrendering information that could put herself and Judas at risk. Worryingly, her initial observations proved there was an apparent support for the Movement's agenda, but as Elizabeth continued to examine her behavior more closely, she noticed an obvious change in manner once Seth's guards approached to accompany her home. When departing, Mary Magdalene displayed a noticeable sense of uncertainty, and it became quite clear to Elizabeth that she was not as content in her role as she had professed. This discovery made Elizabeth feel somewhat more confident, since she believed this was sufficient evidence to suggest that Mary Magdalene could be under duress.

While Judas was alone awaiting Elizabeth's return from making her initial enquiries, he began to imagine all sorts of possibilities relating to the resurrection story; even contemplating the idea that Jesus had somehow survived the crucifixion. He could not resist mulling over such hopeful scenarios, particularly in the anticipation that a breakthrough of some sort was about to occur.

Later that afternoon, Elizabeth returned home and informed Judas of the conclusions she'd drawn when studying Mary Magdalene's behaviour, but also admitted that she had not yet approached her directly. Elizabeth explained how forceful she had appeared, but also noted that her manner seemed to alter quite significantly once she assumed no one was paying attention. Of course, Elizabeth's main concern was whether or not Mary Magdalene believed the story of Judas's betrayal, but her instincts suggested that was probably not the case.

Judas understood Elizabeth's apprehension and encouraged her to begin an approach in an informal way; broaching the betrayal rumour in the casual manner that others in the crowd posed questions. This, he felt, would present the chance for Elizabeth to gauge Mary Magdalene's reaction before disclosing anything further, and even though they both agreed that her response would likely be the official position, Judas was entirely confident that Elizabeth would be able to read between the lines and conclude a lack of conviction on her part.

As the evening wore on, discussion centred on plans for carrying out the next stage of enquiries, but another concern of Elizabeth's needed to be addressed: if Mary Magdalene was under some sort of threat, which they both felt was entirely possible, she may suspect that Elizabeth was setting a trap. As they pondered how they could prove that Elizabeth was not being deceitful, it suddenly occurred to Judas that she could repeat a short turn of phrase that only he and Mary Magdalene had shared. Excited at such an idea coming to mind, Judas became quite animated and began to explain: "In the days when Mary Magdalene needed to feel as though she was of value to the ministry, she and I would travel ahead of Jesus to the next town he was due to visit. Our responsibility was to prepare the way by alerting people of his impending arrival. We both enjoyed it because it was not only an opportunity to be doing something useful, but it was also fun. During this time alone, we teased and gossiped about the ambitious disciples, and generally put the world to rights. However, what is significant, and what Mary Magdalene will certainly recall, is that in jest I always used the phrase, *shall we prepare the way,* as we departed on each of the journeys. Elizabeth, if you were to get close enough to Mary Magdalene and repeat those five words, she would immediately understand it was a coded message from me."

Elizabeth listened carefully to Judas's story, and quite liked the idea of using this expression to see what sort of reaction it produced. Besides which, Judas was so excited at the prospect of finding his friend, Elizabeth knew there was no going back on her promise. She had no choice but to give this a try, but having spent some time observing Mary Magdalene she was now a little more comfortable with the idea. If her reaction was unfavourable, Elizabeth planned to boldly insist there had been a misunderstanding and quickly move on. As it turned out, however, Mary Magdalene's reaction was anything but unfavourable.

* * *

"Shall we prepare the way," Elizabeth whispered while looking directly into Mary Magdalene's eyes.

Slightly surprised and a little uncertain of what she'd heard, Mary Magdalene did not respond at first, but her pained expression told Elizabeth all she needed to know. Cautiously, Elizabeth leaned forward and once again asked, "Shall we prepare the way?"

This time, Mary Magdalene's eyes doubled in size when realising she had not misunderstood; seizing Elizabeth's arm she frantically ushered her to one side, pleading, "Who are you – what are you trying to say?"

Elizabeth, somewhat intimidated by the intensity of her manner, softly replied, "I have a message from a friend."

Mary Magdalene knew without doubt that this was a message from Judas, but despite being wary of attracting the attention of Seth's guards, she failed to regain her composure as she urgently implored, "Take me to him – please, take me to my friend."

Elizabeth was confident that the response she'd received was completely genuine, but she knew they had to be careful of being overheard or watched from a distance, and begged Mary Magdalene to remain calm: "Please, be vigilant – he is badly injured – we need to be extremely careful not to be seen engaged in intense conversation."

Realising Elizabeth was right to be on her guard, Mary Magdalene quickly altered her approach, saying, "Of course – I understand. He is my closest friend — you can completely trust me. I shall meet you here at dusk when I'm alone. Do we have an agreement?"

Elizabeth acknowledged positively, and taking a few steps back, quickly retreated into the crowd. Neither of the women wanted to draw attention to the fact that they were partaking in such a serious exchange, and those snatched few moments were the most they felt they could get away with.

Returning home to Judas, Elizabeth passed on the good news and he could not have been happier. The remainder of the afternoon was spent excitedly contemplating what Mary Magdalene may have to say, but keeping matters in perspective was not easy for Judas. Elizabeth became concerned that his expectations were too high, and encouraged him to focus only on the fact that he was being reunited with his close friend, since anything more could bring much disappointment.

As evening approached, Elizabeth began to feel a little nervous about returning to the town centre, but found comfort when recalling the intensity of Mary Magdalene's reaction and the immediate discretion she had shown. In any event, there was no alternative — she could not let Judas down.

* * *

As dusk began to descend, Elizabeth entered the centre of town in search of the young woman she had acquainted earlier that day. Doing her utmost not to appear apprehensive, she casually glanced around; walking slowly among the few groups of people still wandering throughout the square. All of a sudden a figure approached as if out of nowhere, but it was not until she was almost completely upon her did Elizabeth realise it was Mary Magdalene. Disguised in drab clothing more suited to an elderly person, she made eye contact with Elizabeth and brusquely passed by. Realising that such an approach almost certainly meant Mary Magdalene would follow circumspectly at a distance, Elizabeth slowly proceeded to leave the square while nervously dismissing thoughts about the consequences of them being followed.

Arriving at her home a short time later, Elizabeth rushed to silence Judas who had called out in anticipation, and together they listened carefully until overhearing footsteps approach. Judas could barely tolerate the wait as Elizabeth momentarily left him alone and walked a few feet towards the entranceway. Finding Mary Magdalene warily approaching her home, Elizabeth ushered her to step inside and helped remove her shawl. But as she nervously gathered herself while assuring Elizabeth she'd taken precautions and had not been followed, she suddenly felt alarmed.

Judas had been unable to contain himself, and impatiently called out; beckoning Mary Magdalene to come to him. But his voice sounded unfamiliar, and as she glanced towards Elizabeth looking quite bewildered, it was apparent she had momentarily considered this could all be a hoax.

Elizabeth sensed her anxiety and reassured her by gesturing that she enter the adjoining room. Despite doing her best to remain poised while hesitantly moving forward, Mary Magdalene failed to preserve her composure when coming face to face with Judas. She was immediately overcome at the sight she beheld: he was a shadow of the person she had known and was beyond recognition – the weak voice that had sounded so unfamiliar was a reflection of his physical condition. Dissolving into tears, Mary Magdalene rushed towards Judas and held him as close as she could; sobbing uncontrollably as the relief of finding him took hold.

* * *

For the remainder of the evening, Mary Magdalene provided answers to the multitude of questions Judas posed, and while he was particularly relieved to learn that Martha was safe, the incredulity he felt when told that Jesus had arranged the outcome of his trial was overwhelming. He was distraught when learning the reasons for being excluded from planning meetings, and felt tremendous guilt for the way he had behaved in permitting his overly sensitive ego to get the better of him. Judas now fully understood the extent of the inconvenience and disruption he had caused, and nothing Mary Magdalene could say in any way alleviated his sense of remorse.

For Mary Magdalene, it felt so unfair that Judas had paid such a high price for allowing the insecurities of others to impact his own feelings of self-worth. His entire life had been spent in dedication and unstinting loyalty and support: to Mary Magdalene, this outcome felt so unjust.

* * *

The reunification of Judas and Mary Magdalene began the process of putting together the pieces of this complex puzzle, but of all the discoveries each made during their initial meeting, what shocked and confounded them the most was the conflicting behaviours of Seth. Mary Magdalene was astonished to learn that he had located Judas prior to the crucifixion and arranged for his guards to escort him to safety. Similarly, Judas was taken aback to have it confirmed that the betrayal rumour and the house-to-house search had been coordinated by Seth. When Judas explained how compassionate and reassuring Seth had been, and Mary Magdalene countered his impression with an entirely opposing perspective, neither she nor Judas could even begin to comprehend his contrasting behaviours. All they were able to conclude was how little they understood about the underlying strategies that Seth and his superiors were orchestrating.

As the evening wore on, Judas realised that Mary Magdalene was not going to volunteer to discuss the resurrection story and, in many ways, he too was afraid to broach the subject in fear of his hopes being dashed. Realising that her lack of directness in this regard most likely meant that she had no knowledge of Jesus surviving, Judas nevertheless decided he needed to air his concerns. Cautiously, he asked about the conditions surrounding the resurrection, and with much reservation enquired whether Mary Magdalene had any reason to suspect that Jesus may have lived.

Having previously committed to preserving the secret of the resurrection, Mary Magdalene decided it would be wrong to keep such information from Judas. She had delayed raising the matter due to being concerned he would not approve of her decision, but once the question had been posed she felt confident that Judas was the only person with whom she could share this burden. Composing herself, she proceeded to relate all that she knew:

"Judas, it is true that the body of Jesus is no longer in its tomb, but I am certain he died on the cross. I was there, and I witnessed it all — he could not possibly have survived. Seth showed me the tomb several days after the crucifixion and displayed a vacant cave, claiming it to be where Jesus had been placed. However, my suspicion is that Seth disposed of the body to persuade me to declare I had evidence of a resurrection and recount the story you are familiar with. I have not shared this truth with anyone else – even James and your mother believe I witnessed such an event.

"Seth wanted me to say that an angel appeared at the tomb to announce that the divine son of God had risen to heaven, but will one day return to judge the living and the dead. But the truth is, I did not witness such a visitation and neither have I seen the body of Jesus since it was placed in the tomb. Seth convinced me to work with him to establish this miracle. He persuaded that to do so would ensure Jesus's divinity would never again be questioned, and for all time he would be recognised as the son of God. I agreed to participate because I knew Jesus and Martha had cooperated with Seth, and I wanted to at least ensure Jesus would never be forgotten – I was certain that Jesus and Martha would have wanted me to do whatever I could to ensure the ministry was remembered for all time."

Judas was horrified at this disclosure. He had known that it was most likely the resurrection story was just another *miracle* rumour, similar to those the Movement had perpetrated throughout the ministry, but he had hoped that Mary Magdalene's cooperation was in exchange for something substantial, and not merely the result of her being naïve and succumbing to the persuasions of Seth. Judas could tell she had been completely genuine in her desire to do the right thing, but all the same he was disappointed at her decision and knew that this was the last thing Jesus would have wanted. However, Judas felt that what was done was done, and appreciated there was little to be gained from making Mary Magdalene feel guilty; concluding that one more miracle added to the list was going to make little difference in the scheme of things. Knowing there was much to be resolved and discovered, Judas refrained from reacting to this disclosure and instead focused upon planning what he and Mary Magdalene could do. In attempting to comprehend Seth's motives and conflicting approaches, and to perhaps disrupt whatever plans were in store, it was obvious to them both that the answers to everything lay with Seth, and that is where they centred their efforts.

* * *

In spite of what Mary Magdalene had stated regarding ideas Judas harboured that Jesus may be alive, he stubbornly insisted on revisiting his theory. Hesitantly, he asked, "Mary Magdalene, you have already expressed your conclusions regarding the possibility that Jesus may have lived, but should we not take into account his physical strength and personal conviction – I still speculate that he could have survived and been taken by Seth to another location to facilitate some sort of plan. You said that when revealing the resurrection you were required to claim that Jesus would return to judge the living and the dead. Do you think there is any possibility that Seth may be providing care for Jesus, with the intention of presenting him to the people as miraculously risen from the dead and returned to judge us all?"

Mary Magdalene faltered a little before responding, and thought the possibility through carefully before saying, "Anything is possible, Judas. People are so fearful that they could easily be convinced of such a thing. The leaders of the Movement are influential and intimidating men, and when ignorance and fear exists among the people to such a large extent, it would be difficult for most to argue with whatever scenario they presented. But truthfully, Judas, I cannot see how Jesus could possibly have survived. I witnessed the entire episode, including his burial. He appeared to have died before he was even placed on the cross, and by the time he was removed there was no question. I still believe that Seth's men simply removed his body and buried it elsewhere in preparation for convincing me to support the resurrection story, and I cannot uphold a theory beyond that."

Judas was reluctant to accept Mary Magdalene's opinion, but reminded himself that she had witnessed the crucifixion, and he had not. He knew that had she thought there was any hope of Jesus having survived, she would have clung onto that hope in the same way he had.

However, irrespective of Mary Magdalene's conclusive response to Judas's ideas, he had sown seeds of thought that she had not considered before. Throughout the evening they contemplated various scenarios, but Mary Magdalene kept coming back to the reality of what she had witnessed. On the other hand, Seth's contradictory behaviour, and the fact that many times in the week after the crucifixion he had disappeared for long periods, contributed much to the curiosity that was deepening with each passing hour. There was no doubt in her mind that something unseemly was occurring, and she determined to stop at nothing in identifying what that was.

* * *

Despite how close to the truth Judas and Mary Magdalene's speculation had become, Seth's plans did not involve a scenario as straightforward as keeping Jesus in hiding and one day presenting him as miraculously resurrected from the dead. His actual plan was something no one could ever have imagined.

* * *

Upon returning to the house she was sharing with Mary and James, Mary Magdalene informed them of the good news – she had located Judas. She told of his injuries and confirmed they occurred at the hands of the followers, and while James and Mary were upset to learn what Judas had endured, they were relieved that he was alive. However, when informed that Judas had been rescued from the street by Seth prior to the crucifixion, along with being told the reason why he had not arrived at the Bethany house to escort Martha, they were both extremely confused and distressed. Mary was devastated to learn that Judas had felt so excluded and of no consequence. She had so often given thanks for him joining her family, and was eternally grateful for all the support he'd provided for Jesus throughout his life. While this news was difficult enough for James and Mary to fathom, it was even more inexplicable to learn of the opposing behaviours of Seth. No one could think of any scenario that would explain such circumstances, yet all agreed it was highly likely that something problematic was occurring.

James decided it was now time to escort his mother to Nazareth and was relieved to be leaving Jerusalem. It had taken enormous willpower to refrain from reacting to so many incidents, and the latest news of Judas's injuries and conflicting accounts of Seth's behaviour, was as much as James could stand. He knew Seth was up to something, but while he was responsible for his mother there was nothing he could do. Once he had discharged himself of this duty, he would then be free to begin organising an opposition to the Movement. However, before departing, James and Mary asked if Mary Magdalene could find a way to escort them both to see Judas, and of course she agreed. It was dangerous, but Mary in particular wanted to comfort her son and reassure him of how much he was loved. It was a risk James and Mary Magdalene felt obliged to take.

As Mary Magdalene retired for the evening, she could not help but contemplate numerous potential scenarios, including those Judas had imagined. She felt somewhat in the wrong for not disclosing to James and Mary that the resurrection story was a fabrication, but was fearful of losing their trust; knowing they would not have understood or approved. In an effort to put those concerns aside, Mary Magdalene tried to focus on the future, but as the night wore on her imagination began to take hold. In spite of wanting to remain realistic, she could not help but permit Judas's ideas to take root. Despite repeatedly reminding herself that she had witnessed the crucifixion and that Jesus could not possibly have survived, the prospect that he somehow may have lived was all she could think about.

* * *

Waking the following morning in a feisty and excitable mood, Mary Magdalene decided to get to work immediately. For the first time there was solid information she could begin to research, and she marveled at where this journey might take her. In testing the waters to see if Judas's theories carried weight, Mary Magdalene decided that since a more amenable relationship existed with Seth, there was sufficient familiarity that an enquiry disguised in humour could be worthwhile. However, as it turned out — Seth was in no mood to be manipulated.

Approaching in a casual manner, Mary Magdalene suggested to Seth that perhaps he had not been entirely honest with her. Flirtatiously, she engaged him by saying, "Have you heard the rumour that Jesus survived the crucifixion and that you're nursing him back to health to facilitate a miraculous 'return' at some relevant point in the future?"

Seth turned and glared intently at Mary Magdalene; her insinuations were not amusing to him. Grabbing her, he thrust her towards a wall and fumed, "Who's been spreading such malicious rumour? Tell me immediately."

Astonished by his reaction, Mary Magdalene composed herself quickly since she had not planned for this eventuality. The most she had expected was to be dismissed as ridiculous or laughed at, but as Seth tightened his grip in an effort to solicit a response, Mary Magdalene retorted by making light of her comments, saying, "Seth, don't take me so seriously. I was bored and having a little fun. I hadn't realised you'd lost your sense of humour."

Pushing her aside he released her, while making himself clear in no uncertain terms: "Don't even think such outrageousness. Comments made in jest or as speculation can establish rumour that may be impossible to quash. I have warned you to do as I say if you care for the family of Jesus. There is much at stake. Do not utter such nonsense ever again."

Angrily storming off, while conscious that his reaction to such a suggestion could arouse suspicion, Seth began to appreciate that time was running out. He knew that if rumours did exist, it would only be a matter of time before his superiors found out.

Needless to say, Seth's very obvious panic did not escape Mary Magdalene's notice, and this outburst was certainly not something she could ignore. Questioning herself, she asked whether or not Seth was genuinely concerned about rumour and gossip, or if she could possibly have touched a nerve and come close to the truth. As bad tempered as he often was, Seth had only ever reacted so quickly and violently towards Mary Magdalene once before — when she confronted him for information about Judas after the unproductive search for his body. Now that she understood the complexities behind that reaction, Mary Magdalene felt this similar response could be indicative of the pressure Seth was under relating to schemes that were equally as elaborate.

PART IV – THE RECUPERATION

The faint signs of life detected by the physician caring for Jesus gradually improved as each day passed, with short spells of consciousness occurring despite his weak state. His quarters were an uninspiring, windowless basement room, attended only by nursing staff, and located at the end of a long, narrow corridor. With a guard on duty near the entrance, and another at the far end of the hallway, there was little chance that a passerby would come into contact with Jesus. It was vital that no one question the integrity of Seth's claim that the patient was his long-lost, accused brother, Jeremiah, or that any association with Jesus was even remotely suggested. Since the flogging of criminals occurred numerous times in any one day, Jeremiah's condition would not be considered unusual unless someone began to view the situation as coincidental. Seth's directive that the somewhat humiliating presence of his offending brother be undisclosed, was understood and adhered to by the handful of people responsible for his care. Although some gossip was inevitable, it was generally based upon Seth's shame regarding his delinquent brother, which diverted attention from anything other.

As Jesus's condition began to improve, his spells of wakefulness increased and little by little he became aware of his surroundings. Nevertheless, he was bewildered and suffered traumatic hallucinations as the details of what should have been his final days vividly replayed in his mind. But with no dialogue forthcoming from those who cared for his wounds, Jesus struggled to discern whatever he could from listening in to the conversation of people going about their duties. Unbeknown to Jesus, the nurses and guards were forbidden from engaging their patient in conversation, and had been warned by Seth that his 'brother' was a delusional con-artist he'd taken pity upon, and anything he suggested should therefore be ignored. Being somewhat afraid of their patient and concerned they may fall foul of his antics, the nurses hurried about their duties at various intervals throughout the day, and for the most part left Jesus alone to rest and recuperate. Knowing that a messenger was to be dispatched to Seth the moment Jesus began to show signs of more lengthy periods of consciousness, they were content that no more was expected of them.

A week or so after Jesus's arrival at the Barbelo compound, Seth returned for one of his visits to check on the progress of his supposed brother. As he thundered towards Jesus's room via staircases and hallways, his domineering voice echoed throughout the building, causing Jesus to awake abruptly. He could hear Seth striding passionately in his direction, while bawling complaints and instructions at the fearful personnel who crossed his path. The familiar sound of Seth's voice prompted a sense of panic in Jesus, and his heart began to race as snippets of information about his past began flashing through his now conscious mind.

Brusquely entering the room, Seth demanded an update from the caregivers about their patient's condition, but as they nervously reported the minor progress made, the commanding presence of Seth made it difficult for Jesus to remain composed. Closing his eyes to give the impression of an unconscious state, it took enormous determination to keep his emotions intact as the floodgates of his mind opened up, triggered by the sound of Seth's voice. Jesus could feel himself physically going into shock as the memory of all that had occurred overtook his thoughts like a tidal wave consuming the shore. Using every ounce of strength he could muster to remain quiet, Jesus had the presence of mind to appreciate that he needed time to absorb what was happening and determine exactly what his circumstances were, prior to disclosing his conscious state and being faced with interrogation by Seth.

Fortunately, Seth could not remain at Barbelo for very long since he was preoccupied with events being coordinated in Jerusalem. Once the caregivers confirmed their patient was improving and had not presented problems or engaged them in conversation, Seth sternly reiterated the warning regarding his delusional brother, and departed as abruptly as he'd arrived. The nurses were left in no doubt that Jeremiah's antics should not be entertained, but this fact did not bother Jesus – rather, he was pleased to discover that his caregivers shared his sense of relief at Seth's departure, and while it was clear they were afraid of being on the receiving end of his wrath, it was also apparent they held him in little regard. Overhearing such exchanges was of some comfort to Jesus, as it concerned him little that Seth's staff had been given a poor impression of his character, since that was something he was confident of rectifying, but reading between the lines of conversation, Jesus was pleased to learn it would take little effort on his part to get his caregivers on-side once he felt well enough to begin to make inroads into discovering what was going on.

Even though Jesus was now fully aware of his surroundings, he chose to remain silent for the time being and permitted his mind to come to terms with the confusing circumstances. He appreciated the need to be patient and bide his time, while paying close attention to every word uttered within earshot. He wanted to discover where he was and what lay behind his situation, while using the time wisely to improve his physical strength and allow his mental capacity to return fully. In letting each day pass by patiently, he eventually began to feel more in control of his circumstances.

* * *

Reliving in his mind the weeks prior to the crucifixion and the serving of the sentence itself, was a stressful and emotional time for Jesus. He recalled all of the contingencies he had put in place for his family, and was very preoccupied regarding what they may have faced. As he prayed they had managed to remain one step ahead of the Movement, Jesus appreciated there was little he could do to support them in his present condition, yet felt entirely responsible for whatever horrors he feared they may have suffered.

In continuing to remain quiet in the company of his caregivers and guards, Jesus gleaned considerable information from their discussions. He was particularly amused at overhearing the sarcastic and humorous banter regarding Seth, and intended to use that tone when eventually engaging them and attempting to alter their impression of his character. However, the most fascinating discovery was learning that he was referred to as Jeremiah, and understood to be the long-lost, delinquent brother of Seth. While somewhat confused and amused by such a suggestion, Jesus also appreciated it was a pertinent clue to his circumstances. Clearly, nobody was aware that they were caring for Jesus of Nazareth.

PART V – MARTHA'S REALITY CHECK

Oblivious to all these happenings, Martha continued to make her way to the coast, while still feeling somewhat burdened and overwhelmed by all that had occurred. She saw little purpose in preserving the diaries, despite what James had tried to inspire – for the life of her she could not foresee how they could make an impact, now, or in the future. She believed that the Movement was powerful, ruthless, and ambitious, and would fiercely oppose anyone who attempted to disclose the truth. Her only hope was that people would eventually see the reality of these individuals and their intentions, but deep down she believed the fearful would rather defend the comfort of ignorance, than courageously embrace the truth and all that would entail.

Whenever possible, Martha travelled with others to ensure her safety, since it was rare for women to travel distances unaccompanied. Everywhere she went her eyes moved among the crowd looking for the familiar, kind face of Judas as she prayed for his safety and for them to be reunited. She knew that if Judas were by her side she would feel more positive about the future: he had always been so encouraging, and without fail brought levity to the most demoralising of situations.

* * *

Some two weeks had now passed since the crucifixion, and Martha had decided to settle in a small community for two or three days of rest. She had befriended a family on her travels, and accepted their invitation to spend time with them before continuing her journey. Of course, they didn't know who she was, and Martha did not dare disclose her association with the much talked-about ministry of Jesus, but it was during this short stay that the story of the resurrection and Mary Magdalene's angelic visitation was revealed to her. Martha's hosts casually raised the subject in conversation over dinner one evening, which caused her heart to skip a beat as she tried to remain composed and not draw attention to her reaction. Immediately realising this must have been part of Seth's plan to establish the divinity of

Jesus, Martha was so livid she could barely contain herself – neither she nor Jesus had considered that the Movement would dream up something as dramatic as this.

Her first thoughts were of Mary Magdalene, and Martha questioned the possibility that she had been party to this all along. After all, it was Seth who discovered the brother and sister who'd accommodated her throughout the ministry, so it would not have been too far-fetched to imagine that an episode such as this was part of their agreement. Ultimately, though, she felt this could not be the case, since Mary Magdalene had barely been out of her presence over the years, and on the rare occasions that she had, Judas had accompanied her. Recalling the good words of James regarding her efforts to locate Judas, Martha concluded that Mary Magdalene had in some way been forced into making these claims. She also reflected that when arrangements were being made prior to the arrest of Jesus, Seth had oddly insisted that Mary Magdalene remain in Jerusalem with the other followers, despite the fact that they loathed her. Martha had wanted Mary Magdalene to leave with her, and Seth's refusal to agree had always troubled her. It had not been difficult to eventually draw the conclusion that this scenario was part and parcel of Seth's larger plans, and Mary Magdalene had no doubt been seen as an easy target of coercion once no one was available to support her.

Martha retired for the evening as soon as it felt socially acceptable to do so, since she needed to clear her head and think this situation through. Obviously, she wondered at first if this warranted her return to Jerusalem, and only half-heartedly countered that thought when recalling the advice of James. There had often been turning points throughout the ministry when Jesus knew they had to relinquish control of circumstances they could no longer negotiate, although Martha had not always been easy to convince in such instances. It was often the case that she needed reining in when it came to rectifying misdeeds, since she had tremendous difficulty accepting circumstances that were so clearly unjust. In her mind, therefore, she was already half way back to Jerusalem and was doing little to convince herself otherwise. On the back of reports of Judas's supposed betrayal, she felt this situation was something Seth and the Movement should be held to account for. To have walked away from responding to the fate of Judas had been difficult enough, but to do nothing about these developments was going to require much restraint.

For the next day or so, Martha had no choice but to remain with her new acquaintances, since no transport in either direction was scheduled, which turned out to be very fortunate. Martha was now forced to respond to this situation with clarity, but not having previously made such an important decision alone, she knew this was not going to be easy.

Doing her best to concentrate on the pros and cons of her choices, she found herself beginning to imagine what Jesus would have done. While trying her utmost to look at what she faced with more objectivity, as opposed to the emotional way that had become so familiar in recent times, she discovered that looking at the problem from his perspective rather than her own, produced an entirely different outcome.

In some ways, meditating and praying over this decision had made her feel close to her brother again, and as she closed her eyes and imagined him sitting next to her, she immediately sensed precisely what he would have recommended. With a circumstance as well established as the resurrection story, he would have assessed the situation carefully; determined what could be achieved and what could not, while considering the risks and weighing up the likelihood of success versus the threat involved. Martha knew what his decision would be – God must have a plan, and even though we do not understand what that is, there are times when we have to learn to relinquish control when we know we have none.

Even though it went against everything Martha felt on an emotional level, she concluded it would be futile to fight Seth and his entire Movement singlehandedly. They would simply dispose of her if she arrived in Jerusalem, and the diaries would disappear along with her. Deciding there was nothing to be gained from going back, but potentially much to lose if she did, Martha chose to continue her journey towards the coast, while reminding herself of Jesus's final instructions, and what James had encouraged her to believe – preserving the diaries and bequeathing the truth of the ministry to future generations was all that mattered.

Settling down to sleep, Martha remained restless; over and over in her mind she was relating what she would say to Seth if only she had the chance. She was livid that the Movement had succeeded in getting away with so much: not only had they ridden roughshod over the entire story of Jesus's life, but were now using his death to create absurd scenarios to intimidate people into submitting to their philosophy. While complaining to herself about the despicable nature of what was occurring, Martha began laughing nervously without understanding why. As the laughter became uncontrollable and was soon mixed with tears, an observer would have thought she had become hysterical. As she questioned her own sanity, Martha suddenly began to understand what was happening – it was reality check time.

When things had gone terribly wrong during the ministry, and everyone had concluded it was time to give up the fight on a specific issue, Jesus and Judas had coped with such defeat by turning the situation into something to find humour in. Martha's mind had followed that pattern in a sort of self-activating way, and without consciously realising it, she had moved beyond the anger and reached the point of acceptance. But to feel more positive about accepting defeat, an automatic reflex left over from the days of the ministry seemed to kick in, and she began to look at the resurrection story in a humorous light.

She found herself thinking how completely ridiculous it was for anyone to actually believe in something so entirely absurd. What on earth was wrong with the minds of people that they would take seriously such claims, she questioned. As hysterical laughter took hold, she suggested to herself that if this scenario was not completely and utterly ludicrous, then what was it? Before long, Martha was struggling to keep herself under control and was concerned her hosts would overhear the fits of laughter. No longer feeling angry, she instead had difficulty stifling her amusement over the absurdity of the claims. As she began to imagine the hilarious antics and impersonations of Seth that Jesus and Judas had acted out on so many previous occasions, she could see in her mind's eye how they would have responded to this latest defeat. In the privacy of the Magdala house, and a goblet or two of wine later, Jesus and Judas would have done as they always did: entertain her, Mary Magdalene, and Lazarus with hilarious, sarcastic sketches, mocking Seth and his band of merry men, in an attempt to make everyone feel better about what had occurred. One of their favourite pastimes was to act out the latest 'miracle' rumour, and Martha began to imagine Jesus dressed-up as Mary Magdalene, and Judas in angelic garb imparting words of wisdom to be shared among the vulnerable crowd.

As had always been the case in the past, humour saved the day. Martha was able to move beyond this latest defeat and accept it for what it was: a situation she had no control over, so there was little point in letting it effect her. Realising that this was precisely how Jesus would have wanted her to respond, Martha was able to put her resentment to rest. She determined that if people were going to ignore their intuition and believe in such ridiculous absurdities, the price to be paid for those choices would have to be endured.

Eventually calming down and falling asleep, Martha did so with a new sense of freedom. She acknowledged that she needed to stop taking all of this so seriously, and accepted that her primary responsibility in life had been to work with Jesus and facilitate a series of opportunities for people to learn. However, if mankind ultimately chose that they needed to learn the hard way, then so be it – that was clearly their decision, and there was little more that could be done.

With a newfound energy and confidence, Martha concluded that she needed to leave the past behind and forge a new future for herself. Her only remaining responsibility was to ensure that the diaries were secure for future generations. It would then be up to those people to choose between embracing the truth or continue to indulge in the absurd.

PART VI – TIME FOR SOME ANSWERS

After biding his time, hoping to overhear conversations that in some way shed light on his predicament, Jesus could be forgiven for becoming frustrated. Nothing was forthcoming that revealed why Seth had kept him under lock and key, or why those caring for him were totally unaware of his true identity. Some four weeks into his recovery, Jesus felt strong enough to survive a debate with Seth, so decided it was time to reveal to his caregivers that he was aware of their presence.

The younger of the two nurses was usually the first to arrive in the early hours of the morning, and on the day Jesus chose to speak she was more than a little taken aback. Gently stepping into the room, trying not to cause a disturbance, she was startled as Jesus glanced in her direction and in a strong, commanding manner said, "Good morning."

The young woman shyly reciprocated the gesture and quickly gathered herself, despite feeling a little afraid at being alone with someone she'd heard nothing positive about. But as she hurried about her duties Jesus began to engage her, asking, "Do you mind telling me who I am? I have no recollection of my name or what happened to me. What am I doing in this place, and more importantly, where am I?"

The young nurse nervously replied, admitting she was not supposed to engage her patient in conversation, saying, "I am forbidden from tiring you with conversation, but I shall immediately find someone who can answer your questions."

"No, no," replied Jesus, "please don't bother people on my behalf at such an early hour, but do tell me — from what I have gathered my name is Jeremiah — is that so?

Feeling compelled to respond the young girl admitted, "Yes, I believe so. I have been told you are the brother of Seth, who is the owner of this house."

Jesus furrowed his brow to appear inquisitive before saying, "That's interesting. I do seem to recall having a brother by that name, but I was unsure as to my own name — which is more than a little strange I think!"

Accompanying his remarks with laughter to encourage the young woman to relax, Jesus then continued: "Tell me how I got into this state — my skin is torn — it looks as though I've been flogged a thousand times. The soreness has abated somewhat, but what did I do to deserve this?"

The young girl, now a little more relaxed, confidently informed Jesus he had done nothing wrong: "I am told you were accused of a crime and arrested and sentenced before your brother could vouch for you. He assured the soldiers that you were not the suspect they'd been seeking, and they agreed to release you into his custody."

"So," said Jesus, "I have much to be grateful for. My brother — where is he? I would like to express my gratitude."

Responding cautiously, and uncertain it was acceptable to reveal anything more, the young woman replied, "I believe he is in Jerusalem, and could possibly arrive here this evening. I will make sure someone informs him you are well enough to speak."

Smiling reassuringly, Jesus held out his hand, touching the young girl's arm, saying, "Thank you, my child. Now I must rest."

As the caregiver left the room, she hastily went in search of her superior; explaining the developments and how lucid Jeremiah had suddenly become, which sent the elder of the two women rushing to Jesus's bedside. Composing herself before entering, she was equally as astonished to be confidently greeted with a humorous remark: "I take it your young assistant informed you I wasn't dead," Jesus teased.

Feeling somewhat embarrassed at being amused, she nervously replied, "Yes – I mean no, no – we knew you were alive. It's just that you've been resting and recuperating, so it came as a surprise – a surprise that you so suddenly began to talk with such fluency."

As the nurse fussed around the room, ensuring everything was in its place, Jesus smiled to put her at ease before asking, "Tell me – how long have I been *asleep,* and what has been happening in the world that I've missed?"

The senior caregiver, who was now accompanied by the young girl, began by saying, "Well, you have been here for 28 days and nights, and you were in a bad state when you arrived. We thought we'd lost you a few times, but you're strong – you kept coming back."

Jesus couldn't resist interrupting and jokingly said, "I came back from the dead? I'd better not make a habit of that!"

Little did he appreciate the irony of his remarks, but the humorous and respectful way Jesus engaged the caregivers made them feel relaxed in his company, which was of course his intention.

"So, tell me," asked Jesus with a mischievous intonation, "what have I missed — 28 days does not go by in these parts without some disruption or happenings?"

As the two caregivers looked at one another, suggesting they were unable to think of any notable events to report, they were joined by a guard who demanded to know why they were talking so loudly. He'd not noticed that Jesus was alert and was surprised when he suddenly spoke out, saying, "It's my fault, young man. Don't blame the ladies – they were only responding to my questions regarding what I've missed during my long sleep!"

Without responding, the shocked guard enquired of the caregivers if Seth had been informed of developments in Jeremiah's condition, which they assured him would happen once a messenger was dispatched. As Jesus observed the anxiety the guard displayed, he expressed his amusement at the idea that they were so concerned about Seth: "Why are you so intimidated by my brother? Everyone seems to be afraid of speaking or saying anything without his permission."

The room fell silent until the guard spoke on everyone's behalf, saying, "We answer to Seth, and he's a tough taskmaster. We do one thing wrong, and we're out of a job, and it's not likely we'll work again."

"Oh, I see," said Jesus, "but tell me — are you not permitted to keep me from dying of boredom by discussing matters of interest? Seth will be here later today and I'm sure he'll fill me in, but it would be nice to have a friendly face to spend some time with after all these days alone. Tell me, young man, where is this house located, and how did I get here?"

The guard hesitated, but felt obliged to respond to such an inoffensive question, and said, "I don't know how you arrived here, but when I reported for duty several weeks ago you were here and I was assigned to this position, but no information was provided to me by Seth, although your caregivers told me your name was Jeremiah and said you were Seth's brother, but that is as much as I know. And as for this house — we are in the realm of Barbelo and the house is owned by Seth, who runs his business from here."

Feeling assured that he now had the confidence of the guard, Jesus pushed for a little more information by asking, "And what sort of business is that, may I ask?"

The guard felt rather inept and replied by admitting he had no idea, to which Jesus reassuringly suggested, "That's so typical of my brother. He's so secretive that not even his employees know what they're doing!"

As everyone expressed amusement at Jesus's observations, an immediate bond began to develop between them all, so Jesus wasted no time in taking advantage of the situation. Turning his attention to the now more relaxed guard, he asked if anything interesting had been happening in recent times, or if any troublemakers had caused a stir.

As the guard shook his head thoughtfully, suggesting he could think of nothing of interest, he suddenly recalled the events of four weeks previous, saying, "Yes, there was some scandalous activity recently. Jesus of Nazareth was arrested and put to death, which divided people as many disagreed with the outcome of the trial. And as if that wasn't enough to keep us all occupied, one of his followers — Mary Magdalene — claimed that his body disappeared from the tomb and it is generally believed that an angel appeared before her, declaring that Jesus had risen from the dead to be with God and would one day return to judge us all."

When reminded of this affair by the guard, the two caregivers joined in and all three competed to share what they knew. Jesus's plan had worked perfectly, and as the floodgates opened, Jesus prepared to be educated. Needing to place only a few pertinent questions here and there during deliberations, Jesus was able to solicit all of the information he required. However, the more he discovered, the more difficult it became to uphold a sense of detachment to the issues.

His heart raced as he learned of the accusations against Judas and the rumoured sighting of his body, and the horror he felt at the resurrection story was devastating. But despite his agitation, Jesus managed to preserve his composure and appeared only mildly moved by the information that was conveyed.

Taking in all of this news at once became a little much for Jesus, and he began to feel somewhat unwell. Bringing the conversation to a close by suggesting he needed to rest, he reminded the group not to reveal that the discussion had taken place since he did not want them to risk being punished by Seth. As all three nodded in agreement, each realising they had momentarily forgotten Seth's instructions in that regard, Jesus prompted them by saying, "Our secret," as if to reassure that their lapse was something they did not need be concerned about.

* * *

Once the caregivers and guard had departed, Jesus could barely contain himself: rage consumed his mind when thoughts of what he had just discovered began to sink in. It became clear to Jesus that Seth had fooled them all, and he was certain that those closest to him had probably been murdered or were under threat. When considering the circumstances surrounding the resurrection myth, Jesus felt certain that Mary Magdalene had been coerced into fabricating the tale, and wondered what part this played in Seth's future plans for him. He did not believe that Seth would think he could be persuaded to partake in some bizarre 'event', and could not therefore imagine why he had been kept alive. It was fairly apparent that he needed to be dead if the Movement were to proceed in the direction they intended, and trying to understand their motives for nursing him back to health was in vain. He could never have dreamed up something as incredible as the resurrection, and equally could not imagine what the Movement had planned for his future.

Believing that he was now entirely alone, and that his followers and family would either have been disposed of or escaped the area, Jesus appreciated even more that it was vital he continue to progress physically before participating in a potentially exhausting debate with Seth. Therefore, even though he knew his caregivers would inform Seth of his improved condition, he had no intention of engaging in conversation until he was ready to do so.

PART VII – THE SEARCH BEGINS

As Mary Magdalene contemplated her next move she turned to Judas for inspiration. Arriving unannounced in the dead of night, she quietly entered Elizabeth's house through a back entrance. Judas was more than a little relieved to see her; knowing what a feisty character she was, he'd been concerned she may push Seth too far with catastrophic results. As they greeted one another warmly, Mary Magdalene proceeded to explain Seth's bizarre over-reaction to her informal and lighthearted enquiries, and Judas concurred that this was certainly something that warranted further investigation, but what to do next required some creative thinking.

Elizabeth awoke upon overhearing Judas and Mary Magdalene deep in conversation, and was keen to participate and learn of anything new that had been discovered. When Judas informed her of the latest development, she too agreed that Seth's reaction seemed a little frenzied and definitely should not be ignored. As they each contributed ideas for possible scenarios that may be ongoing, Mary Magdalene recalled an incident with one of Seth's guards. He was responding to her request for information regarding Seth's whereabouts, and referred to the fact that he was travelling to 'the compound'. The guard had not been forthcoming about its location and it was a place that Mary Magdalene had not previously heard mentioned, but she gleaned from the conversation that it seemed to be the headquarters of Seth's operation.

Neither Judas nor Mary Magdalene had previously heard of this place, and only knew that all meetings throughout the ministry were conducted at either the Bethany or Magdala house, and as far as they were aware there had never been an occasion when Jesus or Martha attended somewhere referred to as the compound. However, having lived in Jerusalem all of her life, Elizabeth was familiar with the surrounding area and knew that a place with that name was located in the realm of Barbelo. While she had no knowledge of what business was carried out there, she did know the compound offered employment to many people.

Deciding that this was their only lead, Judas and Mary Magdalene determined that the next task should be to verify that this was Seth's headquarters, as well as set out to investigate the activities carried out there. However, to make such enquiries without causing alarm was not going to be easy. Mary Magdalene was essentially working alone because Judas was incapacitated, and due to the fact she was now so well-known there was little she could achieve incognito. They desperately needed help from someone that would not fall under the umbrella of suspicion for being where they were not meant to be, or asking the pertinent questions that needed to be asked.

In explaining their dilemma to Elizabeth, they hoped she may suggest someone who could be relied upon and would perhaps sympathise with their cause, since not one of the followers could be trusted or confided in. What they needed was an individual who'd be willing to make the enquiries that would likely put Mary Magdalene in danger if she did so herself. Because she had now been ostracised by the followers more than ever, it would take little for her suspicious activities to be reported to Seth, which in turn would mean she was constantly monitored, thereby increasing the risk of Judas and Elizabeth being discovered.

As the group continued to debate every possibility open to them, Elizabeth suddenly interjected with a spontaneous suggestion, saying, "What we need is someone on the inside, and it so happens that I have a relative who once worked at the compound in Barbelo. She cleaned and cooked, but she knows everyone who works there. I'm sure she'd be able to shed light on whatever Seth is up to. In fact, so as to keep her from suspecting my motive for making such enquiries, perhaps I should simply ask if she knows of a temporary servant vacancy that I could apply for. It would gain me access to the compound, and I could attempt to discover more."

Judas and Mary Magdalene were astonished at Elizabeth's suggestion, but thrilled that she was offering to help in this way. She was someone who could not be connected to either of them, and would never be suspected of covert behaviour as she'd had no previous association with the Movement or any other political or religious authority. Not only was Elizabeth the perfect person for the job, but for her to take on this role meant there was no need to increase their personal risk by sharing information with a third party, who could so easily have changed their allegiance when under pressure or persuaded to do so for advantageous reasons.

* * *

Once a thorough examination of the pros and cons of the idea had been conducted, all three agreed this was their only hope of discovering anything significant about the activities of Seth, so the following morning Elizabeth enquired of her friend. It was suggested she present herself at the side entrance of the Barbelo compound, where she could talk directly to the head of household; making mention of the fact that she'd been informed of possible vacancies for service personnel. With Mary Magdalene confident she could find the time to visit Judas twice each day while Elizabeth was away, no time was wasted. It had been four weeks since the crucifixion and they were each feeling a sense of urgency to move forward, so it was agreed that Elizabeth not delay and should proceed immediately towards Barbelo and try to gain employment.

Though confident that Mary Magdalene would provide for Judas, Elizabeth was nevertheless anxious as she travelled to the compound. She was unsure how she would cope once inside, but even more concerned about failing to gain access and disappointing her friends. Upon arrival, however, it became clear that securing employment was not going to be difficult; the head of household greeted her with relief due to staff shortages, and was even more impressed that she had been referred by a valued ex-employee. She was offered a two-week temporary position in the kitchen to cover for someone who'd taken ill, which included accommodation in a rather cramped dormitory with other female staff. However, as with any facility such as this, the people 'downstairs' knew the most about what went on 'upstairs', and while Elizabeth's living arrangements may not have been luxurious, it was the ideal location to overhear gossip and make casual enquiries to see what could be discovered.

* * *

In the intervening time, Jesus had remained circumspect after successfully gathering so much information from his caregivers. Appearing too inquisitive may have raised their suspicions, so he behaved as though their company was enjoyable, but the topic of Jesus of Nazareth was of insufficient interest to promote further debate. As planned, Seth visited Jesus on the evening of the informative conversation but he chose to remain still and 'unconscious' in his company. He needed time to digest all he had learned, and appreciated the need to be physically stronger before tackling Seth. The caregivers admitted that Jesus had become lucid only once or twice, asking to be told of his whereabouts, but Seth nonetheless suspected that Jesus's unconscious state was an act, but there was nothing he could do to prove it.

* * *

The evenings saw Elizabeth exhausted – being constantly on her feet all day in a hot kitchen was tiring for someone of her years, and gossiping with other staff in the evening was not as appealing as collapsing asleep on her bed. During the first few days she learned nothing at all about the business of the Barbelo compound, and was beginning to wonder if she ever would. However, during an early morning duty on the fourth day of her employment a breakthrough of sorts occurred. A soldier arrived in the kitchen, which was an unusual event and caused Elizabeth to gasp in fear – for a moment she thought she'd been discovered. Approaching

Elizabeth, the soldier demanded to know why Jeremiah's breakfast had not been brought to his room, and ranted, "Where is that girl, she knows the routine, Seth will be arriving shortly and we have things to prepare...."

As Elizabeth nervously started to respond, a harried young girl appeared in the doorway. The soldier turned around upon realising she was there and severely reprimanded her; insisting she produce food immediately as he angrily stormed off. The girl rushed into the kitchen and pleaded for Elizabeth's help, then dashed off to make her delivery; returning shortly thereafter looking flustered and upset. Elizabeth comforted her and prepared a hot drink, suggesting they sit for a while and recover from the stressful episode.

When enquiring what all the fuss had been about and asking who Jeremiah was, Elizabeth was taken aback at the response. In a nonchalant way, shrugging her shoulders as if she cared little, the young girl responded, saying, "He's nobody all that important, really – he's Seth's brother – an inconvenience to Seth I think. He seems very irritated that he's here and needing to be cared for, which is why everyone is on edge and Seth is giving us such a difficult time. Apparently, he was wrongly accused of a crime and punished, and Seth brought him here to be nursed back to health."

Elizabeth did not miss a beat, and casually enquired how long Jeremiah had been at the compound, to which the girl replied, "About three or four weeks, I think – I don't know precisely."

Nothing the young girl had said told Elizabeth anything concrete, but intuitively she knew there could be a connection. Even though it seemed like quite a leap to draw such a conclusion, she wondered to herself: "Could Jeremiah be Jesus?" Elizabeth quickly gathered her thoughts and asked, "How is Jeremiah recovering, and how long do you expect he will remain here?"

The young lady responded with even less interest in the subject than she'd shown previously, saying, "I don't know. I'm not permitted beyond the guards. I understand there are two caregivers who alternate throughout the day and night, and neither of them ever come near the kitchen, so I have no idea what he's suffering from or how he's doing."

Not wanting to sound too inquisitive, Elizabeth put the matter to rest and continued with her duties. However, this was somewhat of a breakthrough, and she fully intended to keep her ear to the ground whenever the name Jeremiah was mentioned to see what else she could glean.

* * *

A few more days passed, during which time Jesus became physically much stronger and decided that perhaps it was time for a conversation with Seth. However, he could not resist getting back at him and having a little fun, so when Seth arrived in Jesus's basement room later that afternoon, Jesus was well prepared.

Seth enquired of the caregiver if there had been any signs of improvement in Jeremiah, to which she responded by describing various wounds that were healing, but informed that her patient had not yet spoken to any significant degree. Seth was becoming increasingly frustrated at the lack of response from Jesus and leaned over to closely examine his face, only to be startled when he suddenly opened his eyes wide and stared straight back at him. Seth jumped away in fright, and angrily dismissed the caregiver, who abruptly made herself scarce as she could tell there was about to be a furious argument. All along, Seth had suspected that Jesus was more aware than he was admitting, and he was now incensed to learn his suspicions had merit.

As soon as the caregiver was out of earshot, Seth demanded that Jesus respond, but he couldn't resist enjoying the moment he'd been waiting for. Opening his eyes once more, and with high intonations of sarcasm, he said, "My dearest brother, did you know that I have been visited by an angel in the night, who has kindly informed me of my divine status as the son of God and my miraculous resurrection from the dead?"

Seth was now more infuriated than ever, and responded in a threatening manner, saying, "You're alive because of me, but you'll only remain alive for as long as I decide."

Storming out of the room in a rage, he bawled on top note for the caregivers and guards to report to him immediately. Seth knew Jesus must have been alert for a considerable period of time, and was furious that somehow he had learned of Mary Magdalene's resurrection story. As he raged throughout the compound in the direction of his quarters, Jesus quickly called in one of the guards and instructed that they all stick together and insist no conversations had taken place between them: "The most you should admit is the possibility that I may have overheard others talking in the hallways," he whispered, "he'll accept that and your jobs will be safe."

Elizabeth could not help but overhear the uproar and once again became concerned that she had somehow been found out. She asked anyone who passed by if they knew what was happening, but nobody seemed to know for sure, although most suggested it could be something to do with unsatisfactory care being provided for Jeremiah. Most people had by now learned of the existence of Jeremiah, and knew that Seth had been obsessively concerned about him for weeks, so they assumed this was likely to be what the fuss was about.

* * *

As the terrified guards and caregivers arrived in Seth's office he ripped into them; questioning whether a visitor had been given access to Jeremiah's room, and demanding they admit the truth regarding who had spoken about Jesus of Nazareth. Out of sheer panic, all four denied anything untoward had occurred while remaining tight-lipped about their one encounter, but the senior guard quickly spoke out as Jesus had instructed and said, "We've not engaged with the patient at all. However, the hallways echo, and they're busy with people all throughout the day and sometimes into the night. They talk among each other, and it's possible that if your brother was conscious and aware, he could easily have overheard people gossiping. I assure you that none of us have conversed with the patient as per your strict instructions."

The others all nervously nodded in agreement at this likely scenario, and Seth reluctantly regained his composure. He felt Jesus had probably only heard a few snippets of conversation and was putting two and two together, but he couldn't be sure whether or not he knew much more. Now that Jesus seemed to have regained his health, Seth was under pressure to divulge his plans, but he was nowhere near ready. He had still not located Judas or Martha, and he at least wanted to have made inroads in that direction before approaching Jesus, but it looked as though that was not going to happen.

Seth was under enormous strain from a number of sources, and the lack of conclusive information regarding what Jesus actually knew added to his concerns. He dismissed all four employees from their responsibilities but instructed they be retained at the compound and assigned other duties – the last thing Seth needed was disgruntled employees spreading rumours about 'Jeremiah' in Jerusalem. The head of household gave the now vacant positions to other experienced staff members, and a changing of the guard took place around Jesus, much to his amusement. These people had no idea why they had suddenly been assigned new positions, but were under the same instructions as the previous crew – no conversing with the patient, who is delusional as a result of his lengthy unconscious state.

To Jesus this was nothing more than a nice little challenge to alleviate the boredom. Considerably more fit than the impression he had given, he quickly evaluated his new team of caregivers and guards to establish how best to gain their confidence. He began by ingratiating himself with them, since he could see they were tense as they fumbled around the room trying to discover what was required. In deciding to apologise for Seth's behaviour, Jesus said, "Please relax and don't be so concerned. I am sorry my brother is so on edge, but my health is reasonably good, and it won't be long before I can take care of myself. Seth overreacts – I'll make sure he receives good reports about your conduct, so please treat me as you would a friend. No need to feel anxious in my company – I'm not like Seth – you don't have to worry."

This immediately created an atmosphere in which everyone felt more relaxed and a sensitive bond instantly developed between Jesus and his new guards and caregivers. When that relationship became more secure over the coming days, Jesus intended to slowly engage them in conversation. He needed to learn more about 'Jesus of Nazareth', the gossip surrounding his demise, and his 'miraculous' resurrection from the dead.

* * *

Aware that tensions were becoming increasingly high, Elizabeth kept a low profile throughout the uncertain period surrounding the changeover of responsibilities. Her fellow employees had no idea why Seth was more irritable than ever, but Elizabeth was inclined to believe that Jesus may be connected to the goings-on in some way. As a result, she worried about the danger she may face should Mary Magdalene and Judas be discovered while she was ensconced at the compound, and part of her began to realise that perhaps she'd taken on more than she should. However, appreciating that discovering anything worthwhile would require some ingenuity, Elizabeth did not permit her concerns to overcome her determination to achieve what she'd set out to do.

The head of household did not take long to reassign jobs, and Elizabeth could not believe her good fortune when learning that the demoted caregivers had been assigned kitchen duties and would now be working alongside her. Neither ladies were terribly impressed at such a downgrading, but Elizabeth immediately provided comfort and reassurance in the hope that forming such friendships would eventually create openings to learn more about Jeremiah.

As soon as the anxious atmosphere had calmed down, Elizabeth decided it was perfectly acceptable to ask what all the fuss had been about. With little persuasion, her new acquaintances were more than happy to recount the events surrounding their charge, Jeremiah, explaining they were guilty only of engaging him in casual conversation about matters of little significance.

Elizabeth bided her time when formulating a response, permitting both ladies to air their feelings at being held to account in such a way. When she eventually interrupted the debate she contributed by enquiring, "Did you consider that whatever you discussed might be something Seth didn't want his brother to know?"

After momentarily contemplating Elizabeth's thoughts, they both agreed that could not be the case, with the elder of the two suggesting, "I can't imagine that could be so. It was only casual gossip about local events that were common knowledge, and Jeremiah neither appeared particularly interested, nor raised the matter with us again."

While conscious that it may appear she was dwelling on the subject a little too much, Elizabeth nonetheless tried to extract more specific information as delicately as she could, and asked, "May I enquire what it was you discussed – could it simply be that Seth didn't want his brother upset by something unnecessarily?"

"Oh, I'm not so sure about that," said the younger of the two caregivers with a mildly sarcastic tone, "as soon as Seth realised his brother was alert they argued, and I could clearly overhear raised voices, so I don't believe he was so concerned at him becoming upset or stressed. And as far as I can recall, the main subject we talked about was the trial and death of Jesus of Nazareth and the story of his brother's betrayal and Mary Magdalene's resurrection claim – everyone was talking about that – it was nothing so special that it required us to be secretive."

Elizabeth took a deep breath and tried to remain calm but could feel herself trembling at hearing such news. Not wanting to drop the conversation at such a vital stage, she tentatively asked, "How did Jeremiah react – did he sound surprised at the story of Jesus of Nazareth?"

As the younger of the caregivers responded, she looked towards her superior to discern whether she agreed with her appraisal, and said, "No, I don't recall a particular reaction from Jeremiah, to be honest. He listened without saying too much and didn't raise the subject again, so it couldn't have been of much interest to him."

Elizabeth decided to take a leaf out of 'Jeremiah's' book and casually ended the conversation as if her interest had suddenly waned. She carried on with her duties, encouraging the women to relax now that their ordeal was over, but inside she could barely remain poised.

That night, Elizabeth lay in her bed but could not rest — her mind was racing. She kept asking herself over and over again, "Could the patient possibly be Jesus?" The reality was, however, that the conversation between the caregivers and Jeremiah proved nothing, except that it was clearly upsetting to Seth that such a conversation had taken place. Elizabeth knew she had to do something to obtain evidence that determined one way or the other if her suspicions had any worth, and with only one week of her temporary job remaining, it had to be now.

* * *

Five weeks had passed since the crucifixion, and Elizabeth concluded that if the patient was in fact Jesus, he must be close to recovery. She contemplated that Seth's plans may include Jesus being moved from the compound in the near future, thus she felt it was an urgent necessity to be proactive and take the initiative. Casting her fears and doubts aside, she made enquiries to discover the specifics of the job reassignments to ascertain who had been placed in the position of Jeremiah's caregiver. Having shared private living quarters with the female staff for the past week, Elizabeth had curried favour with most of them, which she hoped would now pay dividends.

As she had anticipated, it turned out that Elizabeth was familiar with the new caregivers, and one young lady in particular had become a reasonably close acquaintance in the previous week; certainly enough that enabled them to gossip without it being considered unusual. Her name was Hannah, and even though she was young and excitable, and possibly not the preferred choice from the standpoint of discretion, Elizabeth felt she had no alternative but to try and use her in some way. Having taken part in general chit-chat during Elizabeth's first week, Hannah had confided her dislike of Seth and remarked on his rude manners and controlling ways, which Elizabeth decided to use to her advantage.

At the first opportunity, Elizabeth approached Hannah and asked how her patient was doing. Engaging her initially in friendly banter, she proceeded to fabricate a story about Seth and Jeremiah's family; asking Hannah if she was aware that Seth had two sisters and four brothers, all of whom he'd disowned and kept secret. As Hannah's eyes lit up to learn such news, Elizabeth sensed immediately that her plan was going to work.

 Confessing to being a friend of one of the family members, Elizabeth got straight to the point and suggested Hannah might like to engage in somewhat of a daring undertaking: "It would be so nice for Jeremiah to know his family is well and thinking about him since Seth will not permit them to visit. How would you feel about secretly passing on such a message to Jeremiah?"

Hannah was astonished to learn that Seth had a secret family, and before Elizabeth could finish her proposal she eagerly offered to participate, saying, "This would be so exciting – I could easily pass on a message to Jeremiah. What do you think I should tell him?"

Elizabeth was delighted with such a positive reaction with so little effort on her part, but appreciated the need to word her instructions carefully. She understood that the risk involved in making this approach could result in her being exposed, which would lead to the eventual discovery of Judas and Mary Magdalene. If Jeremiah turned out to be none other than Seth's brother, Elizabeth believed it possible he may query the approach with Seth, which would commence an unpleasant ending for them all. On the other hand, to let this opportunity go was something she knew Judas and Mary Magdalene would not want her to do. Elizabeth therefore suggested to Hannah that she be as straightforward as possible: "Just keep things very simple, Hannah — I don't want you getting into trouble. Tell Jeremiah that his two sisters and four brothers send their love and have asked if there is anything he needs. But should he react in a spontaneous way and deny he has such a family, try to brush it off as unimportant and suggest your friend must have been mistaken."

Hannah thought for a moment while rehearsing the scenario in her mind, and then raised an important point, saying, "Elizabeth, let's not forget that Jeremiah has been very ill and may be anxious or confused about many things, so he could have forgotten that he has a family, but what if he accepts what I say and then asks who the message is from? Perhaps you should tell me the name of the relative you know, which would hopefully prove that I wasn't fabricating a story."

Elizabeth had to be careful and take into account that Hannah may one day be indiscreet and share details of her exploits with others. But at the same time, she needed to use a name that could easily be identified by Jesus should the patient turn out to be him. Preferring not to suggest the name Judas because it was much talked about at the time, she chose instead to use the name Martha, and responded to Hannah's observations, saying, "You are correct, Hannah — he may well ask for proof, so perhaps you could say that his sister, Martha, is sending the message, but only do so if he appears to otherwise believe you. If he immediately dismisses the idea that he has such a family and suggests you are being mischievous, do not pursue matters; make an apology and leave as soon as you can and report to me. But if he seems to only be asking for further information or proof, tell him Martha is a friend of someone you work with, and then ask if he'd like to pass a message in response. But please be careful, Hannah — you know what Seth is like — if Jeremiah denies your suggestion about his family or appears to have lost his memory as part of his illness, do not push the issue or it will cause untold trouble."

Hannah understood completely, and did not intend to take any risks that would result in being on the receiving end of the wrath of Seth. She was confident about the plan and excited to be involved, and from Elizabeth's perspective, Hannah being so willing to participate was more than she'd hoped for. Even though there was no guarantee that Jeremiah would respond in the way she hoped, Elizabeth knew that attempting to make contact and assess his true identity was something she had to do, and a risk she had to take.

* * *

Hannah was alone with Jesus first-thing every morning, and could hardly wait for the chance to share what she knew. However, in her excitement she didn't quite maintain the careful discretion Elizabeth had instructed, but fortunately that did not matter. As soon as the guard was out of range, Hannah quietly whispered, "Jeremiah — I have a message to pass on from a family friend, but you must promise not to mention this to your brother, Seth, or I will be in such trouble."

Jesus was a little startled at such a revelation, particularly as it came from a young, somewhat excitable girl he'd only recently become acquainted with. Even though his initial reaction was to wonder if this was Seth up to his old tricks, he realised when looking into Hannah's eyes that she exuded innocence and honesty, so in a rather bemused way he whispered back, "Your secret is safe with me."

Almost bursting with nervous energy, Hannah leaned in towards Jesus and said, "I have a message from your family — your two sisters and four brothers said to say hello."

Jesus stared blankly at Hannah and was momentarily speechless and unsure how to respond, but noticing that he seemed unconvinced, Hannah quickly exclaimed, "It is Martha — I work alongside someone who knows your sister, Martha. She asked if there was anything she could do for you, and said to let you know everyone is well."

Had Elizabeth considered that Hannah might so easily divulge such vital information, and not do as instructed and await Jeremiah's reaction, she would probably not have enlisted her help, but fortunately there was nothing to fear from such disclosures. Quickly gathering his thoughts, Jesus overcame his astonishment immediately, saying, "Oh, my dear Martha – how thoughtful of her to contact me. Please – tell Martha I will soon be well enough to meet her. Tell her it won't be long before I can travel, and I will join the family in due course."

The suddenness of Jesus's response surprised Hannah, but she was relieved not to have to convince him further and was very pleased with herself; not only for succeeding in her mission, but for having an entire message to pass back to Elizabeth.

As she rushed to complete her duties in an effort to return to the kitchen and give Elizabeth the news, Jesus cautioned her when leaving, saying, "My child, please take care that you are not overheard passing on my message to your friend. My tedious brother tries to control everything. I understand he wants to see me recuperate, but he has no patience with Martha and would not be pleased to learn of our conversation. However, I'm very grateful to you for passing on this message and taking such a risk in the process."

Hannah understood the need to keep news of this episode from Seth – she'd worked at the Barbelo compound for long enough to know exactly what he was like. Reassuring Jesus of her diligence, she confidently responded, "Don't worry, I'll be very careful. I believe it is good for you to learn that your family is thinking of you – should there be any more messages I will immediately pass them on."

* * *

Hannah returned to the kitchen, bursting with excitement and seeking out Elizabeth immediately, indicating they needed to find time alone to talk: "I have spoken to Jeremiah," she whispered impatiently, "we need to speak privately – he said I should be careful."

Barely able to contain her anxiety, Elizabeth quickly assessed the situation and ushered Hannah to step outside the rear entrance to the kitchen, while eagerly asking to be told what had happened.

"He seemed surprised at first," said Hannah in hushed tones while glancing around to make sure no one could overhear, "so I immediately mentioned the name, Martha, and then he appeared to understand. I didn't need to persuade him — he believed me straight away."

Elizabeth was desperate for information and impatiently demanded, "Yes, but what did he say — was there a message? Did he just say thank you — what did he say, Hannah?"

Hannah was a little bewildered at the angst shown by Elizabeth, so quickly replied, "Oh yes, there was a message. Jeremiah said to tell Martha that he was fine. I think he said he would soon be ready to travel, and would meet the family in due course."

Elizabeth could no longer contain her distress, and with red-faced annoyance she asked, "You 'think' he said he'd soon be ready to travel and meet his family — what do you mean — did he say that or not? Did he say where he'd meet them — he must have said where, Hannah, surely?"

Hannah was quite taken aback at her friend's sense of urgency and abruptly responded, saying, "No, he didn't say 'where', Elizabeth. Why would he? He probably meant he'd meet them at home. He'd be unlikely to mean anywhere else and I didn't think it was my place to ask. Besides, you didn't tell me to question him in such a way — you said to keep things straightforward so that is what I did. I thought you'd be pleased with this result."

Elizabeth realised she was over-reacting and had aroused Hannah's suspicions somewhat, so immediately reined in her emotions, saying, "Of course, Hannah — of course he was referring to meeting the family at home. I apologise — I didn't mean to sound impatient. I will tell Martha the next time I see her, and if she has any more messages I'll let you know."

Another servant suddenly approached, enquiring what the whispering was about, and for a moment Hannah looked as though she could not wait to tell, but Elizabeth's glare told her otherwise. Realising she had to be careful because Hannah was rather immature and easily persuaded, Elizabeth knew this system could not be used for passing serious messages. Nevertheless, she appreciated that what she had achieved was hugely significant: not only had she obtained information that almost certainly meant Jeremiah was Jesus, but also that he intended to meet up with his family soon. Elizabeth was sure that Jesus probably meant he would try to escape, follow the contingency plan, and head to the coast, since he was unlikely to risk travelling to Nazareth or any other locations that had been his home in recent years.

With only a few days remaining before her temporary job expired, Elizabeth needed to think seriously if there was anything more she could achieve before her time at Barbelo was up.

* * *

Jesus was so shell-shocked when Hannah departed that he didn't know what to think. He considered this could be a hoax organised by Seth, and even wondered if his young caregiver could be planning a sequence of supposed secret messages to extract information that would disclose Martha's whereabouts. Jesus knew he needed to be careful, and was confident he had not yet given anything away that could lead to Martha being discovered. However, despite his concerns he believed Hannah was telling the truth, since she did not seem capable of participating in a complex series of exchanges designed to in some way trap him or his family.

Jesus assumed that somehow Martha must have learned what had happened and was trying to contact him, which was a much-needed boost to his morale, but in reality this situation was nothing more than the result of Elizabeth's ingenuity in attempting to discover his identity. At that time, Martha had no idea Jesus was alive and was making her way to the coast alone; she actually knew very little of anything that was transpiring in Jerusalem.

Jesus was now more motivated and determined than ever, and felt the desire to escape the compound as soon as he was strong enough to travel. He had not acknowledged to his caregivers how far he'd progressed physically, and he intended to keep up that pretence a while longer. He knew that once he appeared to be more able, Seth would add extra security and no doubt begin to place expectations upon him for whatever was in the making. However, believing that his family was safe gave Jesus the confidence he needed in preparing to deal with Seth. No matter what threats he made,

Jesus now felt assured they could not possibly be carried out because the message from Hannah indicated his family was safe and well.

Believing that if any more messages were to come from Martha they would take a few days to be received, Jesus used his time wisely. He began to plan an escape, and took the time to observe closely when people changed shifts, exactly when meals were delivered, as well as the intricacies of Seth's schedule. He also decided to be more responsive towards Seth in order to lead him into a false sense of security; giving the impression he would consider cooperating with his plans as long as he understood the purpose behind them. However, the reality was – he'd had enough. As soon as a plan to flee was formulated in his mind, he fully intended to pursue it.

* * *

The next few days went slowly for Elizabeth; for the life of her she could not think what would be an appropriate and safe message to pass through Hannah. She desperately wanted to provide information about Judas's condition and whereabouts, but there was no way Hannah could be trusted with that. In the end, Elizabeth concluded that she'd done all she could, and because it was now approaching six weeks since the crucifixion, she wanted in many ways to leave immediately and raise the alarm. However, she argued with herself that there was merit in seeing through the few remaining days of her employment, since if Jeremiah really was Jesus, there was now an opportunity for him to pass a more significant message via Hannah, particularly once he'd had time to consider his options.

For his part, Jesus had hoped more information would be forthcoming from Hannah, but did not feel confident in using this method of communication to provide explicit details of what he had planned. He was also becoming increasingly frustrated that the rare visits by Seth were not producing any insight into what he had in store, and it was clear to Jesus that Seth was biding his time. However, unbeknown to Seth, so was Jesus. He needed to be fully recovered before an escape was truly feasible, and even though that day was not far off, he had already decided he was not going anywhere until Seth explained why he had been kept alive. He appreciated that the resurrection story did not require his survival, and if anything it placed the 'miracle' in jeopardy, so Jesus was certain Seth must have a complex strategy in mind, and was determined to discover what that was before putting an escape into action.

* * *

As part of developing his break-out, Jesus needed to devise a way of becoming familiar with the layout of the Barbelo compound and discover where it was located in relation to Jerusalem. In befriending the night guard by engaging him in general conversation and making fun of Seth, Jesus managed to extract quite a bit of information about the surrounding area, but in order to discover the layout of the building in readiness for an escape, he needed to persuade the guard to join him in relieving the boredom and exercise around the compound at night. Although reluctant to consider such a thing initially, Jesus was very persuasive and as somewhat of an incentive for the guard, he suggested they always return via the kitchen to look for something interesting to eat and drink. With a little encouragement, the guard finally agreed, and a nightly routine ensued.

On one particular evening, as they approached the kitchen on the return part of their outing, they could see from a distance that it was not in total darkness. The guard became concerned and asked that they immediately retreat, but for Jesus this made the adventure a little more interesting. Much to the guard's dismay, Jesus proceeded to stride on ahead, confidently marching into the kitchen and gesturing a kindly, "Good evening," to the person finishing off her work.

As the woman turned in fright at being approached so suddenly in the dark of night, Jesus smiled to reassure her, saying, "Do not be alarmed – what is your name?"

Nervously, she replied, "Elizabeth – my name is Elizabeth – can I get you something?"

At that moment the frantic guard appeared behind Jesus, suggesting rather impatiently that they should both return to his quarters. Instantly, Elizabeth calculated that this must be the guarded patient – she could hardly believe her eyes — Jesus was standing in front of her, yet she was speechless and could not think of anything to say.

Jesus noted the increased anxiety Elizabeth displayed, which he considered unusual. He thought that if anything her reaction to the guard's presence should have been the opposite: someone who was dealing with an unknown intruder should not have been more nervous at the guard's arrival, but less so.

Continuing to monitor Elizabeth's anxiety, Jesus ignored the guard's request to return to his quarters and settled himself in the kitchen as he glanced around looking for something to eat. Predictably, the guard reacted nervously and mumbled something about potentially losing his job, to which Jesus retorted that he would be better off if he did. As the guard sighed in frustration, he gave up and took a seat — he knew there was no point in arguing with his roguish friend.

"Elizabeth, rest your feet and allow me to provide some refreshments," said Jesus as he strode around the kitchen as if it were his own.

"I couldn't hear of it — please — allow me," responded Elizabeth.

As he continued to observe the unusually nervous reaction to his presence, Jesus decided to take the plunge, and asked, "Are you by any chance a friend of my lovely caregiver, Hannah?"

Elizabeth took a deep breath, since she was sure Jesus was trying to discover if she was the messenger. By now, the guard was paying no attention to the conversation and was focused on eating whatever Jesus passed in his direction, so Elizabeth decided to be bold in her response, saying, "Yes, I am a friend of Hannah — and I am also a friend of Martha."

Jesus's tone instantly became serious as he made eye contact with Elizabeth, before turning towards the guard to see if he'd noticed the exchange.

"Really," said Jesus, doing his best to sound indifferent, "that's interesting. As you may know, Martha took very good care of me for a long time. Next time you see her, tell her — tell her there's a different ending in sight. She'll understand — it's a private joke. She'll laugh at that."

Elizabeth knew full well this was no joke, and replied clearly, "There is a different ending in sight. I'll be sure to pass that on."

There was so much more Elizabeth wanted to say, but she did not dare. The guard was within feet of them both, and she was just grateful he had been momentarily preoccupied before impatiently insisting he and Jesus depart.

Realising how shaken Elizabeth was, Jesus took the few remaining

OLIVIA OSBORNE

moments before leaving to reassure her. Placing his hands on her shoulders, he whispered, "God loves you." Elizabeth could not move a muscle in response. Jesus's energy was overwhelming; his eyes pierced into hers. She had never witnessed such strength, compassion, and determination emanating from one human being in her life. Elizabeth knew that this was a moment she would never forget.

As the two men went on their way she stood in silence, contemplating the enormity of what had just occurred. Having only returned to the kitchen that evening to attend to something minor, Elizabeth was astounded at the coincidence that Jesus and his guard should pass by at precisely that moment. It was times such as this that left her in no doubt she was doing the right thing, and that her instincts had been correct from the start.

With only one more day of employment to fulfill, Elizabeth could not wait to leave Barbelo and let Mary Magdalene and Judas know of what she had learned. When setting out on this mission she had not imagined so much would be discovered, and even though she had no idea what was going to happen next, or how Mary Magdalene was going to cope when dealing with such an outcome, Elizabeth was now confident that things would find a way of working themselves out in the end.

* * *

Early one morning, a day or so after the encounter with Elizabeth in the kitchen, Seth arrived for what Jesus assumed would be another meaningless visit. However, his demeanour was markedly anxious as he approached, which suggested to Jesus that this meeting was going to be quite different to all the others.

Despite Seth being somewhat confused by Jesus's newly acquired non-confrontational approach, he remained determined and focused and was not in the mood to play games. Abruptly diverting from his usual small-talk, Seth got straight to the point.

CHAPTER FOURTEEN

THE MOST UNLIKELY TRUTH EMERGES

y work with you is almost complete," announced Seth as he brusquely dismissed the guard upon entering Jesus's room. "Your work," Jesus retorted sarcastically, "precisely what do you mean by that?"

Glancing at Jesus in an attempt to fully detect his mood before responding, Seth continued: "I have all I need – I have your story and your sacrifice; your divinity is established in the minds of enough people, and further enhancements to the story will be determined as time progresses and situations demand."

Somewhat perplexed, Jesus interrupted, asking, "But what is it you want with me, Seth? All you've achieved could easily have been accomplished with me dead. Why did you bring me here? My family – do they know I'm alive? What is this all about, Seth?"

Observing that Seth was having difficulty gathering his thoughts but recognising all was about to be revealed, Jesus altered his tone and waited in silence as Seth commenced: "I'm going to release you, so don't bother with your plans to escape. I haven't achieved all I would have liked, but you're well enough to go on your way, so there's no longer a reason to detain you. It's too late for you to undo the work of the Movement and there's no point in trying – you would not succeed in any event. They've established control in these parts already; you'd be arrested instantly and they'd assert you were yet another eccentric impostor claiming to be Jesus returned from the dead. Your followers are now convinced of your divinity and they're terrified you'll come back to judge them — they'd be more than happy for you to be condemned as an impostor. The Movement has what they want; I remained faithful to my commitment to them, and now I'm offering you freedom."

Jesus stared at Seth in disbelief, saying, "If you really expect me to believe you're going to let me walk out of here, you will have to provide more convincing information than that, Seth."

With a slight smile on his face, Seth replied, "I did not expect you to believe me – well, not at first, but you will eventually, of that I am sure."

Jesus was not at all amused, and angrily retorted, "Seth, I have known you and your cohorts for too long – no decision is ever made by the Movement without the end-result being of benefit to them and no one else, so please don't waste your time or mine, and get to the point."

"Who said anything about this being a decision of the Movement," Seth snapped back, "this is my own decision, Jesus – mine alone. If you want freedom, you do as I say or we will both be done for."

Being more than a little surprised at this disclosure, Jesus responded, "Your decision alone – oh, come on, Seth. What next – are you going to tell me you kept me alive to relieve your conscience – is that what this is? I find it hard to believe that no one from the Movement has any idea that I'm alive. Surely they have a multitude of absurd ideas they plan to force upon me while under threat – isn't that a little closer to the truth Seth? You can't seriously expect me to believe that I'm suddenly a free man. You know that the moment I step out of here I'd overturn the ridiculous resurrection claims, not to mention the outrageous accusations of betrayal against Judas that only you could be responsible for perpetrating."

Seth took a seat as he permitted Jesus to react in the way he had anticipated, and leaning forward in his chair, staring into the ground, he sighed deeply as he tried to maintain his composure before beginning to explain: "I know there's no reason for you to trust me, or to believe that releasing you is not a trap, but if you listen to what I have to say, you'll know I'm telling the truth. I had made safe arrangements for your family, but I wish you'd trusted me and not made plans of your own. Judas and Martha are missing – I don't know where they are, but I believe that Judas is most likely dead. Things did not go to plan; he didn't do as I asked. He took matters into his own hands and appears to have paid the highest price.

"I did manage to locate him before the trial, but he was collapsed and drunk in an alleyway off the main square in Jerusalem. I brought him around and arranged for my guards to escort him to the safe-house. He promised to stay there until I returned, but things took much longer than I'd anticipated. I suspect he became impatient and anxious, and took his chance to escape when the guard fell asleep, but I really have no idea what happened next. A few of your followers claim to have seen someone resembling Judas beaten and left for dead on the street. I immediately searched the entire vicinity with my men, but there was no sign of him. The most I can hope is that your followers mistakenly identified him, or perhaps someone helped him – I really don't know. That's as much as I can tell you.

"As for Martha – I can't find her either. She didn't arrive at the safe-house after departing from Bethany on the night of the last supper. I have no idea what happened to her; all I hope is that you know where she went. I've searched, but can find no trace. Your mother and James have returned to Nazareth; they are both well. Mary Magdalene is still here in Jerusalem, but she has no idea you're alive. I'm going to encourage her to return to Magdala to be with her brother. Her work is now complete, and it wouldn't be safe for her to remain here alone since matters are going to become more contentious than they are already."

Jesus was somewhat concerned because this did not correspond with the message he'd received from Elizabeth via Hannah, which suggested his entire family was safe. He could only hope that the fact they were missing as far as Seth was concerned simply meant they'd avoided him and escaped. However, he was astounded to learn of the reason Judas was missing from the final gathering at the Bethany house – he found this impossible to believe: it was so completely out of character for him to drink to excess in this way.

Anxiously, Seth waited in anticipation as Jesus absorbed all he'd said, while feeling certain of the question that was to come next.

"You're right, Seth," Jesus began reluctantly, "I do know where Martha went. It was not to your safe-house – it was one of our own choosing. I didn't trust that she would be safe with you. However, I'm concerned mostly about Judas at this point. Did he explain why he'd been drinking so heavily and was unable to carry out his commitments?"

Seth nodded, reluctantly, saying, "Yes, he did explain and I did my best to put him right. I'd hoped to find Martha at the safe-house since she'd have done a better job than I at convincing Judas, but she wasn't there. I had to leave him alone with my guard."

Jesus was still confused and asked, "Convince Judas of what Seth? Had he heard that I'd planned my arrest? What did you need to persuade him of? What was his reason for being so drunk?"

Seth took a deep breath before disclosing what he appreciated was going to be very upsetting to Jesus: "I was as shocked by this as I know you're going to be. Judas hadn't discovered your plans; he'd become disillusioned and depressed, partly due to the stress of the ministry and the way it turned out, but his main anxiety was due to feeling of no value and as though he was someone you felt obliged to have around."

Seth went on to explain in detail all that Judas had shared on that fateful day, which left Jesus completely stunned and lost for words. He could not believe his most beloved brother and friend could have lived with the impression that he was not valued. For Judas to have thought he was pitied and included in the ministry because it was felt he was a responsibility, was the most preposterous idea he'd ever encountered. Initially, Jesus didn't react to Seth's statement, and was so dismayed by the revelation that he hadn't noticed Seth had ceased talking. Shaking his head Jesus said, "This cannot possibly be true, Seth; he knew how much he was valued and needed. Even you knew that. I never agreed to anything without asking Judas first. Is that not true, Seth?"

"Yes, I know that's true," replied Seth rather halfheartedly, "and believe me I explained that to Judas. I told him that never a single meeting ended without you deferring your decision to discuss it with Judas and Martha. He seemed willing to listen, which is why I'd hoped to find Martha at the safe-house — she'd have been able to explain so much more, and dismiss the notion he'd acquired as a result of being continuously taunted by so many of your followers. Unfortunately, it appears that his experiences leading up to the last supper were as much as he could take. He knew from our obvious anxiety that much more was going on than we were admitting, and felt that being asked to escort Martha to the safe-house, and thereby being excluded from the meeting at the Bethany house with the followers, was proof that he wasn't considered an integral part of the ministry. Being charged with doing what he perceived equated to a minder's job, which any one of my guards could have done, made him feel as though his contribution at the meeting was considered negligible. To Judas, it felt as though you were patronising him and placing importance on the assignment of escorting Martha to make him feel as though his service was of value."

Jesus was completely astounded, and even though he tried – he could think of no reason why Seth would make up something like this. For as long as he could recall, Judas had been his closest confidante along with Martha and John. In disbelief, he questioned himself as to how a situation like this could have developed. Turning to Seth, Jesus said, "I need to get out of here and I need to find Judas, but you have to answer my questions. Why did you do this – keep me alive? And why is it that people have been led to believe that Judas betrayed me when you know full well he did not? I understand your incentive behind the resurrection story, but nothing else you've said makes sense. What am I to do once I'm free? You must have a plan, Seth. I need to know, and I need to know now. I can't leave here until you tell me why you kept me alive."

Seth encouraged Jesus to sit calmly while he explained: "You have to know that this outcome is the last thing I wanted to happen. I fully understand why you expected the Movement would harm Judas and Martha, and you were right — it was their intention. However, I personally could never have hurt them, and I think deep down you know that, but I couldn't confide in you. There were things you'd never have agreed to and it was too late – I had to go through with the plans – everything was beyond my control. By the time I understood the extent of the long-term strategy of those in charge of the Movement, matters had progressed too far - much was at stake, and I couldn't stop the chain of events. If I'd stood up to them, they would simply have replaced me with someone who'd have had no problem disposing of you all."

Pausing for breath, Seth came to his feet and paced the room as he got into his stride: "I fully intended to take care of Judas and Martha, but I had to be seen to be fulfilling my role. With Judas safe, I was confident in diverting search parties in the opposite direction. The story of Judas's betrayal, and the hunt for him that ensued, was part of the Movement's original plan and had to take place, but I had not anticipated Judas being drunk and not safely hidden before having to move into that phase of the operation. It was fortunate that I found him beforehand and took him to safety, but it was because I had been instructed to have Judas and Martha disposed of that I needed them hidden. My superiors were keeping a close eye on my activities, and were suspicious of where my sympathies lay due to how much I'd argued on your behalf. However, they couldn't replace me because of the personal relationship we'd developed. I was the go-between, and they knew you'd have been very uncooperative had I suddenly disappeared. The most they could do was maintain a watchful eye on proceedings, which is why I was so anxious when Judas went missing on the evening of the last supper. It was the last thing I needed to happen.

"My plan had been to ensure that Judas and Martha were safe, and when the crucifixion was over I intended to personally escort them away from the area. At that point, I only intended to tell them their lives were in danger from the Movement and that I was supposed to have arranged for their demise. My plan was to meet them again a few days later at a more secure location away from Jerusalem. At that time I'd hoped to give them the news that you were alive and recuperating. Of course, I'd also have had to divulge the betrayal story, but simultaneously I'd have convinced them of what I'm about to convince you.

"The betrayal story was an important and integral part of the Movement's tactics. I had to be seen to go through with it; otherwise, I'd have been disposed of and someone else would have perpetrated the rumour. By me being removed, not only would Judas and Martha have been murdered, but I wouldn't have been able to continue with the rest of my plans, which was to attempt keeping you alive. I openly demonstrated outrage at Judas to your followers and appeared determined to find him, even though I knew he was in hiding and under guard. However, when your followers claimed they'd seen someone resembling Judas on the street, I subsequently learned from my guard that he had escaped the safe-house. All I could do at that point was conduct house-to-house searches in the vicinity he was supposedly seen, and urge your followers to continue the search that was ongoing, but reiterating the importance that Judas be brought to me for questioning. However, my guess is that some of your followers had already discovered him and attacked in revenge. Judas was oblivious to the betrayal story, and when escaping the safe-house he'd not have known he was being searched for. He probably came across a situation with the followers that he didn't understand, but I did everything I could to prevent this from occurring, Jesus – you have to believe me."

Jesus sat in silence, making no gesture of any kind while Seth paused momentarily to gather his thoughts. In realising Jesus was not going to contribute, Seth continued: "My conscience could no longer tolerate participating with the organisation I'd represented to you, so you were correct about that being part of my motivation. I couldn't tell you any of this beforehand because you'd never have agreed to the plans I had to pursue — you'd not have allowed Judas to be portrayed in such a light, or the resurrection story to be established. But my superiors were aware I was weakening; we'd had many arguments and I knew they were watching us all. If there had been any indication that I wasn't going to produce the results required, they'd have disposed of me and some ruthless individual would have taken my place; one who wouldn't have hesitated in murdering you all.

"Of course, I couldn't confide in anyone, and could not promise your family that you'd survive the crucifixion — I only hoped I could judge it effectively. However, I had every chance in succeeding at saving Judas and Martha had things not gone so terribly wrong. That's what is so frustrating – the most difficult challenge was keeping you alive, yet the less complex goal of keeping Judas and Martha safe could not have gone more wrong if I'd tried.

"I'm sorry that the flogging you received was so severe, but I needed you exhausted and unconscious as soon as possible. There had to be an excuse for me to instruct you be brought down from the cross early, and being rendered unconscious and appearing to be dead was the only hope I had of keeping you alive. However, a fraction of good fortune came my way in the form of Pontius Pilate, who appeared to regret participating with the Movement. It was actually he who insisted in front of everyone that the episode be brought to an early conclusion, which meant that the risk of me being accused of doing anything untoward was removed entirely.

"I couldn't confide in you because I knew you'd never have agreed to any of this. If I'd told you ahead of time about the betrayal and resurrection plans, you would have attempted to escape the area with your family and followers, and would undoubtedly have been hunted down and killed. My superiors didn't care how their martyr died; they'd have spun the story to meet their needs.

"Jesus, I promise you, I did my absolute best with a complex set of circumstances that I lost control of, and I am just so sorry I cannot confirm the safety of Judas and Martha."

Seth stopped talking for a few moments as he collected his thoughts, but Jesus remained silent and completely stunned by what he was discovering. All he could think about was the message from Elizabeth indicating his family was safe, but now he had renewed concerns about

Judas, which coincided with the story his guard had offered several weeks earlier. He began to wonder if his family was keeping that from him until he'd fully recovered by asking Elizabeth to suggest all was well. His mind was racing with all sorts of scenarios, but as he tried to regain his composure and prepare for more disclosures, Seth appeared ready to recommence:

"If I'd known at the outset what the long term plans of the Movement were, I'd never have become involved. I'd been led to believe something that was so far from the truth, and by the time I became aware of their ambitions I was implicated to such an extent that I would not have been permitted to walk away – I knew too much. They told me only what I needed to know, Jesus. You have to believe me. They used me, and I know full well they intend to dispose of me now they are aware I've lost admiration for their goals.

"Unfortunately, because the search for Judas went on for so long they became suspicious of why I needed to maintain what they assumed was a pretence, so even though I desperately needed to find Judas I had to call off the search and hope that neither he nor Martha turned up without realising what damage that could do. I have to admit that more could have been done to locate Judas, but by pursuing a search for any longer than was deemed necessary for effect, I was creating questions that were difficult to answer. The more doubts that arose due to my behaviour, the more likely it was that they would dispose of me, which would have resulted in you being discovered.

"Because my superiors believed I'd arranged for Judas and Martha to be killed and that the search for Judas was a ruse to support the betrayal story, I had to explain away the body mistaken for Judas by saying it was a vagrant, and they seemed to accept that. However, if either Judas or Martha is discovered while the two of us remain here in Barbelo, it will be the end of the road for us all. They believe I removed your body from the tomb and disposed of it. Everyone assumed you were dead, and I admit it was a close call. I had no idea whether you were dead or alive, but I knew you were strong, and I knew that as long as I didn't allow you to remain on the cross for too long, I had a chance to let you live. I couldn't have your blood on my hands."

Seth seemed to get lost in his ramblings as he confessed to Jesus what lay behind his motivations: "I thought these disenchanted people who'd organised themselves so well were good and sound. They're from all sorts of backgrounds and cultures and their goals appeared to be of noble cause. I joined them because I liked what I heard and wanted to impress and achieve status within their group. We needed someone different as our icon; someone outspoken and with courage, ideals, and conviction. We needed someone who dared to stand up and say what he felt. I genuinely liked what you stood for. However, I was completely unaware that the Movement had a set of ideals and only required someone with appeal that they could use as a symbol. They intend to take the story of your life and death and use it as a basis for what they want to achieve – total domination over all the people. They will achieve it under the guise of 'spreading the word', but your *word* has already been radically misrepresented and there was nothing I could do to stop them. In the end, I decided more could be achieved by going along with their plans while attempting to create a different outcome for you and your family. If I'd told you everything, you'd have tried to escape, and they'd have hunted all three of you down. You would all have been killed; the Jews would have been blamed, and you'd have been martyred in that way. The plan I developed was the only one where something of substance could be achieved.

"My goal now is to ensure you get out of here. I'll provide you with money, food and clothing to help you on your way, and if you have plans to connect with Martha, then go ahead and do so if it's not too late. If she is alive, I'm certain she will have heard of the resurrection story by now, and possibly the betrayal rumour; the Movement dispersed preachers far and wide to spread the news. Martha will no doubt have guessed that Mary Magdalene was coerced into the resurrection story, but there is no way she would suspect that you are alive and will probably be proceeding alone with whatever plans you had in place."

Seth was exhausted and strained, and became impatient when anticipating a reaction of some sort: "For goodness sake, Jesus – speak. Say something – don't just stare blankly at me in that way."

Appreciating there was no doubt Seth was telling the truth, Jesus responded in a quiet manner, saying, "I understand how this situation could have developed, and how you found yourself in a position of not being able to turn back. And you are correct – I would never have agreed to any of this, particularly not your decision to accuse Judas of such absurd actions.

But tell me — why did they have to blame Judas? Why did betrayal such as that have to come into the picture at all?"

Seth bowed his head and sighed, before revealing what he knew: "Judas was chosen from all of the disciples because he was the closest to you, so his betrayal would be even more abhorrent. He was also the only one who'd be universally accepted by the others as a betrayer, since there was already considerable resentment towards him due to his close relationship with you. It was an easy sell, and one your followers were more than happy to embrace.

"Betrayal became part of the scenario to instill guilt and create a deterrent for those who may consider turning their back on the Movement. Judas is to be an example — an example of weakness, a lack of faith, greed, and betrayal. They want to use him to represent the worst in mankind. They'll portray him as someone nobody else would want to be compared with. They want people to feel that not committing to the rigours of religion equates to succumbing to one of Judas's characteristics. He'll be known as someone who became a coward when the going got tough; someone who turned and walked away in spite of how much you'd done for him. People will be led to believe they are the sinner that is Judas, and you represent the perfection they should seek to achieve. Guilt will be instilled from indoctrination at a young age, and it will be impressed that you died on the cross for us: a flock of worthless sinners who should spend life repenting to demonstrate an appreciation of you. They will make promises of an eternal life, and offer admittance into the kingdom of God in exchange for a commitment to the Movement. In addition, people will be convinced that their sins can be forgiven by leaders of the Movement, who will claim they possess the ability to intercede with God on behalf of the faithful. In other words, the betrayal story is probably the most significant component of your life-story, since on a deep psychological level it will prevent the indoctrinated from walking away — their conscience would not permit it.

Seth looked on with uncertainly as Jesus stood and began pacing the room in an attempt to preserve his composure. He knew that his reaction to these revelations was of paramount importance: if Jesus decided to throw caution to the wind and react blindly to what he was learning, Seth knew that neither of them would survive.

Seething with anger and not knowing where to direct his rage, Jesus confronted Seth, saying, "If you feel so strongly about what the Movement is achieving, why participate in the ridiculous resurrection claims? Why did you coerce Mary Magdalene into this? You could have confided the fact that I was alive to my mother, James, and Mary Magdalene; they'd not have deceived you. Come on Seth, you did have other options."

Seth bowed his head reluctantly. He knew the resurrection story would be upsetting to Jesus, so did his best to explain: "Along with the story of Judas, the resurrection had been an integral part of this phase of your so-called life-story. It had to be seen to occur within a few days of your crucifixion for maximum impact. It was a matter of striking while the iron was hot. Again, I had no choice but to go along with their plans. In fact, it was more important than ever that I did absolutely nothing to upset them and produce the results they required. At that time you'd barely been here three days, and your survival was still uncertain. Judas and Martha were missing, and I was desperately searching for them. If I had refused to proceed with the resurrection plans I'd have lost control over everything, including my own survival. I had no alternative but to participate, as it would have occurred without my assistance. By me not cooperating with the resurrection, you would have been discovered by whoever took over my responsibilities; our lives would have been brought to a brutal end, and an immediate all-out hunt for Judas and Martha would have followed."

In disbelief, Jesus looked at Seth while trying to think of a point he could make, but it was impossible to argue. While it was clear he was telling the truth, Jesus still wondered why Seth hadn't solved many of his problems by confiding in his family: "I do now understand why you needed to proceed with the resurrection plans," Jesus confessed, "but I still don't see why you didn't unburden some of this responsibility by divulging the situation to James and mother. By doing so, you'd at least have been able to contact Martha; they would have shared that information if you'd told them I was alive."

Seth could see why Jesus would imagine things were that straightforward, but he had not taken into account something substantial. Seth sighed as he contemplated explaining, since this was beginning to feel like a long series of excuses, but they were all valid points: "As strange as it may sound, I could not trust your mother, James, or Mary Magdalene. I was certain that someone would eventually inform your mother and James of the rumours regarding Judas, and I knew they'd be furious and hold me personally responsible. If I'd confided in them that you were alive and said

I was trying to save your life, they'd have demanded to be taken to see you as proof, which in itself would have caused problems. While your mother would have been grateful, James would have become out of control with rage and insisted on putting a stop to everything, particularly once learning of the rumour concerning Judas. You know what he's like, Jesus – not only would he not have permitted Mary Magdalene to participate with the resurrection story, which in itself would have brought everything to a disastrous end, but he'd have rounded up every follower he could muster and told them everything.

"James is fearless. He wouldn't have cared if he'd died in the process; he'd have been more than happy to go into battle with the Movement. A serious conflict would have broken out, and we'd all have been murdered – we wouldn't have stood a chance, and even your mother would have been included in the massacre. I had plans for your future, but James wouldn't have seen it like that. He's a warrior – he'd have turned up at Barbelo with an army of followers to retrieve your body, and you probably wouldn't have survived such disruption. My medical team told me you were barely alive, and it could be weeks before they were able to guarantee your survival. James would not have listened to any of my advice. He'd have wanted to use the situation to stop the Movement in their tracks at whatever cost, but we both know they would not stand for their plans being disrupted after so much time, money, and effort had been invested.

"To make matters worse, Judas was missing and James would not only have used the fact that you were still alive to disrupt the Movement's plans, but he'd have taken out his revenge on me personally for the disappearance of Judas. If I were dead, the Movement would have discovered you. I couldn't risk being killed by James or your followers while they took matters into their own hands. An ending such as this at the hands of James would have been disastrous; not only for all of us but, more importantly, for the plans I was trying to put together that would eventually stop the progress of the Movement, and effect change throughout the world in centuries to come. James was the last person I could possibly confide in. I had an ending in sight for you Jesus, and it is the only ending that will see any success worth fighting for, but James would not have seen things that way. I'm so sorry, but you have to believe that I considered every possible option and made decisions based upon the risks involved for us all. I had no one to confide in or seek advice from. The Movement was on my back and watching every move I made, and you were lying here almost dead: I could take no chances. Please believe me. I made the only choices I possibly could when taking everything into consideration."

Jesus listened carefully to Seth's pleas and once again found it difficult to argue. He was right – James would have reacted to the situation rather than respond to it. Jesus knew this state of affairs would probably have pushed James over the edge, and the agreement they had reached before the crucifixion not to react to the Movement's antics would have been the last thing on his mind. Jesus realised fairly quickly that there was no point in looking back – he had to look forward.

"Seth – is there anything I can do," implored Jesus, "please tell me – what can be done to turn this around? If I walk out of here now and announce who I am, telling everyone what you've told me, what would happen? Would that not put a stop to this nonsense?"

Seth shook his head resolutely, saying, "Jesus, there are so many people employed by the Movement that you'd immediately be condemned as a blasphemous impostor and arrested. They aren't going to let you or anyone else ruin their plans at this stage. There are already many men claiming to be you miraculously raised from the dead. They're either ignored or laughed at, and those who persist are stoned into silence or arrested. It's been more than six weeks since the crucifixion and Mary Magdalene was very appealing and convincing. My men have continued to spread rumour, and almost all of your followers have been coerced into preaching the Movement's doctrine for fear you may 'return' as prophesised and judge them poorly. They are so convinced of the resurrection story that they'd be terrified if they recognised you, and would likely run and hide in shame."

Jesus thought momentarily before exclaiming in frustration, "Well, you must have a plan of some sort since you're the master of such things, Seth. What do you suggest I do? Clearly you're going to release me, but you know I don't care what happens to me, so what is there to stop me storming out of here and doing my utmost to convince people of the truth. Even if they think I'm crazy, I'll not stop until they stop me. What else am I supposed to do Seth? You kept me alive – you must have had a reason."

Seth understood Jesus's fury and tried to respond calmly. He did have a plan, and now seemed like a good time to reveal it: "I could neither have your blood on my hands, nor could I permit Judas and Martha to be disposed of in the way it was planned. I believe in you, and I respect your passion and courage. I wanted to give you a chance to oppose these people yourself. The only way you could achieve that was if I kept you alive, then released you to travel far and wide to other lands to continue preaching in the way you have for many years. My people have set the groundwork to manipulate your beliefs to accommodate their agenda. However, I felt that with this knowledge you could spend the remainder of your life travelling all over the world teaching, establishing a following, and sowing the seeds of your philosophy.

"Without a powerful movement such as mine supporting you, it will be impossible to become established in the way in which they intend, but you can cause them a lot of difficulty. Be where they are, and go where they won't go; pre-empt them and make your presence felt. Don't become angry and walk out of here declaring who you are, trying to undo what they've already achieved — that will be fruitless, and you'll be arrested and murdered instantly. By doing as I suggest, you will ultimately be remembered in the histories of cultures all over the world as a prophet whose words they may incorporate into their own religions, which was your intention in the first place. This is the only way you can respond. You cannot stop what has already begun — it's too widespread. However, you can make life much more difficult for them. You can spend the rest of your days establishing your truth in the minds and hearts of people from all over the world, and hopefully one day you will be able to do this alongside Judas and Martha, which had been my plan. Don't waste your life in anger, Jesus — go back to doing what you were sent here to do. Spread God's word of compassion, forgiveness, and understanding, and teach humanity what they need to know.

"Jesus, my guards have been dismissed, and I shall personally escort you from this property later tonight, which will give you time to gather your thoughts."

As Seth stood to leave, he looked directly at Jesus and said, "You will never know how sorry I am. Please go quietly and write your own ending. May God be with you for the remainder of your days."

* * *

Later that evening Seth returned as promised, and having dismissed his guards he personally escorted Jesus to safety through a secret exit at the rear of the compound. However, before leaving, Jesus had something important to say: "Seth, after you departed earlier today I felt overwhelmingly angry at the success the Movement has seen by manipulating my message and my life-story, but then something important occurred to me. Throughout all these years I always reconciled that it must be God's will that they succeed and I fail; otherwise, I'm confident these things simply would not be happening. However, as time moved on and we continued to experience defeat after defeat, I began to lose faith. I couldn't understand why those of such despicable nature and ambition would be allowed to succeed and gain so much momentum.

"However, only today did I begin to understand why they have succeeded and why they will likely find even more success over the years. It is down to the choice people make: the choice between whether they listen to their intuitive voice or allow themselves to be intimidated into believing something irrespective of how ridiculous it is. The immediate and long-term consequence of such negative choices means that the world has decided it needs to experience negativity. However, it occurred to me that perhaps this is the way it is supposed to be. After all, how can bliss be appreciated until negativity has been acquainted? People always seem inclined towards learning the hard way; in part because subconsciously they know there is more to be learned from challenges than there is from an easy passage. It therefore seems that people have been provided with a choice: a choice they have now made, with consequences that will have to be borne out.

"I believe that the truth of my ministry and life will not emerge until such time as the world has endured enough negativity and is ready to embrace bliss. By then, people will be desperately searching for something to believe that their intuition tells them makes sense, rather than believing in something through fear, guilt, and ignorance."

Seth was somewhat taken aback at the way Jesus had drawn such a conclusion, which in effect equated to him making peace with the failure of his ministry and accepting that the Movement was meant to succeed. In agreeing with Jesus that he was probably correct, Seth said, "I believe you may be right, but I'd not considered things in that way before. People were exposed to the opportunity of listening to you as much as the Movement's recruits, so it really boiled down to them believing what they wanted to believe. I would agree that much of what has occurred is down to individual choices as much as it is down to the Movement's tactics, but I am just relieved you are not blaming yourself, since no one could have worked more diligently to create a different outcome."

While Jesus appreciated Seth's supportive response, he could not leave him with the impression that he was blameless: "I made many mistakes throughout the ministry, Seth, and you and I don't have to look very far to see what they were. Years before the ministry began my mother warned that I should do as I teach, and even though I have tried I have not always succeeded; sometimes life simply became too overwhelming. The Movement have asserted my infallibility to such a degree that it will be impossible for anyone to even think of aspiring to such heights. However, I am not the infallible, divine son of God and you know that, Seth. I believe my life had a very specific purpose, and I've done my best to fulfill that, but that's all I believe. Like everyone else, I occasionally made decisions based on fear, which produced negative consequences – something my mother warned me against. For example, if I'd found a few moments at the last gathering with my followers to calmly 'listen' when making those vital decisions, I know my intuition would have said to participate with you as it always had in the past. If I'd done that, Judas and Martha would be together and safe, and you'd now be taking me to them. Just look at how everything has turned out as a result of my fear-driven decision not to trust you.

"My failures should be exposed, Seth, and if you are ever in a position to do so, I would be grateful if you did. Is it not true that we learn the most from our mistakes? Then it is obvious that from my faults, mankind could learn the most. Look at the lessons to be learned as a result of what happened to Judas. Once again, I didn't put into practice what I had taught: to prioritise those closest to us. I, of all people, forgot to do that and put my work first. I took Judas for granted, Seth; there is no getting away from that. I obsessively worried about the ministry and encouraged my followers to believe in themselves and their roles, but not once did I remember to tell Judas what he so desperately needed to hear. I assumed it wasn't necessary; that he somehow knew and believed enough in himself. Just look at the price we've all paid for my errors. There is so much for people to learn from this. I'm clearly living the consequence of what happens when such golden rules are forgotten. It would be wasteful for this not to be recorded in history – it would teach people so much.

"Seth, if you have any influence within the Movement, please encourage them to believe that people will never be able to align themselves with me when I'm declared an infallible, divine being. How can they possibly expect others to attain heights that I myself did not accomplish? I should not be remembered as someone I am not – someone who is impossible to emulate."

Seth appreciated Jesus's honesty and desire to take responsibility for his mistakes, but knew he was placing expectations upon himself that were extraordinary. The circumstances he'd lived through did not come close to what another human being would have to withstand. His so-called mistakes had catastrophic outcomes and certainly held lessons for others to absorb, but the Movement would never consider admitting Jesus was a fallible human being. Seth shook his head as if to admit defeat without even considering Jesus's request: "Jesus, the most you can do is record this truth in Martha's diaries. One day, I am sure they'll emerge when people are truly ready to learn. When they are no longer fearful and dependent upon external authorities to dictate to them emotionally, they will embrace your real story and the invaluable lessons it contains: ones that are really quite simple to incorporate into life and will produce unquantifiable benefits for people to enjoy."

Jesus acknowledged that Seth was probably right; he would be laughed at to suggest to his superiors that mistakes as basic as this be incorporated into his life-story for others to learn, but he had one final request before departing: "Seth – my people – the Jews – it concerns me a great deal that not only will they always be held accountable for my death, but they may always feel a level of guilt without understanding what they feel guilty about. I know that those who heard what I said throughout my trial and sentence were affected, and I only hope they will remember it forever. Can you not at least persuade your superiors to take some responsibility for inciting them to react in this way? If not, my people will pass on to future generations an inherent sense of guilt, but it will be a guilt they cannot comprehend because all they are actually guilty of is reacting in fear and anger to the intimidating rhetoric of the Movement – a completely understandable response. They will also carry forward within their culture a need to overcome or to be in control, because they lost control over a situation that may become pivotal in the history of mankind should the Movement continue to progress as they intend. For my own people to forever be condemned as being responsible for so much is a thought I cannot abide, and is something for which they might be expected to pay for in perpetuity."

Seth stepped forward and touched Jesus's arm with kindness and understanding, saying, "I cannot make any promises, but I will see if it's at all possible to persuade my superiors to announce that the Jews be excused and not held accountable for your crucifixion due to the confusion that existed at the time. Unfortunately, I think the most they would agree to state is that they forgive the Jews because they acted against you out of fear. However, for the Jews to accept they are forgiven would imply they believed you were the son of God as well as admitting they'd been wrong, which I'm sure would be unacceptable to them. I also feel that the Movement's motivation for such a gesture would be to make the Jews appear less sophisticated or less evolved as human beings. They would maintain that the Jews acted fearfully and denied the truth of your divinity, since I believe it is the intention of the Movement to portray them as being inferior and unworthy for this reason. No matter what happens, I fear that your people will always possess an inherent sense of guilt, but will also 'know' they did nothing to feel guilty about; a combination that will never bring them peace. The outcome of such incessant confusion will be for an innate sense of doubt to exist among the Jews for all time, coupled with a determination to uphold their beliefs no matter what. Personally, I don't see the Movement being prepared to alleviate that; rather, they will seize the opportunity to present themselves as superior and more highly evolved. I believe that one day in the future they may claim to forgive the Jews for murdering their icon, but that would only be exploiting them further by being seen to take the moral high ground and appearing to forgive. Jesus, I'm afraid I cannot see that there would be humility or genuineness in their approach, and any suggestions I make will probably be manipulated to achieve their goals."

Reluctantly, Jesus acknowledged that Seth was probably correct and accepted defeat that his suggestion had merit. After a moment or two of awkward silence, both men came to the realisation that it was time to part company. As Jesus offered his hand to bid farewell to Seth, he felt a distinct sense of regret at saying goodbye to his old adversary. Consumed in disbelief at the prospects that lay ahead, Jesus searched his mind for sufficient words of gratitude, but as he did so Seth became overwhelmed, and in gesturing that Jesus should leave, he ushered him on his way.

Filled with a sense of triumph, Seth prayed silently to himself as he stood back and watched Jesus take the first steps into the second part of his life – a life story that has never been told, yet its impression was placed upon every culture in the world, establishing an inherent mistrust of Christianity, which remains in existence today.

CHAPTER FIFTEEN

A NEW LIFE IS BORN

PART I – THE UNFORTUNATE ENCOUNTER

For Elizabeth, her final morning at the compound could not arrive soon enough. She awoke feeling enormous relief and excitement at the prospect of leaving Barbelo, and was thrilled at having achieved so much more than she'd imagined possible.

When heading to the kitchen for the final time to begin her morning chores, Elizabeth passed by the office of the head of household and was somewhat surprised to see her friend, Hannah, among a group of servants being assigned duties for the day. As Elizabeth gestured a greeting, Hannah immediately dashed over to her side, breathlessly reporting that Jeremiah had disappeared: "Elizabeth, he's gone – Jeremiah left abruptly without notice during the night. His room has been abandoned and the guards are no longer there."

Of course, Elizabeth feared the worst and her first thought was that something sinister must have happened, although Hannah had no information in that regard. Swiftly putting aside her initial panic, Elizabeth regained her composure and set about discovering whether anything unseemly had been overheard or witnessed during the night. She quickly concluded it was unlikely Jesus had been murdered, but her main concern was that he had been moved to another location in preparation for whatever was in store. In realising that the staff and guards who had been responsible for Jesus were waiting alongside Hannah to be reassigned positions, Elizabeth joined the group under the pretence she was unwell and wanted to request an early release from her post.

However, despite engaging the staff in talk about the turn of events, all that came to light was that Seth had spent several hours alone with Jesus during the previous day, and some observers admitted overhearing raised voices from time to time. Apart from those rather mundane discoveries, there were no witnesses to anything of a troublesome nature, and most people believed that the brothers had simply argued and 'Jeremiah' had departed for that reason.

While it was a relief for Elizabeth that nothing more improper emerged from her investigations, she nevertheless felt an even greater sense of urgency to leave Barbelo and return to Judas and Mary Magdalene sooner rather than later.

* * *

By the time Elizabeth discovered that Jesus had departed Barbelo he was already far from the immediate vicinity of the compound. He had travelled throughout the night in the direction of the Bethany house, which was the only place he believed would provide some degree of safety. Its remote location afforded him the privacy and seclusion he considered necessary to gather his thoughts, and because the house had only ever been used as a meeting place throughout the ministry, he was confident it would by now have been abandoned and therefore provide the security he needed at such a precarious time. Without giving much thought to the future, Jesus prioritised reaching his destination, with the intention of taking his time in becoming accustomed to his new circumstances while formulating a plan of some sort.

* * *

As Elizabeth departed the claustrophobic atmosphere of the compound, she felt somewhat emotional at the relief she encountered – not until the experience was behind her did she appreciate how stressful it had been. Arriving home was something she much looked forward to, and while immediately proceeding in that direction, the realisation of what had been achieved began to sink in. Living under the strain of being discovered as a spy had not provided Elizabeth with the time to appreciate all that had occurred. It was while deep in thought and contemplating the events of the past two weeks, that she was surprised and relieved to discover Mary Magdalene approaching from the opposite direction. She'd travelled the route in the hope of meeting Elizabeth part-way and escorting her back to Jerusalem. She had been anxious to discover if anything new had been learned, and couldn't bear to wait a moment longer than necessary.

As they greeted one another warmly, the two women sought out a secluded place to sit for a while and exchange news. But what Elizabeth was about to disclose, was beyond anything Mary Magdalene could possibly have dared to hope for.

Listening in amazement to Elizabeth's incredible story, Mary Magdalene was speechless — it was overwhelming and almost impossible for her to comprehend at first. Astounded by what she was learning, she trembled in disbelief as Elizabeth explained each step in her process of discovery. Nevertheless, in spite of what was revealed, Mary Magdalene struggled to accept the notion that the person being described was the person she had witnessed crucified just a few weeks before: it seemed entirely implausible.

Despite her doubts, and after questioning every aspect of Elizabeth's story, Mary Magdalene eventually conceded there were too many coincidences. In the end, she felt compelled to acknowledge that the man Elizabeth had encountered must be Jesus.

* * *

It was early morning when Jesus arrived in Bethany, and the sun was just beginning to rise above the hillside beyond the house. Throughout the years of the ministry, the building had been filled with a vibrant, positive energy, and an atmosphere overflowing with hope, enthusiasm, and gutsy determination. Of course, the walls also housed less comforting memories for Jesus, since it was the home of the last supper, and the location of his final farewell to Martha, as well as the last place he'd known freedom. However, Jesus could not help but smile to himself as he appreciated the fact that the Bethany house was now playing another significant part in his life; in becoming the place he would begin to know freedom again.

With so many memories conjuring up a storm of emotion, Jesus approached the house with mixed feelings. As he entered through the back of the building, he was relieved to at least be in familiar surroundings, even though the sense of abandonment that lingered throughout reflected how he'd felt personally from time to time. It had often been difficult for Jesus to continue to believe that God was on his side, and the turbulence of the latter years of his life had tested his faith in everything he believed to be true.

As Jesus slowly walked throughout the property with only memories of the past filling his thoughts, he began to sense someone else was there. Carefully, he continued towards the front of the building, where he came across half a dozen men lying asleep on the floor. Empty goblets and left-over food lay in a disheveled state, and it was clear the men had used the house as an overnight refuge. Wondering if they were some of his own followers, Jesus hesitantly moved a little closer, and as he did so he recognised that they were.

Part of him wanted to wake them and announce himself, but he recalled the advice of Seth and knew it would be far too much of a risk to take at this stage. Deciding he should depart and find somewhere else to rest, Jesus quietly began retreating, trying not to disturb the men. But just as he approached the exit to the room, one of them suddenly awoke, and abruptly called out, "Who's there?"

Jesus froze to the spot in the hope he was not still within view, but the outburst disturbed two or three of the other men, causing them to join in the call for the intruder to announce himself.

Eventually, Jesus slowly turned around in response to their demands, without having any idea what their reaction would be. He stood completely still and waited for someone to speak, but when realising they'd been stunned into silence Jesus stepped forward to offer assurance. As the men struggled to their feet they began to back away in unreserved horror at the *vision* that had appeared before them.

Realising they were afraid, Jesus motioned towards them in a manner he knew would be familiar as he attempted to calm them, but by now they were terrified and huddled together as they backed away as far as they could;

screaming abusively at what they perceived was either an impostor or a terrifying vision. As they covered their faces in shame, they begged to be left unharmed and pleaded they not be punished for their weakness and lack of personal resolve.

Jesus was frustrated to say the least, but nevertheless did all he could to reassure as he approached the men calmly and repeated phrases he knew would be familiar, but his efforts were futile. The commotion awoke the remaining followers, who jumped to their feet and reacted in the same way; appearing equally as traumatised at what they witnessed – Jesus standing before them in all his glory.

While still somewhat under the influence of a considerable amount of wine, the followers didn't know what to make of this person who resembled Jesus, but their immediate thought was to assume their somewhat slovenly approach to attending to the commitments required by the Movement had resulted in their threat actually occurring. They each concluded that Jesus had done as promised in the miracle of resurrection, and returned from the dead to judge them due to their lack of hands-on support of the Movement's ideology.

The chorus of pleas for Jesus to leave was accompanied by promises to change their ways, but Jesus was shocked to discover that what Seth had warned was true. The story of the resurrection had terrified the followers into submission, yet Jesus found it difficult to fathom that after the many years he'd spent encouraging these men to believe in themselves, within a few short weeks of being under the influence of the early Christians a sense of worthlessness and shame had been instilled.

Jesus continued to reassure the men as much as he could, but eventually he appreciated that for his own safety he should depart, but in doing so he made a final effort to be understood, saying, "I can see you're afraid, but there's nothing to be afraid of. I'm not here to judge you. I only want you to remember what we stood for and my words to you at our last supper together. Don't let them manipulate my message for their own gain. I'll leave you, since I don't like to bring such fear into your eyes. There is nothing for you to fear but fear – please remember that."

As he turned and walked away, Jesus left behind a group of emotionally distressed men, who could barely function as a result of the terror consuming them. As far as they were concerned, what Seth and Mary

Magdalene had prophesised had come true – Jesus had returned from the dead to judge the apathy they'd exhibited in supporting the agenda of the Movement.

From that moment on, this group of followers determined they would be in the forefront of every aspect of the Movement's aspirations, since they had now borne witness to the threat encompassed within the miracle of resurrection.

PART II – JUDAS KNEW IT

Mary Magdalene and Elizabeth arrived home exhausted but elated. To Judas, it felt as though he'd waited a year to see them walk through the door, and when the moment finally arrived he was so relieved that he burst into tears. He could see they were beaming, but was so overcome with emotion that he couldn't begin to fathom why they appeared overjoyed – all he cared about was that they'd returned safely.

Holding Judas's hand, Mary Magdalene began by saying, "Elizabeth's stay at the compound has proven to be of immense value, Judas. She discovered that Jesus is alive – Elizabeth has seen him and spoken with him. He sent a message for Martha to say there was a different ending in sight and promised to meet up with us all soon."

For an instant, Judas was speechless, but the moment Mary Magdalene's words registered fully, he exclaimed, "I knew it – I knew it! Somehow, I knew he was alive — I always knew it. Where is he, Elizabeth – is he a prisoner at the compound?"

"I don't know where he is at this point," replied Elizabeth. "He appeared to leave the compound very suddenly late last night, and from my enquiries it seems he had an argument with Seth, but no one knows with any certainty what the reason was behind his sudden departure. He appeared well enough to have escaped, but it is a little mysterious because he was kept under guard at all times, and my concern had always been that he'd eventually be moved to another location once he was well enough. Even though most people assume he left because of an argument with

Seth, they did not know who he was – he was believed to be Seth's somewhat wayward brother, and that pretense was maintained. I suppose it is possible he escaped, but since leaving the compound it has occurred to me that if he had escaped, surely Seth would have been making his presence felt and an all out search would have been conducted. But because that did not happen, I am now somewhat concerned that he may have been moved under guard to another location. I didn't remain at the compound for any longer than I had to, so have no further information than this."

Mary Magdalene could see that Judas was a little deflated at this uncertain outcome, so injected some positive news by saying, "He knows we are all alive, Judas – Elizabeth managed to get a message to him. He also knows about the resurrection and betrayal stories because his caregivers discussed it with him in general conversation. You know what he's like, Judas – once he's well enough he won't tolerate those circumstances for long, and I'm certain that if he's not already escaped, he'll be making inroads to secure his freedom. And the first thing he'll do after that is try to locate one of us, so we have to remain alert at all times, keep a close watch on Seth, and pay attention to any rumours of sightings that emerge."

As Judas listened to all that Elizabeth and Mary Magdalene had to say, he thought for a moment or two before saying, "Elizabeth, you suggest that the only rumour at the compound was that he argued with Seth and departed, and there was no sign of panic as a result of an escape, but do you not agree that it would be unlikely that Seth would raise everyone's suspicions by causing havoc over his 'escaped' brother, which would make people beg the question as to why he was held prisoner when they'd previously assumed the guards were there to protect him while he was ill? I believe, for that reason, that we have an equal chance that we are dealing with an escape as much as we might be dealing with him being transferred elsewhere – just because there was no panic about an escape from the compound, does not necessarily mean that is not what happened. The only other possible scenario of Seth having murdered Jesus is doubtful – he's just spent weeks on end trying to keep him alive, so it would therefore seem highly unlikely that he would kill him at this point.

"The odds of an escape would be increased if we were to discover that groups of Seth's guards were quietly coordinating searches in and around Jerusalem, but if things are not that apparent and Seth appears to be going about his business as normal, then we can assume he's moved Jesus elsewhere. I think one of the first things we need to do is locate Seth and gauge his mood, and see if we can find out what he's up to – then we will have a better idea of what we're dealing with."

Both Mary Magdalene and Elizabeth appreciated Judas's process of elimination and agreed there was as much likelihood that Jesus had escaped as there was that Seth had moved him, but no one was satisfied to sit around and depend only upon interpreting Seth's behaviour and hypothesising. All three agreed that both possibilities needed to be investigated simultaneously, and because Judas had practically lived inside Jesus's head for his entire life, he tried to imagine that if the scenario involved an escape, what would Jesus be likely to do next?

Thinking aloud, Judas said, "He needs to keep a low profile, so he would never come into Jerusalem itself, but would also be unlikely to leave the area without trying to locate one of us first. If he's heard about the resurrection and betrayal stories, as Elizabeth believes is the case, he'll be extremely careful, but it would be my guess that he would head straight to the nearest place he's most familiar with and feels the safest, which is the Bethany house. It's close to Jerusalem but far enough away for him to feel safe. Thanks to Elizabeth, he will know we're looking for him, and Bethany is the only place in this area we are all familiar with. If my circumstances were similar, that's where I would hide initially. Its discreet location means that people can be heard approaching the property, which provides enough time to hide or get out. There is nowhere else he could find safe refuge, since there is no one he can trust. I'm sure he'll take his chances that the Bethany house is deserted and hope to find at least one of us there."

Mary Magdalene agreed entirely with Judas's assessment of the situation, and after some consultation, it was agreed that while it was important to locate Seth and try to assess what had gone on, there was no point in delaying investigating the other potential scenario of Jesus having escaped. It was decided, therefore, that Mary Magdalene would journey to the Bethany house the following morning to see if she could discover any evidence that Jesus had been there or had left a message for one of them to find. Meanwhile, Elizabeth intended to make enquiries in Jerusalem to ascertain if there was obvious activity of an ongoing search, or if Seth and his guards appeared to be particularly distracted.

* * *

Mary Magdalene's journey to Bethany did not take long, but when a little over halfway she decided to rest for a while. In noticing that a crowd had gathered and people were talking excitedly, she wandered over to see what was happening. When recognising several men as followers of Jesus, she remained at the rear of the group so as not to be seen, but was astonished when hearing their claims. They were hysterically declaring that Jesus had miraculously appeared before them as a vision at the House of Martha in Bethany. As Mary Magdalene listened closely for as many details as possible, she was certain that even though the followers were highly passionate and convincing, and appeared entirely genuine in their urgency to persuade, there was every likelihood that what they had witnessed was not a vision, but was Jesus himself.

Mary Magdalene was ecstatic at this news, and was now certain that Judas's speculation would prove correct – it looked as though Jesus may well have escaped and proceeded directly to the Bethany house. Now very confident of her mission, she immediately set off to complete the second leg her journey.

* * *

Arriving in Bethany in the middle of the afternoon, Mary Magdalene kept her head down and approached the house inconspicuously by using a less-travelled route. In the distance she could see her old home, which now looked tired and unkempt. For a few moments her entire life flashed before her, as the reality of an unbelievable journey began to sink in. But with no time for reflection, Mary Magdalene refocused her energy and continued to advance, while keeping a careful lookout for followers or anyone else who may have taken refuge at the property.

The house was silent and dark, and walking throughout the building Mary Magdalene rather forlornly admitted to the likelihood that Jesus had probably left the area after so clearly traumatising his followers. Sitting alone in the corner of what was now a dusty, cold, damp room, she began to doubt this trip would produce results, and as time wore on she became certain that Jesus would not have felt safe remaining at the Bethany house. Exhausted and saddened, Mary Magdalene wrapped herself in a shawl, curled up in a corner, and cried herself to sleep. The strain of the past few weeks had caught up; her old home brought back many memories, and she succumbed to it all.

* * *

Sometime later, Mary Magdalene awoke with a start. Trying to focus her eyes, she could not believe the sight she beheld: Jesus was kneeling by her side, holding her hand. Suddenly, she became engulfed in the terror she realised the followers must have faced; she couldn't believe this person was who he appeared to be. He looked different somehow — he carried more weight and appeared healthy and relaxed. She could not be sure it was Jesus, until she heard him speak:

"Do not be afraid. Please don't react in the way the others did."

Some things had not changed – his voice, demeanour, kindness, and extraordinary empathy. Mary Magdalene sat upright and looked Jesus squarely in the face, saying, "It is you, I know it's you; please tell me this isn't a dream."

Jesus smiled while shaking his head, which was all the answer she needed. Wrapping her arms around him in complete abandon, she laughed, cried, and screeched with delight.

* * *

Needless to say, the first questions Jesus posed were related to his family's safety, and as soon as Mary Magdalene had regained her composure, he began by asking about Judas: "Do you know anything of Judas – is he alright?"

With a deep sigh, Mary Magdalene explained, "Judas is being taken care of by the lovely Elizabeth, who you met at the compound in Barbelo, but he's not alright. He was fiercely beaten by some of your followers because Seth falsely accused him of betraying you to the authorities. Elizabeth took him in and did her best to take care of him, but I'm afraid his injuries are severe. He can't walk any distance, and even though his legs are healing, the injuries are so brutal that we don't believe he'll walk again. Judas doesn't know this because we didn't want to depress him any more than he already is. The only thing that kept him motivated was the possibility that you were alive – he never gave up and always believed you'd survived."

Obviously, Jesus was upset by this news: he had hoped to learn that Judas was safe and in hiding, rather than discover what Seth had suspected was true. He had taken Elizabeth's message to mean that all was well, but as Mary Magdalene clarified, that message was only to assist Elizabeth in verifying who he was; it wasn't actually a message at all: "Elizabeth was only trying to gauge your reaction," she explained, "she wanted to determine if 'Jeremiah' was in fact you. The message was not from Martha – she knows nothing of what has transpired. Martha only knows of the betrayal story, which was recounted to her by James when he discovered her waiting at the hideout. When she left Jerusalem for the coast, she understood only that Judas was missing. She may have heard the resurrection rumours on her travels, but we can't be sure. James promised Martha that he and I would continue the search for Judas, which was the only way of persuading her to maintain the original plan and journey to the coast."

It was a relief for Jesus to have it confirmed that Martha had at least made it as far as the safe-house and was on her way to the coast, and even though he was concerned that she was travelling alone, the news was better than he'd feared.

There was so much for them each to learn, and for the remainder of the afternoon they put the pieces of this complex puzzle together. Needless to say, Mary Magdalene was particularly fascinated when Jesus explained how he became free of the compound and of the confessions made by Seth. It explained so much of what she and Judas had tried to understand for weeks, and it now seemed that for the most part the situation had come full circle, with the exception of finding Martha.

Even though it was by now late in the evening, Jesus and Mary Magdalene decided it was likely that the Bethany house would undergo investigation now that the followers were convincing people of the vision they'd witnessed, so they both agreed it would be wise to travel throughout the night to Elizabeth's house in Jerusalem, where Jesus could hide alongside Judas for the time being.

⋆ ⋆ ⋆

By the time news of Jesus's *appearance* to his followers at the House of Martha in Bethany reached Seth, it had already been subjected to the rumour mill. The story of the followers' *vision* eventually served to further enhance the general belief in Mary Magdalene's claims, but the visitation by a resurrected Jesus was not an eventuality that had been planned for. The threat that he would *come again to judge the living and the dead* was supposed to be something the Movement held onto indefinitely, not for just a few weeks. Seth knew his superiors would be demanding an explanation for such a claim, so decided to be dismissive of the entire episode.

When Seth was questioned, he confidently reassured that it was most likely the men were inebriated. He suggested that one of them probably dreamt of Jesus and shared the experience; resulting in them all deciding to fabricate a vision in an attempt to establish their importance in the way of Mary Magdalene. With indifference, Seth recommended the men be ignored, saying that without his backing they would be written off as nonentities trying to make a name for themselves.

However, those in authority within the Movement had other ideas. They very much liked this well-timed turn of events, and instructed Seth to support the followers' claim while embellishing the story further. Seth's superiors wanted the circumstances to include that the followers actually witnessed the physical body of Jesus rise up into the clouds with a heavenly force, with the intent to thereafter refer to the episode as *Jesus's ascension into heaven, to be seated at the right hand of God.*

Needless to say, Seth was not at all happy with these developments, and argued vehemently against them. He knew what must have really happened at the Bethany house, and had not been at all surprised that Jesus would travel there in an attempt to locate Judas, but as far as Seth was concerned this latest demand was more than he could take.

He knew that a *miracle* as fantastical as this would be the final string to their bow, and the effect of his endorsement of the ascension storyline would be even more powerful than that of the resurrection. Seth no longer had to concern himself with the security of Jesus, so stood up to his superiors and blatantly refused to cooperate — enough was enough as far as he was concerned.

Seth declared that he wanted nothing more to do with the Movement. He felt they'd become obsessed with seeking opportunities to establish awe and fear in an attempt to intimidate people into being a part of their following. With Jesus now free of the compound, Seth felt it was finally time to make a stand, and as he stormed out of the meeting he utterly refused to back this latest endeavor; telling his superiors in straightforward terms to find someone else to do their malicious work.

* * *

From the time Jesus was free of the Barbelo compound, Seth was never again seen in Jerusalem. He remained at the compound for a day or two after releasing Jesus; making plans for his own future, and relieving some staff of their duties, but with little warning he found himself in the throes of the ascension story dispute. His outburst was overheard by many, and it was assumed that he had either been murdered or abandoned his position and taken flight. Shortly after his disappearance, the compound was dismantled and the staff were let go, but because Seth had been such an unpopular character, few enquiries were made of his whereabouts and his departure was never explained. His superiors had noted his dissent for some time, and the sympathy he often showed towards the predicament of Jesus and Martha was not pleasing to them. It was generally considered not remotely feasible for someone with the knowledge Seth possessed to be allowed to walk away, so most people agreed he had probably been disposed of.

In Seth's place, a number of individuals with considerable authority emerged. They sought out the followers, most of whom needed little persuasion to participate with the Movement. The enhanced version of the ascension story had taken hold, and many were now living in more fear than ever; believing wholeheartedly that there was only one way to repent, receive forgiveness, and be welcomed into the kingdom of God: to dedicate their lives in support of the early Christians, as they took their ambitious plans to the next stage.

PART III – THE REUNION THAT WAS GOODBYE

Upon arriving at Elizabeth's house in the early hours of the morning, Jesus walked into the room where Judas lay, finding his brother sleeping uncomfortably with an appearance he barely recognised. His soul seemed to have been torn from within, and his physical and emotional pain was very apparent.

As Jesus hesitantly approached, Judas awoke suddenly and was startled to discover someone in the room: "Don't be afraid, it's me – please, don't be afraid," said Jesus.

With outstretched arms, Judas sobbed as he begged to be held: "I'm sorry," he cried, "I'm so sorry that I let you down. I didn't mean for that to happen – how can I ever make this up to you?"

Jesus was not known to cry, but on this occasion he was unable to contain his emotions. Embracing his brother, he calmly reassured him, saying, "You've done nothing to be sorry for. I'm the one who is to apologise. I took you for granted, and I didn't take into account that you may be hurting as a result of how my followers behaved towards you. I was too focused on my work; my priorities were in disarray. It is I who was at fault, not you."

Jesus held his brother and best friend as close as he could as they each wept unashamedly. He could see that Judas's legs were twisted and bones protruded the skin; it was horrific to witness. One of the few people Jesus had been able to trust throughout his life, had been destroyed by those who gained so much as a result of their acquaintance. Seeing Judas in this way caused the most unimaginable anguish that Jesus had encountered in his life.

* * *

Once the initial drama and emotion of their reunion subsided, Judas conveyed his inability to accept that Jesus was to blame for his predicament, and insisted he accept full responsibility himself: "None of what has happened to me is your fault," said Judas, "and not for one moment will I have you bear that blame. It was my own insecurities that got the better of me – there is no one at fault but myself. Until I came to live with you as a teenager, I'd always viewed myself as a 'nobody'; someone unlikely to accomplish much of value in life. But almost instantly both you and Martha recognised qualities I didn't even know I had. For the first time in my life you made me feel loved, valued, and respected. You welcomed me into your family as though I'd always been an integral part of it, and what I learned from both you and Martha encouraged me to believe in myself for the first time. Jesus, it was my *choice* to allow the insecurities of the past to take hold at a time when I should have known better. I should have been able to see through the purpose of their ridicule and rise above it, rather than be overcome by it."

Jesus listened respectfully as Judas presented his case for being responsible for the outcome he faced, and recognised his need to accept such accountability. It not only prevented him from feeling self-pity and anger, but Jesus could see that reconciling his predicament in this way had empowered him towards acceptance rather than defeat. For Jesus to have argued the point to compensate in some way for his own feelings of guilt, would have taken away the self-respect Judas had acquired, so he therefore chose only to restate his feelings for his brother: "Judas, I understand what you're saying, and I respect how you've come to terms with your circumstances in this way, but there is something you have to know. Martha and I truly love, value, and respect you, second only to our parents. You are one with us, but we should have made sure we reminded you of that. What you have achieved in coming to terms with your predicament incorporates a vital lesson for us all, but so too does my admission that I neglected to remind one of the most important people in my life that he was loved beyond measure."

Mary Magdalene kept a discreet distance as the two men she loved so much spoke of their mutual devotion, and watched with enormous satisfaction as the physical and emotional pain they'd each endured was released in their embrace. Eventually, their touching and solemn conversation was replaced with laughter, as their more familiar hilariously sarcastic double-act brought levity to the situation. Humbled by the depth of love she had witnessed, Mary Magdalene graciously joined in the celebration as they each toasted the good health of their new friend, Elizabeth, without whom this gathering would never have occurred. As all possible odds had been defied, the reunion that was to become the long goodbye had become a reality.

* * *

Throughout the following week, Jesus remained hidden alongside Judas in Elizabeth's house, while Mary Magdalene maintained her usual schedule of appearances in Jerusalem. It was by now common knowledge that Seth had disappeared, but on the last occasion that he and Mary Magdalene had spoken, he had instructed she prepare to leave Jerusalem and return to her home in Magdala. Seth knew that if Jesus's release was ever discovered she would be at serious risk, so he explained that her role was now complete, informing her it was the responsibility of the Movement to continue to spread word of the resurrection. Seth also recommended that she maintain a low profile away from Jerusalem, and said there was no longer a need for her to speak publicly of what she'd witnessed.

At the time, Mary Magdalene had been suspicious of Seth's motives, but since Jesus explained all that he revealed, it was clear that he truly was concerned for her safety. Those who replaced Seth repeated his instructions, since they no longer needed her witness. The story had taken on a life of its own, and by removing Mary Magdalene from the front line, the Movement would be free to embellish the facts even further.

Mary Magdalene did not argue with the pressure placed upon her to leave, and agreed to end her daily ritual of speaking publicly about the resurrection. The timing of this directive could not have been better, since in promising to leave Jerusalem and return to her hometown of Magdala, Mary Magdalene became free to do as she pleased; creating an opportunity for her to proceed alongside Jesus as he began to formulate plans for the future.

* * *

It was without reservation that Mary Magdalene decided to travel with Jesus to the coast to seek out Martha, Simon, and Joseph, but the anticipation they felt at beginning the next phase of their life was extinguished considerably by the one matter they could not resolve – Judas was entirely incapable of travelling, and by now it had become apparent to all that his ability to walk was always going to be severely impaired and painful. There was no possibility that Judas would be able to join the rest of the family, and for Jesus and Mary Magdalene, this created the most agonising of dilemmas. However, recognising that he would never walk again, and that his lack of mobility was causing other health problems, Judas brought the debate to its painful conclusion and removed the task of that decision from Jesus by stating the obvious – it was simply impossible for him to accompany Jesus and Mary Magdalene to the coast. Elizabeth promised to take care of Judas and no one doubted that, but leaving him alone to the fate of a life with little purpose other than to exist, was more than Jesus could bear.

Distraught at the prospect Judas faced, but knowing that for each day they remained concealed in Elizabeth's house the likelihood of them being discovered increased, Jesus accepted that he needed to move on. In coming to the conclusion that there was no other resolution – Judas and Jesus said their final goodbye.

* * *

When the day arrived for Jesus and Mary Magdalene to depart, all three were only as prepared as it was possible to be. Jesus had given much thought to the purpose for this scenario, bearing in mind history would record his faithful friend had betrayed him in the most awful way. He explained to Judas that he felt God was using him for a purpose they did not yet fully understand, and that this part of his life was a huge sacrifice; they had no choice but to trust that there was a greater rationale at play. Jesus was sure that one day God would find a way for the true story to be told, at a point in the future when the time was right and the world was ready to hear it.

Judas was the most humble human being imaginable, and was not remotely concerned about what history may record – he cared only for his brother, his family, Mary Magdalene, and his precious new friend, Elizabeth. His anguish was not for the life that awaited him; rather, his torment was due to his inability to be present in the lives of those he loved, and be a support to the people he cared for the most in the world.

Their goodbyes were forever, and all three of them knew that. Mary Magdalene spent some time alone with Judas and thanked him for his understanding and patience throughout the years. As she had struggled to mature in the early days of their friendship, he never once allowed her to feel insecure, but always treated her with dignity and respect. Judas had believed in her, and saw beyond the external desires: he knew that inside there was a person to be believed in, and he was proud to declare he'd been right. Holding onto one another for the final time was excruciating, and as Mary Magdalene slowly removed herself from the embrace, she could not bear to look into Judas's face. She tried desperately hard to remember the Judas she had always known, with his wonderfully candid humour and an intellect unappreciated by so many. As Mary Magdalene departed in the arms of Elizabeth, she left Judas and Jesus alone.

Sitting in complete silence with their heads bowed in grief, both prayed silently for insight into how this moment in time could be changed. But as the inevitable tears began to build in Judas's eyes, he quietly said to his beloved brother, "Please leave, please just go – this is too much to bear."

As Jesus reached out to embrace his brother for the final time, he whispered, "This will not have been in vain. I promise to find a way to make sure that is so."

Burying his face in Jesus's hold, Judas could no longer cope with the painful emotion that gripped him. In turning away as tears overflowed his face, he pleaded with Jesus to go on his way.

Remaining quiet for a few moments, Jesus searched his mind for a glimmer of insight into what he could say, but as silent tears appeared in his eyes he could only lean forward and kiss his adored brother on the forehead. Hesitantly, Jesus walked away while struggling to utter the words, "God loves you."

Elizabeth, herself consumed with raw emotion, guided Jesus and Mary Magdalene out of her home for the final time, promising to take good care of their loved one as she watched them disappear into the darkness. In the background she overheard Judas's quiet but constant sobs, and went to his side to comfort him as much as she could. Judas: the weak one, the betrayer who became a victim of greed. Judas: the one who suffered in silence.

* * *

Jerusalem did not miss Mary Magdalene, and it was assumed she had returned to Magdala as instructed. The followers who remained were now under the guidance of those who'd replaced Seth, and in taking complete control of the ministry of Jesus, the early Christians succeeded in turning it into a bizarre and fascinating centerpiece of their doctrine, which facilitated their future prospects and ambitions.

Meanwhile, unbeknown to anyone, Jesus and Mary Magdalene were about to begin an entirely new life. Travelling on a route that would attract the least attention, they headed towards the coast in search of Martha, Joseph, and Simon. Their intention was for the whole group to pursue the original plan of travelling to seek refuge in France.

It had always been intended that Martha would begin a ministry of her own once settled overseas, but there had been a turn of events that she was entirely unaware of. Her future was now going to include Jesus.

CHAPTER SIXTEEN

WHAT THE FUTURE HELD

PART I – MARTHA'S REWARD

*T*he remainder of Martha's journey to the coast provided plenty of opportunity for reflection. Having accepted the reality and purpose of the resurrection story, she no longer felt responsible for putting things right. In preserving a philosophical attitude towards what she could not change, Martha began to focus her attention on what she could.

Knowing that France would be where she eventually settled, she began to think about how to continue the ministry using a style of her own making. Her disposition prevented her from conducting herself in the vibrant manner of Jesus, but she was reasonably confident in achieving her ambitions by allowing her own personality to emerge as she began to find her way. Jesus had always encouraged Martha to be herself; suggesting that people would then intuitively feel they knew her, and thus not hesitate in trusting what she had to say.

By the time Martha reached the coast and located her brothers, Joseph and Simon, she had gradually uncovered a quiet self-confidence and renewed inner peace. No longer burdened with the responsibility of the ministry, she was completely prepared to move forward into the next phase of her life.

* * *

Joseph and Simon had for several months been preparing for the arrival of Martha and Judas, and had set up a small home in readiness. They made a living by fishing and repairing boats and established themselves within the local community, thereby paving the way for their brother and sister to do the same.

They were very relieved when Martha arrived, since the wait had been intense. Benefiting only from rumours emerging from Jerusalem, they had no clue as to what was really happening. Needless to say, they were distressed to learn that Judas had not accompanied Martha, and felt dreadful at being unable to announce the news she had hoped for – that he had made his own way to the coast. Both the betrayal and resurrection rumours had reached Joseph and Simon, and they had hoped Martha would be able to confirm they were untrue, but she was only in a position to share what she had learned from James. Martha did confirm that James and Mary Magdalene were going to pursue the search for Judas, and they could only hope for a positive outcome. All three agreed that Mary Magdalene must have been coerced into making the resurrection claim, but knew there was little they could do about that. It was the fate of Judas that concerned them the most, and being unable to resolve this circumstance was difficult for them each to admit.

As they settled into their new but temporary life, the agreed arrangement to remain at the coastal location for a full year after the crucifixion was adhered to, particularly in view of the fact that Judas was missing. Unless their personal safety was jeopardised in some way, there were no plans to divert from that decision. It was important that Judas be given as much time as possible before they departed for France, but other than wait and hope, there was little else they could do.

As the weeks wore on, Martha, Simon, and Joseph participated in local life while busying themselves with plans for the anticipated journey to France. All sorts of information reached the coast throughout this time, and it was clear that life in Jerusalem was becoming quite volatile between the early Christians, the true followers of Jesus, and the Jewish faithful. Jesus had always insisted that forcing the issue of his divinity would be incredibly troublesome, and even in those early days his prediction was proving to be true. However, Martha believed that the early Christians actually encouraged such discord, since that was how they'd previously so successfully recruited a following. In persuading people of the miracle stories and intimidating them with threats of the wrath of God, they also used the 'victim' approach; suggesting they were not responsible for the uprising and rebellion, but were merely victims of ignorance and misunderstanding, and the fear-driven hatred of others.

With their victories assigned to God's will and losses honoured as sacrifices, it did not take much persuasion for the disenchanted members of society to become sanctimonious believers in their own moral superiority. In embracing indoctrination into a movement that was convinced their way was the only direction for mankind, the followers became entrenched in its ideology, which in succeeding centuries consumed billions of people across the world.

* * *

Martha had little difficulty adapting to her new lifestyle, which was quite relaxed and pleasant compared to anything before. With only everyday domestic tasks needing her attention, along with occasional diary entries to keep records up to date, she felt in many ways as though she was on retreat. Coming to terms with her new-found freedom had not been difficult, and the relief from responsibility was no reason for complaint. The only disappointment Martha felt when closing her eyes at night was that yet another day had gone by and Judas had not appeared, but little did she appreciate that each passing day was bringing her closer to a reality she had not even contemplated.

As Martha went about her daily household responsibilities, her mind was working away and making plans for the future. Obviously, memories of Jesus and Judas dominated her thoughts constantly, and she missed her mother terribly, but as time passed by she started to become accustomed to her new life and was grateful for the company of Simon and Joseph. It had taken many weeks to begin to feel positive about the future, and comfortable in her new environment, but eventually life did begin to feel somewhat normal.

Martha had developed a daily schedule that consisted primarily of maintaining her home and caring for her two brothers while they were out and about earning a living. But on the most routine of evenings when Martha was preparing a meal prior to her brothers returning home, she overheard footsteps approach the house. As she called out her customary greeting, the voice that returned her welcome caused her to gasp in disbelief.

Incapable of physically moving, Martha breathlessly listened; questioning if her mind was playing games. Even though she sensed someone enter the room and begin to approach, she remained stationary; powerless to even consider turning around. As she waited for the person advancing to speak, Martha refused to succumb to the temptation of looking over her shoulder for fear that her impression had been mistaken. But as each moment passed and she sensed someone move a little closer, she braced herself when picturing the impossible in her mind. Shivering uncontrollably, she surrendered to her emotions only when feeling the tender touch of an outstretched hand and a quiet, sensitive voice whispering her name: "Martha."

Turning slowly, Martha was overwhelmed at finding herself looking directly into the eyes of Jesus. As the impact of this momentous occasion overtook her entire being, she collapsed into her brother's arms and wept without excuse. Her body trembled in shock and bewilderment at the sudden appearance of the person she loved the most in the world, but whom she assumed had been lost to her forever.

* * *

Unsurprisingly, it took quite some time for Martha to regain her senses and become composed enough to think clearly. When noticing to her delight that Mary Magdalene was accompanying Jesus, her immediate enquiry was for news of Judas. Even though they both acknowledged he was safe, Martha could sense their sorrow and knew all was not well. In astonishment and disbelief, Martha drifted between staring at the two people standing before her, while cautioning her mind to be patient over the many questions she had. Martha didn't know where or how to begin, since the enormity of what was occurring consumed her entirely.

As all three combined laughter with tears while the relief of reunion took hold and pressures of the past began to dissolve, brothers Joseph and Simon appeared in the doorway. The entire episode repeated itself as the two reacted in astonishment when taking in the scene they confronted. Never in their most vivid imagination had either contemplated such a moment, but their initial inability to respond was instantly replaced with such cheer that no one could have denied their unspeakable joy.

The deep-felt liberation indulged by them all, replaced the stoic self-sacrifice they had each assumed throughout the years. Not for a moment had it occurred to anyone that an outcome such as this was even the remotest of possibilities, yet the gratitude they felt for such a blessing was more than they could express.

There was so much for Jesus and Mary Magdalene to tell, and neither knew where to start, but as the euphoric family group gathered and collected their thoughts, they appreciated that the most relevant place to begin was with the fortunes of Judas.

* * *

Jesus could see the dread developing on Martha's face as he broached the subject, so taking her hand in his, he began: "Judas is alive and being taken care of by a lovely, kind woman named Elizabeth. However, the consequences of the betrayal rumour as relayed to you by James, turned out to be true. Judas was discovered and severely attacked by some of the followers, and as a result is no longer able to walk. As heartbreaking as it was, we had no choice but to leave him behind in Elizabeth's care."

Martha wanted to at least feel some relief that Judas had not been murdered, but she couldn't. She felt such anger and betrayal to have it confirmed that the followers were responsible for this act; it was impossible for her to find any justification for their behaviour. As she sounded out her frustrations with essentially rhetorical questions relating to why Seth would do such a thing, she had not anticipated being responded to with anything other than opinion. Martha had no idea what she was about to discover, and as she looked towards Jesus and Mary Magdalene, expecting them to join in the chorus against Seth, she saw sorrow appear in their eyes in a way she'd not witnessed before. At that moment she realised they had clearly been through far more than they'd so far admitted.

Deciding it was time she pulled herself together and reverted to her usual role of being the person they could rely upon, she toned down her exasperation and gently suggested they tell their story. However, the story they were about to reveal was more astonishing than anything Martha could have envisaged.

* * *

The remainder of the evening was spent listening to what Jesus and Mary Magdalene shared, and as they each took turns in bringing to light the various events that had brought them to this point, Martha, Joseph and Simon could only listen in disbelief.

As the complexities of how the pieces of this intricate puzzle had been put together were explained, it was without doubt the actions of Seth that were the most astounding. They all agreed he was entirely pivotal to the outcome they were benefiting from, since they appreciated that no matter what actions each may have taken individually, without the risks Seth had undertaken no one would have survived.

But for Martha, discovering that Judas was of the impression that he was not valued was equally as shocking to learn. She found it impossible to believe his anxiety and depression had escaped her, and was overcome with guilt and self-doubt. Neither she nor Jesus had recognised the seriousness of the situation, and they both felt such deep regret and overwhelming guilt that their shortcomings had created such an outcome for their most beloved brother: "How did we allow that to happen," Martha questioned, "and why didn't one of us see what was developing?"

Before Jesus could respond, Mary Magdalene felt the need to interrupt. She had spent weeks listening to Jesus indulge in feelings of self-reproach, and could not tolerate the idea that Martha would join her brother in such punishment: "What good is this debate about the outcome for Judas? You can't change things by examining in more detail what is obvious. You'll only feel worse than you already do. I could remind you both of the unbelievable pressure you were under and the continuous defeats you had to endure, but you won't permit that to become an excuse. Is it not understandable that you were overwhelmed when everything you'd worked your entire lives towards was disintegrating in front of you?

"Remember, Judas has to bear at least some, if not most, of the responsibility for this outcome. He admits he should have risen above it all, and he does not in any way hold either of you responsible. He accepts that his behaviour was petty and almost child-like. He should not have needed you both to continuously remind him of things he should by then have known to be true. I took it upon myself to provide him with unstinting emotional support, yet nothing I said had the necessary effect. If anyone should feel guilty for failing it is me, since I was the one fully versed with the situation, yet unable to effect any serious change. But I do not feel the destructive force of guilt, and feel only pity and sorrow. I cannot accept responsibility for the actions of another, and you both have to embrace that stance. You can either continue to allow this to pull you down, or you can use the experience to learn from.

"You both still have so much to achieve. The ministry you thought was your life purpose now appears to have only been a small part of that purpose. We all have work to do, and I know I can speak for Judas when I say he'd be furious if you allowed your feelings over this situation to demoralise you to this extent or, worse still, make you feel like a failure. Remember, Jesus, you have always said that there are more lessons to be learned from our mistakes than our successes. Therefore, let's spend our time wisely. Let's examine the failures from a positive standpoint so we can take those lessons forward into the second ministry instead of only looking at what happened and feeling guilty about it. That is the only way to salute Judas, and to ensure that what he has endured is not in vain."

Martha and Jesus knew there was no point in either of them thinking they would ever come to terms with the fate of Judas, irrespective of the good intentions of Mary Magdalene. All they could do was as she had so eloquently suggested, and endeavour to make up for the mistakes by learning from them. They had to live with their guilt, but they couldn't allow it to diminish their self-esteem to such a degree that they wouldn't be able to continue the ministry. They eventually appreciated that the only way to create value out of the experience was to record this information within the diaries and ensure that these lessons became an integral part of their ministry from that day forward.

The room fell silent after Mary Magdalene's well-spoken delivery, which brought a fitting end to the revelation of a sensational chronicle of events. For Jesus and Mary Magdalene to have, in effect, relived the entire experience was emotionally exhausting for them both, but as they each looked around the table at those present, they still found the reality of the outcome difficult to digest. As they contemplated the many incredible facets of the story as a whole, their moments of private reflection brought with it the conclusion that it was simply meant to be.

While feeling tremendous regret that both Seth and Judas had suffered such terrible fates, and were unable to share in the freedom they were about to embrace, the group declared that all they achieved in the future would be in honour of them both, as they committed to work towards achieving the vision they all had for the future.

* * *

Over the subsequent days everyone set about making final plans for the future, and it was agreed that the sooner they departed from the continent the better. Now that the entire family was accounted for, there was no requirement to wait any longer.

The basic strategy for the remainder of their lives was an undertaking to continue the ministry in one form or another, while covering as much of the world as they could. They hoped to spread word of the *real* ministry in addition to countering the efforts of the early Christians, while openly challenging their teachings and recruiting methods. This had been Seth's vision for the hopeful new life he worked so hard to establish for Jesus, and was an opportunity nobody had thought for a moment they would be so privileged to receive.

As soon as all travel arrangements were in place, everyone but Simon left the coast by boat and headed towards France. Simon then journeyed back to Nazareth and let his mother, James, and Ruth know what had transpired, offering them peace of mind in the knowledge everyone had safely departed for France. Simon also provided James with advice and instructions from Jesus regarding his intentions when mounting a challenge against the early Christians, and asked that he find the time to seek out Judas and Elizabeth to see if there was anything they needed and to let them know everyone had safely moved on.

Upon departing Nazareth, Simon first proceeded to Magdala in an attempt to locate Lazarus, the brother of Mary Magdalene. Amazed by the news Simon delivered, Lazarus decided there and then to abandon his ideas for a ministry of his own, choosing instead to accompany Simon to France to be near his sister.

Once James had ensured his mother and younger sister were safe and provided for in Nazareth, he returned to Jerusalem as had been agreed. After coordinating the support he'd been gathering by word of mouth for some time, he mounted his longstanding campaign to oppose the early Christian movement. Both Jesus and James had always understood this was a battle that could not be won, since the stronghold of the early Christians was far too established. However, the underlying principle was to make a stand, and provide historical evidence of the fact that the very family of Jesus stood against the early Christians, and fought to their deaths for what they believed.

Some eight years after the crucifixion, the beloved mother, Mary, passed away peacefully in the presence of Ruth and other extended family members. Her life had been conducted quietly and without notable event, and she departed this world in the same manner. Mary knew her role in life had been to bear the children she was blessed to receive, and provide them with the upbringing and experiences that facilitated their respective life purposes. She ensured her persona was one that remained virtually anonymous, proving that her humble portrayal of devotion, faith, and true love are qualities that do not necessitate grand declaration.

PART II – JUDAS IS DELIVERED

Judas could have surrendered himself for the remainder of his life to a mere existence with no purpose for being, but instead remained open to being delivered from the personal frailties that wreaked havoc within his life. Jesus had expressed remorse at feeling responsible for Judas's predicament, but without denying him the opportunity to accept responsibility himself. This balanced approach sufficiently relieved Judas of guilt and self-loathing, resulting in the embracing of a more positive mindset.

In Elizabeth's care, Judas lived for a further ten years and eventually passed away peacefully in her loving company. Throughout those years he suffered considerable pain and discomfort, but with a newly acquired frame-of-mind he never permitted himself to dwell on what could have been. Instead, he decided there must be a purpose for his predicament, and by so doing opened himself up to inadvertently discovering what that was.

When Judas initially became incapacitated he felt desolate: unable to be present in the lives of those he loved made his own life unbearable. Self-pity had been a welcome companion at first, but brought with it a sense of worthlessness and fear, which Judas knew he had to overcome. Remembering Jesus's last words before they parted company — *this will not have been in vain. I will find a way to make sure that is so* — Judas was determined to discover for himself the purpose of his predicament, since he felt sure it held lessons for him to learn.

It took some time before Judas began to understand there was a distinct advantage to being physically restricted and incapacitated – he had plenty of time to think. With many hours of each day spent alone, Judas found himself reflecting on life and the many facets of it. He began to appreciate that as a result of his family's encouragement, he had become quite confident in his ability to respond to situations effectively: when observing the challenges others faced, he always managed to find something positive to contribute to any circumstance. But the one distinctive trait that Judas knew he needed to overcome was the inherent characteristic of self-doubt, which was the root cause of the challenging circumstances he faced. The lack of belief in himself didn't extend to all aspects of his life, since Judas had acquired many critical skills of which he'd become very assured, but it was a deep-felt insecurity about who he was as a person, and whether or not he was enough, which caused such turmoil and discontent. Despite often being frustrated that his life was curtailed to such an extent that he felt he was achieving nothing of worth, a chance conversation with a group of people brought about the realisation that the opposite was true.

When eventually strong enough to move around with the aid of a stick, Judas occasionally enjoyed short excursions into town. It was during one such outing that something important dawned on him. He came across a group of men arguing, and it was very apparent that no one would give in to the other's point of view: they clearly perceived it as a sign of weakness to do so. As Judas listened in to the debate, he recognised that for the participants there was nothing to be learned from the discussion itself; rather, the important thing was to win. They were only concerned with what others thought of them, and had to remain on top of their argument no matter what.

It made Judas smile to listen to such a contest, as it was clear that the egos of each of the individuals dominated their contribution entirely. It was that moment when he began to appreciate how much he'd learned during what he had perceived were wasted years. By his own admission, there had been a time when he too would have argued with such intensity, and considered it a weakness to give in to another's stance, so he couldn't criticise their behaviour – in truth, he knew there was little difference between these men and the Judas of old. However, despite being somewhat embarrassed at what he overheard and the personal admissions to himself, he began to realise how much he'd changed.

Judas could not resist but join in the debate, and in so doing his affable style, mixed with humour and irony, brought the men to a standstill. Something about Judas became instantly apparent to them all, and was a quality that Judas himself had been completely unaware of. He possessed a characteristic they admired, but at the same time could not envisage acquiring since the thought filled them with fear. Judas was everything they wished they could be – Judas had become at one with himself.

The response of these men to his approach at this chance meeting made Judas aware for the first time that he was no longer concerned about how he was perceived by others, but only wanted to offer a perspective from his heart and with humility. Being unable to rely upon a physical presence or personal status, and having no desire to manufacture a personality, Judas had learned to depend entirely upon who he actually was. After years of reviewing his life and the attitudes and mistakes that had cost him so much, he came to the realisation that he had always been more than enough.

When reflecting once again upon Jesus's final words before departing, Judas knew that these latter years of his life had not been in vain at all. Quite by chance, the purpose of his predicament became clear – his debilitating condition had provided him with an opportunity to learn so much, and delivered him the most precious gift of all – the ability to be himself, without the fear associated with such condition.

Judas felt blessed – he had become who he truly was. No longer burdened with anger for his shortcomings, he had acquired an understanding of himself, and thereby discovered the freedom of forgiving self.

Judas had learned to be.....

CHAPTER SEVENTEEN

GOD'S CONTINGENCY PLAN

PART I – RELOCATING TO FRANCE

*T*he route to France was long and indirect and included many stopovers in places Jesus was familiar with. During the years he and Judas embarked upon their five-year fact-finding mission, they noted places where they'd been particularly well-received in the event of one day needing to seek refuge. The group had been unsure of precisely where to make their home permanently, and many places throughout Greece, Italy and France were considered before choosing to remain with the original plan of settling in southern France.

By the time the group arrived in this region they had fully recovered from the experiences of the past and were entirely focused upon their future ambitions. They remained together as a group for the first few months, which enabled Jesus to ensure that Martha and Mary Magdalene were safely accommodated before beginning to travel further afield on his own. Having journeyed into France from the Mediterranean Sea via the mighty Rhone Canal, the group investigated many towns on the route and familiarised themselves with the unique local politics of each area. Martha eventually chose to settle in the town of Tarascon, which was a vibrant port bordering the canal and located about 65km inland. The town consisted both of a settled community and one familiar with travellers and traders, due to its location alongside the Rhone. This not only permitted the group to arrive without much notice and come and go as they pleased, but since the canal was the main source of transport used by Jesus when travelling across this area of Europe, Tarascon provided an excellent base for respite throughout the years.

It was agreed that Martha should limit her movements for the remainder of her life to this vicinity of southern France, since it was important that she was safe and able to establish a reputation and strong personal relationships. The information she possessed had to be passed on, and the only way that could be achieved was by developing close friendships with people who could eventually be trusted with the truth of her history.

Martha did not ever lay claim publicly to being the sister of Jesus of Nazareth, which would have served only to draw attention she did not desire. Being the keeper of the truth, Martha needed to be vigilant at all times regarding her relationship with Jesus and the information she possessed. The *truth* she knew was not for her time, but was for centuries into the future when mankind had experienced sufficient negativity and was prepared to embrace bliss. To be poised, willing, and able to listen, humanity needed to be sophisticated enough to comprehend, and courageous enough to make a stand. That time, Martha knew, would be many years away. Her responsibility for the remainder of her life was simply to uphold the message of the ministry within her own teachings, and ensure the diaries were in safe hands before she died.

Being far quieter in nature than Jesus, Martha felt unnatural taking the lead. Talking to crowds in order to continue the ministry took quite some getting used to, but she worked diligently to develop her own style and eventually became comfortable with the idea of engaging small groups or individuals. As her confidence grew, so did the amount of people who sought her out for advice or a word or two of comfort, and eventually Martha became accustomed to sharing her knowledge and teachings with people from every walk of life. Jesus was well known for entering the fray and challenging people's ideals, whereas Martha went about her ministry in a more composed style. She did not possess the extrovert personality of Jesus, but people were nevertheless drawn to her. She exuded inner peace, combined with a demure innocence, which attracted everyone she came across – people became transfixed because she articulated her message in such a beautiful, quiet manner. Jesus knew that Martha would be successful and encouraged her not to even think about adopting his style, saying she should be true to herself and allow her message to come through. As Martha eventually became more adept at teaching, her lessons were delivered straight to the heart of the individuals who needed to hear them.

* * *

Mary Magdalene, who was later joined by her brother, Lazarus, also remained in the south of France, establishing herself in a town not too far from Martha. Still conscious of the fact that the resurrection story was well known, she chose to keep a low profile for the remainder of her life. Mary Magdalene taught others about God, her beliefs, and her spirituality, but she did not talk of her true identity, or her close association with Jesus. She reverted back to her original name, introducing herself as Mary of Bethany, in an effort to distance the past. Mary Magdalene had hoped that by leading a life of relative seclusion, prayer, and contemplation, her name would eventually disappear from history, and her association with the resurrection story would diminish.

The person Mary Magdalene became could not have been more removed from the person she was. Beautiful, and possessed of a calm energy, she attracted the stare of passersby without effort on her part. People suspected her life had a story to it, and many did eventually put two and two together. The unique, beautiful, and reclusive lady now referred to as Mary of Bethany, spoke so graciously of God in a manner of someone with a personal association, thus creating pause for thought among people she came to know. It was not until her death that those who'd been closest to her declared that the striking, serene woman from a land far-removed was the chosen one – Mary Magdalene. People believed that the peace and tranquility she exuded until her final breath could only emanate from a close relationship with God. The love she carried in her heart for Jesus spoke volumes, leaving no one in any doubt as to her true identity.

PART II – WITH THE BENEFIT OF HINDSIGHT

It was almost a year after arriving in France before Jesus felt ready to begin preparations for the next phase of his life. He was content that Martha and Mary Magdalene were safely accommodated, and the anticipation of prospects that lay ahead inspired him to proceed. The period of transition had been of enormous value; with hindsight as a companion, so much had begun to make sense. For Jesus, the lessons of the past became fundamental in forming the future, since he could not deny that the message he was so intent upon teaching was something he had often not adhered to himself. Many problems of the ministry would have been less of a trial of endurance, and far more easily surmountable, had he always remembered his mother's cautious advice to '*do as you teach*'. Jesus was not the first son to confess his mother had been right, and I somehow doubt he will be the last.

Jesus and Martha spent many hours reminiscing while travelling to France and during the settling-in period, but there was one particular conversation that brought so much about the past and present into focus. When contemplating what their life may have developed into had the ministry succeeded, they realised how their initial aims had become entirely obscured by events that not only overtook their aspirations, but entirely removed the founding principles of their original plans. In seeing the reality of the destination they had so blindly proceeded towards, they appreciated just how fortunate they were to have failed. They had set out only to teach people of all cultures and creeds a more sensible and productive way of conducting life, but due to involving themselves with the Movement they became embroiled within the politics of organised religion and unwittingly became a part of it. As they fought to retain their own voice, the message of the ministry became diluted through one compromise after another.

During one such period of reflection, Martha reminded Jesus of a significant day in their childhood. They had been enjoying a favourite pastime of an idyllic walk to a nearby pond, followed by many hours engrossed in conversation as they passed the time discovering more about themselves and the world around them.

On one particular afternoon, Jesus had been casually tossing small pebbles into the water. As he aimlessly watched them skim along the surface before sinking and being absorbed into the silt, he became fascinated by the varying reactions to the way in which he threw the pebble. As he experimented, he started to mull over a parallel that related to the ministry he believed he and Martha would one day pursue.

Jesus noted how the speed of the pebble not only dictated its impact and how long it took to sink, but also the varying ripple-effects and the time it took for the water to return to calm. As they attempted to create an association that offered some sort of path for them to follow, they concluded that each method produced the same end-result since the pebble eventually sank, corresponding with their message being delivered. However, they fretted at being unable to interpret the route that would be preferable and most effective: should the ministry be conducted in a fast and furious style, or delivered gently and in a way that permitted people to learn at their own pace?

Eventually, they decided that the journey was not only as important as the end-result, but perhaps more so. At such a realisation, it became obvious that the slower, more graceful approach is what created opportunities for people to think things through independently, and talk about it to others before the message sank in and became one with them. Whereas the harsh, forceful approach did not offer such opportunity for debate, and in many ways dictated the choices people should make because they had been shocked or intimidated into accepting it.

When Jesus also recognised how the pond had returned to calm much more quickly as a result of the gently tossed pebble, he related this to the lack of disruption he wished to cause. In only desiring to quietly provide food for thought that could be absorbed over time, Jesus realised that the gentle, encouraging approach was the only way forward. Unfortunately, from the moment he became embroiled in fearing he would not be permitted to live long enough to succeed, he essentially abandoned his childhood ambition and allowed the often intimidating realities that come to pass in adulthood to take over his innocent plans. By becoming a part of the Movement, he literally signed up for the supposed benefits of his message being delivered in a fast and furious way. But what that also achieved was confusion, in the same manner of the pebble thrown without caution producing fast-moving ripples that took a long time to calm.

With the benefit of hindsight, Jesus knew that the second part of his life had to be conducted with grace and sensitivity. His message in the future would be gently tossed into the air so it could glide slowly down to earth and be received with barely a ripple felt. By so doing, the principles of the real ministry would subliminally sink into the human conscience without anyone suffering the ripple-effect of the vigorously tossed pebble.

PART III – LET THE SHOW BEGIN

Jesus eventually came to appreciate that even though it hadn't always seemed to be the case, it became clear that there was a 'plan' after all. He now had the opportunity to write his own ending, and within a year of the family settling in southern France, he was advancing towards the second phase of his life. In deciding there was not a culture in the world impossible to reach by one means or another, Jesus set about dedicating the remainder of his days to fulfilling Seth's vision that he should *be where they are, and go where they won't go; pre-empt them and make his presence felt*. And by indulging in the mindset he had decided was best, Jesus also intended to achieve something else he had not throughout the first ministry – he proposed to enjoy it.

The early part of the second ministry was conducted in precisely the way of the first. In appreciating that he needed to review his previous findings and ensure he understood fully the parameters of what people needed to know, Jesus set off on extensive travels to discover just that. He listened to what individuals had to say; assessed their thought processes and how they arrived at conclusions, and then worked out a programme to enable them to focus their minds on a better way of achieving their goals and conducting their everyday life. But there was one major obstacle he had to overcome – the fire and brimstone of the early Christian movement.

It became apparent to Jesus that people were tiring of the sort of rhetoric bandied about by the authorities of all religions. Their representations smacked of threats and a pressure to submit-or-else, which was something Jesus simply could not abide. However, these practices were adopted purely because they were highly successful, since most people fell in line due to erring on the side of caution. Jesus knew they were not supporting and entirely embracing a specific ideology itself, but were afraid to make a stand in case the ever-present threat of God's wrath came upon them.

Jesus could see the negative effect of such controls on individual lives, and knew that cancelling out these consequences was only part of what he needed to achieve. His representations needed to go a step further, and create a positive effect in addition to negating the work of those who had gone before him.

* * *

Jesus found the early part of his second ministry quite fascinating in many regards. He was astonished to discover that the story of Jesus of Nazareth had spread so far and wide, and often encountered preachers attempting to inspire him with erroneous stories about himself, much to his amusement. What was not very amusing, however, was discovering the difficult task of correcting impressions that were so well-established. Many people had been entirely indoctrinated to such an extent that when Jesus spoke of his *real* ministry it was beyond anything they could comprehend. In appreciating he had his work cut out in more ways than one, Jesus decided there was little point in directly challenging the Movement's ideology, so set about approaching the 'problem' in a truly unique way.

After a year or so of travelling throughout France, England, Wales and Ireland, researching ideas for how the new ministry could be accomplished, Jesus developed a system that worked like a dream. In recognising that his original ministry was still as valid as ever, he took the major components of those teachings and crammed them into a one-hour 'session'. Without the luxury of a group of followers to share the responsibility of teaching, and believing it was unwise to remain in one place for extensive periods of time, Jesus needed to devise a plan that was unique and memorable. But more importantly, he believed that in order to succeed, his message needed to be delivered with such delicacy that people would not even realise they were listening to a preacher at all.

In forming a correlation with the pebble throwing story of his youth, Jesus was confident that his playfully clever technique could achieve the desired result. With the intent that his message be casually 'tossed' into the air and unwittingly absorbed by those who heard it, Jesus believed it would find its own time and place to become absorbed into the consciousness of mankind, in the manner of the gently tossed pebble that eventually found its way and settled into the silt.

The one-man 'show' was designed to present the truth that Jesus felt people needed to hear, but with the entire world to cover, most would be forgiven for believing Jesus had set himself an impossible challenge. However, in hoping he had at least thirty years to complete the second ministry, as opposed to the three years he'd given himself for the first, Jesus believed there was more than a good chance he would succeed.

To ensure his message was unforgettable and not just another holier-than-thou preaching session, Jesus used humour, sarcasm, and intonations of grandeur when talking of the Movement's ambitions and delivering the important features of his message. In other words, he entertained the crowd in a way that ensured they would never forget him, or anything he said. He dispelled the myths about Jesus of Nazareth, while instilling his truth as he passionately believed it to be, and challenged the teachings of the Movement in a way that listeners could not take offence, but would have great difficulty denying.

Preachers were ten-a-penny in those days, and most were boring, tedious, and completely unremarkable. Jesus knew he had to be different, and was certain his one-hour 'show' was the most effective way to ensure his message was memorable. Laced with one punch-line after another, Jesus delivered the truth in a way no one had heard before, and with a style they would be highly unlikely to forget.

While the audience may have laughed at his antics, not one person ever wandered from the crowd during the entire hour-long presentation, and no one departed at the end without having learned a huge amount. They believed they were being entertained, rather than talked down to or threatened; resulting in Jesus's reputation becoming so widespread that he emerged as the number one 'celebrity' of his time. People were so captivated by his sense of humour that they took to impersonating him with friends and family, which was precisely what Jesus had hoped would occur. In using audience participation to foster a closer bond and encourage people to relax, Jesus saw extraordinary success at every turn of his journey, no matter what culture he presented himself to.

The opening of his show was the part Jesus enjoyed the most, since he would introduce himself as Jesus, but then try to convince the crowd he was Jesus of Nazareth returned from the dead. He mocked his resurrection and ascension stories, and tried to sell himself as the son of God. These antics managed to instill the ridiculousness of the Movement's claims when considered in such a humorous light, while simultaneously delivering important thoughts for people to contemplate over time as they recounted the story of the unusual and entertaining preacher.

An excerpt from one of Jesus's 'performances'

"Please, please — gather around and make yourselves comfortable. I want you relaxed and lulled into a false sense of security since I'm about to terrify you. Well, you know how it is; we preachers have a job to do. We need you to submit to our authority or live in fear of the wrath of God if you don't! I'm serious — I don't know why you're laughing. I'm a man of God, and I'm here to terrify the living daylights out of you. I need you under my spell. I need you feeling so remorseful and guilty that you can't live with yourself. I need you seeking me out and paying me money. I'll tell you what you need to hear, while convincing that your sins will be forgiven; then we'll all go on our way feeling happy and content! I'm richer, and you're poorer, but hey — that's life!

"Oh, did I just accidentally slip in the 'S' word? I hope that disturbed you. How many 'sins' have you each committed today? Why do you laugh? I don't understand why you would think that's funny. You're sinners — of course you've sinned today — why would you not? You can't live life letting yourselves and your reputations down! The Christian preachers have no doubt convinced you all that you're a flock of worthless sinners who should be full of regret and seeking forgiveness. Did you laugh at them when they said that, or did you shudder with feelings of self-doubt and guilt? Somehow I don't think you laughed.

"I don't know what to do really. I'm not having much luck with this ministry thing; people just don't take me seriously. All they do is roll about laughing. What's a guy supposed to do?

"I'll tell you what, why don't I impart some wisdom. You know the stuff — those Christians are doing it all the time. They quote that guy, Jesus of Nazareth, and before they know it the audience is bowing and scraping and begging for mercy. The Christians offer salvation by welcoming people into their fold; promising they'll be cured of life's ills. But are they? Do you know anyone who's cured; anyone who knows precisely who he is, and what his purpose in life entails? You've all gone quiet and serious on me. Come on, I'm trying to lift you up, not put you down! Perhaps you know someone who claims they 'have it all' and continuously tell you where you're going wrong, but before you know it they're exposed as frauds when their true colours are seen! That's better — I brought a smile to your faces!

"I suppose I was sort of hoping you'd be able to shed some light on why the Christians are succeeding and why that Jesus of Nazareth guy is so damned popular. I hear he droned on and on while harping about being the Messiah — pleeease! There you go again, laughing at my innocent observations. You know what? You're laughing because you know I'm right! The truth is — Jesus of Nazareth was a decent enough guy, but I reckon he'd have lived a bit longer if he'd developed a routine like mine. His hanging on the cross act dried him out in the end, so what good was that?

"Speaking of my namesake, did you know that the purpose of his ministry was to do the opposite of what the Christians are doing? I heard that starting up a new religion was not his

thing, and that his family fought the Christians to the death — now what does that tell you? His real plan was to teach people a few basic facts that they could incorporate into their lives, which would complement whatever religion they practiced. He wanted you to believe in yourself, learn to trust yourself, and know that there is nothing to be fearful of or self-loathing about. He did not intend you be dictated to and led to believe that you're worthless sinners on the one hand, and children of God on the other. What a dichotomy! We are told God loves us as a parent would love a child, yet we are also told we should fear his wrath because we are unworthy know-nothings! How many parents do you know who treat their children like that!

"Those Christians are declaring Jesus of Nazareth their martyred, iconic leader when nothing could be further from the truth. The Christians instill that he died for us, which makes us feel pretty guilty and pathetic. Is that what Jesus intended we endure for his sacrifice — a life of self-reproach? I don't think so — Jesus of Nazareth really worked hard to deliver his message; knowing full well he'd be arrested and crucified in the end thanks to the antics of those Christians. Do you really believe he'd go through all of that just to instill guilt? Do you really think he'd be pleased to know everyone spent the rest of their lives believing they were 'nothing' compared to him; feeling bad about themselves if they didn't meet his standards? From what I know, I think he'd have a blue fit if he knew what was happening in his name. He'd be so incensed that I reckon he'd come back from the dead just to prove his point!

"I've heard from those 'in-the-know' that Jesus worked his entire life to teach what you need to understand, and I reckon that if he was alive today he'd kick the backsides of the people trying to intimidate you into believing in their authority to be God's representative on earth; offering you eternal life in exchange for your commitment. Who do they think they are!

"I don't think for one moment that God thinks you're worthless sinners, and I'm damned sure Jesus of Nazareth didn't. The loving God within is more than happy to point you in the right direction and help you avoid making mistakes. You just have to ask, and you'll be shown the way; that's what Jesus used to say all the time. Being human is difficult enough, and we don't need those Christians making it more so. Please just remember — think with your heart as well as your head. Remember to always ask yourself if what you're doing is the right thing, and let your conscience decide. Follow that golden rule and you'll never go wrong."

* * *

Jesus perfected his presentation in many languages by cajoling people he met along the way into helping him translate his speeches. He took his multi-lingual one-man show on the road for the remaining thirty-plus years of his life, travelling from the British Isles, throughout Europe, the Middle East, and some parts of Central Asia. Two thousand years ago, much of the world's estimated population of between 170 and 300 million lived in these areas. With presentations to hundreds of people taking place two to four times per day, quite a percentage of people would have experienced the performance over the years, and even more would have heard of it during the thirty-year period of the second ministry. The verbal transmission of stories, known as the *oral tradition*, was an effective form of communication at that time. Information was transmitted from one group to another and one generation to the next, in the form of stories or song. Without the distractions that consume so many of our waking hours today, people engaged in the oral tradition of story-telling between family and friends for hours upon hours each day. Jesus's hilarious presentations became one of the most popular storytelling activities, and even though people did not take him seriously as a preacher, the message he attempted to deliver subliminally became part of the consciousness of generations of people who heard the stories.

You may wonder what motivated Jesus to dedicate every moment of the second half of his life to achieving this ambition. After all, he wasn't establishing a religion, even though he certainly established a following. But neither was he just biding his time, nor merely having fun while traipsing around the world as an entertainer of sorts. As will be revealed in upcoming chapters, the second ministry was more vital and important to our destiny than anything the first ministry came close to achieving.

CHAPTER EIGHTEEN

AN OPPORTUNITY TO UNDERSTAND

*J*esus travelled extensively throughout the thirty years of the second ministry, and returned to southern France to visit his family whenever possible. He managed to secure passage to whatever destination he desired by using his appeal to befriend and make the acquaintance of those he met. Without fail, he was accommodated each night of his life in someone's home or within a comfortable campfire group, with ample food and wine on offer at both. Of course, none of this was done with mischievous intent; rather, it was simply a mathematical equation and a desire not to waste time.

Jesus had calculated that within the thirty years he believed he might expect to live, the hours of darkness, rest, and sleep amounted to almost 50% of that time – or potentially 15 years of his life. To his way of thinking, this was an unforgiveable waste that could not be ignored. Having convinced himself that he could preach and travel for most of the thirty year period, he therefore felt there was no alternative but to seek out a solution for utilising as many of those 'dead' hours as possible, and putting them to good effect.

When taking into account that most family homes housed at least two generations and sometimes three, Jesus calculated that on the occasions he secured housing for the night, it was likely that those numbers would triple or quadruple as extended family and friends gathered to join in the event. He then determined that to secure such overnight accommodation with a family or group of individuals for each of the remaining nights of his life, he could conservatively estimate being in the company of a minimum of 20 people per evening, for several hours on end. Over a 30 year period that amounted to a captive audience of at least 219,000 people, all of whom would be 'entertained' by Jesus during these so-called 'dead' hours that would otherwise have been a waste.

Not only was this far preferable to sleeping rough, but this large audience was very worthwhile. These people spoke proudly of their triumph at having the well-known 'entertainer' as their private guest, and they talked for generations to come about their experience. While such reflections merely recalled his humorous one-liners and the ironies that emerged as a result, they had no clue about what they'd really signed up for – Jesus's philosophy of life being sewn as seeds of thought into the minds of thousands upon thousands of people.

While the oral tradition was not quite as efficient as the communication technology we are accustomed to, it was nevertheless highly effective in its day and contributed a great deal to Jesus's message being ingeniously spread throughout the continents.

* * *

On a particularly unexceptional afternoon, some fifteen years into the second ministry, Jesus benefited from a rather extraordinary accident of fate. He was travelling on the continent of Europe, and discovered he was not alone in establishing his truth. In overhearing an elderly gentleman preaching words of wisdom similar to his own, Jesus casually joined the onlookers to learn more of what this like-minded preacher had to say.

Half-expecting only to have stumbled across yet another occasion to step in and oppose, Jesus listened and waited for an opening to challenge and counter. However, to his astonishment the disheveled, elderly man was talking his talk. As he forcefully condemned Christian preachers, Jesus wondered if the old man had overheard one of his entertaining 'sessions' and taken it upon himself to 'spread the word' in his own way.

After a while, Jesus could not resist the temptation to become involved in the debate, so out of curiosity he spoke up and asked the preacher a question: "If you say the miracle stories of resurrection and ascension are untrue, who then was responsible for the atrocity of removing a dead man from his burial place?"

The preacher instantly fell silent, much to Jesus's surprise: he hadn't considered it such a difficult question for the old man to contemplate, or even dismiss if he'd wanted to. His non-reaction made people feel uncomfortable and many began to turn and look curiously at Jesus, but the preacher wasn't concerned by what his audience thought and began brushing people aside as he shuffled his way through the crowd towards Jesus.

Supported by a stick and squinting as he approached, the man eventually came to a halt in front of Jesus, and after a further few moments of up-close scrutiny, he slowly nodded his head as if agreeing with himself, before saying, "I thought so — I knew I recognised that voice. I couldn't leave you to do this job on your own, now could I?"

Jesus was momentarily speechless and literally gasped for air as he realised who was standing before him: "Seth," he stammered, "am I seeing things — I didn't recognise you. I assumed they'd murdered you — I can't believe you're alive. I'm so pleased to see you after all these years."

Seth was equally as pleased to see Jesus, but not quite in a mood effervescent enough to admit it. In reclaiming his previously profound voice, he snappily responded: "In those days I was a fast mover, and they didn't move fast enough — simple as that. I can't say I'm all that pleased to be alive though. I can barely see or walk, and I've spent my life wandering from place to place trying to clear my conscience, and now you turn up and start making things difficult for me."

Jesus laughed so much that most of those standing nearby joined in, but without knowing what was so amusing. He was astonished at such a chance meeting after so many years, and spontaneously abandoned the formality they'd previously shared. Reaching out to Seth, Jesus embraced him forcefully and shook his hand while saying, "I'm glad to hear you haven't changed, Seth — always prepared to take me on as usual."

The crowd began to disperse once they realised the occasion was merely two old friends who'd run into one another, and as they did so Seth acknowledged his work for the day was done. He shuffled around a little as he quietly muttered something to himself and patted Jesus a friendly farewell and went on his way. But Jesus could not let such an occasion pass without it being marked, and walked alongside Seth, encouraging him to wait a while and talk.

It was clear to Jesus that Seth felt a little embarrassed, but when he eventually stopped, he turned and looked at Jesus with a friendly smile across his sad and aged expression, and said, "This is enough for me, Jesus. I now know. Throughout all these years I've wondered — I wondered if you made it, or if you did something insane and got caught up in it all again.

So, this is enough – I'll be on my way. I'm sorry I caused you so much heartache. I can't change the past and I can do no more, so I'll be on my way, Jesus – farewell."

As Seth turned and began to depart again, Jesus noticed tears form in his eyes and began trailing alongside him; gently speaking to reassure him: "Seth, if I were to say that you did more than enough, would that make you feel any better? You kept me alive, and you gave me the opportunity to write my own ending, and that's what I'm doing; you don't need to do any more."

Seth stopped for a moment, and stood with his head hung low as tears gently fell, while Jesus continued: "Despite what you may think, Seth, what happened is what was supposed to happen. I truly believe the lessons of the ministry will not be learned for a long time to come. As we discussed on our last night together, I still think that the world needs first to experience negativity before it can appreciate bliss. Eventually people will show they can stand up to those who labour to control them, and they'll encourage those in authority to listen and meet the true needs of mankind. But until then, the world will have to be patient and endure what it has chosen to withstand."

Now that Jesus had Seth's attention he wanted to bring some levity to the conversation and a smile to Seth's face, and proceeded by saying, "Now, don't get me wrong, Seth – for the record, I think some of your decisions were far from the greatest in the world – you don't get off that lightly! How could you have fallen for such nonsense and not seen straight through their propaganda?"

As quick as a flash, Seth responded, "I wasn't the only one who fell for it – let's not forget how quick you were to embrace their sales pitch, Jesus!"

"Well, that's more like it, Seth," replied Jesus in mock relief, "you *are* on form after all – you had me worried for a moment – I thought you'd lost your fighting spirit!"

As both men laughed and took one or two more digs at each other's expense, they simultaneously had a moment's pause as they realised it was the first time they'd shared humorous banter. But without making reference to such, Jesus continued to persuade Seth of what he believed he needed to understand: "Seth, you don't need to make up for something you did wrong. The important thing is that throughout the period of the ministry you learned from everything you experienced, and that is really all that matters. What occurred back then was the 'plan', but the experience itself was a learning one — not only for you, but for me, and for everyone else who was involved. All that will happen in the long term is that the world will have a choice to make: to listen to them, or learn from us."

Jesus continued to speak for some time to convince Seth he was forgiven, and did so with such empathy and compassion, it took all of Seth's strength to remain composed. Seth interjected with questions about Martha and Judas, and was relieved to learn that at least Martha had escaped unhurt, although very saddened to hear of the outcome for Judas. But all throughout the conversation, Seth kept asking himself how Jesus could be so forgiving after all that had happened – the disastrous outcome for the ministry, and his best friend and brother being so badly hurt. For the life of him, Seth could not understand how someone could forgive all of that.

Seth began to feel tired and needed to find somewhere to sit; he was trembling and struggling to respond effectively. As he gathered his thoughts and made himself comfortable, he decided to take a leaf out of Jesus's book and lighten the situation: "So, Jesus – I've listened carefully to all you have to say, and if what you suggest is true, and overall I really did nothing all that wrong, then explain this oh wise one – why is it that you look tall, fit, and healthy, and I ended up a crippled, half-blind old man?"

Jesus laughed and jokingly responded, saying, "Well Seth, the truth is – some of us have it, and some of us don't!"

As the two men shook hands warmly and called a truce, they agreed that clearing the air had paved the way for a more relaxed time and perhaps a little fun. For the next few days Jesus and Seth became somewhat of a double-act, engaging in a spot of team-work and mock debates as they put the world to rights and presented the crowds with a double helping of 'entertainment'. Jesus also took the time to teach Seth a few of his most valuable tricks of the trade, and showed him exactly how to secure comfortable accommodation and an ample supply of food and wine in exchange for an evening of exemplary story-telling. Jesus even suggested that Seth should add a few interesting real-life stories to his repertoire, such as reflecting upon the fact that *Jesus of Nazareth* survived to live another day. Seth agreed that could very well put him in high demand, and afford him the sort of pampering Jesus had become accustomed to over the years.

* * *

A close bond developed between Jesus and Seth throughout this enjoyable interlude, and from Jesus's perspective a far more in-depth understanding emerged; not only of Seth personally, but of behind-the-scenes antics of the founding members of the Movement. Some of what Jesus discovered was chilling, and it was only now that he fully appreciated the extent of the risks Seth had taken to save him and his family. The weeks after the crucifixion had been fraught with danger, and when Seth explained just how close to disaster his entire plan had become, Jesus appreciated how fortunate he had been.

Much to Jesus's amazement, it transpired in conversation that shortly after the ascension episode, Seth's superiors discovered evidence of Jeremiah's existence. Seth reminded Jesus of the fact that his allegiance to the Movement had been wavering for some time, but despite the concerns of his superiors, they could not respond to the growing mutual conflict when in the throes of setting up the betrayal and resurrection stories. However, the unanticipated episode known as the ascension miracle brought matters rapidly to a head. In abandoning his post so suddenly due to the dispute, Seth did not have time to rid Barbelo of all the evidence relating to *Jeremiah*. He had spent the first few days after Jesus's departure secretly preparing to close down his operation and prioritising paying off and letting go the key staff that had been responsible for Jeremiah's care. But as Seth explained to Jesus, the Barbelo compound was not merely closed down and abandoned after Seth's suspected murder as Jesus had assumed, but underwent a thorough search and investigation, during which considerable evidence emerged of the existence of Jeremiah.

When Seth escaped Barbelo, he knew that his best option was not to run, but to hide. Disguised as a vagrant inhabiting local woodland, Seth managed to keep his whereabouts unknown. However, living among these people enabled him to remain abreast of developments by participating in gossip about local goings-on. The siege on Barbelo had been big news, and as rumour flourished people tried to understand what all the fuss was about, but the only person truly able to interpret the information emerging was Seth. From what he was able to gather, he knew with certainty that the Movement had learned of the existence of Jeremiah and the wounds he had suffered, as well as the fact that his arrival and departure coincided with the timing of the crucifixion and ascension.

Seth had expected an all-out manhunt for Jesus would ensue, since even the most elementary of investigators would have surmised who Jeremiah really was, but significantly that did not occur. Within a very short period of time the episode appeared to be forgotten, as though it was of no consequence at all. Seth concluded that leaders of the Movement had decided it was not in their interest to attempt locating Jesus and his family, choosing instead to permit them to disappear into oblivion. It seems the Movement had been placed in the no-win position Jesus and Martha had endured for so many years. It would have been impossible to send hundreds of soldiers on a manhunt without telling them who they were searching for, and inevitably such news would have become public knowledge. For the Movement to do anything other than let the matter drop, would have destroyed every aspect of the foundations they'd laid for their institution.

Jesus was amazed to discover it had been known all along that he had lived, but the Movement had been too afraid to do anything about it. Seth and Jesus could barely contain their amusement at drawing the conclusion that for all these years, while the early Christians had been threatening that Jesus would one day 'return', it was in fact they who were terrified of his 'return' to completely destroy what they had founded.

While this news was highly amusing to Jesus, far more significant was Seth discovering that the second ministry of Jesus was destined to have an effect so far-reaching, that not in their most vivid imagination could the early Christians perceive what that would be. It wasn't his *return* they should have feared – it was the fact that he had no intention of leaving, but was intent upon being ever-present in a way they could never conceive.

* * *

Before parting company, Seth needed to ask Jesus for one more piece of advice: "How do you do it," he asked. "How do you find it within yourself to forgive me after what I put you through? You seem to excuse it by convincing yourself it was all part of a bigger 'plan', but look at what you went through, and look at what Judas suffered. How can you forgive me to the extent that we can be together and laugh like old friends? I know I couldn't if I were in your position."

Jesus thought momentarily before saying, "Seth, how would it be if I, who came to teach the world about forgiveness and understanding, was unable to do the same? I am supposed to demonstrate such things by sowing seeds of thought into people's minds, which hopefully one day will become a part of them. Remaining angry with you wouldn't be such a good example to set, now would it? Having said that, don't forget to keep things in perspective. I'm able to forgive your part in the horrendous acts that occurred because of how much 'life' experience I have, but it is important to remember that you should not expect to immediately attain the same capacity for forgiveness. Firstly, you need plenty of experience working with the philosophy I'm about to explain, and you need to learn of the benefits by experimenting with less significant issues that make you angry. For example, you could practice my theory by trying to forgive the tailor who made that awful tunic you're wearing! By practicing overcoming anger, gaining understanding, and discovering forgiveness, my philosophy will become a natural part of you. Then you will be prepared to deal with the more difficult challenges that inevitably present throughout life.

"I know forgiveness seems elusive to most who've been hurt, but that's because they believe an inability to forgive is the issue. However, it is anger that is the issue — anger needs to be reconciled before forgiveness occurs as a natural part of the process. You neither have to condone a person's behaviour, nor find some justification for their actions in order to forgive. Either of which are almost impossible tasks when someone is in emotional pain. What you can do, however, is begin a process that will alleviate the anger. Analyse the situation and the perpetrator's circumstances; view it all from their perspective, or if necessary their weakness of character's perspective. This will not excuse their actions, but it will explain them.

"Their acts may have been determined or thoughtless, and character weaknesses such as inferiority and low self-esteem, or emotions such as jealousy and anger may have compounded the circumstances, making it extremely difficult for an individual to act in good conscience. These character traits themselves are attributable to a long list of other negative inborn credentials; you have to feel pity for the person, Seth, not anger. Regardless of their motivation, an internal turmoil directly impacts their decision-making capability. As a person of good conscience, you should be able to find compassion for an individual with such processes of thought. You wouldn't want to be in his shoes, now would you? Once you've analysed the situation in this way you will discover that you've gained an understanding of how the person arrived at the decision to act in such an insensitive and negative manner. They couldn't help themselves. This is not an excuse, Seth, but it is a fact – there are people who never avail themselves of the opportunity to learn simply because they have never been shown how, and do not possess the basic intellect to figure it out for themselves.

"Before I go on, you need to remember that this is a process — not a quick fix. If whatever it is that is making you feel resentment and anger feels overwhelming, it will take time for this process to work. A commitment to succeed is required, so don't give up — the benefit to you in the long run will be unquantifiable.

"When I was resolving my feelings towards you, Seth, I worked towards gaining an understanding of you in this way; almost instantly the anger began to abate, and eventually disappeared altogether. How could I remain angry at someone I felt sorry for? What I had to do first was accept that my anger was directed towards you personally; the anger was not directed towards the events themselves – they were not the cause of my anger and emotional pain, you were.

"Having reconciled my anger towards you, the reminiscence of the upsetting experiences started to diminish since my focus had turned towards understanding what motivated you personally, which over time made the offending episodes pale into insignificance – forgiveness was on the horizon!

"Healing can occur, as long as you choose to allow it, but we must not forget to deny the victim mentality and preserve self-respect, and accept responsibility for what occurred when circumstances were partly created by our own actions or decisions. It is a choice to forgive, as it is a choice not to, but the burden we carry throughout life when not getting to grips with this process is overwhelming. However, focusing on the more difficult aspect of forgiving in itself is too daunting, but when addressing anger in this way, forgiveness can occur as an involuntary consequence of reaching an understanding and overcoming anger. Once you reconcile your anger, there's no longer anything to forgive. Forgiveness becomes a non-event: healing has occurred.

"It is true to say that time is a great healer, but only if it is used wisely. In choosing to remain angry, your attitude towards every other aspect of life is affected. Anger becomes a part of who you are; you, in essence, become an angry, resentful person. Now, why would anyone want that to happen?

"In fact, if you think about it, Seth, in some ways it's rather selfish to forgive. Go ahead – call me selfish for forgiving and not wanting to carry around the burden of anger and resentment for the remainder of my life – I wasn't that brave! It is I, and those whom I love, that have benefited from my ability to overcome anger by gaining understanding and stumbling across forgiveness. Don't you forget that Seth — I wasn't doing you any favours. I did it for myself – I forgave for purely selfish reasons."

Seth shook his head while smiling to himself, saying, "Forgiveness is a selfish act — I'll remember that line!"

* * *

Having spent several days exclusively in the company of Jesus, Seth had learned more about himself and about life than in his entire existence. He now felt more empowered than ever to teach anyone he could find, and spent the remainder of his days doing just that.

CHAPTER NINETEEN

THE INSIGHTFUL MOTIVATION

Out of necessity, the second ministry of Jesus needed to be memorable and had to possess the vital ingredient of longevity. By including the dynamic of humour in his presentations, Jesus fashioned his own method of subliminal teaching. *Humour sells* became the motto of his campaign, and by employing what is now regarded as one of the most effective tools in establishing permanence for a product or an idea, Jesus was way ahead of his time.

Perceived as a lighthearted, entertaining preacher, Jesus affected the thought processes of everyone who witnessed his 'show' or heard of it from those who had. It was an absolute given that people would incorporate into their lives aspects of what they learned, mostly due to the memorable nature of the teachings and the humorous way they were conducted. Jesus's entire philosophy of life became part of the mind-set of all those he engaged.

Story-tellers of the oral tradition repeated for generations the anecdotes of the entertaining preacher, which became a vital component of their repertoire. As a consequence, for centuries beyond Jesus's death his message was delivered into the hearts and minds of multitudes of people throughout the world. Simultaneously, however, the religion of Christianity was making great inroads towards achieving its own ambitions, and as a result the respective philosophies of Jesus and the early Christians, which were advocated side by side throughout many hundreds of years, continuously clashed and contradicted. The unrecognised entity of Jesus's subliminal teaching became a part of the mass human consciousness in the same manner as religious indoctrination, and was fundamental in the disputes responsible for the many battles waged against the early Christians as they fought to establish themselves.

The teachings of the second ministry passed subconsciously from one generation to the next, very much in the way other knowledge, customs, habits, and mannerisms are transferred. This inherent understanding is today contributing directly to the decline of support and respect for the institution of Christianity. On some level we all 'know' something is being kept from us, which is due to our subconscious mind possessing an innate intelligence that has been passed throughout the ages. We do not doubt or question because we lack faith; rather, it is because we subconsciously know the truth. Each time the integrity of those in power within the various factions of Christianity is questioned – usually as a result of the truth of atrocities emerging – it serves only to validate what most already suspect. As we each slowly but surely permit our inherent intelligence to ascend above what we have been programmed to believe, we will gradually move beyond the confusion and frustration of 'knowing' something is missing, and will eventually discover precisely what that is.

* * *

Jesus knew that during his time, people would not be courageous or sophisticated enough to stand against those so intent upon changing the world in the most insidious of ways, but he also believed that as time and the centuries advanced it was inevitable there would be a revolt. He was certain such rebellion would eventually reverse the emotional hold of Christianity, and their future existence would be entirely dependent upon their ability to earn and deserve the support they had surreptitiously acquired. However, their ability to succeed in recognising the truth of their decline was something Jesus felt was unlikely, since he believed their innate sense of entitlement would be the final pre-cursor to their downfall. In predicting that those who had so erroneously used his name and image would one day be forced to reveal their past misdeeds and plead for forgiveness, the notorious *Day of Judgment* was something Jesus believed was their fate alone. It is humanity as a whole that will preside as judge and jury, while determining the fate of those who have so much to answer for.

As the church continues to wage war with its image, and competing factions progress its decline even further, those with an expanding intellect are abandoning their association with its philosophy and acquiring the independent thought and personal accountability that Jesus subliminally instilled in our ancestors. This has always been an inherent part of our awareness, but was suffocated in guilt and negativity until recently. With the constraints of the past rapidly dissolving, and the church's indoctrination techniques failing as each generation progresses, it is finally time for the truth to emerge.

While there is still some way to go before populations have the courage to prevent the dictates of powerful religious leaders from cultivating their minds, the seemingly chaotic transitions we see in society today are positive, despite how it appears. The massive social change that has occurred over the past century is evidence that a dramatic shift in direction is underway, which needs to occur to facilitate the growth of the human mind. It can be likened to a teenager rebelling and learning to think for himself, rather than live within the constraints of being told what to think, do, and say. If the religion of Christianity had chosen the way of Jesus – to guide, educate, and encourage rather than dictate and control – they would be enjoying an easier passage through this evolutionary age, and the human race would be benefiting from acquiring such wisdom rather than having to endure the painful process of discovering it for themselves.

Irrespective of our culture or creed, we should all by now be able to see the consequence of a lack of rational thought permitting the mind to be influenced by ambitious individuals with a despicable agenda. While the more challenging road of independent thought that Jesus encouraged may appear to be courageous, it is in reality no more than deciding to think for oneself: a normal characteristic employed in all other areas of life.

Fortunately, the journey towards *bliss* is well underway, even though that may be difficult to believe. As the years progress, individuals will begin to see those in leadership of religion and politics with a less obscured view. People will begin to realise that we as human beings have nothing against one another, but it is those who harness our collective mind and speak for us who have created such discord. The process of self-discovery has already begun within the Christian religion, and can be witnessed in the old world by a decline in support, the consequent financial devastation, and a lack of recruits into the priesthood. The new world is in the throes of coping with fashionable factions, whose leaders are continuously exposed for what they are. They abandoned tried and tested methods of indoctrination in exchange for friendlier more inviting techniques, but the underlying principles are no different, and slowly but surely time is being called on them all, as and when their fraudulence and impropriety is exposed.

We have a world besieged by conflicts that cannot be won by any one country, culture, or creed, and a human race that has no idea how it could have come to this. All that is actually required now, is for each of us to decide that this is not the way we want to live.

* * *

While this book may be replete with new information and alternative perspectives to consider, the majority of people will not feel as though it is 'new', even though the entire story is not one they have heard before. The 'familiarity' with the story, and the perspective upon life it presents, will feel completely natural and appear obvious, logical, and sensible to anyone who has chosen to read it with an open mind. In other words, this story is already very familiar, since the details of it have been transferred throughout the generations on an innate level through our subconscious minds. The awareness most people possess will be triggered or 'woken up' when reading this book, and should be recognised on some inexplicable level as true. The subliminal teachings were inherently conveyed throughout the centuries until mankind evolved intellectually and became consciously aware of what it intuitively knew to be true. As long as fear does not become part of the equation when considering the facts, answers to so many previously unanswered questions should become apparent, since there is nothing to fear from this story but fear itself.

Jesus was a unique human being, with an important message for mankind, and all he tried to do was deliver it. However, the goals of the first ministry pale into insignificance when compared to the aspirations and achievements of the second. Jesus was determined to not only effect monumental change within the mind-set of humanity, but to ultimately overturn those who had destroyed his first ministry. As a result, we now have an opportunity to effect change in a way never before conceived. We possess a freedom of mind and spirit, and are evolved and sophisticated enough to determine our own destiny. We no longer live in fear of religious authorities, or within the constraints of absurd doctrines that dictate what we should believe. We are capable of thinking for ourselves without fear or prejudice; intellectualising that inherent part of our being that Jesus instilled in our ancestors some two thousand years ago.

A human aspect of our nature is to be curious, but it is the prevailing confusion that states the time for answers is here. We have experienced the negativity and learned from it; now we can begin to embrace the bliss. Learning the invaluable lessons provided in the *real ministry,* and understanding precisely what the life of Jesus was supposed to teach, is the beginning of our journey towards bliss.

Seth had suggested that Jesus should write his own ending — and that he certainly did.

CHAPTER TWENTY

TIME TO GO HOME

*T*he second ministry in comparison with the first was an entirely different experience for Jesus. By not remaining in one place for too long, the authorities had no reason to be concerned that he may become disruptive, and for the most part his presence remained unobtrusive within the hundreds of communities he visited throughout the years. In fact, in many ways he had reverted to being the excitable teenager; going from one place to the next and causing a stir before moving on, having left behind plenty of food for thought.

It is rare indeed for individuals, cultures, or other religions to condemn Jesus himself, but the same cannot be said of the religious institution that hails him as their icon. This no doubt relates to the fact that despite Jesus and Christianity being perceived as conjoined, there is an intuitive sense among the vast majority of people that they are not. The sympathy and respect emanating from other cultures towards Jesus personally, could be explained by historical accounts that reference he spent time in their presence in the years after the crucifixion. This would suggest that his teachings became part of their history and their subconscious memory as a whole. Along with those of us residing in predominantly Christian cultures, a knowledge of some sort exists that is difficult for them to define, but will not permit them to condemn the man himself, irrespective of their feelings about the religion that claim him as theirs.

The leadership of the early Christians eventually heard of the man named Jesus who travelled the world discrediting their assertions, and many among them correctly suspected who it could be. However, they could not accuse this individual of being Jesus of Nazareth since that would have destroyed their lofty ambitions, but neither could they bring themselves to deal with this 'version' of Jesus in the ruthless manner they were inclined towards when faced with opposition.

Ultimately, these individuals were governed by a fear of the wrath of God, and even though their aspirations overtook their conscience as they convinced themselves that their goals were pure, they were too afraid to consider tempting fate once again. The whisperings of the findings at Barbelo created intrigue for many, and when coupled with the knowledge of how they had conspired to establish their icon, the only palatable decision for leaders of the Movement was to instruct their preachers to ignore the 'new' Jesus and pretend he did not exist. By paying him no attention whatsoever, they felt he would eventually disappear and be forgotten.

Despite the audacity they displayed, the leaders of the Movement knew Jesus had agreed to his end in an attempt to distance himself from them and protect his family and followers from threat. As a result, guilt permeated their conscience in spite of their tendency towards denial. In the further knowledge that it appeared Jesus had in fact survived the crucifixion, or had truly *returned from the dead*, fear took over every aspect of their being. As a result, anger and resentment became a part of their mind-set as they lost the psychological battle to ignore or justify their actions. In an effort to alleviate such debilitating emotions, they passed the guilt and insecurity onto their flock — a problem shared was a problem halved. By pointing the finger of blame, while stating that Jesus's crucifixion was for their benefit, and the result of the sinfulness of humanity, the flock became known as worthless sinners, expected to dedicate their lives to submissive atonement.

This approach deflected the guilt of those in power by laying blame at the feet of the innocent converts who knew no better, while simultaneously providing an outlet for their guilt and fear-induced anger. The Movement's preachers vented their feelings with lectures that were consumed in damnation and focused upon eternal punishment in hell, thereby instilling the same fear of the wrath of God in their followers as they themselves possessed.

It is fortunate that with the passage of time, the majority of people instinctively understand they have done nothing to feel guilty or fearful about, and as a result have abandoned the subliminally held belief that they are responsible for helping the church carry its burden of guilt. In recent years the church has generally toned down its angry rhetoric in an effort to preserve the support it requires, but people are conscious of that nuance and the reasons for it, so it has little effect. Society has moved on, and people are no longer intimidated or threatened by such authorities and feel free to speak their mind. This new found confidence has ensured that the church is held accountable for its misdeeds; not only for historic atrocities, but for equally outrageous modern-day deplorable acts.

In spite of the fact that most of us are free of guilt regarding the life and death of Jesus, these emotions are still apparent in today's leaders and their more staunch followers. This is relatively easy to detect in that anger, condescension, sarcasm, and smugness are often used to defend accusation, as well as the more fashionable idea of employing in debate the admission of mistakes that rarely includes a plea for clemency, but more often than not comprises of explanation and excuse. However, if we are to learn anything from the past and from what Jesus really tried to teach, taking the moral high ground, overcoming anger, and stumbling across forgiveness as Jesus explained to Seth, would be the appropriate course to take. As the church is already learning; it is no longer the case that we need them – they need us. For their fortunes to reverse they are going to have to change, and even though the people of two thousand years ago may not have been brave enough to make a stand, it is clear that the people of today are.

* * *

The last year of Jesus's life was spent in northern Italy. He was well known and loved by everyone in the community for his frankness and sense of humour, even in old age. Two elderly sisters took him under their wings and cared for him during the latter months of his life, and together they enjoyed reminiscing about all they'd experienced. Jesus would often share stories about his family, the ministry, and his life in general, and was particularly entertaining when explaining the truth behind some of the more well known 'miracles' assigned to him. He confided in many people during the latter stages of his life and admitted his true identity, which nobody doubted for a moment. It confirmed rumours that had been rife for years, and most felt privileged to be included in this tightly knit circle of people who 'knew'. His secret was kept safe for centuries within groups and societies all over Italy and France, since no one dare speak of their beliefs in public. The true life-story of Jesus has been well known by many people for thousands of years, including the powers that be within Christianity.

* * *

Jesus knew that his life was coming to a close, but was also aware that his new companions needed to be prepared and should know he was content that his time was near. To relieve their worries, he would tease them constantly about which one of the three would die first, and their retort would usually be along the lines of wishing he would just get on with it instead of only threatening to do so. There were even occasions when he would pretend to be 'gone' but suddenly sit upright and frighten the life out of them; mocking his 'return from the dead' scenario and causing them to double up in laughter.

Jesus *went home* peacefully in his sleep at the age of 67. His companions attempted to wake him, but did not succeed. They had hoped he was up to his old tricks, but he was not. Without fanfare of any sort, Jesus departed our world in the same hushed, calm manner of his birth. An implicit and agonising void was profoundly suffered by all who knew him, and that same void has resided in the consciousness of the world ever since.

Jesus would be disappointed to be remembered as a serene and holy individual when he possessed such a gregarious personality and intelligent sense of humour. His intellect was such that no one could compete, but without a sense of fun and the ability to see humour in almost everything, he would never have achieved a thing. He used to remind himself that this is only life - it's not such a big deal — just get through it, do your best, and eventually it will be time to go home.

CHAPTER TWENTY-ONE

DREAMS OF SLEEP

*T*he sense of abandonment that prevails and the search for answers that continues, is indicative of a deep loss innately felt by so many for so long. Christianity's threat that Jesus will one day return to judge us all provides neither nourishment nor comfort to our soul. He will not return for Christianity's benefit to judge us, or to prove their claims to the world. His return will be in a manner that has previously been inconceivable to the conscious mind, until now.

In the Voice of Jesus

"The intrinsic fear among mankind as a consequence of indoctrination made it impossible for so many to listen: you were too afraid to hear. You have now demonstrated by your defiance that you are ready to listen; refusing conformity, you are determined to think for yourself. No longer are you afraid, but you question; demanding that those in power be called to justice for their fraudulence and indiscretion. To me, this signifies a desire that is beyond listening; it is a desire to hear, which is why I have chosen to speak.

"My 'return', as suggested by the Christian religion, will not occur for the simple reason that I never actually left. My physical body expired once the purpose of my life on earth was complete, but my soul, like yours, lived on; blending with the powerful light energy you refer to as God, which exists within the composition of your soul. My ability to communicate with you became greater after physical death because I am as much a part of you, as you are of me — we are all one. I did not fear death when I knew my time was near; rather I embraced it because of the opportunities it held.

"My name is known in every corner of the world, irrespective of the religious affiliation each culture supports, because in death I became one with you all. I am still in the thoughts of all mankind some two thousand years after I lived as a result of my soul maintaining communication with each of yours on an intuitive level. This is why there will be no 'return' as such — I did not leave; do not be intimidated by empty threats from the religion that purports to represent me.

"This book, and others that will follow, have a specific purpose, which may not be immediately apparent. They will not be sowing seeds of thought as you may perceive; rather, they are food for thought. The seeds I sowed in the subconscious mind of your ancestors many years ago have been subliminally communicated throughout the generations. It is now time for the seeds I sowed to be nurtured; to develop, and flourish.

"Hopefully you should intuitively comprehend as true all that you read, as long as you are able to do so without fear. Once your mind receives the nourishment it so desires as a result of this learning experience, growth and a new awareness and maturity will begin to develop on an innate level. You will begin to participate in life in a way you have never before considered. The more this learning experience sinks into your conscious mind, the more growth will become apparent; the roots that have grown from the seeds I sowed will begin to flourish.

"The beginning of this process coincided with the beginning of the demise of the Christian religion some sixty or so years ago. We are now ready to take a resolute path into the future, which will take us all in a direction we have not before been. I say 'us all' not only because I am taking this journey with you, but because 'all' are welcome to participate. This journey will have no limitations created by religion or culture, and it will not require a commitment to or a denial of either.

"Irrespective of how difficult life often feels, please remember that you are not alone; there is no need to be afraid. I am here, and in the future my presence will become very apparent within the hearts, conscious minds, and souls of all people from all cultures. However, it is my wish not to distance anyone from their associations or traditions. I wish only to encourage an enhanced perspective on life and a way of conducting life that would benefit all. My commitment is to humanity as a whole, not the institution of Christianity, and my goal is to satisfy the curiosity that exists within all of mankind. I want you to know who I am, who you are, and that my relationship with you is as one.

"You will dream of me and of what I wish for you. When you hear my voice, tell a friend so he too can hear. When you learn from me, share by example. Do not relate my message to that of historic associations, but relate to it irrespective of such. You are not to be afraid; rather, you are to feel reassured. You are not to feel like the 'chosen one'; instead, you are to feel as one.

"Until now it has been a rare occurrence for me to appear in your waking mind or in your dreams of sleep. That is, in part, because I was waiting until you were ready to hear what I had to say, but it is also because I know you need proof. The sudden occurrence of waking thoughts and dreams of sleep will be the evidence you will no doubt seek: evidence that your new perspective on life is beginning to take root.

"My call to all people is to hear my voice, which will come from within. In your waking hours and dreams of sleep I will be there, as I always have.

"Be still and know that I am, and you are....."

CHAPTER TWENTY-TWO

IN CONCLUSION

The world we are living in appears to be in much conflict: misunderstanding and a lack of tolerance and compassion seem to prevail to an extent we have not witnessed before. Many believe that the earth itself could be disintegrating before our eyes, and the challenges we face due to the multi-cultural nature of society today can be overwhelming for many. The apparent lack of moral boundaries, where mention of making choices of conscience would be met with a curious stare, understandably leaves many feeling as if there is little point in trying any more.

Christian church authority figures often describe the current social climate as being one of rapid moral decline, resulting in what they perceive as a broken society. They suggest that the impression many give of thoughtlessness and selfishness demonstrates social immorality and a lack of personal responsibility. The church believes that these circumstances are a direct consequence of so many abandoning the Christian religious doctrine and values, and it is content to blame 'society' for its ills. However, in refusing to recognise where the true responsibility lies, the church has failed to understand why such departures have occurred.

Society cannot be 'fixed' by embracing a solitary source of influence and returning to the conviction of submitting to the church's doctrine: a luxurious position those in religious authority maintained for many centuries, which is precisely the reason why society is as 'ill' as the church perceives it to be. Our ancestors were not taught to understand who they were and why they were here. They were not shown how to trust their intuitive inner voice, thereby establishing a connection with themselves and with God; a process in and of itself that would institute the values and moral boundaries so many believe have been eroded. The church neither embraced the recommendations of Jesus's real ministry, nor did it bear in mind his guidance and evolve into an institution designed solely for people to rely upon to provide spiritual guidance when sought. The religious authority preferred instead to indoctrinate a belief system that convinced people they were inferior, weak, worthless sinners who were incapable of making choices of good conscience for themselves. Establishing emotional dependence upon the church for instructive guidance on every aspect of life was perceived as the road to success: it was considered by those in authority to be the most likely way they would expand as an institution.

To accommodate such ambition, the masses were literally named the 'flock', and intimidated into blindly following direction like sheep. Consequently, no belief in self was established; no understanding of the process of conscious thought was learned, and a fear was instilled that anyone who dared to consider abandoning the flock would find himself relegated to the status of a lost sheep – someone with no sense of direction and no ability to find his own way.

While many of us feel a sense of being 'lost' from time to time and in varying degrees, we intuitively know that returning to the flock is not the answer; we know we need to learn to think for ourselves – after all, we are human beings, we are not sheep. Therefore, the climate that currently prevails should be described as one of transition, not one of decline. Society is not broken, but it is preoccupied, thinking, questioning, experimenting, making mistakes, changing, and searching for answers more than ever before. What many perceive to be an ongoing social, moral decline is nothing more than confusion as a consequence of mankind's stubborn determination to gain a better understanding of life, and an unwillingness to return to the days of old.

Such rebellion stems from an inherent frustration. Questions relating to the 'reason' for the life we live have never been addressed, since everything Jesus actually taught was completely ignored by the early Christian movement. Embracing the real ministry will ultimately provide a greater understanding of the purpose of life and establish new meaning for everyday experiences. In turn, this will eventually create a society that is more at peace with itself; one that will automatically project the caring and thoughtful nature many have forgotten they naturally possess. For that to evolve, we need to have a little faith – a faith in ourselves.

* * *

Our time here on earth was never intended to be a picnic; it is an opportunity to benefit from growth and the evolution of our soul. In life, there are challenges and difficulties to be overcome, and it is those very experiences that incorporate the lessons which contribute to our personal development. The maturing and progress it is hoped will occur, is preparation for a *life* in eternity that is beyond the comprehension of the human conscious mind.

At this point in the history of mankind, we are in a position where we can reflect upon the past and assess whether massive positive change could have been effected in the world if our ancestors had made different choices. Alternatively, we could consider that by experiencing such difficulty for so long, we have availed ourselves of a monumental amount of learning opportunities, which has established human evolution to the degree we now have. We are no longer afraid of governments or religious institutions; we are educated and sophisticated enough to see what is wrong, and prepared and capable enough to put it right, if we so choose.

Individuals establishing personal attitudes that demonstrate a positive and constructive way of conducting life will establish change within society, and that will be reflected in the attitudes of governments and religions. Placing high expectations upon ourselves will empower us to place those same expectations upon those in authority. Contrary to popular belief, it is not the other way around; it is no longer political and religious leaders who effect change by instituting all sorts of unnecessary laws, it is we as individuals who have the power to effect change. When controlled and told what to do, we naturally rebel, but we would respond positively if the example we set was well received by those in authority, who, in turn, would feel encouraged and obligated to support our ideals. In other words, if we want to see change in the world, we have to make it happen.

We all need to reprioritise and understand that satisfaction and happiness are not things we need to strive for; rather, they are things we should simply accept. They are available free of charge to all who find a way to make their time here on earth of value to another, and thereby of value to self. Deep personal satisfaction with life and true happiness is only a heartbeat away. All we need to do is decide we would like to receive it.

This book is meant to enlighten you to the truth of your history and inspire you to stand up from the crowd of hungry people and set an example for all to follow. Contribute positively to the lives of your family, your neighbours, and your communities. Encourage young people to become involved in what they can do instead of relegating them as ineffectual: their feelings of self worth will improve when they can see value in their efforts, since to feel of value means it is no longer feasible to feel inconsequential. The ripple effect of the pebble we all gently toss into the pond will contribute to the world as a whole, and change will occur. It is up to us to let our voices be heard, so go ahead and write your own ending, but remember — have the serenity to accept the things you cannot change, the courage to change the things you can, and the wisdom to know the difference. The key is in the wisdom.

PostScript

PostScript

Part I – The Birth of Jesus

The Marriage of Mary and Joseph

*J*oseph and Mary met when they were about four or five years of age. Their families knew one another, and as young children they played together. Both were quite unique when compared with other children, and possessed a sense of calm not evident in their peers. While their friends negotiated their way throughout life, establishing personalities and competing with one another, Joseph and Mary seemed to possess a deep intellect and sense of knowing. Their highly evolved souls were apparent even at a young age, but their parents did not perceive them as such: they simply felt fortunate to have such beautiful, well-behaved children.

The experiences of Mary and Joseph do not warrant every word they said being turned into *gospel*, but that does not mean they were in any way less evolved as souls than Jesus. They knew who they were; understood their life's purpose, and knew nothing else mattered.

Joseph was only 19 when he declared his love for Mary and from that moment on it was accepted they would be together forever. The marriage had received the blessing of both families, so it was a matter of allowing the engagement period to commence, while making plans for a happy celebration of their union.

The love shared between Joseph and Mary was a true love, and besides being responsible for bearing Jesus and his siblings, their life was supposed to symbolise *true love* for all to observe and aspire to. However, the truth of their relationship was completely distorted by the Christian church to accommodate their decision that Jesus be recognised as the divine son of God, born of a virgin. As a consequence, an understanding of the components of true love was neither represented nor taught to mankind. Today, most people cannot distinguish the difference between true love and the romantic *falling in love*, and of those who have some awareness of the concept, most regrettably consider it unrealistic and unattainable.

The Conception Mystery Resolved

One of the most renowned miracle stories is the immaculate conception of the Virgin Mary. The propagated myth states that before Joseph and Mary were married, Joseph experienced an angelic visitation, wherein he was instructed to take Mary as his wife. He was informed she had conceived a child by the Holy Spirit, who would be born a son and was to be named Jesus. Joseph was further instructed that Jesus was the son of God, and as such had been miraculously conceived by a virgin. Joseph was therefore expected to maintain the purity and virginal status of the vessel that bore the son of God, and was instructed to abstain from physical expressions of love towards his wife.

Needless to say, the truth is closer to something we could more easily relate to, and is more beautiful than anything we have been presented with before. Joseph did indeed experience a dream, but in a manner that is familiar to us all in that it included relatable information with regard to what was happening in his life. Joseph dreamt he was to take Mary as his wife and was informed they would conceive a son who should be named Jesus. Joseph also learned that Jesus was an extraordinary soul whose life would prove to be highly spiritual in nature. He was so taken aback by this vivid experience that he shared details of it with Mary, much in the way we would share with friends or family details of an unusual dream we might encounter.

The instruction to *take Mary as his wife* was something Joseph already intended, and on their wedding night he proposed to do as any man who loved his new bride, and *take* Mary as his wife in a physical expression of his true love. The dream Joseph experienced did not include a warning of an immaculate conception, and did not require that Joseph be expected to forever sacrifice physically expressing his love to maintain the virginity of his wife. Rather, it was simply a matter of Joseph and Mary being provided with information about the direction their life was to take, much in the way most of us have such experiences from time to time.

The wedding of Joseph and Mary was a beautiful, joyous occasion, and when marriage vows were exchanged their enchanting voices echoed in the hearts of everyone: the truth and depth of their love was so passionate and intense it was conspicuous to all. Their wedding night of innocent intimacy was a beautiful experience for Joseph and his virgin bride. The first physical expression of their true love created a special child they were to name Jesus. This innocent young couple consummated their relationship with a depth of true love and intimacy, which can only be described as a holy and miraculously spiritual moment in time.

The real miracle that occurred the moment the child Jesus was conceived was of an exceptionally deep, true love, and a level of caring intimacy beyond the comprehension of most. It is the *love* we all seek, but will be unlikely to accomplish since we have never been taught how.

The Birth of the Child Jesus

The biblical version of the birth of Jesus is a magical and romantic tale. Joseph and Mary are depicted travelling across country to Bethlehem and arriving at a remotely located inn. Upon being informed that no accommodation is available, they are offered shelter in an adjacent barn where animals roam freely. Among these simple surroundings the child Jesus is born and laid on a bed of hay in a manger (an animal feeding trough). Encircled only by the night sky and twinkling stars, the Holy Family are joined by three shepherds who arrive on camel-back having travelled throughout the night under the guidance of stars to worship at the child's birthplace.

While this enchanting tale is inoffensive it is also incorrect. Had the true story been recounted throughout the ages, it would have produced a moving anecdote that would have endured forever, rather than a tale that is justifiably doubted and constantly challenged for its authenticity.

Throughout Mary's pregnancy Joseph continued to have dreams that were often quite dramatic in nature, but rather than being afraid he felt reassured, since the dreams always provided guidance and support. It was the result of an inspiration in one of the dreams that it was decided the expectant young couple would spend time with a relative during the latter months of Mary's pregnancy. This was also partly due to the fact that around the time of the birth of Jesus, prophets in the vicinity were predicting the impending birth of a special child, and even though Joseph and Mary found it entirely implausible that the rumours could possibly relate to their child, they both felt happier removing themselves to a safe haven where they could escape the rather contentious atmosphere that existed in the surrounding cities.

Several months prior to the birth of Jesus, Joseph and Mary had taken up residence in what would be described today as a cottage located behind a large house. The homes belonged to a mother and daughter who were trusted family members of Joseph. They were comfortable dwellings, positioned in a quiet, rural setting, and before long the newlyweds felt very much at home. These properties were not situated in the town of Bethlehem but were to the north-west of that area and near the coast – they were actually closer to the town of Nazareth than Bethlehem. The little cottage was rarely used other than when visitors were passing through, but Joseph and Mary made it feel like home for the last few months of the pregnancy. As would any young couple in love and enjoying this stage of their life, they excitedly made plans for their future and took pleasure in one another's company while awaiting the birth of their child. They remembered to pray for the safe delivery of their baby and asked for help with all that was expected of them. Although Joseph and Mary believed that we are all essentially children of God, they did not perceive their child to be anything other than their own, despite the unusual series of dreams that suggested he was in some way destined to leave his mark upon mankind.

Jesus was born on a warm summer evening, and that important day saw Joseph and Mary partaking in what had become their normal routine. Having joined their hosts in the main house for breakfast and discussed plans they each had for the day, Mary proceeded to assist with light household chores and cooking, while Joseph helped in the garden and carried out some general maintenance work. In the late afternoon Joseph and Mary retired to their cottage to rest before dinner, and it was during this respite that Mary felt she was going into labour and alerted Joseph to summon the two female family members.

Arriving at the cottage with everything they needed to assist in the delivery, the women prepared Mary for the birth. They encouraged her to relax and remain calm and focused, while doing whatever they could to make her comfortable. Once everyone was settled, all that remained was to let nature take its course, but it was at this moment that silence fell, and an energy overtook that was so consuming, no one dared speak.

Mary's eyes were closed for most of the time and she remained quiet and calm in a meditative sort of way, while Joseph nervously looked on from a distance and prayed silently to himself. The women taking care of Mary had delivered many children before, but never had they witnessed anything like this — the ambience was overwhelmingly spiritual and intense. For those present, the energy that encompassed the room was highly emotional: none of those witnessing the birth of Jesus had been prepared for what occurred — it was the closest they had ever felt to God.

In an atmosphere of serene silence, all those present awaited the birth of a child destined to accommodate the highly evolved soul of Jesus. As the child was delivered safely into our world, a spiritual moment of inconceivable hushed splendor reigned as the spectacular soul of Jesus was ushered by a heavenly force, becoming one with the beautiful child at his moment of birth.

The silence was broken only by a gentle cry from the newborn baby, accompanied by silent tears of joy from all those present. As Joseph approached his wife, he took her hand in his, while the two women bathed the child and wrapped him in a cloth. As Jesus was handed into the care of his mother for the first time, Joseph reached out and touched his precious son. Together as one, this exceptional family lay silently in reflective contemplation. What their future held they could not begin to imagine, but Joseph and Mary knew without doubt that they were in the presence of an extraordinary child.

The most highly evolved soul to inhabit the earth had been born.

PostScript

Part II – The Gospel according to…?

$\mathcal{T}$he four gospels of the Bible *according to* Matthew, Mark, Luke and John were produced in their original form between forty and one hundred years after the crucifixion. Centuries later, in 325 AD, they were chosen from among hundreds of texts produced by numerous writers at the Movement's behest. None of the authors of these works lived during the time of Jesus and were therefore neither apostles, nor individuals with first-hand knowledge of the ministry. However, the writers presumed their work represented the truth, since their source of information was the leadership of the early Christian movement. In reality, however, they had been instructed to produce texts that represented what the Movement considered was suitable in relation to their ambitions.

Those who competed for the coveted position of their works being chosen as best representing the ethos of the Movement, had no idea they were dealing with a highly organised quasi-political force that had been in existence for many years before Jesus began his ministry. The authors believed that the Movement comprised of followers of Jesus and their descendants, and had absolutely no idea they were individuals intent upon creating history rather than representing it. As a result, they naively worked diligently to impress the decision-makers by producing what they were told was required, and did so in the hope of achieving the honour of their literary work becoming known as *the word of God,* and perceived forever as *gospel truth.*

* * *

Approximately 250 years after the original versions of the gospels had been fashioned, the Bible was constructed during a protracted and contentious process known as the First Council of Nicaea. It was a complicated procedure that involved hundreds of church authority figures; all of whom had travelled far and wide to attend the conference. While being presided over by the Roman Emperor, Constantine I, the attendees were responsible for reviewing the historic textual material available to them. Their conference did not conclude until a general consensus was reached by the gathering, and a declaration made regarding which of the texts would be used to represent the absolute word of God for the future of mankind.

As decisions were being made, argumentative and pontificating debate prevailed, and behind-the-scenes negotiations became fierce: the engagement in deceitful bribery and corruption was astounding. The priority of most Council attendees was not benevolent in nature; rather it was to curry favour with the powerful and demanding Emperor, Constantine I. Intense conflict was the order of the day, as attendees grappled and fought over every minor detail and lobbied for financial or political benefits in exchange for supporting certain positions. As a result, not one of the texts under consideration was accepted 'as is', but all were significantly altered to meet whatever demands were tabled, particularly those of the Emperor. While the decisions were theoretically to secure a blueprint for the Movement's mission statement, in truth they related only to satisfying the desires of a powerful and demanding leader, whose ambition overall was to secure more wealth and influence.

The atmosphere at Nicaea was hardly conducive to establishing the world's most powerful religion in the name of God: impatience, jealousy, discord, persecution and bigotry reigned. Yet in this very atmosphere in the year 325 AD, the four *gospels according to Matthew, Mark, Luke, and John* were chosen to represent God's word for the betterment of mankind.

★ ★ ★

For centuries Christians have been instructed not to dare question or doubt the gospels as being anything other than God's word and a faithful account of the life and ministry of Jesus, and further instructed only to accept the church's interpretation of biblical text due to unease that an 'incorrect' message may be construed. In fear of attracting the wrath of God, the flock adhered to the church's indoctrination techniques, which to date has successfully compelled billions of people across the world to commit to its ideology.

PostScript

Part III – The Making of a Miracle

While the miracle story relating to the *feeding of the five thousand* was clarified earlier in this book, many such stories are not translatable in that way. This is due to most of them being complete fabrications, with one or two others relating to Jesus doing something unintentionally. In one particular instance, Jesus took the opportunity to lightheartedly deride such episodes by pretending he'd performed a miracle. The account known as *turning water into wine* occurred at a social gathering and was intended as a humorous tease by Jesus. Having been sent to fetch water in the assumption that all the wine had been consumed, he came across two jugs of wine in a dark corner of a cellar. Much to everyone's delight, he returned to the gathering with wine instead of water, and mockingly announced that he'd miraculously transformed it. This intentionally comical episode was repeated in jest by those who were present, but taken seriously by many who were not. Each time the story was repeated it was exaggerated for effect, before eventually transforming itself into a *miraculous* episode to be revered.

Another well-known incident related to Jesus supposedly *walking on water*. In this case he did not deliberately do anything to mischievously trick people, but a group of fishermen actually believed they saw Jesus *walk on water*, since from their vantage point that is how it looked. When bearing in mind that the eyesight of most people was probably even less perfect than it is today, and aids such as spectacles did not exist, it is very easy to imagine how the horizon could play such tricks, particularly with those who were always on the look-out for an episode that would associate them with a miracle. Witnessing such an incident was considered a blessing from God, so many of the followers went out of their way to make something out of nothing, thereby creating a mysterious anecdote that could be added to their story-telling repertoire to produce intrigue.

* * *

Besides the *miracles* that are translatable into real and meaningful events, and those that are not for the aforementioned reasons, the ambiguity surrounding Jesus's gift of healing has also been the cause of much dispute. When Jesus was credited with a healing episode, it more often than not included dramatic exaggerations for effect, but Jesus did have such a capacity, although it was not something he viewed as miraculous.

It is true to say that some individuals are more sensitised than others, and are gifted with the ability to feel the energy that vibrates from a person's physical body and soul. By being able to deduce that such energy is negative, a healer can assist in diagnosing what is the root cause of a physical ailment. The source of most ailments is directly linked to the wellbeing of the mind, and detecting what is causing such imbalance and offering to support the patient in overcoming the dis-ease, is all that a healer actually does. This is achieved either through help that is psychological in nature, or by the laying on of hands in a way that induces the physical relaxation of muscles and of the mind. Such practices are as prevalent today as they were in Jesus's time, and are considered as a therapeutic and complimentary support to traditional medical intervention, which is how they should be viewed. Many people who are unwell find such therapies to be an extremely valuable part of their recovery, and most are sensible enough to appreciate they should not be conducted in isolation, but as part of a health care programme.

As you might expect, Jesus was an excellent *healer* in that a patient felt somewhat recovered simply by being in the presence of such a charismatic and highly evolved soul. He was naturally gifted in making a diagnosis and putting people on the road to recovery, and used both his skill of communication and empathy, as well as the gentle touch of his hands. He exuded an indescribable positivity, which brought about relaxation of the muscles and the mind in a moment, and when combined with his moving and often overwhelming presence, it did not take much effort on his part to make others feel far better than they had for a long time.

Those who were unwell or depressed were stimulated by his caring approach and the confidence they felt in his presence. Jesus established trust with all those he helped, and consequently was able to get to the root cause of ailments and help a patient begin to recover. Because most of those Jesus encountered immediately felt better within themselves, and did as a result make an improvement at some point, they believed it was a miracle and recounted such episodes to others in that way.

The healing Jesus actually conducted was primarily of the mind, and by helping resolve such issues, the physical ailments manifesting as a result of dis-ease began to improve. The 'laying on of hands' for which he is associated, is similar to a therapeutic massage treatment commonly prescribed today for both physical and emotional wellbeing. In essence, Jesus assisted in 'healing' by explaining to individuals precisely what they needed to know, which helped them come to terms with areas of their life that were wreaking havoc on their emotional and physical health. To many, this no doubt felt like a miracle.

PostScript

Part IV – Jesus and Mary Magdalene – The Truth

*F*or thousands of years, the relationship between Jesus and Mary Magdalene has been the subject of speculation and intrigue: even Jesus cannot escape humanity's insatiable appetite for gossip and sensationalism. The subliminal reason for our interest in this relationship is to satisfy two things: an instinctive desire to humanise Jesus, and a yearning for an enhanced understanding of the complex components of romantic love. On a subconscious level, there is a feeling that if we could relate personally to Jesus in at least one way, perhaps the message he tried to deliver would be more accessible. We *know* his message is missing, and in an attempt to access it we try to get into his head; creating fantasies to generate a connection or an understanding of the man in a way that relates to our own life. Nevertheless, even though many want to believe in the romantic relationship rumour, the majority intuitively knows it is untrue.

In spite of how unrealistic it may feel, Jesus did not entertain a romantic or sexual relationship with anyone throughout his life. The role Mary Magdalene played in the life of Jesus was considerable, as has been revealed, but it did not include romance. Such feelings towards Jesus were certainly expressed by Mary Magdalene, which was the cause of much consternation among the followers, but those feelings were never fulfilled in the way it is often contended. Mary Magdalene initially became an integral part of the ministry to ensure she was kept occupied and on side, entirely for reasons surrounding the security of Martha. As a consequence, Jesus was required to use considerable tact and diplomacy in dealing with her advances and the subsequent resentment of the other followers, but never did he consider taking advantage of such circumstances, which would have been entirely inappropriate and unbecoming to even consider.

Jesus's life was driven by purpose, and every second was focused upon what he had to achieve. Romantic relationships are highly consuming to maintain, and Jesus was certainly not the type of person to partake in casual, meaningless relationships, since he had the utmost respect for women. Not only was there no time available for him to dedicate to such matters, but he had no natural desire to seek out a partner or enter into courtships in the manner most of us are inclined. Not only did such relationships not incorporate any aspect of his life's purpose, but they also held no experiences that required learning on his part, and the comfort derived from sexual gratification was not a component of life for this unique human being: this highly evolved soul was above such basic needs.

* * *

Mary Magdalene became a devout follower of Jesus after experiencing the so-called 'miracle' of her brother, Lazarus. Nevertheless, the apostles believed her involvement had ulterior motives, such as the eminence of association with Jesus and the prospect of romance. The fact is, the apostles were correct on both counts, hence the reason for their intense irritation at Jesus for appearing not to recognise these facts and dismiss Mary Magdalene from the inner circle. However, Jesus wanted to be sensitive towards her feelings, while also considering his personal reputation, the concerns of close supporters, and the risk to Martha's security in the event that a rejected Mary Magdalene put that under threat. For all of these reasons, Jesus needed to find a compromise that would ensure Mary Magdalene understood the extent of their relationship, and that the followers were satisfied with his stance, while also guaranteeing Martha's alias and safekeeping remained intact. Under the circumstances, the most Jesus felt able to do was express himself in the only way he knew how: to show compassion and understanding, but above all else to show love and to teach. Speaking privately to Mary Magdalene, Jesus gently tried to persuade her:

"Mary, you display such devotion and love towards me, which is both inspiring and worrisome: to see such generosity of spirit inspires me, but to see such devotion where your gestures cannot be reciprocated in kind, concerns me. You are placing your heart in great jeopardy when you behave in this way. Situations such as this should not only be considered from the heart; there needs to be a mixture of mind with heart.

"Giving so much of yourself to one person means there will be insufficient love remaining

within to give to others. For example, if a woman loves her husband in an imbalanced way, she will not have enough time, energy, or love to devote to her children, mother, father, siblings, friends, or self. If her husband demands her love be such, he is not the definition of a husband at all.

"My desire is to meet your needs by loving you for who you are. I hope to teach you to believe in yourself by providing nourishment for your soul and instilling a sense of inner peace and well-being, but I cannot give of myself in a manner that would create further imbalance in your mind and heart; I hope you understand.

"I do love you Mary Magdalene, but my role is to give of myself and to teach love to all of those I engage. I have no desire to take from another person what they are not in a position to give. You are still learning to love and respect self, and that will take time. I am nourished from the giving of love. I am here to give.

"In your hour of need I hope these thoughts appear in your tears like tiny pearls of wisdom; it is not my intent to cause hurt to one that I love."

* * *

Because the truth of this relationship was not recorded in history, conspiracy theories abound; intuitively people know they have been deceived. Pertinent details were omitted and embellishments were deliberately added, which facilitated rumours of romance. Even though the church gives the impression it is furious that this relationship now causes such debate, they have only themselves to blame – it was they who purposely established the ambiguity in the first place.

It was known that people would be significantly drawn to such affairs of the heart, and the indeterminate nature of the biblical relationship was a tantalising source for imaginative invention. There was a time when these subliminal insinuations created a welcome distraction from the truth being sought, which was their purpose in the first place. However, in many regards the story has taken on a life of its own. In recent years in particular it has become a focal point and spawned umpteen books, documentaries, and films; clearly not an outcome foreseen by the early Christians. No longer simply a distraction purposely created to preoccupy curious historical researchers; it is now a major issue that the church finds itself spending an inordinate amount of time and money trying to dispel.

The irony is that the person coerced into supporting the story that contributed the most to Christianity's ability to succeed, is the person who has come back to haunt them. It is the world's obsession with Mary Magdalene that will eventually lead to the truth, and it is that which causes such anxiety today among those in religious authority. In an attempt to bring an end to such investigations, they proclaim outrage at the blasphemous suggestion that Jesus partook in a sexual relationship, and are working tirelessly to undo the damage created by their predecessors. They appreciate that encouraging such a line of enquiry was convenient to employ centuries ago, and provided the necessary distraction from the less colourful story of Martha, but in this day and age it will not remain the diversion it was designed for. Researchers who study the life of Mary Magdalene will always be left with the same amount of inexplicable loose ends, uncertainty, and intuitive suspicion, and sooner or later they will have no alternative but to search elsewhere for the answers they seek.

For centuries, the world has been looking in the wrong place: the story of Mary Magdalene has not been *covered up* as we have intentionally been led to believe – rather, the story of Mary Magdalene is the cover.